CONSEQUENCES

Muriel Bolger is a well-known freelance journalist and editor. Award-winning travel writer and Irish Travel Writer of the Year 2006, she has written three guidebooks on Dublin. Her latest work is a look at Dublin writers, which she wrote to tie in with UNESCO's designation of Dublin as a City of Literature. She lives in Dublin. *Consequences* is her first novel.

CONSEQUENCES

MURIEL BOLGER

HACHETTE
BOOKS
IRELAND

Copyright © 2011 Muriel Bolger

First published in 2011 by Hachette Books Ireland
First published in paperback in 2011 by Hachette Books Ireland
A Hachette UK Company

1

The right of Muriel Bolger to be identified as the Author of the Work has
been asserted by her in accordance with the Copyright, Designs and Patents
Act, 1988.

A CIP catalogue record for this title is available from the British Library.

ISBN 978 1 444 73302 0

Typeset in Times New Roman by Hachette Books Ireland
Cover design by Red Rattle Design
Printed and bound by CPI Group (UK) Ltd, Croydon, CR0 4YY

Hachette Books Ireland policy is to use papers that are natural, renewable and
recyclable products and made from wood grown in sustainable forests. The
logging and manufacturing processes are expected to conform to the
environmental regulations of the country of origin.

Hachette Books Ireland
8 Castlecourt Centre
Castleknock
Dublin 15
Ireland

www.hachette.ie

A division of Hachette UK
338 Euston Road, London NW1 3BH
England

For my many absent friends, whose memories still live on and make me smile frequently, and for Glenn, Jillian and Graham, with much love.

ONE

June 2006

Sharonne didn't bother to call goodbye or wish Derek luck. She slammed the hall door behind her. He heard the screech of the tyres as she rounded the bend in their driveway, the revving while the gates opened and then the ensuing engine roar as she disappeared down the leafy road in their quiet Dublin suburb.

Derek had woken up as the morning sun had sliced through the wooden blinds and reached the bed. It was the day of the Captain's Prize and he was looking forward to an outing with his mates, Conor, Rory and Liam, who was the only bachelor among them. They had a bet on that Derek would win today. The previous year's event had almost been washed off with the last few players forfeiting their chances by crying off before drowning on the fairways. The little stream that meandered through the course – and swallowed golf balls with a vengeance – had burst its banks, leaving the eighth and tenth greens unplayable for weeks. But today was sunny and clear skied, with no chance of the flood recurring.

'Morning, honey,' Derek had said to Sharonne as she came in to the kitchen. He stroked his goatee, something he did quite subconsciously. His greeting had been returned with a grunt. His wife had changed the spelling of her name to Sharon-NE when she'd gone into PR. She thought it would add a little air of mystique and distinguish her from all the other Sharons in the business.

'What has you so happy?' she'd snapped.

'No kids. A bit of peace and quiet, the competition and all that. Aren't you looking forward to the dinner?'

'I suppose,' she'd muttered. 'I've a lot to do first though.'

'Work?' he'd asked.

'No. Today is me time.'

'Would you like a fry-up?' he'd enquired, waving the frying pan in the air.

'Don't be ridiculous. Since when do I eat fry-ups?'

'I suppose Conor will regale us with more tales of the shenanigans at the tribunal – he can be very funny about the goings on there.'

'Maeve will probably be wearing something mumsy,' Sharonne had said by way of reply.

He hadn't reacted.

This had become a pattern ever since Sharonne had discovered that Derek had gone out with Maeve before they'd met. True, he still had a soft spot for Maeve, but once she had been introduced to Conor, he'd known he didn't have a chance. That pair had fallen for each other in a proverbial *coup de foudre* and they still acted like two lovebirds. The guys had met in college and kept in touch through golf.

'Yes, something mumsy,' Sharonne had goaded.

'What do you mean by mumsy?' Derek had risen to the bait, even though he'd sworn the last time that he never would again.

'Mumsy – you know – like an earth mother in a floral duvet. Old before her time. She'll probably turn up in a safe, floaty thing, to cover her big thighs.'

'She doesn't have big thighs,' he had exploded, no longer holding back his anger. 'You know, I actually thought they were your friends too, but obviously I was very wrong there.'

'I just say what I feel. Anyway, Maeve can do no wrong in your eyes, can she?'

He had said nothing, concentrating on turning the sausages over on the pan. That was when she had flounced out, making a grand exit.

Derek put his breakfast on a plate and sat down to eat, savouring the silence, which was rare in his houseful of women.

***

Sharonne arrived at Brush Strokes with only minutes to spare for her appointment. Hervé greeted her, scissors clipping rhythmically in his right hand, a habit that irritated Sharonne beyond belief, but she knew she couldn't say anything or he might take out his artistic tantrums on her. He blew air kisses behind her ears with little popping sounds and in his best inner-Dublin, pseudo-French accent, welcomed her and escorted her to her chair, mincing along on his high-rise heels.

'Cherie, are we colouring, highlighting, treating, cutting – what would la belle Sharonne like today?' Clicking the scissors again, Hervé called one of his minions to wash 'Madom's' hair, before he worked his magic.

Sharonne thought of Maeve again who, it seemed, everyone but she wanted to canonise. What she hadn't let her husband know was that she hated feeling threatened by Maeve. Perhaps if he'd told her about their relationship himself and not let her find out what everyone else already knew, Sharonne would have been able to dismiss it. She'd never even known they had dated until he confessed one New Year's Eve. They'd been playing a truth or dare type of game after a few too many glasses of the Widow Clicquot's bubbles. That was what really rankled – that and the fact that Maeve and he were still really close.

Why hadn't she been able to tell Derek that she'd do him proud tonight, that she had a knockout new outfit to wear? Was it because she knew she was determined to give Maeve a run for her money or that she really did feel threatened by this former girlfriend?

***

Maeve and Conor lived in a secluded, period house in Killiney. It hadn't been their first home, but when Conor had begun his rapid climb up the legal ladder, they had moved there a few years earlier. Much as she enjoyed her job at the clinic, Maeve loved her weekends. She enjoyed nothing better than pottering around her garden, especially at this time of the year, when the roses were out and the leaves were still a freshly minted green. She stopped every now and then to look down on the sea, and today was a glorious day for doing that.

She decided to paint her nails out on the patio. She settled herself with the newspaper, the only way to stop her getting up and pulling a weed, or doing a bit of deadheading somewhere in the beds and smudging the polish before it dried. The garden in a way had become her baby. She listened to the birds and the sound of a neighbour's ride-on mower doing its repetitive circuit. This was the sort of decadently lazy Saturday that she most enjoyed. She inhaled the smell of the newly cut grass wafting from the other side of the hedge and wondered how Conor was playing. Maybe he'd take the prize again this year. I must ring Trish, she thought, but her phone buzzed on the table at that moment.

'Hi, Trish, I was just thinking about you,' said Maeve. She'd been friends with Trish since schooldays and when Maeve had started going out with Conor, he had introduced Trish to Rory and it hadn't been long before they'd become an item.

'Well, that's telepathy for you. Have you a new gúna for the do tonight?' Trish asked.

'I have,' said Maeve. 'What about you?'

'I've just gone mad and splurged. I bought new shoes too. I daren't tell Rory what I spent so I threw the receipts away! He'd go mad if he knew how much they cost. You know what he's like, always going on about saving the pennies.'

Maeve did. She and Conor often talked about Rory's stinginess and he'd told her that the guys in the golf club were saying the previous week that he'd never allow himself to win the Captain's Prize because he'd have to buy the drinks afterwards.

'Is Liam bringing anyone to the dinner?' Maeve asked.

'Not that I heard, but you never know with him – always full of surprises.'

'Right, I have to fly, have to pick the kids up from the tennis club. See you later.'

***

As always, it was chaotic in the Collins' household in Glenageary and this evening was no exception. Rory had come home, very happy with his round of golf. Trish's niece had arrived to baby-sit. Their eldest son, Barry, at almost sixteen, was at an age where he felt offended by such an indignity and argued that he was old enough to be in charge. That was what worried Rory and Trish – he was old enough – old enough to have some pals in and to visit the drinks cupboard. They'd been told tales of this happening from his school – of kids topping up the gin and vodka bottles with water after they had had their fill and Trish was adamant that it wouldn't happen in their home. Louise and Toni, their other two children, loved having their cousin over. She was in her final year at school and was 'cool' in their eyes. She gave them French manicures and showed them how to use make-up.

'Everything Liam touches seems to turn to gold these days,' Rory said when they were getting ready to go out.

'What makes you say that?'

'He's just landed another hotel development – with a new client in Cyprus – five star all the way.'

'Well, that's great, isn't it? I mean – he works really hard,' she said.

'We all work really hard.'

'You know that's not what I meant. You can't complain. You have some nice contracts on the books too and Liam has no commitments, no kids or school fees, no mortgages, no wife …'

'I'm not about to give her up,' he said as she disappeared into the bathroom.

'Good,' she called out.

He followed her into the bathroom.

'You know, I've just been thinking, there's Derek with his finger in the Palm Island development in Dubai and a new bank headquarters in the Dublin Docklands. Maybe I should have expanded abroad more.'

'I don't think so – and leave me with those three downstairs.' She laughed. 'We're doing fine as we are.'

Rory was doing well. He owned his own highly successful architectural practice and with the way the construction industry was booming and running away with itself, there were good times ahead for all of them, despite the fact that one or two economists were saying the bubble would burst sooner rather than later. He was making sure he'd salted away enough just in case.

'You better get a move on Rory, or the taxi'll be here,' Trish said. The surfaces around her sink were scattered with make-up as she stood in front of her mirror. Rory's side was free of everything except his aftershave. She was wearing an open wrap over her black underwear.

'I hate these strapless bras, I always feel I'm going to fall out of them,' she said, tugging it up higher.

'Need any help?' asked Rory, putting his arms around her and nuzzling her.

'Not the kind you have in mind, not now anyway,' she said, 'Maybe later …'

'Aha, I'm on a promise …' he said doing up his bowtie.

Trish went back to their bedroom and slipped on her dress.

'You look terrific,' her husband said.

'Thank you – and I feel it too.'

***

'Perfect timing,' said Derek. 'There's Maeve and Conor in

front of us. Derek was taking money from his wallet when Sharonne shrieked.

'My God, I'm not going in there! Look at her – look at what she's wearing,' she said grabbing hold of his arm.

'She looks terrific,' said Derek.

'She looks terrific!' echoed Sharonne.

'Don't say you're going to throw one of your tantrums. You both look great.' He tried a recovery but it drove Sharonne into an even greater rage.

'Look at her will you, you blind fool. She's wearing my outfit.'

'For Christ's sake get a grip. Pretend you don't notice. It's only a dress and it doesn't look the same to me. It's not even the same colour. Yours is purple.'

'It's burgundy, not purple,' she said irrationally, 'and I'm going home. I have to change.'

'For once, will you realise the world doesn't revolve around you. What would you tell a client to do if this happened to them?'

She gave him a withering look. 'I'm not a client and I'm going home.'

'If you want to go that's your call. I'm not going with you. Could you not try, for my sake, to be … nice?'

'If you go in there without me, you needn't expect me to come back.'

'Fine! I won't. I'm going to enjoy myself.'

'As if I bloody well care.'

The taxi man kept his eyes straight ahead.

'Oh honey, don't I just know that? Thank you for asking me how I played. It's the first time I've ever won the Captain's Prize. Thanks for your support, but I'm not going to let you spoil tonight because of your insane jealously of Maeve.'

Conor approached. 'Hi there, you two.'

Derek got out of the taxi.

'Sharonne's having one of her petulant moments,' he said,

shooting a menacing look back at his wife, who was still in the car. 'She's deciding whether or not to grace us with her presence.'

Conor laughed. 'Grace us with her presence? Umm. It can't be that bad?' he said. 'And you know I don't handle divorce cases.'

'Well that could all change and this could be your first,' he said. 'It seems our wives are wearing similar dresses. And mine is not very happy with the situation.' He took a note from his wallet and handed it to the driver.

'That's not sufficient grounds for another world war, is it?' asked Conor.

'Maybe not in global terms but, in the world of Sharonne, it seems to be of nuclear proportions.' Derek went over to Maeve.

'You look stunning, as always,' he said, hugging her warmly. 'And,' he whispered, 'Sharonne's on the warpath – be prepared!'

'I hear congratulations are in order,' Maeve said while Conor was coaxing Sharonne out of the car.

'Snap, Sharonne,' said Maeve, 'I see we've been shopping in the same place. I only hope I look as good in this as you do.'

Sharonne could hardly speak with anger. 'Now that I see it on you, I'm not sure I really like the cut,' was her reply.

'Come on, let's get you ladies inside for a drink,' Conor said.

They headed upstairs to the bar, which overlooked the eighteenth green. It was a blissful summer's evening and they took their cocktails out onto the veranda where Rory and Trish were already sitting.

'I'm really looking forward to the holiday in Mijas,' Maeve said to Trish, referring to the two-week holiday the friends took together every summer. 'I can't wait either,' Trish replied. 'Hey look, here's Liam – with a stunner. I told you he'd surprise us.' They all laughed.

Liam had a striking-looking girl by his side, one they hadn't met before. She stretched out her hand to Maeve and said, 'I'm Noelle, and I don't play golf.'

Liam said, 'That sounds like a confession. "Hello, I'm Liam and I'm a gambler or a serial womaniser or some such."'

'Well, it *is* in a way, because my parents, three brothers and two sisters-in-law all play and when any of them get together my eyes are inclined to glaze over. So I just thought I should warn you that if that happens I don't need medication, just a change of topic!'

Sharonne chimed, 'Mine will probably glaze over before yours,' before adding, 'with boredom.'

Liam interrupted, 'Now Shar, we're not that dull.' He went on, unaware of the reason for Sharonne's bad temper. 'We can always talk about things like who's fleecing who in the seedy world of finance that you represent.' She shot him a filthy look, glanced at her watch and asked, 'Will they never get on with speeches?'

Noelle turned to Trish, 'That dress is a stunner. I wish I could wear black.'

Sharonne butted in, 'There's so much of it here this evening it's hard to tell who's serving staff and who isn't.'

Trish smiled sweetly at her and said, 'Well, I'm not on duty tonight, so you can rule me out!' Her one-shoulder black dress fitted her like a second skin. She didn't usually buy designer labels and was the envy of many of her friends as she always had the knack of knowing what to buy, whether from a chain or department store.

Maeve said, 'You do look fantastic, Trish. That was worth every penny.'

Trish replied, 'When I saw it in the boutique in Donnybrook, I decided I was going to splurge. I dipped into my running away money to buy it. Designer dresses don't fit into any of Rory's accounting systems so I'll have to pretend it came from Next.'

Derek was the centre of attention with club members coming up to congratulate him on his win. Sharonne did her public relations bit of smiling and being nice to them all, but her smile never reached her eyes and took on a frozen look as Derek made his acceptance speech. He finished it up by saying, 'We were all getting worried that Conor might make it three in a row and feared that the only way we would be able to stop him would be to vote for him to be vice captain, but with so many builders in the club that may not have been an easy vote to get passed!'

There was laughter all around. Everyone knew that the developers were the ones being investigated in the tribunals and some of them there that evening might yet end up in the witness box being cross-examined by Conor.

Derek went back to the table amid guffaws and wisecracks. He was a popular winner. He was a good sportsman, good at tennis, had played rugby for his school and college and run a few marathons in his time, yet he was never fanatical about anything only his work. Sharonne clapped half-heartedly but with no evidence of delight as she watched Maeve show real pleasure at his victory. She didn't sit beside him at the table, or beside Maeve, and as soon as the soup was served she feigned a migraine, excused herself and went to ask the barman to call a taxi. When she joined the table again she turned on Maeve, 'You should do something with your hair. Maybe lighten it a bit to give it a lift. I could give you the number of the guy who does mine – he's great at shaping.'

Trish and Rory exchanged looks and Trish stretched her foot under the table kicking Maeve not to react, while she said pointedly, 'Don't you dare go blonde. You're not old enough to do that yet. Look around here. It's like a Barbie reunion.'

'… a Barbie reunion,' echoed Conor.

'Now that you mention it, it could be,' laughed Liam, 'Not old enough to go blonde – I like that.'

'What do you mean old enough?' Sharonne rounded on him.

'Well, all my mother's friends who got tired of trying to hide the grey roots turned blonde in their old age. Talk about the

Golden Girls – they called themselves the Flaxen Floozies!'

'They didn't!' said Noelle.

'They did. They had the X factor all right – Botox, detox and intox, the highlights in their lives. It was all Auntie Anne's fault. She came home after living for years in the States with all these crazes and the others followed suit. Well, she'd had three husbands and confessed to a few lovers too, so they felt she knew something they didn't, scandalised and all as they were by her.'

Before Sharonne could make any further comment, a waiter signalled the arrival of her taxi. Her parting shot to Derek was, 'Well, you enjoy your evening.'

'Oh, I will. Now,' he muttered to himself, getting up and walking her to the door. 'Don't wait up for me. It'll be a late one.'

Astounded at her bitchiness and knowing full well there was no migraine, Noelle asked, 'I couldn't help but notice that you are wearing the same dresses. Is that what that was all about?'

'Apparently so,' Liam replied before Trish could. 'She has her moments and sometimes it doesn't take too much to trigger them!' The guys all felt sorry for Derek.

'No glazed eyes tonight, then?' Trish asked.

Noelle laughed, 'I might have been missing out if club nights are all like this.'

'Happily they're not.'

'What a bitch. Men have left their wives for less!' Conor muttered to Maeve.

Derek came back to the table and, as he passed by Maeve's chair he ended everyone's awkwardness about the situation when he stopped and said, 'Now more wine anyone? This is supposed to be a celebration.'

Although conversations started up again Derek knew Sharonne had gone one step too far. He and the men were all dressed identically in black suits and bowties and they weren't running home to change. What was the big deal anyway? But he knew that it hadn't just been the dress that had rankled with her.

***

When Derek got home that night, Sharonne was fast asleep, or pretending to be. He stood looking at her comatose form and realised he didn't like her much any more. When had this happened, he wondered, this change of heart? They used to be so good together. He acknowledged that their activities in the bedroom had become too metred, like everything else in her life. He was not accommodated when she wasn't in the mood. Accommodated. Had it really come to this, that he found himself looking at his wife and thinking words like that? No, he decided, I've had enough of this. He went to one of the guest bedrooms, undressed, climbed beneath the duvet and lay thinking. Sleep was a long way off as he reflected on their friends and their lifestyles. If she kept up this behaviour, it would make things very awkward when it came to the holiday in a few weeks time.

He knew that Sharonne was a high-maintenance woman. She hadn't ever wanted children either. She used to say women never looked the same after they'd been stretched. Derek had been thrilled when she'd become pregnant. She hadn't been – she'd freaked. She hadn't missed taking her contraceptive pill, she'd assured him of that. But she had had a violent reaction to mussels after a meal one weekend and had been sick for a few days. 'That's what did it,' the doctor told Derek, 'the food poisoning and the retching had the effect of rendering the dosage ineffective for a short period, and so your wife is pregnant.'

'It's good to have your family when you're young,' the doctor said after he'd broken the news to them that they were going to have not one, but two. 'So many women are waiting until well into their thirties before starting.'

'At least I'll get it all over with in one fell swoop,' had been Sharonne's reaction to the news. 'I wouldn't like to have an only child, like me, and would have felt pressured to have a second one. I always felt responsible for my parents. If they were arguing, I felt it was my fault and when they were old, I had no one to share the visits and the anxieties with. I even felt guilty for wanting to travel, I felt like I was abandoning them.'

'So twins seem like a perfect solution for you,' the doctor had said to them. 'They can gang up on you when they are teenagers.'

Derek hadn't really been surprised when she'd told the obstetrician then, 'When you're delivering them you can tie my tubes too?'

'Isn't that a little extreme?' Derek had asked. 'You might change your mind later on.'

'I won't,' had been her resolute reply.

She was a good mother to Megan and Sandy, Derek conceded. Much as he was annoyed with Sharonne, he knew that neither one of them would do anything to rattle the girls' lives.

TWO

'I'm off now, Conor,' Maeve said as she gathered her keys and bag.

'Is it not a bit on the early side for you?' he asked.

'I want to get in before the new patients and they seem to arrive earlier and earlier on Mondays, especially when they are coming from the country,' she said.

'They probably all listen to AA Roadwatch and are terrified of being caught in a traffic jam so they set out at the crack of dawn.'

'Probably, but they don't feel so lost when there's someone there to greet them.'

Maeve worked at a private clinic, as receptionist to a consultant oncologist who was much in demand for his vanguard approach to cancer.

From her office window, she enjoyed a view across Dublin Bay to Howth, a view interrupted only by a passing train. In summer, the sea was dotted with yachts from the numerous clubs that delineated the wealthier suburbs of the city. This morning the tide was out, and she was sitting staring, unseeing, when Stan Rosenthal came in behind her.

'Morning, Maeve. Had a good weekend?'

'Yes, and you? How did the game go on Saturday?' Stan was a member in a different club to her husband, but they often played in the Opens at each other's courses.

'Good. I hear Derek pipped Conor at the last hole. About time he let someone else win that trophy,' he joked.

'You've been listening to gossip,' Maeve said.

'Never!' he laughed. 'But I played with Liam yesterday and he was telling me. Heard about the ding-dong at the dinner too. Must have been a good night.'

'Memorable,' said Maeve.

'I don't know how he stays married to that woman, or how he plays golf with a frozen shoulder.'

'I didn't know he had a frozen shoulder,' she said.

'Well, wouldn't you have if you had to sleep with that frosty face at your back every night?' Stan quipped.

'That's terrible,' she laughed.

'Just true,' he answered. 'At times like these, I'm delighted to be single again. Breda did me a favour by leaving before I had to take that step. And I'm glad that, despite your best efforts, I'm still in that happy single state. Having my work as my wife is a much better solution for me!'

He ducked from her mock punch. Everyone knew what Breda, or Chandeliers, was like. They called her that because she seemed to live her life going from one glittering do to another, always dripping in bling – real and fake together.

No man was safe in her presence, even with a wife or girlfriend on his arm. Since their very public divorce she'd appeared regularly in the gossip columns at some society bash or other and she seemed to have a penchant for dark-eyed, Arab-type escorts. When any of their friends ran in to her it was to have to endure a litany of, 'I was at dinner in the Egyptian embassy last week and the ambassador told me …' or 'the attaché, you know he's single, asked me to be his hostess at their national day party …'

'Do you know what she's up to now?' Stan asked. 'She's recently got involved in a charity for Palestinian orphans or a rescue effort for child camel jockeys or some such good cause. She seems to think this will be her social entrée into the foreign service circle,' he laughed. 'Now all she talks about is, "When I was staying in the Irish embassy during the Dubai Classic this year … or wherever.'

Maeve was thinking that this sounded just like her. She knew Breda well.

'I hate to admit to it,' Stan continued, 'but my mother was right about her, you know. She always said Breda was more in love with the idea of being married to a surgeon than with this particular surgeon. I should have listened to her! Oh hell and damnation. Has it come to this? I never thought I'd say that about my mother. I think it's time I got back to work.'

He grinned as he picked up the files Maeve had left on the edge of her desk earlier and took them into his consulting room just as the first patient arrived.

The morning seemed to drag, which was unusual. Normally it was over without Maeve noticing. She felt tired and thought that she must be getting old, late nights never used to affect her like this.

As Stan, her boss, was operating in another hospital that afternoon, Maeve finished her paperwork early and decided to call in to Trish on her way home. She rang and told her to put the kettle on, promising to bring some Danish pastries.

When Trish opened the door she teased, 'Oh, Maeve – that hair – you should do something about it. I see you haven't been to the studio yet!' They fell around the place laughing.

'Hervé will be so-oooo disappointed.'

'Poor Derek. I felt so sorry for him,' Trish said. 'How does he put up with her? She was furious about the dress, which really was fabulous by the way, and that's all that was wrong with her. But you'd think she'd have the cop on to hide it.'

'She doesn't realise how lucky she is, with a successful business, those gorgeous girls and a good husband,' Maeve said.

Over mugs of tea, they talked of their approaching holiday to Spain. It had become something of a ritual, all the friends taking these few weeks off together to spend in Maeve and Conor's villa.

'If I were you – but I'm not, I'm not charitable and kind and forgiving – but if I were you and Conor, I wouldn't invite them this year. Teach her a lesson, that would.'

'That wouldn't be fair on Derek and, besides, who'd make up the fourball? The guys would hate the change in the routine and they were friends long before she arrived on the scene.'

'Well, just invite him then.'

'I think pretending it never happened is the best plan,' said Maeve.

They drained the last of the tea and picked up the crumbs from their pastries on damp fingertips.

'Thanks for popping in. The kids will be back soon so I better get organised too.'

'Well I'm going home for a nap.'

Trish laughed – 'A nap? You're always on the go – putting the rest of us to shame with your limitless energy.'

'Well, today I'm feeling lazy.'

When Conor came home from an early adjournment of the proceedings, he ruffled her hair. She stirred and stretched. She'd dozed off watching *The Weakest Link*.

'We should put Sharonne into that,' he said sitting down beside her and pointing at the TV. 'Anne Robinson would cut her down to size. In fact, I wonder if I could get her on to my team – she'd be great at intimidating some of the chancers we're up against.'

'You should write and ask her,' Maeve replied. Then she told him she'd popped in to see Trish that afternoon. 'She thinks Sharonne may not want to come to Mijas with us.'

'All the better. She's quite a harridan, isn't she? Derek deserves a break.'

'Did you hear from him today?'

'Yes and no! He left a message and when I called him back, he was at a planning meeting. I'll give him a shout later. We need to get those flights confirmed.'

THREE

Liam Coffey had had a frantic week and he was really looking forward to chilling out with his friends. His work as a quantity surveyor had taken him to London on Monday and Tuesday, then he'd flown to Cyprus and had just arrived back home on Friday. He'd gone straight to the office to check up on a few things, before heading off to Mijas the following morning. The light on his answer phone was flashing in a frenzy – one, two, three, four, five, six – eleven calls. He pressed the button as he poured a gin and tonic. The last one said, 'Hi, Conor here, we'll pick you up on the way to the airport, 6.30 sharp in the morning. Don't forget to set the alarm clock.'

'Righto,' he muttered out loud. He sliced a wedge of lemon and popped it in his drink, taking it through to his bedroom, picking up his case as he went along. He set the glass down and emptied the contents of his bag onto the bed, barely noticing the panorama of glittering lights that spread out beyond his penthouse windows.

'Josie, my Mrs Wonderful,' he said out loud as he took a fresh pile of short-sleeved shirts off a shelf in his wardrobe, gathered some slacks and golfing shorts, an armful of underwear and balled socks and placed them neatly in his case. What would I do without her? he mused. A quick shower and I'm in the sack, he thought, glancing at the bedside clock, which read 1.30 am. I should be able to catch four hours if I'm lucky.

In Cyprus, he had gone through the contracts and costings for a new golf development, owned by a very successful German consortium. It was to encompass luxurious villas, a small shopping centre, a gym, tennis club and a golf course. There were only a few other courses on the island and really they would be in a different league when this one opened up. With the deals signed and out of the way, a night of celebration had followed.

The musicians in their white shirts with voluminous sleeves and wide red sashes had started playing Zorba's dance. At its opening leisurely pace, Liam had tapped his foot in time with the slow movements, but was quickly dragged onto the floor.

Da da – Begin on left foot. Step forward. Da da – Tap ball of right foot next to left heel.

Da da da da da – Swing right leg and kick it slightly forward. As Theodorakis's music gained momentum, high-lifting steps, squats and double steps were added, the musicians' fingers speeded up on the strings of the bouzoukis and the crowd clicked their fingers to the rhythm. The Cypriots clapped in time before applauding his hilarious efforts to keep up.

Both Stavros, the marketing director, and Aldora, the publicity woman for the project, fancied the pants off him. They hung on his every word each time he came to the island. Aldora showed him the steps and he was urged in one direction, then another, dancing with everyone, except the leering Stavros! Liam only managed to avoid that by taking the hand of the older, very overweight waitress and swirling her around and around to the pulse of the instruments. She was captivated. Liam could do that to anyone. He was a man's man and a ladies' one too. Macho and sporty, he had had a sequence of glamorous women in his life, several verging on being serious. Liam was a collector – he collected people wherever he went – never letting them go once they became part of his world.

After the musicians had gone home, he and Aldora, who had practically hand-bagged Stavros to get rid of him, had gone for a walk along the beach at Limassol.

'You speak English with an American accent. Did you live there?' he asked.

'Yes, for several years. My family moved there after the Turkish invasion in 1974, but I always wanted to come back. They used to live in Nicosia, now in occupied Cyprus, as you know.' He loved the way she pronounced the city's name. 'When the Turks arrived my family left, literally taking only their nightclothes and some food. They went to their summer house, a little place in the hills, and never went back home.'

'That's terrible. Did you stay there long?' he asked.

'No. It wasn't safe to stay so we fled with my grandparents. They really believed they'd be back home in a few days, but we never even went back to get our clothes. It was very sad. We haven't got one family photograph. Our grandparents left everything too. I did have my teddy bear though,' she smiled. 'My mother grabbed that when she took me out of the cot and I don't think I've gone anywhere without him since. He even came back from the States.'

'I had a teddy too. He was called Barney,' volunteered Liam, suddenly remembering his scruffy, much-loved childhood companion. 'But what happened to your home?'

'Have you been to Nicosia?' she asked.

He nodded.

'You can actually see the house behind the barricades. It's in the no-man's zone between the occupied part and free Nicosia. The roof has collapsed in places and it's just lying there, derelict. The houses were all looted years ago and now they are just shells. My parents couldn't accept what was happening and they emigrated to the States.'

'I can't imagine what it must be like to be suddenly separated from everything you own,' he said.

'It wasn't easy. Even starting a new life wasn't easy for the older people. They had very little English, especially people like my grandparents. Some of them never learned and that was to our advantage because they still spoke Greek at home. That made it possible for us to come back.'

They sat down on a sun lounger, the sound of the lapping waves lazily breaking the silence.

'What brought you back?'

'I met Nico. His family came from Famagusta. Our backgrounds were the same, only a Turkish family now lives in his home and his mother lives in Paphos. We fell madly in love and used to spend hours talking about coming home. We got engaged and decided that was the right time. Nico's an accountant so he was able to find work easily and he joined a Limassol hotel group. Because of my English I got a job with Harris, the solicitor for this new golf course development. He needed someone with English to handle the large contracts.'

'Were you living together?'

'Good God, no!' she said. 'That's still frowned on here, but you know, I think if we had we'd still be with each other,' she said sadly.

'How come?' asked Liam.

'The same things that happens to nearly all relationships which flounder in Cyprus,' she said.

'Which is?'

'He met someone who didn't have brown eyes and black hair. The Cypriot men go mad for anyone who looks different.'

'But Cypriot women and men are stunning. I envy them their sallow skin and colouring. We Irish are a mottled lot – with pasty skin and freckles; we burn in the sun and half of us have watery blue eyes. And as for ginger hair – well forget it!' he said, patting his unruly crown. 'Irish men find dark hair really attractive.'

Aldora smiled a sad smile. 'You're just being kind. Seriously, it is a real difficulty for women on the island. The Cypriot men are always attracted to those who look different, so fair hair and fair skins are like beacons and you only have to look around to see how many of them visit the island constantly. Every week or two, they have a new crop to fall in love with. And these women are willing to sleep with them too. Men here don't see dark colouring and virtue as nice – to them that's too ordinary and we are too repressed.'

'Nico obviously didn't mind,' said Liam.

'Yes, I thought so too until I discovered he was having an affair with his secretary in the office and that he was sleeping with her too. She's Dutch, tall, leggy, fair and available. She also lives in the hotel. I never suspected anything because Nico used to go away often to do audits at the other hotels.'

'How did you find out?' Liam urged gently.

'It was his mother who told me. She thought he was staying out to sleep over with me and she was determined to tell me what a depraved woman I was, leading her darling son astray.'

'The meddling old bitch,' he said, taking both her hands in his.

'In fairness she was shocked when she realised what she'd done. She would prefer to have a Cypriot daughter-in-law than a Dutch one any day – even one who had supposedly led her son astray.'

'How long ago was that?'

'Almost two years.' She laughed. 'They're engaged now and, as you see, I'm completely over it, don't you think?' She looked at him, her eyes glistening in the moonlight. He drew her towards him and cuddled her for a while, neither saying anything.

'What about you?' she asked, breaking the silence. 'You don't wear a ring – are you married, divorced or what?'

'Or what, I suppose,' he laughed. 'I'm in recovery too! I never wanted to settle down, I was always on the move and after today I'll be in Cyprus more often so perhaps we can meet up when I'm over – if you'd like.'

'I'd like that very much,' she said, 'but tell me about your broken heart – if you want to.'

'I met Helen at Charles de Gaulle airport – waiting for a very delayed flight. We got talking. She was in overseas property, something we discovered when, after a drink, we found we were seated beside each other on the flight back to Dublin. I'd seen her that morning on the flight over. She had dark eyes and dark hair,' he said, and Aldora laughed.

'Perhaps men are the same the world over – looking for what is different. Maybe it's a one-upmanship thing: they like to have something that's different from their friends.'

'I must think about that some time,' he said, 'but not now.'

'So what happened? How long did you know each other?'

'We met in early December and saw each other every chance we could.'

'That must be difficult if you both travel a lot.'

'Yes. It was. Time was so precious that we made the most of every minute of it, meeting for snatched weekends in Dublin, Paris and Rome. We even managed to co-ordinate a visit to Bermuda and took a week there together.'

'How romantic. That sounds fantastic.'

'It was. The stuff of Hollywood romances and I admit I was obsessed with her. That had never happened to me before and I thought she felt the same. We often discussed it although she was always reticent, never really committing to anything, I was convinced I'd win her over and decided the first anniversary was the one to do it on.'

'What did you do?'

'I went overboard,' he said pensively, 'I proposed to her at the spot where we'd met in Charles de Gaulle airport.'

'Oh, Liam, that is so romantic.'

'It wasn't. She turned me down!'

'Oh my God. What did you do?'

'We got on the plane, ate our meal like the civilised beings we are. I have never seen her since we parted at Dublin airport.'

'My God! Why? What did she say?' It was Aldora's turn to take Liam's hands in hers.

'She told me she had a past. I told her it didn't matter. She said it did. I tried to convince her that it was behind her – us – but she had never told me she had a daughter, who is now ten and who lives with her grandmother. The father never knew. She had been in her final year in college and he'd just been accepted for an internship in a hospital in England. They'd only been together for a handful of months.'

'But surely she is not going to let that stop her being happy again,' Aldora said in disbelief.

'She never told him. She'd never seen him after she discovered she was pregnant, until a month before I proposed. They had begun seeing each other again. She said she was going to tell me that night on the way home from Paris. He had just been introduced to his daughter that week for the first time.'

'That's so sad,' said Aldora.

'I misread all the signs that weekend. I thought she was just tired, worked up about Christmas. I never suspected what turmoil she was going through, nor that she would want to finish with me. I was so wrapped up in getting the romantic scene just right. It had to be fate, she'd said. The girl's father just walked into the agency where she works looking for a property to buy in Ireland. He had been in the States, specialising, and now, recently divorced, he'd been offered a consultancy back in Dublin.'

'Was she remorseful? How did she think you'd take that bit of news for Christmas?' asked Aldora.

'No. Just said she never intended for it to happen. But she felt the old magnetism was still there between them and she owed it to her daughter to give it her best shot. That was the last time we spoke. I sent her flowers for her birthday, but she never acknowledged them.' His voice was sad. 'You know they say actions speak louder than words and, I have to admit, I am one for the grand gestures – always have been. Next time, if there ever is one, I'll send dandelions.'

They sat there and hugged each other as the dawn began to lighten the sky over the Mediterranean, each cherishing the new contact, but locked in their private pasts, wanting to forget, but still afraid to move on.

Now, as he threw the last few toiletries in his case, he was looking forward to his break in Spain, to some good golf and to seeing Aldora on his next visit to Cyprus.

He set his alarm clock.

FOUR

After a lengthy delay at Dublin airport – the French air traffic controllers acting up again – they had made it to the villa in Mijas on the Costa del Sol in Spain. Derek was on his own. Sharonne had decided the FitzGerald-Reglob deal was too important to leave for any of the lesser mortals in her office to handle. Secretly, Derek was relieved. Things between them were still a bit on the cool side since the famous night of the identical dresses, dubbed so by Liam. And if Sharonne was in one of her moods, she would ruin everything.

The villa was idyllic, with four en-suite bedrooms, a huge reception room, a large patio and the inviting pool. When they had first seen it, Maeve's eyes had lit up as she walked from room to room, exclaiming at the views down to the sea and, on that mistless day, right across towards Africa. For Conor, there'd been the added bonus that from the back veranda the verdant ninth fairway and the tree-dotted golf course spread out like an open invitation.

'It's perfect,' she'd said, 'and big enough for us to have lots of kids and their friends all here together. But can we really afford it?'

'Of course we can,' Conor had replied confidently, kissing the top of her head. He had just won a protracted, high-profile libel case and had been handsomely rewarded for his erudite and often-witty skills, which saw the arguments of the plaintiff's counsel tumble one by one.

They had spent a month in Mijas that summer and Maeve had decorated the villa in cool sherbet colours of pistachio and lime. The sofa and chairs were lemon with splashes of contrast in the French-blue cushions. Outside, a wooden veranda ran the whole length of the front, wrapping around the end of the house past the main bedroom. The pool was lined with azure tiles, which always made it look inviting. It was set a little way off in a slight hollow so that no one could see it from the course – affording more privacy than the others in the secluded complex. She loved the sounds at night-time, when the frogs courted and the sprinklers came on to keep the putting greens up to championship standard.

Conor and Maeve managed to get to Spain several times every year, usually taking a three-week stint as their annual vacation. In between their visits, the property was never rented out, but left at the disposal of their family and friends. The lots of children they had envisaged never materialised, a fact they had come to terms with, after a round of miscarriages and false alarms. All this seemed to have brought them closer together, if that had been possible. Conor adored Maeve. His eyes followed her wherever she went. Maeve was the perfect companion for him too, able to read when he was stressed and knowing instinctively how to defray anxiety and introduce some levity. They worked well as a team. Trish and Rory often speculated privately that perhaps this was because they had no children, that they had more time to devote to each other.

'Are we all in our usual rooms?' asked Liam, hovering in the hallway with his bags.

'Yes, you all know your way around so just settle in and make yourselves at home,' Maeve said.

She followed Conor, who had had taken their luggage through into their room and was looking out at the view that stretched in front of him.

'This is what I love, the pool outside, the golf course next door and the smell of the sunshine,' he said.

'I'm so glad we bought this place when we did,' said Maeve, 'and to think I thought it was too big then. Do you know what I love about it most? Being able to have our friends enjoy it with us.'

'I agree. and I'm going to make the most of these two weeks,' Conor said, eyeing the water in the pool. 'It's been manic for the past few months and it looks as though we're going to be going back to even more of the same. If only you knew how often my mind wanders to this place when I'm sitting in that stuffy courtroom …'

Moving back into the living room, Maeve called out for everyone to go out to the pool. 'Time for some vino and a start on the tans – that's an order.'

'We don't need to be told twice,' Rory said, following Maeve and Trish who were carrying out some bottles and glasses. Maeve went back in to get the canapés she had asked Marise to prepare. Marise always made sure the villa was ready for them when they arrived. Trish had already changed into poolside wear and was just taking off her robe when Rory came up behind her and put his arms around her playfully. She twisted to face him, lost her balance and they toppled over and fell into the water together. The others joined them.

When they had climbed out, Conor poured the wine and proposed a toast. 'To freedom from clients, emails, mobile phones and deadlines.'

'And children,' said Trish.

'And children,' they chorused as they clinked glasses.

Later on the veranda while waiting for everyone to get ready to go out to dinner, Rory said to Trish, 'You know, Derek seems to have got the work/relaxation balance just right and he's making more than a good living out of it.'

'We don't do too badly,' said Trish.

'By my calculations, he has an awful lot more than us to

spend. He has an expanding overseas property portfolio, new top spec cars every year for himself and Sharonne, lots of breaks, the kids in the best private school around, ponies. All he's lacking is the helicopter.'

'Who's lacking a helicopter, apart from me?' asked Liam, joining them.

'Derek mentioned that if he had one, it would actually save his company money at this point as his project managers spend a few hours every day just trying to get from one site to another.'

'I think Derek is too prudent to make that sort of investment, especially now,' said Liam.

Maeve and Conor emerged. 'What sort of investment – am I missing out on something here?

'Rory thinks Derek should have a helicopter,' Trish said.

'What a great idea. You could take us all to the races in it,' Maeve said to Derek as he joined them. 'I've always fancied myself arriving that way.'

'You and Sharonne both,' Derek said, rubbing his jawline where he had shaved off his beard. It was the first time his wife's name had been mentioned. 'If I ever get one, you'll be the first to go up in it,' he laughed. 'But I'm not sure how that would go down with the tabloids when they discover that the state's top barrister and his wife are taking junkets! They'd go mad.'

As was their habit on their first evening in Spain, they had decided to go to dinner in the nearby town, at their favourite restaurant, El Caballo Loco. Maeve was just eight when she had first gone there and still vividly remembered the impressions made by the narrow twisting cobbled streets and the burro taxis, which were really just donkeys that carried people and their goods up the steep streets. Later, for Conor and her, it became their special place. El Caballo Loco was their spot, a little restaurant that the locals favoured and which, over the years, had become a favourite with them too.

'Isn't life good? I so love this annual get together,' said Maeve. 'Imagine, we've been doing it for five years already!'

Oddly enough, none of the women in the group had taken up golf. Maeve had had a few lessons, even had her own set of clubs and had gone with Conor on a Sunday evening to bang a bucket or two of balls in the practice bays at the club, but other than that, she'd never bothered. Trish didn't see the point of 'making little red flags' her goal in life. Besides, she was far too busy with her teenagers to take that much time off. The lads were intent on getting in a round of golf most days, if the women didn't object to being abandoned altogether.

Maeve and Trish didn't. They were equally determined to spend the time as lazily as they could, tanning by the pool, ploughing their way through airport novels, perusing the market stalls, sipping wine and cocktails and generally enjoying each other's company. Trish and Rory's kids were safely in the Gaeltacht, for what was supposed to be total immersion in the Irish language.

El Caballo Loco was nothing showy and was consistently the same. Red and white check tablecloths and napkins, candles in wax-draped bottles, a guitarist perched in the same seat in the same corner, as though he never left. The proprietors greeted the group as long-lost friends.

'¡Bienvenidos Señora Maeve y Señor Conor! ¡Bienvenidos todos!'

'Xavier and Isabella, it's great to see you again.'

Embraces followed before they were ushered to the table in the window. They were scarcely seated before Liam had caught the attention of two good-looking women – Finns, he guessed, from the strange guttural sounds they were uttering. Despite his numerous business trips to Finland, he could only remember a few words of this lingo – ravintola, which meant restaurant, and kiitos paljon, or thank you very much. One of the women kept smiling a perfect smile any time he happened to glance in her direction, something he did with increasing frequency during the evening.

'I think you've made an impression,' Maeve whispered to him. Liam laughed.

'No, I think it's Derek she fancies,' Rory said.

'I hope not! Can you just imagine how we'd explain that to Sharonne!'

'It would serve her right,' said Liam. 'She doesn't appreciate how good life is for her.'

Between the joviality at their table and the machinations of Xavier and his matchmaking wife, the two beauties eventually joined them for after-dinner drinks – drinks that stretched on and on. The women were indeed Finnish and worked in the European Commission in Brussels. The taller of the two, Agneta, was due to complete her tour of duty in a few months' time and head back to Helsinki; Anna Maria had another two years to run. This trip to Mijas had become an annual event for them too. They both played golf and promised to meet the guys for a match during the week. It was very late when they eventually headed back to the villa, having seen their new friends back to their apartment block en route.

'Tee time is 9.30 and I want no excuses for being late,' Liam called as he retired.

Trish and Maeve gave each other a good night hug. 'See you at the pool whenever.'

'Yeah – whenever. And don't you guys dare wake us up when you're leaving,' Trish said.

'Come on, wife, I have plans for you tonight,' Rory said to Trish, taking her hand.

'Isn't it amazing what the sight of a bit of flesh will do to a man?' she said, to no one in particular.

'Or the thought of no teenagers walking in on us,' Rory added.

Bedroom doors closed and the villa gradually quietened.

Conor curled around Maeve, who said, 'Well, did you miss Sharonne?'

Conor laughed, 'No! Did you?'

'Not a bit, but I do hope they are not growing too far apart – they do have the twins to consider.'

I'm sure it'll not get to that,' said Conor. 'Besides, it might do them both good to have a bit of time away from each other.'

'I bet he's next door thinking the same thing!' said Maeve.

'Probably,' Conor agreed.

'Do you think Liam is wondering how Helen's doing, or do you think he'd take her back if things don't work out with her daughter's father?' she asked.

'I don't honestly know.'

'He was telling me about Aldora on the plane – he met her in Cyprus and has promised to meet up with her on his next trip there,' said Maeve. 'She phoned him today, when we were waiting for our luggage to come through at the airport.'

'Aha, quite the little detective, aren't you?' he said, pulling her closer to him. 'As you seem to know what everyone else is thinking, do you have any idea what's on my mind?'

She snuggled closer to him and said, 'I think I have a very good idea.'

***

The days passed under cloud-free skies, the breeze on the hillside keeping the temperatures bearable.

'Isn't it amazing how quickly you sink into relaxation when you are removed from your normal day to day habits,' Derek said to Liam and Rory. None of them had noticed he had shaved off his beard.

'If we could do this all year round, do you think we'd get tired of it?' asked Liam.

'I'd like the opportunity to try it and see,' said Rory.

The days flew by. They visited the port and walked by the marinas, admiring the ostentatious yachts. They foraged in the markets and dined in an assortment of tavernas, enjoying the fresh fish and local food. They caught up with some friends they had made over the years, some of whom were Irish who rarely came back to Ireland. The Finnish women had become part of their little group and, when not golfing, they joined Trish and Maeve at the poolside, where all sorts of female theories and opinions, along with books and magazines, were exchanged. They teased Maeve about her facility to power nap while they all chattered around her.

'You better not talk about me because I'm listening all the time,' she joked.

***

It was Wednesday and, as was the custom, breakfast was a leisurely affair and taken when they felt like it. Liam, Conor and Rory were lolling by the pool, watching the mists evaporate in the distance as the sun's heat intensified. 'It's going to be a scorcher today. I'm going to head to the vineyard to stock up,' Conor said.

'Great idea,' Liam said. 'Let's make a day of it and lunch is on me.'

'There's no need for that,' said Maeve.

'Yes there is! And there'll be no more discussion about it,' he insisted.

About an hour later, Maeve, Derek, Trish, Rory and Liam climbed onto the scarred seats of the old Jeep that Conor kept there for just such excursions and they all headed into the countryside.

The low buildings of Bodegas Manuel were shaded by a long band of pine trees. The walls were painted in a soft honey colour and, behind them, rows and rows of vines sliced the fields in every direction. There was always a bustle about the place, especially in autumn when the harvest took place and the grape pickers and owners celebrated.

'I love the timelessness of these places – to think they were making wines thousands and thousands of years ago and in exactly the same way,' said Maeve. 'Do you ever wonder who first decided to squash them and dance on them and then have the patience to wait until they fermented?'

'I think it was some old codger in Macedonia who discovered that secret, and thank God he did,' laughed Rory.

They went into the winery's shop and were spotted immediately by the owner, who, after welcoming them, insisted that they try some of his newest produce. They were taken through to a tasting room, bypassing the little cinema where visitors could watch a short film on the whole process at Bodegas Manuel. They had seen it before. They slid along the banquette to sample the offerings from the cellars.

'They've obviously been doing more swallowing than spitting,' said Liam, nodding towards a noisy group of tourists sitting at the next table.

There were no windows in there. The walls were covered with mounted barrel ends and awards, and panels from wine boxes. There were candles lighting on the tables. It felt very cold to be out of the heat of the day.

Wearing a striped ribbon around his neck, from which hung a silver tastevin, the owner began his spiel. This was his show and he was going to give it his best. He proudly held a bottle so that each of them in turn could read the label. He buffed the already gleaming glasses and with a flourish poured the velvety liquid into the ornate little cup, drank a little and did a bit of sloshing and swirling in his mouth, then with a faraway look pensively spat the contents into a spittoon. Only then did he pour some wine into their glasses for them to try.

After the tasting, they made their way back into the sleek, well-lit shop. Conor set about ordering, knowing exactly what he wanted. Liam was off discussing other labels, while Trish was engaged in conversation with an assistant.

'What are you doing?' Rory asked her.

'Buying two cases of the red,' she replied.

'We're flying home remember, you can't take them with you.'

'They're not for us. They're for Conor and Maeve.'

'You don't need to buy all that.'

'Yes, we do, Rory. For God's sake, we're staying at their villa for nothing!'

'Get them a few bottles of the Cava—'

'What a good idea! We'll take a case of the pink cava, too, that one there,' she pointed. 'We've had it before and liked it.'

'You want … ?

'Si, todos, todos – los tres.' Turning to Rory she said, 'You do have your credit card with you, don't you?' When he had handed it reluctantly to the assistant, she walked off to join Liam.

'We're going to have lunch in your restaurant,' Conor told the manager, leaving his keys for them to load the wine they'd bought, and they headed back outside into the brightness. They found a table under a large umbrella and sat back to enjoy the sounds, the birdsong, the scenery, the tapas and each other's company.

'I could stay here for ever,' said Trish.

'No you couldn't,' Maeve replied. 'You'd get tired of it very quickly – and you'd miss the kids.'

'Kids! What kids?' laughed Rory.

'Oh, Maeve, why did you remind me? For a minute, I was eighteen again and with no ties and no responsibilities. Now I'm back to being a mother and a wife, with only eight more days holiday to enjoy.'

'And there's nothing to stop us having wild and frequent sex till then,' said Rory.

'Please wait until we get back to the villa,' laughed Liam, signalling to the young waiter who was hovering around them.

FIVE

Thursday brought an even hotter day. By evening it was positively clammy, the sky filling with darkening storm clouds as they turned in for the night. Maeve couldn't sleep. She turned this way and that before getting out of bed and walking to the open double doors that led to the terrace. It started to rain and she slid the door over to keep it out. Going into the kitchen, she poured herself a drink of orange juice and sat down in a wicker chair to watch the lightning as it lit up the sea in the distance. As a child, she had been terrified of thunder and her mother had spent many a sleepless night telling her that thunder was harmless. It was lightning that caused any damage. But the magic of its flashes, and the brightness as it zigzagged across the sky always excited her. Conor slept, oblivious to the tempest that nature was producing.

Something, she could never afterwards explain what, made her put her fingers on a particular spot on one of her breasts and she felt it – a lump. Maeve had never examined her breasts in her life, despite all the magazine articles and stories she had heard and the stream of patients who visited Stan every week in the clinic.

Outside, the thunder rumbled and walloped with a deafening all-pervasive noise and the lightning lit up the landscape again and again. She slid back into bed. Conor snored while her mind raced. It's only a lump and most lumps are nothing. It's just the time of the month, breasts change then, she tried to tell herself.

She did a check on the other side, going back again and again to see if they felt any different. How can you possibly tell – breasts are lumpy, she thought. But it was different. No! I'm imagining it. I'll put it out of my mind and talk to Stan when I get back. No, I can't go to him. I know him too well. I have to work with him. I'll go to someone else. I'd feel a right fool if it was nothing, having stripped off in front of him. She continued to fret.

The weather seemed to beat time with her thoughts – rational and calm one minute, only to erupt into a crescendo of anxiety, panic and frenzy the next. She'd tell Conor. No! She would not. She would let him have his holiday. She'd ask Trish. No! She wouldn't. She'd keep this to herself until she knew she had the all clear.

I feel great, she told herself. There's nothing wrong with me. Before I went to bed tonight, I was perfect. I have been a little tired lately – no, no, that's definitely my imagination clicking in. I'm older now. I can't expect to have the energy of a twenty-year-old anymore. I'm almost forty. I used to think that was old age. Perhaps a tonic … I don't need a tonic …

She got out of bed again and went back into the kitchen to make a cup of tea. The Irish answer to any crisis, she thought. As the storm was passing, she took it outside to the decking and sat under the awning. When she eventually came back in, Conor was spread-eagled on his back, still snoring. She moved his arm out of the way and slid in beside him.

***

The morning broke with blue skies and full sunshine. The only sign of the night's pyrotechnics and deluge were little pools on the uneven surface of the tiles that had still not dried up in the increasing heat.

'That was some night,' said Liam, reaching for the percolator in the kitchen.

Rory cocked his eyebrow.

'Was it?' he asked, wondering whether Liam was alluding to the storm or the Finns.

'I'm thinking of hiring a car tomorrow and heading up to Granada with Agneta and Anna Maria. Anyone like to join us?' Liam asked. 'What about you ladies? There's no point in asking the guys.'

'Why is there no point in asking the guys?' said Conor. 'That's a very sexist attitude to take.'

'Sexy more like! He just wants to have four beautiful women to himself for the day,' said Derek.

'I've never been to the Alhambra. It's something I promise myself I'll do every time I'm out here, yet I never seem to manage it. I'd love to come along,' said Rory. 'We'll need two cars though.'

'I hate those people carrier things. Let's get those little Jeeps and enjoy the sunshine. Lord knows, we'll get little enough chance of open-top driving when we get back home.'

'Great idea,' said Trish. 'I'm game. I know I've been there before, but there's a great air of magic and history to the place.'

'I thought you had to book months in advance to get inside,' Conor said.

'When has a little detail like that ever stopped Liam?' asked Trish. 'He could talk his way into heaven and back out of it again if he had to.'

'Well, as it happens I do have a friend ...'

'He has a friend ... ' echoed Conor.

'... who has another friend, who just happens to be an old girlfriend, who just happens to have another friend who happens to work in a hotel, who happens to have a friend in the tourist board, who just might happen to have some passes in her handbag ...' said Trish.

'Well, it's not quite as complicated as that,' Liam grinned and headed towards the veranda. 'I'll just need to make a few phone calls.'

When he returned he said, 'I managed to get us some press passes, but you'll have to pretend to be travel writers.'

'Pretend to be travel writers … here we go again!' Conor teased, while Trish and Maeve exchanged I-told-you-so looks.

'I just used my loquacious charms on my friend Consuela – who happens to work for the tourist office. She can wangle it – because we are an international press party of prestigious Finnish and Irish journalists!'

'You're a con man,' said Rory. 'You never cease to amaze me.'

'I asked her to join us afterwards. I hope that's all right with everyone.'

They all agreed that was a fair trade off.

'Come on lads, we've transport to organise for tomorrow.'

'Won't we be up for impersonation?' Trish asked.

'Christ, don't even joke about that,' Conor said. 'You never know when these things come back to bite you.'

'Can I ask you something? About your work. What's in all those boxes your team carries in and out of the court hearings every day?' Trish asked.

'Our sandwiches!' said Conor. 'The food is bloody awful in the canteen!'

SIX

Derek called Sharonne every day. Sometimes, she was too busy to talk to him. Today when he phoned, she was waiting impatiently for a taxi to arrive. She had examined her perfectly ruby-tipped fingernails, patted her Hervé'd hair and admired, for the hundredth time, her new Loeffler Randall shoes and bag, specially ordered through Harrods. When she'd seen them one night on a series of *The World's Most Expensive*, she knew she just had to have them. They relegated her Blahniks to almost chain-store status. She'd also bought the twins some designer threads. After all, Derek was off enjoying himself in Spain, wasn't he?

Judging from his phone call, they seemed to be having a great time. She would have liked a spell in the sun too, and in a way regretted her decision to forego the trip.

'Why don't you hop on a plane and come out to join us for the weekend?' Derek urged, part of him wanting her to say yes, the other secretly enjoying the freedom from her barbed comments and bored looks. Guiltily, he added, 'It'd do you good to have a little break and they're having all the usual suspects over on Saturday night too.'

Sharonne muttered something Derek couldn't make out, so he continued, 'Liam's managed to get himself not one, but two blonde beauties, Finns this time, and they've been hanging around with us. They're great fun. You'd enjoy them.'

'I must fly, Derek, my taxi's here.'

'I'll talk to you tomorrow. Think about coming out, Shar, and enjoy your evening.'

'OK, I'll see what I can arrange.'

Hanging around indeed – did he think he was seventeen again? She topped up her lipgloss and dropped the tube into her bag before opening the door. Sharonne considered this contract to be far too important to let her employees get too involved, even though she was sure that her assistant Sadie would be quite capable of looking after most of it. She felt it would lead to further opportunities and if that meant dealing directly with these big guns, she would. She was going to dine with Bob Dawson and his European associates.

The taxi drew up outside the Merrion Hotel, a sleek limo preventing it actually stopping at the steps of Restaurant Patrick Guilbaud. She didn't mind, her curiosity to see who was getting the star treatment prevailed. She stepped out of the car swinging her long legs together in an elegant way, just as she had learned at finishing school. In reality, she had never attended finishing school, but was an unpaid student teacher for a term in a girl's boarding school in Nîmes, where they ran a finishing school for 'young ladies of nobility', as the prospectus termed it. With a watchful eye, she had gleaned all sorts of tips and had watched the seven wealthy students whose parents paid for such lessons. Their expensive tuition covered such skills as learning how to walk, sit, stand and move with ease, grace and decorum. It hadn't been the nuns who had taught her to show so much flesh. Never enough to be too revealing, just enough to be alluring, she thought as she caught the admiring glance of a passer-by, whose female companion didn't seem too pleased at the amount of attention he was giving her.

The uniformed hotel doorman greeted her as she walked past. She couldn't believe her eyes: Pierce Brosnan and his wife had stepped out of the limo in front of her and were heading up the steps into Guilbaud's too. Quickening her step, she caught up with them – he smiled at her as he held the door open – that crinkly smile that made his eyes twinkle and hearts go flutter the world over.

'Thank you, Mr Bond,' she said, as Bob came out from the elegant foyer to greet her, 'Sharonne! You look delightful.'

Delightful! I was trying to look fantastic, sensational, even a little sexy, she thought, instantly forgetting about Pierce Brosnan as two other men stood up from one of the plush sofas in the little ante-room bar.

'Let me introduce you to Jonathan Whyte – he looks after the UK – and to Christian de Villepin, Paris-based, but in charge of European affairs.' She offered her hand and smiled brightly at them both.

'I'm sure you're no strangers to Dublin,' she said.

'No, we're here quite often,' said Christian, eyeing her up and down approvingly. 'And if things go as I hope,' he paused for an instant, 'we'll be spending a lot more time here in the foreseeable future.' She felt he was looking into her soul.

I don't believe it, so typically French, he's actually flirting with me, she thought, and we've hardly even heard each other's names. A flush crept up her neck under his scrutiny. It was a long time since she had felt so engaged by a man's gaze. They were welcomed by the maître d' and shown to a table in the corner, from where they could see the whole dining room, yet could be apart from it. Guilbaud's was the place to dine and be seen doing so. She was seated between Bob and Christian and had the Brosnan table firmly in her line of vision. It was set for four and she wondered who might be joining them.

They then spent some time in deliberation over the menu and finally ordered. Bob left the wine choice to Christian. That irritated Sharonne. Not all Frenchmen are wine experts, she thought. She also fumed because inevitably when she was in the company of men, they seldom consulted her on the wine selection. She had become interested in wines when she first went to France – an interest that she had pursued over the years with wine courses and short vineyard breaks. In fact, she was probably more knowledgeable on the matter than most of the men with whom she ate dinner. After a further scan of the list, Christian chose a Cheval Blanc from the St Emilion region and some Chateau Margaux, a real French extravagance. Both met with her approval. Then they got down to business.

Bob, in command as always, briefly outlined the problems they were expecting with the upcoming takeover. He was representing a well-established investment management company that FitzGerald-Reglob was about to acquire. Due diligence and all the usual investigations had shown no irregularities and, as this was the second such acquisition in as many years, things had been expected to go smoothly. However, one of the company directors with whom Bob had been in college had called him one day and there had been an urgency in his voice. They had met and he'd told Bob that he felt there were too many things not adding up at FitzGerald-Reglob. He'd stressed the importance that no one should get wind of his concerns until an unbroken chain of evidence had been established. He had been collecting various documents for a while and he had reiterated that it would be far too easy to destroy evidence if those involved got even the most vague hint that they or their practices were under scrutiny.

'But where do the European offices come into all this?' asked Jonathan.

'There's a strong link with some of the banking institutions in Luxemburg and Monaco. There are also some French investors involved, although they are probably totally unaware of any underhand dealings.'

'Am I supposed to believe the same applies to the UK and the Channel Isles?'

'You've got it in one. But it's bigger than that. We have to get the Stateside people involved too, to cover all angles. I'm not pretending this is going to be an easy task,' said Christian.

Sharonne could have sworn Christian's foot had touched hers under the table. Surely not!

'Secrecy and discretion are tantamount in such investigations,' Christian added, looking steadily at Sharonne. Then it happened again – this time she knew it was no accident. His foot lingered against hers.

'Heads will roll when this is uncovered. In fact, I would go so far as to say a few companies will probably fall, so no one must know what we are looking for.'

She found herself fiddling with her napkin, too aware of Christian's glances and equally aware that this was not a social occasion and that she must keep her professional demeanour intact.

'Sharonne,' he said, 'this is where you will come in.' All she could think of was the Carte Noir coffee advert that used to be on television, the one where the woman gets carried away when sitting across the table from David Ginola – the part where he brings her back to earth with that outrageously smouldering sexual glance as he turns his head ever so slightly to one side, cocks his eyebrow and says 'aromatique'. Concentrate you fool, Sharonne told herself.

'This is where I will depend on you.' Bob outlined some of the problems. 'After the acquisition the previous year, they had transferred many of the smaller existing investment accounts to the new division. Apparently, some of the clients had had tax "difficulties", which had needed to be straightened out and FitzGerald had said that he'd look after those clients personally. All very plausible at the time. Now we know why he did it. Bogus offshore accounts, tax evasion and embezzlement – FitzGerald and Reglob think they are a dynamic duo who've got away with trousering millions in cash. It's up to us to make sure they don't. And we also know that this is only the tip of the iceberg; consequently, there is no way this takeover can go ahead, but, in stalling it, we have to come up with a smokescreen so no one gets suspicious.'

Bob continued, 'We'll need you, Sharonne, to set up meetings to smooth out the way, issue statements, etc. The media will be over this story like ants when they realise what's been going on. That pair have been very cunning in the way they've operated, but their investors won't be too pleased when they discover their monies have gone.' He expanded on a few of the problems he foresaw. 'We know we are dealing with something very big here. Their senior partner is also an accountant and a company lawyer – a formidable combination and, as such, he's familiar with ways around the law. We'll have to go softly and not let them know we are on to anything out of the ordinary. If this goes through as we would like, and legitimately at that, we all stand to make a tidy sum of money.

Sharonne nodded, understanding the brief perfectly.

'This is not going to happen overnight. We're going to need all your time for the next year or more and because of the US involvement, it's not going to be a nine-to-five effort, but rather a 24/7 one as the need arises,' said Christian.

'Sharonne knows the score,' said Bob to the other two. 'She's a real professional. We've worked together in the past. Successfully too,' he nodded in her direction as she smiled affirmatively.

Very successfully, she thought, eyeing the emerald ring she'd bought with some of the proceeds.

Christian raised his glass and clinked it against hers. 'To a successful and, let's hope, a not too dirty takeover.'

Sharonne felt a faint quickening of her pulse. She toyed with her dessert, Citrus Fromage Blanc and Orange Sorbet. She sat back in her chair and sipped the last of the dessert wine Christian had chosen, the mellow yellow Beaumes de Venise. Business out of the way, conversation was easy and witty. They might be charming men to spend an evening with, but Sharonne was no fool. She was going to be paid handsomely but no one was under the illusion that she would earn her money easily. She would be at their beck and call continuously.

'I'll give you a lift Sharonne,' said Bob, once the dinner was finished, asking the waiter to hail taxis. 'Talk to you all on Monday,' he called as the visitors went out to their car.

'It was nice to meet you,' said the Englishman formally, shaking her hand.

Christian held her hand a moment too long, before raising it to his lips. 'I look forward to working with you. No doubt, we'll be seeing a lot more of each other.'

'No doubt,' she replied and, as he walked away, she smiled.

'That went very well I think,' said Bob as he and Sharonne got into the taxi. 'They're nice guys, they know their stuff too. Christian can be a bit ruthless. He's a great ladies' man, so be warned, don't fall for his charms. He collects beautiful women like you.'

She ignored that remark. He was one to talk!

'It's really going to be crazy once we get things rolling so, if I were you, I'd enjoy the next few weeks, get as much R&R as you can because, after that, as Christian said, it could be around the clock and we'll own your soul and your diary.

'That's the penalty of doing business with New York and LA – they're awake when we should be sleeping,' she said, making a snap decision. 'Derek's in Mijas – I thought I might go out for the weekend, if I can get a flight.'

'That's a great idea. I'd love a break myself, but Judy and the kids have some gymkhana or other that I must attend.'

Twenty minutes later, they pulled up outside her house. 'You know, having horses is an even more onerous occupation than dealing with MBO's and takeovers, especially when you're the only one who can tow the horsebox competently.'

'You chauvinist,' she laughed.

'Make the most of the weekend,' he said as he walked her to the front door.

As she headed up the staircase to bed, her mind was in a spin replaying the evening – editing out most of Bob and Jonathan's roles and scarcely remembering that a real live 007 had held the door open for her. She couldn't wait to tell the twins that. Yes, she was going to enjoy the challenges ahead, she thought as she stretched out between the cool sheets. 'I'm no pushover, Monsieur Christian. It'll take more than a glass of Chateau Margaux to get around me, cheri!'

SEVEN

'Another sunny day in paradise,' was how Derek greeted the morning, 'and a whole week still to go.'

'That means bottles of factor fifty for me,' said Liam, 'and a few of aftersun. My genteel skin was not meant for exposure. My ancestors must have been troglodytes who had survived so long in their caves that when they eventually came out, they weren't able to tolerate sunlight.'

The others, already subtly bronzed, were standing by the pool munching warm croissants and coffee, ready for their excursion.

'Who do we have to thank for these?' Derek asked, knowing that it wouldn't be Rory. Before anyone else was dressed, Liam had collected the pastries from the village.

It wasn't that Rory minded acts of generosity – so long as none of his money was involved. Acutely aware that he was shorter than his two friends, Rory was standing, or posing, as was his wont, with one shoulder raised to add some stature. It was a habit he had developed growing up with two brothers who were much taller than he was. He was just five feet eight, they both topped six foot. In a suit, this posture worked, with the added act of keeping one hand in his trouser pocket to support his raised shoulder. Shoes with slightly thicker heels helped too, but his attempts looked out of place in shorts, a T-shirt and flip-flops.

It was still cool and that distinctive early-morning smell which heralds a glorious day along the Mediterranean permeated the air. The mists were beginning to evaporate and the mountains were just about visible in the distance. Birds tried to out-shout each other above the whoosh of the sprinklers on the nearby golf course. A few intrepid ones hovered, waiting for falling crumbs.

Trish tore off a small corner of pastry and threw it on the ground. The birds descended, like a scene from a movie, to squabble and fight over it.

'Don't encourage them,' Maeve said as she shooed them away, 'or we'll never be able to eat outside in the day time.'

'Well, that'll confuse them,' said Conor, as they all joined in. The birds took off in a single noisy flight as though wired invisibly together.

'They're probably saying, "bloody foreigners" to each other,' Rory said.

'Time to collect the Finns,' Liam said. 'If you get ahead of us, ring and let us know where you're stopping for coffee.'

'Will do,' said Rory, who was already in the driver's seat, as the others climbed in to the Jeep. They then followed Liam and Derek down the winding road to the main thoroughfare.

***

They headed north, stopping about an hour later. The Sierra Nevada peaks were now quite clear in the brighter light.

Maeve piped up, 'In my new-found capacity as a travel journalist, I, at least, can appear to be knowledgeable about the area,' she said. 'I may even be able to fool the tourist people into thinking I did my research before coming along today.

She had spent some time in Granada as an au pair. She would always remember the Murcias, her family for those four months, telling her time and again that this was the most visited site in Spain. She explained to Anna Maria and Agneta, 'I was going through a romantic phase back then, young, impressionable and abroad on my own for the first time – not to mention the crush I had on Juan Murcia.'

'Who was he?' asked Anna Maria.

'Just the pompous son of the house, who had a giant superiority complex, puffed up and kept inflated by an adoring mamma who wouldn't let him lift a finger. He was reading history at the Universidad of Granada. This, he proudly told everyone who would listen, had been in existence since 1531 – sixty-one years before Trinity College in Dublin had opened.'

'Is that true?' asked Agneta.

'Oh yes. Everything he said was true! He was a tour guide for the summer and I hung on his every word. Looking back, he was an arrogant little upstart who, after only three weeks in Dublin, knew more about it than I did, and possibly still do! You'd think Trinity was a mud hut or a hedge school to hear him dismiss it.'

Now I really have to come to Dublin and see it for myself,' said Agneta.

Maeve remembered being intrigued by the breadth of Spain's historic past – the tales of yesteryear, the opulence and the architecture that survived centuries of invasion and strife. All of these things were to mark the embryonic stages of her enduring love affair with all things Spanish.

Some time later, they parked in the designated area and walked the last stage to the Alhambra. Liam, with an air of authority, led them all straight to the top of the queue and after lots of devastating smiles and much arm waving in their direction, they were ushered ahead of the inquisitive tourists, into the hallowed cloisters.

'As important international journalists you cannot be expected to stand in line for hours,' Liam teased, as Anna Maria and Agneta persuaded them all to join a tour so that they could learn something of the history.

'Certainly,' he said, leading them by another long queue which was waiting at a sign that read: 'Next Tour in Five

Minutes'. He turned to the crowd and said, 'This tour has priority – personajes muy importantes, visiting VIPs. Thank you. Thank you so much. Gracias, gracias, muchas gracias.'

A bespectacled guide, taken in by his bluff, greeted them and led them off to the first stop. She had eyebrows that were constantly halfway up her forehead as though she had just been startled; she enunciated every syllable as though she was saying it for the first time and then seemed even more surprised that it had actually come out right. Right? Well, that was the subject of conjecture later.

'Granada is one of the pearls of the Spain. Most visited by tourists from all the worldwide. The long-time capital of Moorish Andalusia has to offer the most important reminds of this epoch in history of Spain, with world-famous Alhambra at the peak of the list.'

The Finns, flanking Liam, tried to suppress their giggles at the imperfections in the guide's English: theirs was word perfect.

She continued as she led them through the arched cloisters, appearing even more astonished at having found the famed arches in the first place. 'If you looking at the stones, you will begin to know how the castile name Calat Alhambra begins. It is red castile and from the shimmering red stone it arrives at its name …'

And so it continued, its legends and tales being lost in a mumbo jumbo of mistranslation and misinterpretation. Liam remarked to Maeve, 'Your version is much better! Makes you wonder if any history is true at all if every time it's retold it loses this much.'

Agneta couldn't take any more. Doubled up with laughter, she pretended a coughing fit and retreated to the back of the crowd that had followed them. An hour and a half later, having wandered through the passages and cobbled alleys, the guide was still in full spate. They managed to take their leave as she continued, oblivious. 'Breath the centuries of history around you anywhere. Don't miss to visit our famous cuevas in the mountain of the monastery of Sacromonte, where some of the gypsies habitat there still making magnificent artisany nowadays.'

They drove some way to dine at a little restaurant on the twisty road outside Toledo, feasting on local wine and tapas of various chorizos and olives, peppers, lemon chicken and the local specialty, Trevélez ham. Consuela, Liam's friend from the tourist office, joined them there and he was in his element. He had the knack of being genuinely interested in the people he met and, consequently, he always met interesting people. They told her about the guide.

'Which one did you have? Do you remember the name?'

'Mercedes.'

'Oh. I should have warned you off her. She's very intense.'

'Ah ha,' said Liam, 'the penalty of being travel writers – there's no such thing as a free ticket! You have to endure the lectures, the endless dates and details and then there are questions at the end to see if you were listening.'

'You're joking,' said Trish in mock horror.

'No. I'm not. Some of your esteemed readers may want to find out where to go to procure "magnificent artisany", and they'll expect you to know. Besides, you blew your cover by not asking for a press pack as you left. They usually give you one and in them you find every scintilla of information you have already got from the guide and more. And the bonus is that by the end of a press trip, you have to pay excess baggage on the weight of all the bumph you've collected.'

'How do you know all this?' asked Anna Maria.

Conor said, 'Because in my considered opinion I suspect it's not the first time he's used the travel writer guise.' Liam just grinned in response.

The snow-frosted Sierra Nevada had developed a collar of cloud, but its beauty was lost on Maeve. She was preoccupied.

'Are you all right? You seem very quiet,' said Conor.

'Yes I'm fine, really I am,' she replied, 'Just reminiscing …'

She had to stem the urge to visit the washroom and do another check to see if the lump had disappeared, but it had been there at breakfast time, and when they stopped for refreshments that morning.

'Tell Consuela about the time you sold timeshares in Malaga,' Rory urged Anna Maria.

'Oh please, Rory, you don't want to hear that story again,' she laughed. 'I'm sure the others don't either.'

'We haven't heard it,' said Trish. 'You must have told it when you were playing golf.'

'I was only out of school and thought it would be really adventurous to go working in Spain for the summer. Agneta and another school friend came down from Helsinki and we were poached on the first day as we sat on the beach. This little man, he always dressed in black and had a moustache that looked as if it has been painted on, promised us free accommodation, lots of time off to tan and even more money than we would have got from au pairing. All we had to do was encourage visitors to come to the presentation on his timeshares.'

Agneta interrupted, 'Poor innocents. We were thrilled and moved into one of the apartments with three girls from England. It only took a few days for us to realise that once we got the unsuspecting tourists in, luring them with promises of free champagne and a sangria barbecue on the beach at dusk, they would be kept there for about three hours listening to a very persuasive sales pitch.'

'I think that is the worst job of all. Did you sell many?'

'Not one,' said Anna Maria. 'After a few weeks, without a sale, we told the little man in black we were going to leave and he tried to charge us rent for the accommodation and told us he'd have us arrested if we left. We waited until the presentation the next day, sneaked back, grabbed our rucksacks and were leaving to go to the next town when we saw him arriving back in his car. The English girls were still waiting for their taxi.'

'What happened?'

'We lay down on the back seat on top of each other until he had passed. The taxi man thought we were mad. We took jobs as chambermaids after that. Any time I've been through Malaga since, I keep waiting to see that odious little man coming around every corner at me! I often wonder if the English girls managed to escape or if they were sold into the slave trade!'

Anna Maria's story sparked off other reminiscences of summer holiday jobs, of nights spent sleeping on beaches in Greece, of inter-railing, hitch-hiking and other such adventures.

'If I ever thought my kids would do any of those things I'd kill them,' laughed Trish, who had been the wildest of them all.

'Just you wait another few years and they'll be doing the same,' said Agneta. 'My mother thought I was staying with a respectable family. I don't know if she ever really found out what we got up to.'

It was late when they got back. They had persuaded Consuela to come down to Mijas the following Friday for the barbecue. She hadn't needed much arm-twisting. They dropped Anna Maria and Agneta off at their complex, returned the Jeeps and walked back up the hill to the villa.

Maeve said, 'That was a great day, but I think I'll turn in.'

'It's not like you to be first to hit the sack,' said Rory.

'… the first to hit the sack? Is this a not-so-veiled invitation?' Conor winked at his wife.

'No it isn't,' she laughed. 'I think I got too much sun today or maybe too much vino or a combination of both. Please don't let me spoil the mood. Go out on the terrace and have a nightcap. I'll see you all in the morning.'

EIGHT

It was Friday morning and, as had become another of their holiday rituals, Conor and Maeve were preparing to host a mid-holiday barbecue at the villa. Over the years, it had grown, as had their circle of friends in the area.

'Well, I think we've got things under control out there,' said Rory, coming in from the patio with charcoal-blackened hands. 'Everything's set for tonight. Let's hope Sharonne will be as easy to manage.'

He and Conor had just been assembling the barbecue. They had a large gas one but Conor always felt there was something nicer about food cooked on real charcoal, and, besides, they would need the extra capacity for the crowd they were expecting. Derek had already left for the airport to pick up Sharonne.

'Easy to manage,' laughed Conor, 'that'll be a first. But I think Derek is genuinely looking forward to seeing her again. Was that Liam I heard drive off too?' Conor turned to Trish. She was wrapping knives and forks up in coloured flowery napkins.

'Yes, he's gone to collect the Finns. They offered to go off to the market and get the last-minute salad stuff and pick up bread on the way back.'

'Hasn't Liam become very cosy with the two of them, but I can't figure out which one he fancies, if either.'

'You never can tell with Liam. I'm not even sure he's got over Helen yet. He never talks about her anymore, but I've never known him to be so serious about anyone before or indeed to take a break-up so badly. He's changed since,' Rory said, putting on coffee to percolate.

Maeve was busy. She left the chicken to marinate in a lemony basil mix, put the calamari and prawns in other dishes and began amassing the ingredients necessary to create her paella, the centrepiece of these evenings. She never followed recipes, just added a dash of this, a handful of that, but the results were unfailingly delicious.

'He really thought he had a future with Helen. He was even talking about settling down and having kids.'

'… settling down and having kids. Yeah, that was a new departure. I never heard him talk like that before,' said Conor.

'He's getting broody, looking for an heir to continue the line – perhaps Agneta or Anna Maria might oblige,' said Maeve.

'Do you see them as settling down material?'

'Maybe with the right guy. Should I try propositioning them?' asked Conor.

'Humph – do you think they'd have you?' Maeve pushed him aside. 'With Liam as competition.'

'You're a hussy,' he said chasing her around the table.

'Get back to work – we've thirty people coming in a few hours and, as you know, it's impossible to get good staff at short notice.'

'Better kiss and make up then,' said Conor running a charcoaled finger down her cheek.'

Rory and Trish were drinking coffee on the terrace, enjoying each other's company.

'I do miss the kids, but this is bliss, isn't it? I'm afraid to think about what they're getting up to in the Gaeltacht,' said Trish.

Rory, smiling, put his arm around her shoulder and said, 'Omnifarious things no doubt, and you can be sure that whatever those things will be, they will be no worse than we did at their age, and we survived.'

'So long as they keep an eye on Toni, it being her first time away from home on her own …'

'Technically speaking she's not on her own – she's with her siblings.'

'Yes, but can you honestly see Barry wanting to hang around with his younger sisters? Come on, with all those youngsters together and hormones hopping all over the place, he'll most likely disown or, at best, ignore them!'

'And for what it's worth, I think there are some hopping hormones going on around here too.' He gave her a squeeze.

'Behave yourself,' she laughed as she pushed him away, and they went back inside. They came in on the tail end of a conversation in the kitchen.

'… Besides, I think our Liam seems to have a new girlfriend,' Conor was saying, 'in Cyprus. He's mentioned her several times and was texting her this morning before breakfast.'

'Hmm, interesting,' muttered Maeve, who always thought it was such a waste that Liam hadn't got a long-term partner. 'He hasn't mentioned her to me.'

'Wise man. Probably trying to avoid the Irish Inquisition from you pair of nosey parkers!'

'The Finns are real babes, aren't they?' said Rory, teasing his wife.

Before Trish could react, she noticed the dusty cloud that Derek's Jeep was throwing up behind it as it made its way up the end of the road by the golf course.

'Oh-oh, here comes trouble. Brace yourselves. Double-N E is about to descend!'

'Rory, be nice.'

'I hate these Spanish flights,' Sharonne was complaining the second she walked into the house. 'They're always full of overexcited, spoiled brats who no one wants to control. As their parents get more tanked, they are left to run amok up and down the aisles. The noise was terrible.' Then, as though remembering that she was still in the bad books, she smiled. 'I decided I couldn't stay away.'

'You're more than welcome,' said Maeve.

'I haven't seen any of you for ages. You all look really bronzed. I believe the weather's been great.' She smiled again parting perfectly painted lips to reveal her perfectly veneered teeth. She never admitted to having this dental work done, but in a framed photo of her in their dining room back home, taken on the night of her debs' ball, a gap is clearly visible between her front teeth.

'It's been terrific here and having nothing to do has made it even better. I hear you've been up to your tonsils with work,' Maeve said. 'Relax and make yourself at home – you know where everything is. The others won't be arriving until six-ish so you've time for a swim if you'd like to freshen up.'

'That sounds like a great idea. I'm wrecked, so perhaps a swim would do me the world of good.'

She was still in the warm water with Derek when Liam came back with Agneta and Anna Maria, laden down with food from the market. Liam called out introductions as they walked by the pool and Sharonne took in the tanned, natural beauties.

'This is going to be fun,' Liam said, depositing the baguettes on the table in the kitchen. 'I have a hunch bullfighting could be a less extreme sport by the end of the night!'

'Be nice everyone,' said Maeve.

'Perhaps we should have invited some banderilleros in case we need to use some diversionary tactics,' muttered Rory.

Sharonne chose that minute to make an entrance, a fluffy towel casually draped across one shoulder and dripping water on the marble tiles in the kitchen.

'So these are the two Finns you've been hanging around

with all week,' she said, appraising them from head to toe and dismissing them just as quickly.

'I'm Agneta Baltaar and I'm delighted to meet you.' Agneta offered Sharonne her hand. 'And this is Anna Maria Kauppila. Derek has not told us nearly enough about you.'

'Really?' she said. 'How fascinating. I'll catch up with you both later – must do my hair before the guests arrive.' Her look implied that they could do with doing the same.

'I see you lost the beard again,' she said to her husband as she exited. 'Makes you look younger.'

'So that's what's different about you,' said Trish, 'and we never noticed.'

'I suppose I should be flattered that my wife did,' Derek said dubiously.

***

Later, Conor posed for photos between Agneta and Anna Maria, wearing to all intents and purposes nothing but a frilly apron. It barely covered his shorts and had the words 'Kiss the Cook' emblazoned across the front of it in bright, sparkling purple and red. Maeve and he had bought it the market one year for a laugh and it was taken out in ritualistic fashion each time they entertained at the villa.

The coals on the barbecue were reddening down nicely. Their friends were beginning to appear, among them some Irish who had moved to Spain permanently, others who summered there in their own villas or apartments. Xavier and Isabella from the restaurant arrived with an unexpected guest.

'We brought Pablo with us to play some music. It's impossible to buy wine for you people – you have better ones than I serve in the restaurant, si? And, as for that paella I can smell, I am afraid that you may decide to open up in opposition and I will have no customers left, no? So this,' he said, indicating to Pablo the guitar player from El Caballo Loco, 'is my party contribution instead, si?'

'… Party contribution,' said Conor. 'What a great idea.'

'What are they going to do in the restaurant without him tonight?' asked Rory.

'Do not worry. His cousin plays for him when he has to go to weddings and funerals. They look so alike no one ever notices either. And this is more important than them, si?'

'Si,' said Pablo, resplendent in his black waistcoat with heavy silver thread embroidery, red cummerbund and black flared trousers. He carried not one but two guitar cases.

'He always brings a spare in case anyone else wants to join in, si?'

As the other guests arrived, more introductions were made. Some newly made acquaintances and their partners from the rounds of golf over the past five days had been invited and it never took long for someone to realise they knew or were related to one of the other guests. Consuela brought her boyfriend, Carlos, and in no time at all it was the usual, boisterous, good-humoured occasion that was the hallmark of any of Conor and Maeve's bashes.

The evening was perfect, as only balmy, scented evenings in the south of Spain can be. Deck chairs and loungers had been positioned all around the poolside and patio as well as on the veranda, and the tables were lit with little red-glass storm lamps. Citronella torches burned in the grass verges to keep the mosquitoes away. The sun, like a large nectarine, slipped slowly down into the darkening sea behind stripes of blue and pale orange clouds, before the light finally disappeared. This nightly miracle set off some silent alarm clock that awakened the frogs, activating their distinctive noisy chorus.

Derek was already beginning to regret his insistence that Sharonne should fly out for the weekend. He sensed that Liam was on watch, a peacemaker in case he was needed, but as he circulated, he soon realised that Sharonne had met her match in Agneta and he stood back by the temporary bar to enjoy the sparring.

'It must be dreadfully boring living in Finland in the winter,' Sharonne said. 'I always associate people from northern latitudes with being cold and unemotional – they must get it from all the snow and eating so much pickled fish.'

Agneta smiled. 'Yes, we do love cold things – cold vodka, skiing, ice-skating and rolling around in the snow – naked,' she said, a deadpan expression on her face. 'These things cool our passionate natures and keep us under control.'

'I can't imagine you rolling naked in the snow,' Sharonne said, taking in Agneta's figure-hugging wraparound belly top and cerise hipster trousers.

'I can,' said Derek, who had still not quite forgiven her for her attitude towards his friends.

Sharonne shot him a filthy look.'Do you have saunas in your houses?' she asked.

Here's the subtext, thought Liam.

'Yes. We do. I'm sure you'd love it. They are great for purifying the skin and giving you a healthy glow. In our home, we always had a family sauna on a Friday night. Now it's fashionable in Finland for girls' nights and bachelor and bachelorette parties too, to go to one of the big centres and celebrate there in the pools and spas. We always do it on our birthdays too and often stay overnight. It's really great fun.'

'When's your birthday? I'd like to be invited,' said Liam, putting his arm casually around Agneta's waist. She slapped him away and laughed.

'You're welcome any time – you know that, but not to my birthday sauna.'

'You'd never be able to handle all those women,' said Rory.

'No, he wouldn't,' said Trish, 'but I bet he'd welcome the opportunity of trying, wouldn't you, Liam? And talking of birthdays, you have a big one coming up soon, haven't you?' Trish said.

'When is that?' asked Anna Maria.

'Not for a couple of months,' Liam replied. 'It's in October.'

'It's the big four zero' said Maeve, quietly.

'… ah the big four zero. That's facing us all,' said Conor.

'Well, he has to have a party for that, doesn't he? You could come to Helsinki or Brussels to celebrate,' suggested Agneta.

They all agreed, but Liam said, 'No. If you want to witness me growing older, then you can do it in Dublin. Come over and we'll party together.'

'Well, Agneta and I will certainly come. We keep threatening to go to Ireland, don't we?' said Anna Maria.

'So will we,' said Consuela, nodding to her boyfriend. 'We keep saying the same.'

'I think that's a great idea,' said Liam. 'But let's make a pact. No presents. Just yourselves.'

'Um, we'll see about that,' Agneta said. 'But we'll be there for definite. You can count on us.'

'Come and get it,' called Conor from the far corner. 'Grub's up!'

The array of food elicited many compliments. 'It was a joint effort,' said Maeve, standing beside her husband, 'everyone pitched in so I can't take all the credit.'

Conor announced that before anyone was served they had to have a toast. Glasses were filled and charged. 'To us and our old and new friends.'

The Finns chorused 'Kippis', the Irish 'Sláinte,' the Spanish 'Salut'. Rory, standing beside Anna Maria, called, 'Go mbeirimid beo ag an am seo arís.'

'What on earth does that mean?' she asked.

'It's Irish or Gaelic and it's a traditional toast, a prayer really. It translates something like "may we all be alive this time next year".'

'That's beautiful. Will you write that down for me?' Anna Maria asked Rory, and they went inside to get some paper.

'Let's drink to that,' said Trish fervently. 'And to Liam's party in Dublin. You're not going to wriggle out of that, you know!'

'I promise you I won't. I'm looking forward to it already,' said Agneta.

Pablo's fingers skimmed the strings of his flamenco guitar with the speed of a hummingbird's wings, while toes tapped and hips swayed to the infectious rhythms of the music. The wine went down easily and so did any inhibitions. The second guitar was passed around and the party gathered a momentum of its own.

'I'm looking forward to coming to Dublin,' Agneta said to Sharonne, who didn't want to get into a discussion on age and birthdays. She knew full well it was going to be Liam's fortieth. It meant hers was only a few months after.

'I'm going to be up to my eyes in work for the next few months,' she said, avoiding looking at Derek.

'At weekends?' asked Anna Maria.

'Especially at weekends. I have some clients who seem to spend the weekdays in Europe or the States, flying in on Friday nights to catch up on operations in Ireland.'

'That's a pity. It doesn't leave you much time for your girls; twins, aren't they?'

'Yes, they are, and they understand. Besides, Derek will be around much more this winter and he's great with them.'

A small group from Ireland were discussing the ongoing Docklands development, while Derek was voicing fears that no one was listening to the economists, a few of whom had started predicting a crash as early as 2008 or 2009.

'I hope that won't happen before I make a few million, like you,' said Rory.

Derek put this hand on his shoulder. 'So do I!' he laughed. 'So do I.'

NINE

Maeve went back to work on Monday, determined to talk to Stan Rosenthal about the lump that had been coming between her and sleep for the past week.

He breezed in the door, larger than life for all his short stature. 'Wow, you look great. How was the holiday?' he asked.

'Great. Super weather. The guys got in loads of golf and we girls enjoyed shopping, sightseeing and sunbathing. What more could anyone ask for?' she said.

'Not a lot. Welcome back to the real world. I've got to warn you it's going to be pretty hectic around here for the next while. Rashid Baroud was in a car smash last Wednesday. Luckily he only broke his wrist, but he'll not be able to operate for a couple of months. A few of us have agreed to share his workload. As you know, most of his patients don't have the time to be bumped onto waiting lists.'

'That's awful, Stan. If there's anything I can do, let me know.'

'You can bank on that,' he said, gathering up an armful of files. 'Into battle.'

The console on her desk buzzed its discreet tone, to Maeve's relief. She felt now was not the time to broach the subject with Stan. He's already working to a punishing diary, she realised, as she watched him disappear into his consulting rooms. Stan also had a secretary who typed up the medical reports. At half ten, as usual, Maeve went downstairs to get some coffee and met her friend Dorothy on the stairs. She worked on the floor below, also for an oncologist.

'Dot, can I ask you a favour?'

'Ask away, but before you do I have to say you look fantastic. It's so unfair. You tan to gorgeous in a few weeks. You know if you weren't so nice, I'd hate you!'

They laughed.

'Looks can be deceptive,' she said.

'What is it? Are you OK? Is anything wrong with Conor?'

'Yes, everything's OK. At least I hope so, and Conor's fine. At least, I don't know. Do you think Mary would fit me in for an appointment? I just need reassurance on something.'

'Of course. I'll ask her. Maeve, what's the trouble? Or would you rather I hadn't asked that?'

'No, that's no problem. I think I have a lump – a breast lump. No, I know I have one, but I need to have it verified. I was going to ask Stan but I really feel I can't. I'd die of mortification if it turned out to be nothing, having been examined by him.'

'Lord, there's no need to feel like that. Lots of women think they have lumps and they turn out to be nothing. Doctors get that all the time, but I know where you're coming from. I'd probably be exactly the same if my boss were a man. When did you find it?'

'In Spain, fittingly in the middle of a sensational lightning storm. I was so freaked, I could actually see how the Romans used to read portents and omens in the weather. I was sure they were heralding the end of the world for me. Melodramatic or what? I haven't told Conor yet.'

'You poor thing. How did you keep it to yourself?'

'I felt I couldn't go blurting it out in front of the whole gang.

Besides, why spoil everyone's holidays for what might still turn out to be a false alarm?'

When they had got their coffees and were going back upstairs, Dorothy's parting words were, 'I'll give you a bell and let you know when Mary can fit you in. I could say try not to worry, but I won't!'

'I know. I can't help it, and Dot, thanks. It's such a relief to tell someone.'

'You'll be fine,' she said, giving Maeve as big a hug as she could manage with her hands full of goodies.

About an hour later Dorothy called Maeve. 'Can you get away? We've had a no-show and Mary said she'll see you.'

'I'll just wait till I've given the patient who's in with Stan his next appointment and I'll be down. Thanks a million.'

Maeve broke out in a sweat and her hands started shaking. 'Get a grip girl. It's only an examination. It'll be over in a few minutes and you'll know the worst.'

Stan's door opened and he emerged, following a strapping young man in biker's leathers.

'Maeve, can you book John in for me?' Stan turned to his patient. 'Maeve will talk to the oncology nurse and between you, you can decide what dates are best.' He gave her a note of what was needed and extended his hand to the young man and shook his firmly. 'Good luck. We'll fight this thing together,' he said reassuringly, 'and we'll beat it too.'

'You betcha,' the leathered figure replied, grinning back. 'I've a lot of living to do still.'

'So have I,' she thought, trying to concentrate on how he must be feeling. Once Maeve had made the necessary arrangements for him she told Stan's secretary she had to go to the lab for some results and would be away from the desk for a bit. She hurried down the stairs to Mary Lynch's rooms.

'It's strange, but although all these consultation suites are the same, they are different somehow. I've never actually sat on this side of the desk before, nor experienced the nerves either,' she said to Dorothy.

'There's no need to be nervous, Maeve,' said Mary Lynch coming out from her consulting room. 'Come on through.'

The surgeon opened the conversation by going directly to the point. 'Dorothy tells me you think you have found a lump, but before I examine you I'll just take a little history if that's all right,' she said.

Maeve answered all Mary's questions. No, no one in her family had had breast cancer. No, she didn't examine herself regularly. She didn't smoke, etc. When the doctor had finished making notes she looked up and said, 'Shall we have a look?'

She indicated to the couch. Maeve unbuttoned her blouse, undid the hooks on her bra, uncovering her untanned breasts, which contrasted starkly to her otherwise bronzed torso.

'A wise lady,' said Mary, 'not sunbathing topless. Young women don't realise the risk they are putting themselves into getting exposure there. I'm just going to examine both breasts first and then you can tell me what you are worried about.'

Deftly her finger explored, gently kneading some spots more than others, inspecting the nipples and returning to the exact spot that Maeve felt was the alien one. Mary nodded. 'Is that it? Is that what you felt?'

'Yes,' said Maeve swallowing hard, knowing in her heart of hearts that there was a problem.

'Well, there is something there. Some of these lumps are simply caused by fibrocystic disease, which sounds a lot worse than it is. They are ducts which fill up with fluid and they are almost always benign, so if you can bear with a little discomfort I'll put a needle in and we can see if that's what it is.' She prepped the syringe and, rubbing the skin with a moistened wipe, inserted a needle into the lump.

'I hardly felt that,' said Maeve, her body relaxing as Mary removed the needle.

'The advances of modern medicine – the needles are so fine now they make our lives so much easier. I remember seeing needles in medical school that looked as though they should only have been used on horses instead of humans.'

She studied the vial. 'That's not very conclusive, Maeve, however a mammogram will tell us more. Try not to worry, it doesn't mean the worst. If we do have to do anything we usually perform a lumpectomy, depending on the spread and the depth of the roots. In fact some women who are prone to breast tumours have these quite frequently. But that's jumping the gun. Let's have the scan done first and then we'll know what we are dealing with. I'll see if they can fit you in today or tomorrow and we'll talk again.'

'Thank you, Mary, I really appreciate that.'

'I know it's easy for me to tell you not to worry, but please try not to. A large percentage of my patients present like this and it turns out to be nothing sinister.'

Maeve went back to her office, somewhat shell-shocked. She hadn't thought this through. A lump was a lump, but being prone to them, having several lumpectomies, a partial removal, or a total mastectomy – she hadn't given any of those headspace. It was as though she had been holding on for confirmation before allowing herself to think any further. Now that the lump was confirmed she just knew something in her equilibrium had shifted and it wasn't ever going to go back to where it had been.

Her first urge was to ring Conor. She needed his support, but he hated hospitals, was no good around blood, drips and bedside scenes. In fact it was always she who visited their friends when they were ill or had had surgery. She felt he had paid his dues in that respect.

No, she decided, I'll wait till the results of the mammogram before I say anything to him.

TEN

Dot called during the afternoon and told her they had got her a slot for her mammography first thing the following day, adding that Mary had obviously pulled the staff card trick with one of her contacts who happened to know Maeve too. She had volunteered to go in early and do the scan for her.

When they were getting ready for bed that night Conor remarked, 'Maeve, you're not yourself these past few days, are you?'

'Sure, you know what it's like coming back from holidays – leaving the sun and the nothing-to-do-ness behind. It's always hard to get back into the stride. Besides, we're just especially busy because Stan has Rashid's patients to slot in. I think I'll go in a bit earlier tomorrow to get on top of things.'

'Does that man know how lucky he is to have such dedication from his staff?' he teased.

'I'll be sure to tell him in the morning,' she replied.

'No, I'll tell him for you, he's playing with Liam in the Open next Saturday. I saw his name on the board yesterday.'

They got into bed and reached for each other with a comfortable closeness that thirteen years of marriage had brought.

Maeve didn't sleep very well and was awake long before the alarm sounded. She had showered, dressed and had the coffee made by the time Conor appeared. They chatted over breakfast and headed off in their different directions.

At the mammography clinic, she gave the necessary details and was led into a cubicle with a quite inconspicuous-looking machine in one corner. She had often heard of this procedure and was almost ashamed to admit to never having had herself screened before. Maybe if I had I wouldn't be in such a panic, she thought. Some of her friends said it was like having your breast squeezed into a sandwich maker, only worse. Others said that if you were well endowed it didn't hurt as much as if you had nothing on top.

'There's no need to be scared – this is not painful – more uncomfortable, but if you can bear with it for a few minutes, it'll be all over before you know it,' said Aoife, the radiographer, disappearing behind a partition at one end of the room. 'Just hold still for a few seconds till I take that picture. Good, that's OK.' She came back out.

'Now, let's take it from another angle.' Releasing the pressure, she explained, 'I'm just moving these plates to get a better lateral view.' She realigned them, checked their position. 'Great – just hold there for a few minutes again,' she said, disappearing again. 'Great – now we'll do the other side. Might as well give you the full treatment while you're here, then you can get dressed. We'll just have a quick look at these to make sure they are OK. Then you can head off to work.'

'When will I have the results?'

'Let me see. Mary Lynch has requested immediate notification so once the radiologist comes in, he'll be on the phone to her. He'll be here later. Don't worry I've had two lumpectomies myself, both benign!' she reassured her.

'Thanks for that,' said Maeve. 'My mind is playing all sorts of games with me since I found the lump.'

'I can honestly say I know what you're going through,' Aoife said, opening the door for her, 'and it is a very scary time.'

Maeve made her way to her office, forcing smiles and

bonhomie at everyone. The minutes dragged. She couldn't concentrate. Every time her phone buzzed its jingly tone, she froze. Just before going down for coffee, she got the call she had been waiting for.

'Mary Lynch here, Maeve. I have your results if you'd like to drop down to me, whenever you get a minute and we can talk about them.'

'Yes, yes thank you. I was just going down for coffee, so is now a good time?'

'Why not bring me one too? White, no sugar.'

Dorothy showed her straight in to Mary's room.

'Well?' asked Maeve. 'Is it good news or is it bad news?'

'A bit of both, I suppose,' said the surgeon, studying her screen before swivelling it around towards Maeve. 'There's definitely a tumour here,' she pointed to the grey image before zooming in for a closer look, 'and from what I can see from these images, it's more deeply rooted than I would have hoped. It's impossible to say at this stage if it's benign or malignant, but, either way, I'm afraid you are facing surgery. From my point of view, Maeve, it's always preferable to operate as soon as we can in cases like yours. I know you work for Stan and you may prefer to have him take care of you. If you do that's not a problem at all, but whichever of us you decide you want, there is no time to be lost.'

'Will I lose my breast?' she asked hesitantly, afraid of the answer she knew she would get.

'It is a possibility. We'll have a pretty good idea once we analyse the growth, sometimes it takes a lab report, but with implants and prosthesis nowadays, even the possibility of a reconstruction a little further down the line, that is not as major a problem as before. Have you discussed this with your husband?'

'No, I haven't even told him about finding the lump yet. He hates hospitals and I didn't want to say anything until I was sure.'

'Don't try to be too brave. This is not easy news to deal with. Do you mind my asking if you have a strong relationship?'

'Of course I don't mind you asking. We have a great marriage. We couldn't have children though, and I often think that brought us closer.'

'What was the cause of the infertility?'

'Infertility wasn't the problem, it was holding on to the baby that was. We went through the heartache of three miscarriages, and all that entails. When I was told I had developed endometriosis, we knew that was it and had almost got around to accepting it would never happen. Then I discovered I was pregnant again, against all the odds, but it was an ectopic pregnancy. That was heart-breaking for both of us.'

You've been through a lot,' she said, making some more notes as she listened, 'and I know news like this is always a shock. I'm here if either you or your husband have any questions. Give him my number at home too and tell him to ring, any time. Some men have difficulties coming to terms with this operation. Most, when the shock subsides, accept it with good grace and see it as a lifesaver. Some don't like talking about it in front of their wives either. However, there is counselling there if it's needed – and that goes for you too.' While she spoke, Mary wrote her numbers on a piece of paper, which she now handed to Maeve.

'You're very kind,' said Maeve.

'No,' she said, matter of factly. 'A lot of women have issues with losing a breast. Some feel violated, and mutilated; others feel thankful it's just a removable part that is affected. But let's cross that bridge if, and when, we come to it. Could I suggest you go back upstairs and have a chat with Stan? Tell him about the mammogram results and sort your dates out with him, then ring me. Remember if you want him to look after you that's OK by me. Equally, I'm at your disposal if you'd prefer me to take you on.'

She put her hand reassuringly on Maeve's shoulder as she

led her out of the consulting room. Dorothy was on the phone as she walked by, so Maeve just smiled at her. She paused on the stairs to collect her thoughts. Should she tell Conor first? Or should she talk to Stan. She looked down at her breast and thought, 'One of us may have to go and it's not going to be me. You're spare parts. I can live without you.'

Back in the office, she waited until Stan had finished with his last patient. The secretary had her earphones on and was tapping away happily on her keypad. Maeve had never realised until this moment that many of those letters were to people who had just been given the same news she now had. Stan opened the door to see a female patient out.

'Bye, Jean, I'll see you again in six months.'

'Thank you again, for everything. You've given me back my life.'

'Just doing my job,' he said, as he helped her into her coat. Maeve followed him into his rooms.

'Stan, I need to tell you something …' she began.

'Oh no, you're not going to leave me—'

'No, it's not that. Let's hope it's not that …'

***

By the time Maeve got home that evening, a bed had been booked for the following week and her surgery scheduled for Saturday morning. She cooked Conor's favourite dinner of steak and stir-fry vegetables and made an apple tart. She had opened a bottle of Gaillac, leaving it to breathe until they were eating.

'Umm, something smells good and it's not just you,' Conor said as he gave her a hug. 'You spoil me – half the guys in the firm are going home to takeaway dinners and half the women are going home to order them.'

'I know,' she smiled back, 'but you're worth it. Besides I need to talk to you and, you know what they say, the number one rule in marriage is that you never tell your man anything before you feed him.'

'Sounds ominous, you're not having an affair with Stan, are you?'

She swiped the tea towel at him.

'No, but I might now that you've suggested it. It sounds like a great idea. A little bit of fumbling between appointments and some illicit lunchtime sex behind the filing cabinet!'

'… "Illicit lunchtime sex behind the filing cabinet!"' Conor had a habit of repeating key phrases, something Trish assumed he had developed as part of his training in law – a device to enable him time to formulate his thoughts or gather his arguments into a logical sequence before saying something inappropriate. However, Maeve adamantly refused to tell him what she wanted to talk about until he had finished a second piece of dessert and she had got up from the table and started to clear the dishes into the kitchen.

'OK. Let's have it. You want to have the garden landscaped, go on a shopping spree to New York with the girls …' he prompted.

'Well, yes to both of those, but not in that order. Conor, I have to have an operation.'

'An operation? What for?'

'I found a lump in my left breast when we were in Spain. They're going to remove it. Next week.'

'A lump. My God! Why didn't you tell me? When did you find it?'

'I lied about having to go in early this morning. I had the mammogram done first thing. I went to see Mary Lynch yesterday, you know her, and Stan knows now. I told him today once I found out. I know I should have told you first, but I didn't want to tell you over the phone. Mary managed to get me on the theatre list for Saturday week. She's going to operate.'

'Operate? Why couldn't you tell me before?'

'I don't know. I think I was afraid that, if I said anything it would make it real. Now it is anyway.'

Conor just sat there. It seemed an age before he asked, 'How serious is it? Why aren't you letting Stan do the operation?'

'I thought I'd be too embarrassed, so I went to Mary instead. She was really sweet and kept telling me if I wanted Stan to look after me that'd be OK with her.'

'You still haven't told me how serious it is.'

'Conor, there is a deep-seated growth and if worst comes to the worst, I may lose my breast.' She studied his face for any signs of horror or revulsion at the prospect. There were none.

'Babe, I'll be here for you no matter what. You'll always be the most beautiful woman in the world to me.' He went over to Maeve and folded her in his arms, rocking her gently. 'I'm just so sorry you have to go through this and that you kept it to yourself till now.'

'So am I.'

'I thought they only did mastectomies nowadays if the person has cancer – they don't know that yet, do they?'

'There is definitely something there – they can tell from the X-rays. What they don't know is the extent of it.'

At that point, the week's pent-up anxiety and dread overcame Maeve and she cried. Conor continued to hold and rock her. She could sense the fear curling and uncurling in the pit of his stomach, as it did in hers.

'This can't be happening. Why you? I feel so angry,' he said. 'I don't know what to say.'

Neither did she, so she just stayed nestled in his arms while her tears soaked his shirt.

***

Trish was in the utility room sorting the piles of washing the kids had brought back the previous evening from their trip to the Gaeltacht. There were mildewed shirts and shorts, stiff socks, which she could swear Barry had worn for the whole thirty days, and everything she lifted left little pools of sand behind. Louise implied that there was really no need to launder any of her things as all her clothes were 'so not in'. What she really needed was a whole new wardrobe if she was to rate in the street-cred stakes, while Toni, who had just started to stretch and develop, refused to wear cast-offs and really did have nothing to fit her any more.

Maeve had phoned.

'What are you up to?' she asked.

'The usual after the holiday frenzy. The kids are back and there are sports bags, teenage paraphernalia and clothes all over the place. Rory's off to Brussels for a few days, lucky sod, while I'm left with three hyperactive adolescents. Those lazy hours at the pool are fast becoming a dim and distant memory. Why aren't you at work? I didn't realise you'd taken this week off too.'

'I haven't. I'm on a bit of unscheduled leave. Can you meet me for lunch?'

Maeve had gone in that morning and Stan had told her to take that day and the next few days off and get herself prepared for her operation. He said he'd call on Rashid's receptionist to stand in and, besides, the temp who usually did holiday relief for Maeve knew her way around the office and would be delighted with the extra shifts.

Trish sensed there was something not quite right.

'Come over here. The kids are all out, no doubt swapping tales of their latest conquests, which I really prefer not to know about,' she laughed, 'so we'll not be disturbed.'

'If you're sure, Trish.'

'Of course I am. I'll just toss a salad or something light and we can have a natter.'

A short time later, Maeve arrived at Trish's house, looking tired beneath her tan. They sat in the breakfast room, the doors open to the lawn with its daisies and bald patches from football and penalty shootouts into imaginary goalmouths between the hedges.

Trish said to Maeve, 'The joys of kids, eh? Not like your manicured lawns and flower-filled beds.'

'It looks well … well used,' she laughed.

'That it is,' said Trish. 'Come on, spill it. What's the matter? You didn't come here to talk about my garden?'

Maeve told her the news.

'Good God, Maeve. When did you find this out?'

'In the villa, the night of the thunderstorm. I mean that's when I first found it. I just found out about the operation yesterday.'

'But you never said a word.'

'No, I wasn't even sure. I mean physically I wasn't sure, but mentally I think I knew it was there. It's hard to explain.'

Trish stood up, her eyes brimming with tears, and she hugged Maeve. She didn't hold back. There was no need for pretence. No words were necessary.

When Trish was serving up lunch, the phone rang. 'That'll be Rory,' she said. 'He's off later this afternoon. Can I tell him?'

'No, don't. It'll keep till he gets back,' said Maeve.

She fiddled with her salad as Trish talked, and from the one-sided snatches of conversation, Maeve knew that Conor had already told his friend. He probably needed to do that, she conceded. He'd need to confide in someone too. After the phone call, the women talked for a long time.

'In one way I'm dreading the weekend, in another I'm willing it to arrive sooner than it will, so that I'll know the reality of what I have to begin to deal with.'

Trish offered to take her to the hospital on Friday, but Maeve felt that Conor might prefer to do it himself. 'I'll let you know,' she said as they parted company.

'Keep the best side out and, who knows, it may well be a false alarm.'

'Who knows?'

'I'm here if you need me, you know that,' Trish said, putting her arm around her friend.

Maeve smiled. 'I do and you'll probably be sick to death of me whinging on your shoulder.'

***

Rory was just leaving the office. He headed to his car in his coveted city-centre parking place. He was off to Brussels for meetings with the DeLonghi Hotel board regarding a proposed new property in Brussels, where such space seldom became available. He had arranged to meet Anna Maria, but he hadn't told anyone.

He looked at his watch for the third time in as many minutes. Was she looking forward to their meeting as much as he was? He felt excited and uneasy. He also felt guilty about not mentioning anything to Trish. Why he hadn't, he couldn't say. Anyway, he told himself, there was no harm in meeting a friend in a foreign city, was there?

ELEVEN

Rory rang Trish from his hotel room that night, as he always did when away from home. He was meeting Anna Maria in fifteen minutes in a little bar just off the gilded Grand-Place.

'Any news?' he asked.

'No. I still can't quite believe it about Maeve. It's really upset me.'

Blast it. How could he have forgotten to mention that himself? He knew how she felt about Maeve and it should have been top of his thoughts. 'It may be nothing too serious. She's lucky to have you. Just be there for her. How are the kids?'

'Great. The usual. You know how it is. Barry wants to go to town to meet his new friends and is in sulky-silent mode because I said no! Louise is mooning around dropping 'Gearóid this' and 'Gearóid that' into every sentence. I think she's fallen in love with this Gearóid and the fact that he's from Wexford isn't helping. And there's worse.'

'It can get any worse?' laughed Rory.

'Yep. David, you know David from Barry's class at school, well he's going around with the collar of his sports shirt turned up and Barry and Louise are giving him a hard time about it. They keep asking him if he's hiding something. David, as you know just goes bright red when anyone even looks at him, so he reacts by pulling the collar up even higher, hiding – wait for it – a love bite!

'My God, that brings back memories of Coláiste Chonnacht, all right. I learned more about girls there than Irish.'

'Maybe I should have gone there. All I learned where I went was how to play 'Báidín Fheilimí' on the tin whistle and how to do jigs and reels like 'The Walls of Limerick' at the céilis.'

'I wouldn't like to tell you what we got up to.'

'I can guess,' she said. 'Well, you're lucky to be in a nice hotel with someone cooking your food and the chance to have an early night with a good book. I wouldn't mind changing places until the kids get back to normal again.'

'Stick with it, you're doing a grand job,' he said, promising to ring the next day, a twinge of unease unsettling him. He should have told Trish he was meeting Anna Maria. It wasn't too late; he could pretend they had just bumped into each other. It was the most natural thing in the world for them to meet when he was in Brussels, and he really didn't know, or didn't allow himself to acknowledge, why he had held back on telling her. He knew he was turning this meeting into something furtive and clandestine – a deception, leaving it open to interpretations that might never arise.

Deep down, however, Rory knew this was no ordinary catch-up for a drink with a friend to while away an hour or two when away from home. He admitted to himself it was much more of a date.

He now was having misgivings at having arranged it. He knew from the minute he had met Anna Maria that he was attracted to her – from that first night in El Caballo Loco in Mijas. He'd admired her sporty figure on the golf course – sexy in her Bermuda shorts and matching sleeveless polo shirts. She moved with a cool confidence in a very sensuous way and tossed her hair unselfconsciously. But heck, who wouldn't have admired her? He'd seen heads turn anywhere they had gone. She was drop-dead gorgeous, he rationalised. So too was Agneta. Liam was in constant touch with Agneta and had talked about her to him yesterday. Rory never mentioned to him that he had phoned Anna Maria or that he intended meeting her. He remembered how he had felt at the barbecue in Mijas weeks earlier, when she had brushed against him in the kitchen in the villa. Definitely there had been chemistry there. He had felt it, and was sure he had seen it in her eyes too.

His saner self told him he could always cancel, tell her his meetings had run on, stay in his room and watch BBC World, but the male predator in him took over. He was excited at the prospect of seeing her again – this time on her own territory. She was one of the breeds of Euro commuters – highly motivated, multilingual, efficient and capable. A woman of the world, she used this capital as her workstation.

He showered, dressed in a lightweight Pierre Cardin suit and open-necked shirt and left the hotel. She was waiting, clad in a flimsy floral top in deep turquoise, which accentuated her tanned skin and naturally blonde hair. Her tailored trousers were detergent-ad white and she wore strappy sandals with impossibly tall, transparent, spindly heels.

He knew the minute he saw her that the magnetism was there. He hadn't imagined it. He had wanted to kiss her at the barbecue, when they had gone inside the house together. He'd sensed that she had wanted it too. Now here they were, both running their eyes over each other as if checking that their memories hadn't lied. There was no awkwardness filling the spaces since their last meeting and, immediately, they delighted in each other's company, neither knowing where the evening would lead. They chatted like old friends, talking about the holiday in Spain, their likes and dislikes, their work, and then got on to all the personal things they hadn't got around to discussing in the villa.

'Where would you like to go?' he asked. 'This is almost your town, so you must know the best places.'

'I do,' she said, and told him about the newest ice bar. They headed there and found a table. The sheet of ice behind the army of waistcoated bartenders shimmered as diminutive white beams of light twinkled and caught the frozen facets of the surface. Elsewhere, the bar was dark, with black walls and pools of silvery light shining on the glass tables. White candles floated in black containers and a jazz pianist played in one corner. After a drink, they headed to a restaurant, one he had chosen, one where he had dined with clients before and which he remembered as being intimate and atmospheric – one where he could use his company credit card.

Rory noticed the curvaceous shape of Anna Maria's buttocks and the faint outline of her thong as she went ahead of him into the moodily lit dining room. He knew he was playing with fire, but felt he could control the situation. He wished he'd told Trish. They had no secrets. She trusted him implicitly, and told him so frequently. Rory was not the sort to play around. In fact, he was the one who decried such behaviour by some of his mates in the golf club.

When they were seated Anna Maria asked, as if reading his mind, 'You didn't tell Trish or the others we were meeting, did you?'

'No,' he said, and she flashed a beguiling smile across the table at him, holding his gaze.

'That's good,' she said coyly. 'I didn't tell Agneta either.' She reached across and put her hand over his. Rory felt a flicker of desire at her touch, a tingle that excited him. She moved her hand away while the waiter took their order. When the wine was served, she deliberately and slowly ran her fingers up and down the stem of the glass. Afterwards Rory had no recollection at all of what he had eaten.

It had rained when they were dining; one of those unrelenting showers that dump buckets of water in seconds and then stops just as quickly. They turned into the Grand-Place to the spectacle of the gilded buildings in the square making magical reflections on the wet cobbled stones and in little pockets of water between them.

'Can't you see how this place inspired Baudelaire to write?' Anna Maria asked.

'It is beautiful,' he said admiring, as always, the eclectic facades of the seventeenth-century buildings. She stumbled as one of her spindly heels caught in the uneven surface. Rory put out his hand to steady her and she took his arm. Her apartment was too close to bother with a taxi. Just as they arrived, the heavens opened again.

'Come in,' she paused for a heartbeat, 'until the shower passes.' He followed.

'So, this is where you hide out,' he said, suddenly out of his depth and feeling unsure. It was an unusual position in which to find himself. Rory was always in control, reading every situation in an instant. It was a talent that had made him so successful in business, yet here he was like the proverbial fish out of water, not knowing how to act. Should he sit on the sofa or one of the armchairs? He stayed standing.

'Yes, most of us at the commission just live in Brussels for five days a week and we high-tail it out of the city at 4 o'clock on Fridays. The exodus we call it – the airport is like the last day of college, with us all heading home in different directions.'

'Don't you get tired living out of a suitcase?' he asked.

'I don't take one with me. I have duplicates of essentials like toiletries and footwear and two different wardrobes in Helsinki and here so that I don't have to spend hours in queues checking in and hauling baggage everywhere with me.'

'Clever.'

'Efficient. It works a treat,' she said. 'Speaking of treats, what would you like for a nightcap?'

She sidled up to him, so close he could smell the scent from her hair. He reached to touch it.

'Sit down and relax,' she said.

As she fixed them brandies, Rory commented on her apartment, which had been given the Finnish minimalist-design treatment. In complete contrast, the walls were hung with modern art in sultry colours and light-coloured, wooden frames.

'I see you like my artwork. I did bring it from Finland. And my glassware too,' she said. 'I love these Iittala pieces. Are you familiar with Alvar Aalto, the designer?' she said, picking up an oddly shaped turquoise bowl. 'This is one of his signature pieces, a compulsory wedding gift back home.'

'Are you – were you married?'

'No, but I decided I wanted one of these and it was easier to buy it for myself than wait to find a husband.'

'I have to admit I never heard of Alto Ava … Alvar … of him – it is a him? I'm a bit of a philistine,' he joked, 'that's Trish's department.' Why had he mentioned Trish?

She replaced the piece on the shelf. The whole ambience in here reflected Anna Maria's calm demeanour. Rory was feeling anything but calm. The paintings had passion – a passion he just knew lay below the surface of this woman. Damn it. I'm nervous. Grow up lad, he told himself, this is par for the course with these high flyers. She probably entertains like this every other day and I'm just reading the signals wrong. Anna Maria leaned over the settee and handed him his glass, her soft hair brushing against his cheek. His pulse quickened, her scent intoxicating him. Now that didn't seem accidental at all. She came around and sat beside him.

'To us,' she said, clinking the rim of her glass to his, fixing him with a soulful look.

'To us,' he replied, taking a swallow and putting the glass down too heavily on the coffee table.

She put her hand on his leg, and he felt as though she had seared him with a hot iron. He wanted her so badly. He put his hand on top of hers. She reached up and kissed him full on the lips, pulling away to read his reaction. He didn't need a second invitation. He kissed gently at first, then more deeply and insistently. She began to open the buttons on his shirt, one by one. He offered no resistance. Unwilling to pull away, he began to undo her flimsy blouse. Taking his hand, she stood up and led him into the bedroom. Within minutes, they were naked. With a practised manoeuvre, she tossed the duvet aside and rolled onto the undersheet. Rory climbed in beside her, touching, exploring, their senses exploding with each discovery. She cried, moaning with pleasure. At that moment, a passing thought of Trish crossed his mind, as he realised they weren't able to make these animal sounds now that the kids had got old enough to hear them. That thought brought him back to reality and with a wave of guilt his erection died instantly. What the hell am I doing here? he thought. He pushed her aside.

'What's the matter?' she asked, reaching down to caress him.

'Anna Maria, I'm sorry. I'm so sorry. You're gorgeous and desirable. I shouldn't have done that. I shouldn't have come here. I'm married. I've never cheated on Trish.'

'No one knows. She needn't know,' said Anna Maria, her hands still working on him skilfully.

'I'll know,' he said, sitting on the edge of the bed.

'Look, stay and let's talk,' she urged, pressing her cheek to his shoulder and folding her arms around his chest.

'No, I'm going back to the hotel. I'm really, really sorry. I think it's best if we don't meet again.'

He dressed hastily, retrieving his clothes as he went through to the lounge. He walked out into the rainy night, ignoring the heavy drops. 'Christ, what was I thinking about?'

TWELVE

It was just a month since their holiday but so much had
happened. Maeve's operation was over. She was in the
recovery ward off the theatre when Mary Lynch came out to
speak to Conor, still in her green scrubs.

'Conor, come in and sit down,' she said, leading him into a
tiny impersonal office.

'There is no way to make this any easier. Maeve has cancer.
We did a frozen biopsy and the indications are that she has
indeed got a malignancy.'

' … got a malignancy. Christ. No! She's never been sick in
her life. Could you be mistaken?'

'No, I wish we were.'

'But can it be cured, treated even?'

'Conor, I really should be waiting until Maeve is fully
recovered from the anaesthetic to tell you this, but she has
cancer in both breasts.'

' … in both breasts? You mean you had to remove them
both?' he began to shake. This could not be happening.

'As you know, she signed a consent form before we operated
giving us permission to proceed if necessary, but because this
has all happened so quickly, I thought it would be best to give
her a little time to prepare her somewhat rather than just
waking up today to find out the worst, but we will have to

operate within the week if we are to have any hope of containing it.'

'She's not going to die, is she? I couldn't live without her. Christ, that sounds so selfish, but I just can't take this in.'

'That's not selfish. It's natural to feel like that. Unfortunately, the cancer she has is the most invasive sort. We'll do all we can to contain it.'

' ... we can *contain* it? Can we not beat it? I mean can it be zapped or whatever they do now. What about all these miracle drugs I keep reading about in the papers?'

'I can't pretend to play God, Conor. It's serious, but with treatment and proper aftercare she can look forward to about five years.'

' ... about five years. Do we have to tell her that?'

'Maeve is an intelligent woman. She'll want to know. In all probability, we'll have to follow up her operation with some chemotherapy and radiotherapy. We'll have a better idea then. The treatment in itself can be pretty tough going. And can have some unpleasant side effects. Then there are times between sessions where we have to wait for long periods to do scans and that can be hard – the waiting and not knowing. She's going to need all the tender loving care you, her family and friends can muster.'

'She'll get that, I can promise you,' he said. 'I can't believe this. Can I go see her now?'

'Yes. Just for a minute. She'll still be groggy from the anaesthetic and may not make much sense. Conor, do you want me to tell her what we found or would you rather do it? I can ask Stan to be there too if you like, or ask him to call in to her later when she's fully awake as I'm sure she'll have lots of questions, once she starts thinking about it.'

'Do whatever you think is best for her, Mary, and thank you.'

Mary left him at the door of the recovery area and he approached his wife's bed, remembering only too vividly the same scenario when she had lost their baby and almost her life too after the last pregnancy. He quashed his revulsion to the antiseptic smells and the clinical drips. He had to be strong to get her through this.

'Maeve. Maeve. It's me, Conor,' he said, leaning down and kissing her cheek. She opened her eyes, half-focused on his face and smiled, stretching her hand out to find his.

'Hi there,' she said, as though she had cotton wool in her mouth. She moved her hands in slow motion up over the blanket and said, 'I still have two.'

He put his hands on top of hers and said, 'Yes, you have, you still have two, babe.'

She closed her eyes and went back to sleep, still smiling. Conor left the hospital, climbed into his car and sobbed, as he hadn't done since he was a kid. He then phoned Trish and asked her if she would come in later with him for moral support – for both of them. He was worried that he might not be so brave when faced with the reality of what was going to happen. She insisted he came to her house straight away.

***

Later, they were sitting at either side of Maeve's bed. She was now fully awake and waiting for Mary's visit. She had promised to come back about now and break the news to her. Maeve seemed totally unaware of how her world was about to shift off its axis.

'I thought you were supposed to be in at the tribunal this afternoon?' she said to Conor.

'It's just legal arguments, so I got Jason to cover for me.'

The door opened and in Mary came. Maeve introduced Trish and Mary sat down on the side of the bed. Conor had not let go of his wife's hand.

'Well? Tell me the worst,' said Maeve.

'I'm afraid, Maeve, you have cancer. Unfortunately, though, there's a little more to it – it's in both breasts and we suspect in some of the lymph nodes under your right arm. There's no easy way to tell you this, but you need to have a double mastectomy and those rogue nodes will have to be removed too if we're going to beat it.'

'Oh God. It's that bad?' she said, almost as though she had been expecting the worst. 'Can you get it all by doing that or is it too late?'

'Let's not be pessimistic. It's impossible to tell just yet. We'll know more after the surgery. The lymph nodes are the filters along the fluid canals and it's their job to trap cancer cells before they reach other parts of the body. Whatever we find will be followed up by radio and chemo treatments and we'll be monitoring your progress constantly.'

'Will I lose my hair?' she asked, before adding, 'what a stupid thing to ask. I mean – that's nothing in comparison … It's not really the most important issue.'

'It's almost the first question everyone asks though,' said Mary. 'In all probability, you will lose your hair, but it will grow back. There is a treatment we've been using with good results. It's called the Cold Cap. It's highly successful in some cases for the prevention of hair loss, but there's no need to think about that just yet.'

'I've never heard of it,' said Maeve.

'Nor have I,' said Trish.

'This Cold Cap … how does that work?' asked Conor.

'It is literally what it says, a cold cap. It's more a helmet really that prevents as much of the chemotherapy drug getting to your scalp as possible. It works by chilling your head. The cold restricts the blood supply so the drug doesn't reach the hair follicles.'

'That sounds like such a simple but great idea,' said Maeve.

'The best ones often are. In theory, it sounds ideal but some people cannot tolerate the cold. It means the treatments take a little longer to administer and it's not the most pleasant thing in the world. The cap must go on fifteen minutes before chemo begins so it starts restricting the blood flow first, and it has to be kept on for the duration of the treatment, and then for up to an hour after. But this isn't something to think about now – we can deal with those things further down the line.'

'Does it always work?' asked Maeve.

'Frankly, no! And it's not always compatible with some of the chemo drugs we use, but there has been about an eighty to eighty-five per cent success rate recorded to date.'

'Babe, you've surgery to get over first and you may not feel like any more discomfort when that's out of the way, so let's just concentrate on that for the moment.'

'Conor's right, Maeve. We can do your surgery on Tuesday, but if you feel that is too soon and you want more time to think about it and get used to the idea we can delay it for a week, no more … It's up to you.'

'Let's do it on Tuesday and get it over with,' she said. 'What's the point in waiting?'

'Is that too much of a hurry to take things in?' asked Conor.

'No. I think I already knew what was ahead. My breasts are spare parts at this stage. I can live without them and I can always have a reconstruction to make me look like Dolly Parton later on. Besides, gravity was beginning to take over and they were starting to sag a little!'

'I don't know if I would be so brave,' said Trish, who had been strangely silent throughout all these exchanges. The shock was beginning to sink in.

'When you see my new ones, you'll be pestering Mary to do the same for you, you'll be so jealous.'

'We'll do a few more scans and bloods and I'll get one of the oncology team to come in to you and you can ask any questions you may have. Conor, you can talk to someone if you like too.'

He declined, not knowing where to begin. They all thanked

Mary and as she left she said, 'I'll pop in to see you tomorrow, Maeve.'

The next few days were unreal. Maeve and Conor spent many hours talking and being quiet together, both trying to protect each other from what was ahead. They were grateful that, because of their contacts, they had been spared long delays for action and therefore hadn't had to endure the anxiety that comes with having to wait. Conor knew he would never forget that room with its geometric-patterned curtains, the television with the tinny sound, the noise of the trolleys as they trundled along the corridor delivering meals on wheels, as Maeve called them. He was sick with worry.

***

Maeve's operation was over, and although hardly fully awake from the anaesthetic and still in the recovery room, she immediately wanted to see how she looked.

'Lie still,' a voice from some middle distance echoed and a hand caressed hers. 'You've had your operation, Maeve, and everything went according to plan.'

She tried to talk, but only sounds came out as though in slow motion. 'Go back to sleep now, Maeve, there's nothing to worry about. We're here looking after you and we'll bring you back to your room in a little while.' She fell back asleep.

Her mind was confused and as she became more lucid, her thoughts began to make sense to her again. She moved her hands to feel her new shape and even though the dressings and bandages bulked her up a bit she could still feel the unbelievable flatness where her breasts had been.

None of the supermodels have breasts at all – for them the androgynous look is desirable, her thoughts wandered. I have to be philosophical – if they were a straight swap for my life then the price is not too high. I have to be strong to get through the chemo and I know that's going to be tough. I have to be strong for Conor too. I know how he hates all this trucking with hospitals, but it's about to become a big part of our normality. We've managed before and we'll get through this together too. We have to.

***

The day had that distinctive September quality to it, misty and with a mellow fragrance. It was Maeve's favourite time of the year and she lay looking out at the hospital grounds. An enormous chestnut tree close by was heavy with ripening conkers. Trish phoned to see how she was.

'I'm doing great, really,' she said. 'High as a kite on the drugs and my arm is bit sore to lift, but I suppose that's to be expected. How are the brood? Did they all go back to school OK?'

'Yes, thank goodness, but not without incident. All the high drama, looking for books and pens, bits of uniforms and sports gear missing. They think we're made of money. I keep telling them what I'd like to do with it instead and that quietens them down for a bit. Honestly, I think they were easier when they were toddlers.'

'You're obviously up to your eyes. Don't come in to see me today.'

'Now listen here, I'll come in unless I'm told not to, and as you're in no position to fight with me, I'll see you later. Rory sends his love by the way.'

'That's nice, and you're very bossy!'

THIRTEEN

What had started out as an idea for a modest celebration for Liam's fortieth birthday was turning into quite an affair. Unbeknownst to him, Carol, his PA, and some of his friends from the office had got on to their advertising agency and booked a large billboard in Donnybrook for the actual date. This was going to show a twenty-year old Liam on skis negotiating a steep incline with the words, 'It's all downhill from here' in two-foot-high writing across the top. They had other surprises in the pipeline too.

Liam himself was looking forward to getting all his friends to Dublin for the big night. Numerous girl friends, past and present, work colleagues, as well as golf club associates, had all accepted. Liam's work currently saw him flitting back and forward to Cyprus regularly and, as promised, he always met Aldora. The two had formed a great bond, but not of the romantic kind, yet whenever he was there, they spent all their free time together. She had promised to come too, saying she was looking forward to coming to Dublin for the party and meeting some of his eligible friends. He had of course invited the Finns.

Anna Maria was the only one who was showing any signs of reluctance to committing to the date.

'She has to come. This whole party idea was Anna Maria's

and yours – don't you remember? At the barbecue in Spain?' he urged when he was talking to Agneta.

'I do, but I don't think she'll be able to make it,' she said.

'Why not?

'Well. It's a bit awkward.'

'How do you mean, awkward?' Had they had a falling out, he wondered.

'Oh, I'll tell you when I see you.'

'Trying to be mysterious, are we?'

'No, nothing like that. How's Maeve doing?' she asked, changing the subject in a way that made Liam think he had missed a bit of the conversation.

'She's being Maeve, stoic and good humoured, leaving hospital at the end of next week, but she'll have a nurse at home for a bit as she won't be allowed to lift or carry anything. Then I believe she'll start having her chemo,' he said. 'She's determined to be at the party.'

'She's really amazing,' said Agneta. 'I don't think I'd have that strength. I go to pieces when I have to have a routine check-up in case they discover anything.'

'Yes, she is,' said Liam. 'She really is and she's looking forward to seeing you both again'

'Well, as I said, I may be coming on my own.'

'You still haven't told me why.'

'I'd rather not,' she said evasively, 'at least not yet.'

When Liam had finished the phone call, he sat at his desk for a while trying to figure out what was going on. He and Anna Maria always had good fun sparring on the phone and he hoped he hadn't said anything to offend her. Surely Anna Maria couldn't be jealous that he and Agneta were closer. He'd give her a call later and see if he could suss out the reason for her change of heart. He'd try to talk her into being there for the celebrations. He decided he'd wait until he got home from the office that night before ringing her.

***

'Oh sir, we have two messages for you,' the uniformed concierge said as Rory checked into the hotel in Brussels. It had been a week since his last visit.

'Thank you,' he said, taking the little envelopes from the man. Both, he suspected, were from Anna Maria. He waited until he got to his room before opening them.

'Please call. We need to talk,' said the first. The second read, 'Please call, Rory.' He had arrived that morning and gone straight to a meeting as he normally would have done. He had been determined not to see Anna Maria again.

'Holy shit,' he said out loud as he scrunched up the notes and threw them in the waste bin. He went straight to the computerised bar, took out two miniature bottles of gin and emptied them into the large tumbler. He splashed a bottle of tonic into it and took a long slug, not bothering to go to the machine at the end of the corridor to get ice. A minute later, he reached into the bin and retrieved the two notes. One was dated the day after he had left the previous week – the other at 4.30 that afternoon.

Despite the vows he'd made to himself, he knew he wanted to see Anna Maria – badly. Besides, he really ought to apologise to her for what had happened. Then he thought, who'd know if anything happened? They could keep it between them. What harm would a little licentious fun do? He knew there would be no strings attached from her side. Lust, sex and satisfaction – she wouldn't be looking for anything more. He knew she'd toy with him, as indeed he might with her, but they both knew the rules. He met women like her all the time in business. Gorgeous, efficient, desirable. He'd seen his colleagues and friends have one or multiple night stands: he also knew several who had mistresses tucked away. Most of their wives never knew – or chose not to in some cases – but he had never approved. God, wasn't it easy to be sanctimonious when you hadn't been smitten, he thought.

Sitting in the impersonal hotel room, the relentless Brussels weekday traffic humming in the background, he could imagine Anna Maria writing the note, 'Please call, Rory.' He could hear her faintly accented words, smell her scent, remember her kisses, the feel of her warm breath on his shoulder.

He took another sip from his drink as he tried to blot out his conduct and the look of disbelief on her face when he had said he had to leave. He could still see her sitting up in bed surrounded by the crumpled sheets, her hair a silvery halo.

He looked at his watch – 7.30 pm – the time he usually called Trish when he was away. He picked up the phone to dial, to get the latest on her day and the kids. He sat there for a minute with the handset to his ear, then slowly replaced it and finished his drink. He couldn't talk to her now. His mind was in turmoil. He decided to shower, but even the force of the power jets didn't soothe him as they normally would.

He'd been like this all week, full of reproach, self-recrimination, indecision and, yes, guilt. He'd bitten the head off everyone in his office and his PA was still sulking at his uncharacteristic behaviour.

He had avoided any real conversation with his workmates, afraid to give anything away. He'd even been at odds with the guys when they'd played their fourball on Saturday and it had showed in his game. He'd had a disastrous round. He felt he was acting a part, trying to be light-hearted, trying to be loving, trying to be concerned – all actions which would have been totally natural to him before last Thursday. Now he was acutely aware of everything he said and did, terrified he'd give anything away. Trish, preoccupied with concerns for Maeve, hadn't appeared to spot anything different. If she had, she'd said nothing, but he had noticed her looking at him quizzically once or twice – at least he thought he had.

Stepping out of the shower, he pulled on the monogrammed robe, impatient at the ways the sleeves were tucked into the pockets and the belt double knotted to make it look as though a person had slipped away magically from inside it. He picked up the phone again. He punched the number in and it was picked up almost immediately.

'It's me,' he said.

'I knew you'd call,' Anna Maria replied.

'So did I.'

FOURTEEN

Sharonne was at her desk going through the ever-growing pile of paperwork about the FitzGerald-Reglob takeover. Bit by bit, she was discovering just why the shareholders were in for a major shock, not to mention monumental losses on their investments, which should have been secure and maturing. It was a considerable file, with some quite complicated paper trails – many going nowhere of consequence. She had an imminent meeting coming up with Bob, which both Christian and Jonathan were flying in to attend. The thoughts of meeting Christian again made her think of her hair. She buzzed Sadie. 'Make sure you have my 8 am appointment confirmed with Hervé. I want to look my best for this meeting.'

'You always look great,' said Sadie.

'Well, I'm playing in a man's world and I need to know I look my best to be taken seriously. I know there are those who say you don't need to get to the top – but that's where I intend going. I don't believe that because I'm a woman I have to wear tweeds, my hair in a bun and a pencil tucked into it to make an impact.'

Sadie just laughed. There was no danger of that happening, she thought.

Derek phoned her a short time later. He was really upset by Maeve's surgery and had just been talking to Conor. She and

Derek were supposed to be going out to a dinner that evening with some of Derek's colleagues, but he said he really wasn't in the mood.

'I'm just as happy to get out of that,' she said. 'Fix up another date with them. But why don't you and I have an early bird on the way home, somewhere quiet, where we can talk. We haven't done that for ages.'

He hesitated for a fraction before agreeing. She was finding the pressure of the FitzGerald-Reglob deal was taking up all her energy and was surprised to find how much the news of Maeve had affected her too. In fact, the news had devastated the whole circle of friends and they all reacted differently.

She wasn't too proud of her exhibition the night of the Captain's Prize, but there was no way she was ever going to let any of the others know that, so she had just brazened it out and pretended it never happened. No one had brought it up in Spain and she felt she had gained some ground by turning up for the weekend. She'd enjoyed it too.

She and Derek met at their local Italian and got a quiet table in the corner. 'Maeve's illness has made me feel very vulnerable,' she confessed while they were eating.

'Why? You're not feeling off colour are you?' Derek asked.

'No, but you know how I hate illness. We had years of nursing my dad with his 'bad heart'. I used to think that was like a bad apple with a bruised bit that would get bigger and more rotten the longer you left it in the fruit bowl. I hadn't understood about valves and arteries and bypass surgery until I was much older. And then I thought he was better for ever when he had his operation.'

'That was really tough on you and your mother.'

'I'll never forget the phone call the next day. I knew when I answered it that it was bad news. Why, I'll never understand. I can still hear my mother repeat the word "aneurysm – an aneurysm". When she put the phone down she just stared at me. I suppose she was wondering how she was going to tell me we had lost Dad, but I knew.'

'Surgery is much more sophisticated now,' said Derek.

'I know, but that doesn't stop me being terrified at the very thought of it.'

'You know Shar, sometimes, it's the lesser of two evils.'

'I know that, in here,' she said, putting her hand on her chest. 'But the thoughts of letting a complete stranger carve me up freaks me out.'

'They have slicker procedures and keep coming up with all sorts of new cosmetic aids nowadays,' he said.

'I know that and I know I'm probably being irrational too, but I saw some black and white photographs in an exhibition once of two lovers kneeling facing each other on their bed. The woman had only one breast. Where the other one had been was just a long shining track of silvered scar tissue reaching from her breastbone right around under her arm to her back. That really shocked me. Now all I keep thinking of is Maeve looking like that and how she will cope.'

'She will. She's strong. So is Conor.' He reached over to take her hand. 'They'll do it together, as we would if we had to.'

'It's so unfair.'

'I know it is, but let's hope they have got it in time. If that's the case, then the surgery will seem like a small price to pay,' Derek tried to reassure her. 'I mean small in the context of the other option. We just have to be positive for Conor and for her,' he said.

'Do you ever think how you would react if it was me?'

'I never did until this happened, and now I hope I never will have to,' he replied.

'You know, Derek, you're good for me.'

'I hope that too.'

'Let's skip coffee and have it at home.'

'Good idea,' he said and went off to pay the bill. While she waited for him to come with her coat, she reflected on how things were still a bit strained between them and on how they seemed to talk through the twins rather than to each other these days. She'd have to work on that.

The next morning she rang the hospital to see if they permitted flowers in the wards. Then she ordered some to be sent to Maeve, before settling to the business of the day, her mind occupied with getting the finer points of her notes and research into coherent logical sequences. She was excited at the prospect of meeting Christian again. They talked frequently on the phone, his manner always flirtatious, even seductive, that sexy French accent doing strange things to her senses.

This project was taking up a lot of her time. She was determined to impress Christian, and the team, with her efficiency. This meeting was her chance to shine, show them what she was really capable of. She had Sadie busy photocopying and checking details in her report. She set up meetings with the relevant solicitors and an international company lawyer. She had booked a room in the Merrion Hotel, one with video conferencing facilities in case they needed to talk to the company department heads in New York or LA.

Satisfied that she had everything in place, she felt she could relax a little.

***

Rory walked through the airport corridors in Brussels, the place as always abuzz with commuters. He passed the jewellery, perfume, lace and chocolate boutiques. He went back and bought Trish a big box of Godiva hazelnut pralines. He knew she loved them but, riddled with guilt, he also knew it would take more than a box of luscious chocolates to put things right in his mind. He headed for the business class lounge. He checked his watch and rang her. 'I'll be home in less than two and a half hours, if we take off on time.'

'I've had a manic day. I had to bring Louise for her braces

and spent hours at the dentist. I've already bribed the three of them with a promise of a Chinese. I'll make you something when you get here,' Trish said.

'You're a gem,' he said, feeling like a murderer.

'Well, I know as you didn't get a chance to ring last night that things must have been rough for you,' she said.

'Oh God, what have I done?' Rory said to himself, remembering the panic he'd felt when the phone had rung in Anna Maria's apartment last night while they were lying side by side in their post-coital glow.

They'd just made love for the second time – the first had been a rushed, lustful frenzy – Rory had been fearful that he'd be unable to perform after the previous week's disaster, but he need not have worried. The second time had been a slow and sensuous arousal, culminating in a tender possession, which had left them both totally sated. Then the phone had buzzed beside Anna Maria's bed.

'I have to take that. I'm on press rota tonight,' she said, reaching over his bare torso to get to the phone.

'Yes, Anna Maria here … Oh Liam, hello. I'm so glad it's you. I thought it might be some crisis or other … Oh, you know, to do with the speculation around the ECB interest rates. Yes, yes. I'm very well. How are you? She made a face at Rory, rotating her finger to indicate that he was going on and on. Theatrically, Rory put his index finger up and ran it across his neck telling her to get rid of him. She slapped his hand away as he started to fondle her breast.

'Your birthday? Yes. No, of course I haven't forgotten. Liam, can I call you tomorrow?' she asked. 'Yes, yes, no I mean you're not disturbing me but, yes, I do have someone with me. I'll call you tomorrow. Promise. Promise. Goodnight.' She put the phone down and straddled Rory again.

'That was just Liam.'

'I gathered as much,' said Rory, pulling her gently to him. 'Does he ring you often?'

'Not as often as he rings Agneta. I think he's fallen for her.'

'And I think I've fallen for you,' he said, as they began another session of discovery.

Now he was on his way home to face the consequences. He usually found the quiet of the business class lounge helped him unwind but not this evening. His mind kept going back to the previous night. He couldn't concentrate, his mood careering between guilt and elation. Will I be able to hide this deception from Trish? he wondered.

***

Since Maeve had come home from hospital, every time Trish visited she brought some offering or other with her. Today, it was an already cooked casserole. Often it was a batch of fruit scones or an apple pie. Trish dismissed these acts of friendship as nothing, 'Just something for your freezer, in case you don't feel up to doing anything after your treatment,' she'd say. Trish had taken to bringing Maeve in for her treatments, collecting her too.

'I must have the best stocked freezer on the road,' laughed Maeve, whose appetite was painfully small as the result of the regime. She usually felt fine for a few days until the effects hit her. Then her appetite and sleep patterns went haywire and she was overcome with a dreadful fatigue. Stan gave her great encouragement, popping in frequently on his way home from the clinic and insisting that she ate, even bird-like portions, to keep up her strength.

'I have to keep an eye on my right-hand woman,' he told Trish, who was just leaving. 'I need her to come back to me in fighting form.'

'I bet you don't even miss me,' said Maeve.

'We couldn't find a file today. Are you sure you're not having work sent home to you?' he teased.

'As if.' Her eyes turned grave with concern and she confronted him. 'Stan, please level with me. Do you honestly think I'll be back – that I'll make a full recovery?'

'You want honesty, you'll get it from me, Maeve, you know that.' He took her hands in his.

'You can say anything in front of Trish. In fact, I wish you would, then we can all know what's going on.'

'Truthfully it's too early to say for definite. But we do think the root of the problem has been removed. However, that won't rule out other cancerous cells starting up somewhere else. That's why you're on this course of chemo to make sure we head them off before they have the chance to take hold. We'll be monitoring everything carefully and if it works you should be back scourging me about my bad note-taking and illegible writing in no time at all.'

'And if it doesn't?'

'Let's take this one step at a time. If it doesn't go as we want it to, then it's on to plan B.'

***

Maeve had been given lots of information on special post-mastectomy bras and wig suppliers. Now that she was coming to terms with the idea, she phoned Trish. 'It's time to go shopping for my extra-cranial prosthesis,' Maeve said.

'Your what?'

'It's fancy talk for a wig. I should be going to one of the specialist places on the list they gave me, but I'm not ready for that yet.'

Friends had offered advice but the best of all was the piece she got from Nessa, her oncology nurse. 'If you decide to get a wig, go for something zany that will make you feel good about yourself. Buy two if you can and you'll be able to change your look with your mood. Your own hair will grow back so you needn't spend a fortune on them.'

That was their mission this morning. In the car Trish teased, 'Let's get something that looks like Hervé'd done it.'

'You know, Trish, Sharonne has been really kind, considerate to me even, since all this happened. It's like she's had a wake-up call or something, or maybe at last she realises that there was nothing furtive between Derek and me.'

'And about time too,' said Trish. "That one could be really nice if she stopped trying so hard to be nasty.'

'Maybe we should include her more.'

'I think that treatment has affected your brain,' laughed Trish.

'No, I mean in the plans for Liam's birthday, give her a mission, she'd love that. Put her in charge of something. Maybe we have been a bit exclusive with her.'

'She's the one who excluded herself.'

'I know,' said Maeve, 'but I think we should give her the opportunity, that's all.'

'OK, boss. We'll do it your way,' said Trish, pulling into the parking spot.

Ignoring the recommended specialists, Trish and Maeve had set off instead to a theatrical costumiers, one where they had hired outfits for fancy dress parties in the past. The man who served them was wearing the worst wig either of them had ever seen, with a three-inch-high quiff and a solid helmet appearance. They both had to struggle not to laugh when they saw him. It was a peculiar inky greenish-black colour, which clashed horrendously with his bushy ginger brows that almost met in the middle.

'I wonder if he takes it off when he goes to bed,' said Trish, picking a shoulder-length carroty model off a stand on the counter. 'Look, you could have a Texas high hairdo with this. Try it. Just like those in *Dallas*. Do you remember them? Sue Ellen and Pamela and Charlene – their hair added about six inches to their height – compensation for the ridiculous shoulder pads no doubt.'

'That must have made it hard finding tall male actors. Didn't Clark Gable stand on a biscuit tin or something when he was making *Gone with the Wind*?'

'No!'

'I'm sure I read that somewhere.'

At the far end of the shop, three women were trying on blonde styles.

'Look,' said Maeve, 'they're not women. They're men. Transvestites.'

'No they're not.'

'They are. Look at the shorter one – he has an enormous Adam's apple.'

'My God, you're right. They are,' said Trish. 'Pretend you're interested in buying this one,' she said, handing Maeve a tightly crimped Charleston-style concoction. 'I want to watch them in action.'

'They may have Adam's apples but look at those legs – it's so unfair – they're fantastic.'

'What do Adam's apples do?' asked Trish.

'I've often wondered that myself, but I think it has something to do with the thyroid.'

'No, that's definitely not my colour,' said Maeve, as Trish pulled out a Shirley Temple ringlet version in golden yellow. She put her hands in the air and started miming 'On the Good Ship Lollipop'.

'There's one over here just like your own – look.'

'You know, Trish, I think I'll go mad for once and try something completely different, maybe something really short.'

They spent another hour trying on every wig in the place – some merely accentuated Maeve's pallor, which was obvious since her surgery, others flattered with a gamine appeal. Eventually, when they left, she was sporting a new short bob in ash blonde with highlights. She almost had to wrestle for it as one of the group of transvestites had spotted it at exactly the same time and decided he wanted it too. Trish pulled him aside and explained why Maeve should have it. He was lovely about it and insisted it looked much better on her. Then the others joined in and the decision was made by committee.

Maeve lost her own hair as dramatically as had been predicted. She woke up one morning to find clumps of it on the pillow. She had cried then. Once it had started, it kept coming out in handfuls. The strands seemed to lace themselves around her fingers, as though reluctant to be consigned to the bin. She stood in front of the mirror in her bathroom and looked in sadness, not wanting to believe what she was seeing, bare patches of scalp peeping through. She took a scissors to it and cut it all off. When she had composed herself she phoned Trish.

'I need to go out wearing my new hair and I need moral support,' she said. 'I'll drive over and collect you.'

'You really look fabulous. It really suits you,' said Trish when she opened the door. 'Maybe I should have bought one too. It might make Rory look at me in a new light.'

FIFTEEN

'Conor, come out and play a few holes this evening,' Derek said. 'It'll do you good to get out in the fresh air for a bit.'

'I'm not very good company at the moment, but I supppose Maeve has some of the girls from the clinic coming over after work so I may just take you up on that and escape for a while. Leave them alone to talk.'

They'd arranged to meet at five thirty and were just walking down the first fairway when Derek asked, 'How are you coping with all that's going on?'

'Truthfully Derek, I'm still a bit shell-shocked. It really hasn't sunk in on one level. I mean apart from the obvious of seeing Maeve without her breasts and not being able to imagine what that must be like for her, I can't begin or maybe I'm just too scared to allow myself think any further than that.'

'I can just imagine. It's knocked us all for six,' said Derek, 'and I know Sharonne is stunned by it. She's no good at dealing with hospitals and illness.'

'I'm not the best myself,' said Conor, 'but do you know what, it's even worse when you get home and they're not there. When Maeve was still in hospital, it was somehow easier to deal with, surrounded by nurses and people who understood. Now, in a peculiar way, I feel as though we have been cut loose to fend for ourselves.'

'That's understandable.'

'I feel, rightly or wrongly, that Maeve is constantly wondering if I'm turned off by how she looks now. If I try to get close, she moves away. If I stay away will she feel rejected? And I don't know how to ask her or even if I should?'

'It must be one hell of an ordeal to have to come to terms with,' said Derek. 'I'm sure she's probably still struggling with all that herself.' He remembered Sharonne's description of that photograph where the woman had had her breast removed, and how Mary had said that some women regard such surgery as 'violation and mutilation' and was inclined to agree with it.

'I'm afraid to go too near her in case I'm rushing things.'

'Have you spoken about it?'

'No, that's the weirdest thing, I can't – I just feel it's not the right time yet.'

'Conor, we're all here for you, for both of you, you must know that.'

'I'm not explaining myself very well. I know you and all our friends are there and Sharonne has been very thoughtful sending flowers and goodies around, but it's as if Maeve and I have a common enemy, one that is going to defeat us in the end, but who is going to put us through hell first.'

'That's perfectly understandable. You're still in shock, but surely you're being too fatalistic?'

'Perhaps. This has been a real wake-up call, Derek. You know we never really appreciate our wives as we should. I know I love Maeve, but I feel if I were to lose her I would never have told her often enough how much she actually meant in my life.'

'I'm as guilty as you are there,' said Derek, thinking of when he had last told Sharonne he loved her. He'd been too busy scoring points against her recently, points she probably hadn't really deserved. Points because she always spoke her mind and got her own way, but as he walked along the course, his thoughts were that these were the qualities he had admired in her when he'd first met her. They were also the assets which made her so successful in the predominantly male world in which she worked.

As they finsihed their game and the early autumn evening closed in, Conor asked, 'What do you make of Rory these days? He doesn't seem to be himself. Is business going OK for him?'

'As far as I know. He's doing well – he's got some new project on the continent. He's probably just preoccupied with that,' said Derek. 'Anyway you know what he's like, even if he were coining it in it'd never be enough for him.'

'True,' said Conor, chipping his ball onto the eighteenth green before asking, 'Can you believe Liam will be forty next month?'

'No. He's the first. The girls are having great fun organising his party,' said Derek. 'Seem to have a few surprises lined up because any time I walk into a room and they're on the phone to each other they change the topic.'

'That's going to be a good bash,' said Conor. 'Maeve is determined to be there. Isn't it hard to believe we've all known each other over twenty years? It doesn't feel like it at all.'

'Yep, and what's even more unbelievable is that we'll all be following him in the next few months. Forty – I suppose it'll be downhill for us all after that,' he laughed.

SIXTEEN

Sharonne took a taxi to Bob's office in Dún Laoghaire. She was wearing a smart business suit and carried a navy Ted Lapidus briefcase. She arrived minutes before her appointed time and met Christian stepping out of a taxi.

'Bonjour, cherie,' he said taking her hand in his. 'Ça va bien?'

'Bien sur, merci,' she said as he stood back to allow her to pass him into the building. They shared the lift to the spacious suite of offices. She felt her pulse quickening, all too aware that they were confined in such a small space. Christian just stood there looking cool and smiling directly at her as though he could read her thoughts. She was relieved when the lift reached their floor. He stood aside as they went into the reception area, her heels tap-tapping on the tiles as she walked. Bob appeared immediately, greeted them and led them to the boardroom. After a few pleasantries they got down to business.

'This is turning into something of a nightmare,' Bob started. 'We have reason to suspect that some of the missing funds have been laundered through Pieter Reglob's arm of the business and dropped back into the FitzGerald side through off-shore dealings. We've had a due diligence team working on the figures that were issued prior to the takeover bid and it seems that they too had been doctored or concealed – or both – we're not sure which yet.'

'Are we getting regular reports from the legal team?' asked Christian.

'Yes,' said Bob, 'and Sharonne has sat in on some of the meetings. The media hounds are baying at the door, waiting for the smallest whiff of skulduggery. If news leaks out now and we haven't declared our knowledge of it, it will seem that we were in cahoots with them all the time. It will be difficult to convince anyone, least of all the press and shareholders, that we are legitimate. We can't afford to let them away with it, or to lose this deal either. We've already spent months of time and investment on it. It'll be a major scandal if it breaks before we're ready, or indeed before we've had time to put damage limitations in place first.' He turned to Sharonne. 'It's imperative that you continue to fend off any questions, distract from any indication or suggestion of underhand dealings and give absolutely nothing away.'

'Yes, I do realise that. I was actually thinking perhaps we could send out a decoy – a smoke screen of sorts. Axiom Associates is coming on the market in the next few months. I heard this from a friend of a friend, a reliable source.'

'How will that help us?' asked Christian.

'Well, I was thinking. What if we created a leak and enough evidence to let the press think we are a contender for that, then it would make them think these meetings are about Axiom and not the FitzGerald-Reglob business at all.'

'Has there been an announcement yet?' asked Bob. 'This company had one of Ireland's shadiest politicians on its board in the past,' he explained to Christian. 'He had to relinquish his interests when a business journalist leaked that he was still very much involved, despite all the lip service to transparency and the ban on holding on to other businesses while in office. It seemed he, had transferred all his shares to his girlfriend's name and that was leaked too. His wife is going ballistic, demanding an immediate divorce.'

'We French are much more civilised about that sort of thing,' said Christian.

'I think you may enjoy the irony of this when you hear that this politician was one of the ones who was in favour of a four-year wait after irrevocable breakdown before divorce would be granted in Ireland,' explained Bob.

'How primitive,' said Christian.

'Anyway, that's just a bit of background. Sharonne, has anything been released about Axiom yet?'

'No, absolutely nothing public yet.'

'That's a smart move. But how do we proceed?' asked Christian.

She reached into her briefcase and took out another file, one that contained her proposals, with sufficient facts and figures to erect a considerably murky screen.

'We may have to openly declare our interest to make it seem legitimate. Just say the word and this can be filtered out to a few of the key business writers through the right channels,' she said.

'I am impressed,' said Christian. Sharonne felt herself glow.

Bob continued, 'Meanwhile, can we get the due diligence procedures reactivated on the FitzGerald-Reglob front, starting with the original figures offered when the buyout was first mooted in the Reglob camp? That way I'm sure, now that we know what we are looking for, it'll be easier to find where the discrepancies started. If they did start there, then we have them over a barrel for misrepresentation and fraud and Murphy Lestrange could get the company at a considerable markdown, if we trade this information to keep it out of the papers.'

'This goes back to about three years ago before Reglob started his frequent trips to the Caymans,' said Christian.

'It was also before he bought that Georgian pile in Killiney, out of shareholders' funds and profits,' said Sharonne.

And so the meeting went on, breaking only for lunch. The day was bright and sunny and Bob suggested they walk down Dún Laoghaire pier to clear their heads before the afternoon session. As they did, Christian told Sharonne about his barge on the Dordogne and how he loved to spend his weekends there when he wasn't flying around the world. 'You should come down some time,' he invited.

'Perhaps I will,' she said, holding his gaze for a fraction longer than necessary.

They broke promptly at three as Christian had to make the airport by five. She tried not so show her disappointment at the fact that he would not be staying over until the next day as she had hoped to have dinner with him that night. She thought of her yet-to-be-worn Odette Christiane dress hanging in the wardrobe. It hugged her figure and she loved the midnight blue colour, the asymmetrical hem and the double strap over one shoulder. That would have to wait till he was back again in two weeks to get its first airing. She wasn't going to wear it for Derek, not the way things were between them.

***

'I'm so glad I bought the wig when I did,' Maeve told Trish on the phone. 'They said four weeks and I'm almost like an egg this morning and it's not a pretty sight. I don't know how Sinead O'Connor shaved her head voluntarily. I couldn't go out looking like this, but, then, I don't look like her.'

They talked on, Trish telling her about the latest in the continuing drama of life with three teenagers. Barry had left his sports gear – the new holdall, new rugby boots and kit as well as his new tracksuit – on the bus and it hadn't been turned in at the lost property office.

'What did Rory think of that?' asked Maeve.

'I don't know. I don't think he cares,' she added.

'What do you mean, he doesn't care?' she probed, knowing Rory would have a fit at having to fork out another small fortune a few weeks into the term.

'Nothing. Everything. I don't know.'

'Are you OK? Come round for coffee.'

'Are you sure you're up to it? I could do with a chat,' said

Trish. 'I really need someone to tell me I've lost the plot and that I'm imagining things.'

Trish stopped off at a new Italian deli and bought some ciabatta and the fillings for lunch and arrived at Maeve's house. Pressing the security code on the pad on the pillar, the gates slowly parted, opening to reveal the well-tended garden. The beds were still filled with swathes of colour. An artificial heron perched on one leg by the pond, protector of the fish that lived there. Trish felt a twinge of sadness. Maeve had everything money could buy and she was lovely with it, yet the gods who had smiled on her for so long seemed to have let her fall from their care and now she was in freefall. She wished with all her might that Maeve's cancer would be stopped.

Maeve had put the delicate china mugs out on a glass-topped wicker table in the conservatory. They were the ones that Trish had given her for her last birthday, decorated with little stylised topiary trees and a perfect match for the room. They both loved this space with its woven furniture and oversized cushions in pale yellows and greens. A colourful stuffed parrot hung from the tallest point of the vaulted ceiling and a red one sat on a perch in a large white wire birdcage. It always looked summery in here, even on rainy grey days, and it was here they headed straight after preparing lunch in the kitchen.

Trish started to talk about the garden, but her friend interrupted her. 'Trish, what's going on? You're not sick are you?'

'No, why?'

'You just aren't yourself.'

'Maeve, you're going to think I'm a crazy, pixelated woman, but I think Rory is up to something.'

'What do you mean, "up to something"? Do you mean at work – some shady dealings?' They were all too aware of the sort of trouble that could bring, immersed as the country was in illegal planning and bribes.

'No, I wish it were that. That would be simpler. I think he's having an affair.'

'Oh that's ridiculous. I never heard the like. You two are great together. I know he has an eye for the ladies but I've never seen him do anything out of order the way some guys do. Whatever gave you that impression?'

'I can sense it. He's changed. He's different and I can't really explain why. He avoids mealtimes with the family. He's always taking phone calls on the mobile, walking out of the room when it rings. I just know. I sense it in here,' she said, beating her chest with her fist.

'Trish, I think you're imagining things.'

'I know I'm not. He's changed his aftershave and there is something different in our relationship. Has Conor said anything?'

'Not a word, and I'm sure that's because there's nothing to say about it. Look, why don't you confront him? Maybe he has work worries that he doesn't want to tell you about. Think about it. He never brings his work home with him, does he?'

'No. It's something I've always admired: the way he can leave it behind and not worry about it till he's in there the next day. The advantages of having partners, he says. They allow him delegate.'

'I bet it's something like that.'

'Yeah – maybe you're right. And I have been a bit preoccupied with the kids too, what with all the rigmarole of getting them ready to go back to school.'

'Just ask him.

'Yeah – I'll talk to him when he comes home tonight.'

SEVENTEEN

'Do you want to tell me what's going on?' Liam asked Rory.

The monthly medal competition was in full swing. They had all been so busy this year that it was a rarity for the four of them to compete with each other. They were fighting it out over two strokes as they came down the fourteenth fairway. Liam and Rory strode along in the direction of their last shots, which had landed only a few metres apart from each other.

'What do you mean?' Rory asked, 'Going on where?' He fudged his shot, thinking, Christ, Anna Maria must have told Agneta about us. The stupid bitch.

She hadn't, but Liam had put two and two together. Agneta had been too evasive with him, which was totally out of character and was enough to make him suspicious. He had a hunch that Rory was with Anna Maria when he phoned Brussels that night and that was why she had got so flustered. Rory's reaction had guilt written all over it so he pushed him further.

'With you and Anna Maria?'

'I don't know what you're talking about.'

'I think you do. Rory, I know it's none of my business …'

'You're absolutely right. It's not, so just butt out!' he said. He waited for Conor to take his shot before he headed towards his ball. He lined it up and hit it with such an unmerciful wallop that it overshot the green and plugged into the sand in the far bunker. His expletives coloured the air. He stood aside while Liam took his swing, a beautiful stroke that read the lie of the green perfectly and left the ball coasting towards the flag before rolling in with a satisfying plop. A birdie, which would put him firmly in the lead.

'Rory,' said Liam, catching up to him.

'I told you – butt out! It's none of your business.'

'I accept that, but you and Trish are my friends. Have you thought this through? You're playing with fire. Do you want to jeopardise your marriage and your family for a fling?'

'I've no intentions of doing any such thing. Just don't go there! Now let me play my game.' He headed off around the back of the green and Liam decided he'd said enough. Enough, he hoped, to make Rory think about the consequences. Enough also, he feared, to fracture a long friendship.

***

Maeve and Conor agreed to join Trish and Rory, and Derek and Sharonne to confirm the arrangements for Liam's birthday. It was Maeve's first foray out for an evening since her surgery. Liam had wanted to celebrate his fortieth with twenty or so friends, but the numbers had grown out of all proportion. The problem, as Maeve had so rightly pointed out, was that Liam had a handful of friends everywhere he went. So they had decided that as so many were coming in from abroad for a few days that they should make a proper weekend event of it.

'We'll have to show them all a few of the sights,' said Trish.

'Let's organise transport and take everyone down to Glendalough on the Saturday morning. We'll arrange for a walk, a picnic – weather permitting – back to the hotels in time for a little rest before the tarting up for the birthday party,' suggested Sharonne.

'Well, as the expert in schedules and plans, I am perfectly happy to leave all that in your hands,' said Liam.

'We should make dinner at eight thirty.'

'Sounds great to me,' said Liam, 'You know I kind of like having a committee organising things for me, especially one made up of such glamorous ladies.'

'I wish I had one,' said Conor.

'Look who's talking? Haven't you got a team of poor minions devilling for you for nothing.'

'Just getting my own back on the world for all the days I spent following wigs and gowns around and doing all the tedious searches in the Law Library.'

'Hold on, lads, enough of the self-pity. We can't do this on our own,' Trish said. 'We need to know everyone who should be invited, so Liam, we need you to give us all the addresses, emails will do, of anyone you'd like to see there. We'll put a programme together and send it out with the invites.'

'Sounds great,' said Liam again.

Sharonne chimed in, 'Now for the sensitive bit, where are your friends going to stay? Are they paying for that? Should we give them a few options for those who might prefer a B&B?'

'I'll take the tab for the hotel,' said Liam. 'Leave that to me and I'll sort it out. I'll email you details tomorrow and you can include them in the invites.

'God, isn't it great to be loaded?' said Rory. Trish shot him a dirty look. Derek and Conor exchanged glances.

'I suppose you guys will all want to factor in some golf on Sunday morning too,' said Sharonne.

'I wouldn't be too sure about that – it's likely to be a very late night,' said Liam.

'Yes, but some of your friends won't have been to Ireland before and they might want to play at least one course,' said Derek.

'Why don't we give them the option – a game of not-too-early golf or brunch and shopping in Grafton Street to give them a real flavour of Dublin life?' offered Trish.

'Now that's what I call a perfect solution,' said Liam.

'I haven't done that in ages,' said Maeve. 'It'll be great and this party is going to be a chance for me to see if blondes really do have more fun,' she said, tossing her artificial hair.

'I've nothing to wear,' said Sharonne, excusing herself to go to the loo, 'I must try to make time to buy something suitable.'

Liam raised an eyebrow at Maeve and Trish, all of them remembering the last time they had been at a function together, and they all started talking at once.

'Well, I haven't exactly been in the mood for shopping lately, so I suppose I'll be recycling something,' said Maeve.

'You always look great,' said Derek. 'You don't need fine feathers.'

'Yes I do – especially now,' she added a little wistfully.

'You never did, Maeve,' Conor said, stroking her arm. 'You were always just one of those special people whose beauty shines through.'

'Would you ever stop? I'm not dead yet you know. Save your eulogies, I intend to be around for a long time.'

'I didn't mean that.'

'I know you didn't, stupid, but you'd better watch your step, because when I parade around in my blonde hair at this party, you may well have some serious contenders for my affection!' she teased.

'They'll have to form a queue and be vetted by me,' said Conor.

'Form a queue for what?' asked Sharonne coming back to the table.

'To dance with the blonde at the party.'

'Which blonde would that be?' she asked, still getting annoyed every time Derek mentioned the Finns' names. No one answered her.

'I'd love to have Anna Maria and Agneta to stay with us for

that weekend, Conor. What do you think? Should I invite them? It would be much nicer for them than a hotel.'

'It's a lovely idea, sweetheart, but I really think you should hold off on the house guests for another few months, till you're back on your feet again,' he said gently.

She agreed when she thought about it. It wouldn't even be two months since her surgery, but she wanted to get back to normality as quickly as she could.

Liam shifted in his seat ever so slightly, fixed Rory with a stare and said, 'I'm not sure if Anna Maria will be coming.'

'Why not?'

'I don't know, pressure of work or something.'

'Why don't you try to use your powers of persuasion? I'm sure you'll get her to change her mind' said Maeve.

'Perhaps,' Liam said noncommittally. 'But it's very kind of you to think about hosting them. I'll let them know you suggested it and that we vetoed it.'

'I hope they'll both come. I'm really looking forward to seeing them again,' said Trish. 'Aren't you Rory? We had such a laugh with them in Spain.'

'Yeah,' he said. 'Anyone for another drink?' he asked, changing the subject.

As he walked towards the bar, Conor said, 'Rory's buying? What's got into him?'

Everyone but Trish laughed.

Conor followed him to the bar. 'How are tricks, Rory? Hear you landed a big contract in Belgium?'

This threw him off guard. First there was Liam's interference this morning. He'd been furious all day; furious with Anna Maria for blabbing to Agneta; furious that he'd been caught out the first time he'd ever stepped out of line, and furious now because he felt like the odd one out in this group of friends and he knew he had put himself there.

'Yeah, just heard yesterday that it'll be even bigger. It was supposed to be one hotel in Brussels but they now are talking about five five-star hotels in total across the Benelux territories.'

'… the Benelux territories? That's great news, and good not to have all your eggs in an Irish basket. Things can't go on as they are here for ever. The country's too small to sustain that level of growth.'

'Don't say anything to the others yet, because I haven't got around to telling Trish that I'm thinking of setting up an office over there.'

'Mum's the word,' said Conor as they carried the drinks back to the table.

EIGHTEEN

It was Liam's birthday and his friends, several of whom were first-time visitors to Ireland, were entranced with the countryside as they walked around Glendalough. The afternoon had been great, a glorious autumnal outing with the Wicklow Mountains showing off to the full and the fallen leaves crisp underfoot. They did a bracing climb up to St Patrick's Bed where Liam told them, 'We're a feisty breed, we Irish. This is where our saints slept and we built these round towers without cranes. Lots of our monks lived as hermits to keep them away from the wiles of scheming females and the temptations of the flesh.'

'Pay no attention to him,' said Trish, filling them in on the real story of this ancient monastic settlement. On the way back down to the pub on the other side of the weir, they stopped to see if they could make their fingers touch around a Celtic cross in the graveyard.

'We always did this when we came here as kids,' Trish said, trying to embrace the cold stone. She couldn't.

'That was before we had bosoms to get in the way,' said Sharonne. She caught Trish's eye and said, 'Oh, I never thought.'

'Don't worry, I say things like that all the time too.'

Conor and Maeve had arranged to meet the others in the pub

and were already drinking Irish coffees when the invasion arrived. More introductions were made and time slipped pleasantly by until the transport arrived to take them back to the city to prepare for the evening's party.

The giant billboard in Donnybrook had been a great hit, it had even been picked up by one of Sharonne's friends in the media and had made it into one of the evening papers with the caption 'Who is this guy?'

The Four Seasons had done everything Sharonne had instructed them to do. There were exotic flower arrangements towering above their pedestals on the consoles, with smaller versions taking centre stage on the dining tables. Waiters hovered with little trays of sparkling champagne. The guests looked the part – the men in their tuxes, the women rivalling the flower arrangements in colour and splendour. Sharonne had certainly woven her magic and every detail had been thought of. She had decided to wear her Odette Christiane dress and knew no one in the room would have the same one. She was almost as tall as Derek in her skyscraper sandals. The party was about to begin in earnest. Liam greeted everyone as they arrived, really glad he'd succumbed to the pressure of having this celebration with his friends.

'Wow, wow, wow! I never realised there were so many good-looking women in my life,' he laughed, looking around. 'The place looks terrific.'

'Time you settled down with one of them,' cajoled Derek.

'How can I? It's impossible to choose between them. They're all gorgeous.'

Agneta smiled at him above her glass and winked, while Judy, his fifty-something divorced secretary who had a new short hairstyle, sat patiently by, sipping her third vodka and orange juice. She still held secret fantasies that one day he would come in, notice her as if for the first time and be totally bowled over, whisking her off, Meg Ryan-style, to a life of love and passion and happy ever afters. She knew he never would, but there was no prohibition on dreams, was there?

Liam had that effect on women. He never committed though. He almost had with Helen, and was only now getting back to his former self after that split.

Trish was standing with some friends at the bar when she caught sight of Rory laughing at some witty remark. Maeve was right, she decided, I was imagining things. He's in great form again. I'm glad I said nothing. His moodiness must have been work related and I definitely must have been hormonal, maybe even early menopausal, to have got into such knots like that. She caught his eye and raised her glass. He tilted his towards her in reply.

Agneta, Maeve and Aldora were chatting. 'You're so brave, and I love the blonde hair,' Agneta said to Maeve, 'it suits you!'

'You know, I'm getting to like the colour myself! When, and if, my own grows back I might consider doing this permanently.'

'I might even try it myself,' said Aldora, 'although I did dye it once when I was a teenager and it turned out the colour of sunflowers, with a greenish tinge. My mother had to bring me to the hairdressers to have it fixed and she made me pay for it out of my pocket money. I've never forgiven her.'

'Why is it we always want what we can't have? I'd give anything to be dark – to be different from everyone else in my family,' said Agneta and Conor, passing by, joined in and said, 'I'd give anything just to have hair – again!'

They all laughed.

'I don't think it's that bad. Besides isn't it true that bald men are supposed to be the sexiest?'

'Only if they're really hairy all over,' said Aldora. 'Something to do with excess testosterone levels in their body.'

'Oh yeah, that's me,' said Conor, 'like the Wild Man from Borneo underneath.'

'OK, sexy, you can let some of the air out of your head and sit down – they're signalling they're ready to serve dinner,' laughed Maeve.

The meal was excellent, each dish a masterpiece, warm foie gras served with a Sauterne. The main course was boeuf Wellington, followed by a lime sorbet before a sinfully delicious chocolate roulade appeared for dessert. Liam had insisted that after every course, the men would move two places to their right and the ladies two to their left so that everyone got a chance to talk to everyone else. They all agreed it had been a great idea and the conversations and banter were lively and laugher-filled. The birthday cake arrived at the table – in the shape of Liam's favourite toy – a red Ferrari. It had an iced registration plate reading 'Liam 40'. Champagne flowed again and a phone rang somewhere at the table.

Not mine, Trish thought thankfully. She was seated between Derek and Pat, a colleague of Liam's.

'I'm always concerned when we leave our teenagers at home for an evening. They're too big now for babysitters, but big enough to get into all sorts of other troubles.'

'Yeah, I remember the things we used to get up to when my parents went out!' Pat said.

'Thanks for that reassurance,' laughed Trish.

Derek said, 'Relax, yours are very responsible.'

'They were yesterday, but who know what they'll do today? Overnight Barry has turned into a monosyllabic moody teenager whose sole vocabulary consists of "money" and "no". Oh, he does have a three-word phrase too. "Get a life!"'

'Brings back memories,' Derek said, and everyone agreed.

Conor led the table in a rowdy rendition of 'Happy Birthday', followed by demands for a speech. Just before Liam started talking, Trish heard the unmistakable double beep of a text message arriving.

'That's definitely you,' said the young man on her left. She fumbled with the little purse as discreetly as possible and, holding the iPhone in her lap, touched the screen to read the message: 'hi luvr mss u wnt u v badly am'.

Obviously a wrong number, was her first reaction. Then she

froze – this wasn't her phone. She remembered picking it up off
the bed after she had put her lipstick into the little beaded
evening bag just as the taxi arrived to collect them. The
realisation began to seep through her like a cold grey wave and
she felt the blood drain from her face. It was Rory's. They had
identical models – freebies when he changed the office
communication systems. This message was for Rory. She felt
sick. She began to shake. Wanted to scream at him at the far end
of the table. She touched the screen again. Who was it from?
AM. AM what or where? she wondered. Was there going to be
more? Obviously the message had been sent before it was
completed. She did that all the time. She needed time to think.
Maybe it was a wrong number. She was jumping to conclusions.

When Liam finished his speech, of which she heard not one
single word, there was loud shouting and cheering, hand
clapping and more toasts. She seized that moment to leave the
table and headed for the Ladies. Inside the marble
surroundings she locked herself into one of the cubicles.
Taking the phone out of her bag she checked to see if it was
Rory's before she read the message again.

I knew it. I was right all along. I knew there was something
going on. Eyes burning with unshed tears, she felt as though
she had been kicked in the stomach. Check the number, she
thought. She scrolled down, messages, time of call, number –
no number showed. She sat down on the toilet seat and wept.
The world she knew had just disappeared. She felt as though a
large bubble had burst inside her and she knew with a strange
sense of conviction that life would never be the same again, no
matter what happened. She heard someone open the outer door
and stifled her sobs.

Maeve's voice called out.

'Trish, Trish, are you in there? Are you all right?'

'Yes, I'll be out in a minute,' she answered.

When she emerged Maeve said, 'Trish, You look dreadful.
You're as white as a sheet. What happened?'

'I must have had too much to drink. I don't feel very well,' she lied. 'I need to go home.'

But Maeve knew her too well and without heeding this feeble excuse she reached out and hugged Trish. 'That's not true, is it?'

'No,' said Trish, starting to cry again.

She fished in her bag, produced the phone and handed it to Maeve, saying, 'I was right. I knew it. Read that.'

Not understanding, Maeve took the wafer-thin mobile. She read the message and read it again, before saying anything.

'Oh my God, no! I don't believe it. There has to be a reasonable explanation. It's probably a prank. A random text. Who'd send that to you?'

'It wasn't meant for me. It's Rory's phone. I took it by mistake and the message just came through. He must have mine.'

'What are you going to do?'

'I don't know, but I'm not going back in there because I couldn't face him, or anyone for that matter, and I'm not going to spoil Liam's night for him.'

'Look, it's been a hectic day. I'm feeling pretty tired, why don't we take a taxi back to my place. I'll tell them you're bringing me home and that I wouldn't want Conor to miss out on his best friend's night. No one will suspect a thing. Wait here.'

When she came back Trish asked, 'What did Rory say?'

'I didn't tell him. I just told Conor you were coming home with me and that he needn't rush. I asked him to tell Rory you were bringing me home. Now let's try and sort this out together. There has to be some logical explanation.

***

Back in Maeve's cosy sitting room, Trish read the message again on the screen. Maeve had put the kettle on, got a warm wrap for Trish and sat beside her on the sofa.

'Let me see that again,' she said, reading it carefully in case she had missed anything and then handing it back. She was at a loss for what to say.

'Have you any idea who it's from?' she asked.

'Not a clue. It's not signed so whoever sent it must assume he'll know who it's from.'

'I have an idea. Why don't you reply? Ask where she is and what she's doing? That may give you a clue.'

Desperate to find out more – no matter how unsavoury, Trish was already tapping the keys: 'miss u2 c u'. When she sent the message she said in a voice devoid of all modulation, 'Do you think he's been making love to her?'

Maeve replied, 'Look, Trish, don't jump to conclusions. As I said, it could be a random crank text – the way people make crank phone calls. Some twisted person trying to cause trouble and just punching in numbers willy-nilly.'

'Do you really think so?'

'No, but I don't think it's from a lover either. Rory's not the type. Has he ever given you any reason to suspect anything? Anything at all?'

'No, but I just know,' she said.

The phone beeped again. Hesitatingly, Trish picked it up, afraid of what she would discover – confirmation perhaps of her worst fears. The message read 'c u – radson as plan – til 2mrw 11 am'.

'Oh thank goodness, it's not for him at all. The guys are playing golf in the morning.' She looked at Maeve with relief. 'You must think I'm an idiot,' she said, and then burst out crying again.

But Rory wasn't playing golf. He'd told Conor earlier there was a crisis of some sort with the Brussels job. Some drawings had gone missing and he had to go in to the office to try to track them or their duplicates down, so he scratched his name from the game. Conor had told Maeve about it before they had left for the party.

Maeve said nothing. She was out of her depth. She just sat there with a comforting hand on Trish's arm. She didn't know what to do. She wanted to rant and rave, but divided loyalties dictated that she say nothing. Conor was Rory's best friend since long before she ever met him. She was Trish's; besides, she couldn't believe that Rory would be off having a bit on the side, he wasn't like that. She needed to talk to Conor, but knew she'd have to wait. She decided to try to stay awake until he came in to ask him, although it was unlikely he knew anything or he would have told her. Between tears and tea, Trish kept staring at the screen, 'Oh my God! Maeve, I'm blind. I know who sent this. It's Anna Maria – that's why she didn't come to the party. I thought AM at the end of the first message was where they were going to say something else and sent the message before they finished writing it. I do that all the time with texts. When I read this I read it as 11 am – morning time – but it's not. AM is Anna Maria. It's from Anna Maria. And I bet she's in Dublin.'

'You're jumping to conclusions again.'

'I'm not,' said Trish with determination, a sixth sense washing over her. She knew she couldn't involve Maeve any more, because of the bond between Conor and Rory, but she had just thought of a plan.

'It's way past your bedtime, Maeve. I'm going to call a taxi and head home. I have some serious thinking to do before I confront Rory. That is, if I decide to confront him at all. I may just let him hang himself.'

'Sleep on it if you can – things usually look better in the morning. Will you be all right?'

'I will and thanks, Maeve. I'm sorry for ruining your evening.'

'You didn't. I was just about ready to crash anyway.' Trish hugged her friend and stepped out into the starless night and into the taxi. Back in her bedroom – the kids all asleep – she took out the phone again. She knew what she was going to do. She tapped in a message. The Radisson – that could be anywhere, maybe even Brussels, but she was certain it was the Dublin one.

She wrote, 'cn mkc it Orangerie x'.

It was one thirty. If she were already in bed then she mightn't get this till the next morning. If it were for someone else, the reply would tell her. However, just as Trish had finished brushing her teeth the reply beeped through 'c u then x am'.

There it was, the 'am' again.

'That bitch! The conniving, scheming bitch!' Trish said out loud, flinging the offending phone on the duvet. She picked up the landline and dialled directory enquiries asking for the number of the hotel in Dublin. When the receptionist answered, Trish asked if she could leave a message for Miss Anna Maria Kauppila. When he asked her what the message was, Trish knew Anna Maria was staying at the hotel, so she hung up. 'I knew it. I just knew it.'

Sleep evaded her that night, as her mind hatched schemes of how to get back at Anna Maria. But Trish knew she needed absolute proof before she could do anything. She had to be sure. She heard a car draw up outside – it was Rory coming home from the party. She turned the phone to silent, curled up and pretended to be asleep. Within minutes of his climbing in beside her, his deep, even breathing told her he was asleep.

Now her anger turned towards this husband of hers, and she wanted to hurt him. Hurt him as she was hurting and stop him ever cheating again. The fact that he wasn't even aware of her pain made her hurt even more – he was snoring through her agony. She climbed out of bed and retrieved her phone. It was on the dressing table where he had left it with his keys. He was oblivious to the fact that he had taken his wife's one with him. She wiped the messages from his phone, placed it on the table beside his keys and crawled back into bed.

NINETEEN

Conor brought Maeve her breakfast in bed. It was another crisp autumn morning with an early mist rolling across the lawn from the sea.

'It was a pity you had to miss the end of the party. It was a great night. I hope you didn't overdo things yesterday.'

'No, it was great and I really did enjoy myself, but, Conor, I need to talk to you.'

'Sounds ominous,' he said, placing the tray down on the bed, his gut twisting. Don't tell me she's found another lump, somewhere else. 'Are you OK?' he asked.

'Yes, it's not about me – for a change – so relax,' she smiled at him.

'Then it can't be very important,' he said, reaching over to kiss her before climbing carefully back in beside her.

'Conor, is Rory carrying on?'

'What do you mean – carrying on?'

'Conor – does "carrying on" have any other meaning? Having an affair, playing offside, cheating on Trish. You know well what I mean.'

'Why do you ask that?'

'Will you stop answering my questions with another? I'll spell it out for you. Is Rory having an affair?'

'What makes you think that?'

'Conor! You're doing it again.'

'Doing what?'

'Trish thinks he's involved with someone.'

'Whatever gave her that idea?'

'That's another question and you still haven't answered mine – a straight yes or no, please.'

'Now that you mention it, he has been a bit odd lately. Secretive and uncharacteristically bad tempered, but there could have been all sorts of reasons for that. He's been really busy with some hot deals, opening the new European office and doing a lot of travelling – maybe he's just burned out. I was telling him the other day he should take a month off, let Des run things for a bit. There's no point expanding just for the sake of it – he should be enjoying the benefits too. But another woman? I don't think so.'

'Trish has had her suspicions for a little while and last night something happened to confirm them. She took Rory's phone to the party by mistake and during Liam's speech, she got a text message, an intimate text message. That's why we left. She was too upset to go back in so we came home here. She answered the message and got a reply. Both finished with the word 'am' and at first she though the message had cut off in mid-sentence. Then she decided that 'am' is Anna Maria – and that's why she didn't come to the party.'

'Oh, Christ, Rory has been going to Brussels a lot more lately, but I thought that was all work related. Come to think of it, Liam and he have been a bit at odds with each other and he talks to Agneta all the time. Maeve, I think you might be right. He and Liam had a right ding-dong on the course last week and I wondered what it was about. Liam must know something.'

'Trish thinks he's playing golf with all of you this morning – I didn't tell her he had cancelled.'

'But that doesn't mean anything.'

'Yes it does, because the text confirmed a meeting this morning and we think Anna Maria's in Dublin.'

'What gives you that idea?'

'The very fact that Agneta and Anna Maria are both highly organised. They'd have booked their tickets to come to Liam's party weeks ago, and if Anna Maria and Rory are having a fling, then it makes sense that she'd come to Dublin to see him anyway. She probably couldn't face us all so chickened out of going to the party. I bet that Rory is going to meet her this morning, when he's supposed to be in his office. I didn't allow myself think any further than that. I needed to talk to you first. What can we do? We just can't sit here and pretend nothing is happening.'

'Look, let's get our facts straight first. We may be jumping to conclusions. There may be a perfectly reasonable explanation. I'll have a chat with Liam and see what he says.'

'I'm not sure if Trish will still want to join the ladies for that shopping trip to Grafton Street this morning. Should I ring her or wait till she calls me?'

'Wait till she rings,' Conor advised.

***

Trish didn't ring. Instead she got up earlier than normal, showered and put some effort into her make-up, doing her best to conceal the black circles under her eyes and the puffy lids that told the world she'd been crying. None of her kids were about – they didn't do mornings, especially Sundays. If anyone asked, she was going to stick by the lie that Maeve had been tired the previous evening and that she had volunteered to leave with her. She felt that would buy her some time.

She left the house at about a quarter to ten, just as she heard Rory stirring upstairs, and she headed for the hotel. She drove around the upper, outdoor car park to see if there were spaces and there were several. She knew Rory wouldn't go to the lower level. He was the sort who would park in the doorway if they'd let him. She parked in the lower car park, in the spot farthest from the entrance, so that Rory wouldn't notice her car. As she walked in to the hotel, a sudden gust of wind caught the water from the fountain and she had to move quickly to avoid the spray. She went up the short flight of steps, through the double doors and in to the right to find a niche beneath the old choir balcony. Here it was relatively secluded and still had the air of a sanctuary. This part of the hotel had been a monastery at one time. She picked up a newspaper on her way. From this vantage point, she could monitor everyone coming and going into the Orangerie and unless they deliberately did a one-eighty-degree turn, they wouldn't see her.

This was her place, where she and her friends often met for coffee and scones. It was a popular venue for the ladies who munch, and for those who nibbled on lettuce leaves as they discussed their diets and then spoiled them all with the yummy desserts. Outside the tiered formal gardens spread out before her, but today she didn't notice them.

She ordered a pot of coffee and opened the paper. The minutes ticked by. She must have read the headline a dozen times and yet she hadn't absorbed a single word. She kept looking at her watch. Then she heard a voice say, 'Yes, thank you. I have reserved a table. I am waiting for a friend to join me.'

Trish froze. She'd know that accent anywhere – perfect English with just that slightly different inflection. She watched Anna Maria being escorted through to the outer sanctum. She was seated just out of view. Trish could see her handbag, which she had placed on the seat beside her.

'A friend.' My husband, you mean! I have a good mind to go over and tell that scheming bitch what I think of her, she thought. How could he, she kept thinking. How could he do this to us?

However, she knew she needed aboslute proof before she could take any steps to sort it out. She still didn't know what she was going to do – one minute she was determined to confront Rory; the next she thought, the least said the soonest mended. Maybe there was an innocent explanation, and then she'd remember the message, 'hi luvr mss u wnt u', and she'd feel a wave of despair and nausea wash over her again. She wanted to go into the conservatory and empty the coffee pot over Anna Maria. With solid reserve she waited and waited – palms sweating and feeling cold in the over-heated hotel. It was the longest half hour of her life. She saw Anna Maria reach into her bag and withdraw her telephone.

Eventually, Rory arrived at the hotel. Trish sensed his presence before she saw him. He spotted Anna Maria instantly, and headed straight for the Orangerie, with a silly grin plastered all over his face. He leaned down and kissed her on the mouth. She held his hand as he slid into the seat beside her.

He can't take his eyes off her, Trish realised. When did this start? He was smiling and holding her gaze. She moved to see them from a better vantage point, and felt physically sick as she watched Anna Maria put her hand up to his cheek. He kissed her, more slowly this time. He didn't seem to care if anyone saw them like this – it was almost as though he was making a public declaration – I have a lover, look everyone. Trish felt a black cloud descend on her, a strong pain radiated from her chest. She slid a ten euro note into the leather folder that held the bill and left.

She could barely see the way back to her car as tears welled and spilled. She put her head on the steering wheel and cried desperate moaning sobs. What was she going to do now? She knew she couldn't go back home until she had calmed down … and she was supposed to be meeting Maeve and the others in town for brunch.

She couldn't. Could she?

***

'So has Rory been having an affair?' Conor asked Liam directly as they walked down the third fairway. It was the first chance he had to mention it. He and Conor were playing a mixed fourball with Agneta and Consuela. Liam didn't reply for a second, then said, 'Jesus, does Trish know?'

'So it's true?'

'How the hell did you find out? How did Trish find out?'

'She's not stupid. I reserve that category for myself. Does everyone know except me?' asked Conor.

'As far as I'm aware no one knows but Agneta. I have had my suspicions though. Actually more than that. I confronted him a few weeks ago and he went mad and told me in no uncertain terms to keep my meddling nose out of his business.'

'So it is Anna Maria?'

Liam nodded. 'Look,' he indicated behind him, 'we're holding up play. Let's discuss this later.'

'Did he cry off the game because you knew?' asked Conor.

'He doesn't know I do, yet, but by God, he soon will.'

There was no chance for them to continue the discussion. Even in the men's locker room most of the group were still on a high from the evening before. The plan was that the golfers were going on to catch up with the others and then get something to eat at the Horseshoe Bar in the Shelbourne Hotel. The shoppers were already ensconced in the bar when they arrived. There were lots of Avoca and Kilkenny carrier bags under the chairs, evidence of a fruitful few hours, and they were enjoying Irish coffees while discussing their purchases.

'Glad to see you've been helping the economy,' said Liam. 'I'll get a round in. Is it the same again for everyone?'

'I'll give you a hand,' said Conor, following him to the bar. 'What's going on? I don't see Trish in there and I told Rory to come along when he sorted things out in the office.'

'I doubt we'll see him, though,' said Liam. 'Look, between

us, I think Anna Maria is in Dublin, and he's with her. I figured that much out, but how did Trish find out?

'She took Rory's phone to the party last night instead of her own and read an explicit text from Anna Maria. As far as I know, he doesn't know Trish knows, although he must have missed his phone by now and that's probably why he's not here.'

'Where's Trish?'

'She told Maeve she'd be here only an hour ago, so I'm sure she's on her way.'

Sharonne appeared behind them. 'What's the deep and meaningful about? Our glasses are drying over there.'

They laughed. 'You're just in time to help carry these back,' said Liam, abandoning the discussion. At that moment Trish arrived, wearing more make-up than usual.

'Where's Rory?' asked Liam.

'He sends his apologies. He's not able to make it – some problem that is taking him to Brussels for a crisis breakfast meeting tomorrow. He managed to get a flight out and is on his way to the airport right now. He said he really enjoyed the party by the way.'

Liam got her a drink while Maeve made room on the banquette beside her.

'What's going on?' she whispered.

'I decided to pretend I knew nothing and take some breathing space. I need to sort my head out.'

Sharonne caught the end of the conversation and said, 'You look a little ropey. Too much to drink last night?'

'Hair of the dog!' said Liam as he plonked a drink in front of her. 'You'll feel better tomorrow.'

'I hope I do,' she said.

Sharonne said, 'Liam tell me, what's it like to be forty?'

'Sure darling, you won't have to wait that long to find out for yourself – aren't you just seven or eight weeks behind me?' he said as he went back to the bar.

Sharonne couldn't believe her ears. Liam was never usually abrasive. 'What is wrong with everyone today?' she muttered and went back to folding the cream into her Irish coffee.

TWENTY

It was half past three. Sharonne picked up a CD from her desk and, angling it to catch the best light, used it as a mirror to apply her lip liner and then her lipstick. She licked her forefinger and smoothed her eyebrows, before putting the disc back in its case. She was meeting Bob and his legal team at four.

The FitzGerald-Reglob project was going better than she had hoped. Her media friends had come up trumps, especially her gym companion, Ros, who did the daily business report on national radio each morning. She hinted at developments in the rival company, giving just enough information to put the business bush telegraphs in motion. The meeting was taking place in The Merrion, which was just around the corner from the offices of the firm of solicitors they used. On her way in, she was greeted by name by both the concierge and the receptionist. A consummate professional, Sharonne knew how to work a room, any room, to make her presence felt. She spotted Bob at a corner table with two other suits and joined them.

'Sharonne, as you know, has been invaluable as the vanguard. She's been great in the diversionary tactics department during the past few months. I think if we can keep this going for another while, until we have a watertight case prepared, we may just pull this off. Then we can set the facts out before the shareholders.'

'And that's when the fun will start,' said one of the lawyers.

'I think that by then we'll have enough safety nets in place to save us from plummeting too far,' Sharonne said, riffling through the sheaf of papers she had taken from her briefcase.

'Delighted you could make it,' she heard Bob say. When she looked up, she looked straight into Christian's intense Gallic eyes. She hadn't expected him to be there.

'I didn't think I would. The London meetings went on for ever and I thought we wouldn't get a flight until this evening.' He inclined his head in her direction as he issued a general greeting, took a chair from the adjoining table and went back for another before sitting down. 'Françoise is with me.'

Sharonnne thought, who the hell is Françoise? She looked towards Bob, who didn't seem at all surprised at this announcement, but before she could agonise any more, Christian continued.

'You will be pleased with what I've discovered,' he said, pausing for optimum effect. 'The FitzGeralds had not one, but two accounts in the Caymans. One has been closed since the day the takeover was provisionally signed. The other was opened that same day – with the exact figure in funds being lodged. The second is listed in his wife's maiden name, Russell.'

The way Christian rolled his rs and emphasised the ls made Sharonne tingle. 'That's where the resources that were siphoned have ended up.'

'How did that come to light?' Bob asked.

'With Françoise's help – over a boozy dinner with two of the FitzGeralds' closest "friends". She could have procured the bank account numbers if she'd asked – and all in return for pit tickets for the Monaco Grand Prix – simple!'

'Simple?' Sharonne said, annoyed, although she knew not why. Yes, she did. It was the way he kept referring to the elusive Françoise that rankled. Was she another one of those trophies on his belt that Bob had warned her about?

'Yes, very simple,' he replied, leaning towards her. 'They are so typiquement nouveaux riches, real social climbers, the easiest people of all to manipulate. Madame F. met Alonso at a dinner once and now drops his name into every conversation,' he said with much gesturing. 'Those sort of people just want to be able to tell their friends they've been to a grand prix, while I'm sure they wouldn't know a Formula One car from a stock car.'

'I'd kill to get to a grand prix myself,' said one of the lawyers. 'I wonder could I sell info on any of our clients?'

'Forget it,' said his partner, 'I've just been going through the list in my head, and it's a no-no!'

Christian laughed, 'Sort this deal out to our advantage and I'll send you both to the final race of the season in Brazil. That's a deal.'

The two young men sat up taller in their seats, looking at each other, not knowing if he was serious or not, but if there was a chance.

'Françoise will fill you in on all the details when she comes down. She has just gone to the room to freshen up.'

'You're both staying here?' Sharonne asked, hating herself for doing it. She had been delighted to see him. She hadn't known he was going to be in Dublin this week. Nor had he mentioned it when they last spoke on Monday. Now, he arrived – with a woman.

'Yes, it's Françoise's first time in Dublin, so I thought nothing but the best for her. After all, she deserves a reward for her part in procuring these gems of information, n'est-ce pas?'

The guys all agreed. Christian, meantime, removed his PowerBook from his briefcase and began hitting keys, moving on to addressing another issue.

Sharonne saw Françoise approach – a sophisticated businesswoman who took the art of dressing Chanel-style to new degrees. There was a scent of Dior about her too. In unison the men all rose to their feet, straightening ties and buttoning up their jackets for the greetings. Sharonne smiled a rictus smile at her, already regarding her as Enemy Number One and deciding not to stand up as Christian leaned over to make the introductions.

'Sharonne. You have not yet met Françoise Vercluse. Françoise, this is Sharonne, about whom we spoke.'

'Yes, hello. Christian has mentioned you often. I look forward to working together with you,' she said. 'I work with him in the Paris office.'

'He never mentioned you,' she retorted.

Sharonne looked at Christian. He was studying the reaction of the two women as they met, a smile playing around his mouth. Was that smile a genuine, *I hope they'll get on as it will make this business a lot easier if they do* one, or *a let's see the claws come out now* sort of smile? Sharonne couldn't tell, but she suspected he was enjoying this.

'I am sure Sharonne will fill you in on developments at her end and that you two will get on well together.'

Some hope, Sharonne thought, as she forced herself to concentrate on the matter in hand. They finished up at about six, something that further annoyed Sharonne, as she'd now have to face the crawl that was rush hour traffic. Christian had not invited her to join them for dinner either. Even if he had, she had already decided, there would have been another entry in her diary for that night. There was no way she was going to be available on his whim. She headed for the gym, drank two smoothies, had a swim, a sauna and a massage, not one of which did her any good. She was as tense leaving as when she arrived, and by the time she got home she had missed saying goodnight to the twins.

Derek was watching the end of a match when she got home. 'How was your day?'

'Shitty, and yours?'

'Pretty crappy too, if you must know. Fancy a drink?' he asked.

He wanted to discuss the phone call he'd had with Conor that afternoon, but sensed this was not the right time.

'How did your meeting go?'

'Productive, really.' Sharonne told him about the Cayman accounts revelation and couldn't resist an assault on Françoise's arrival.

'He brought his assistante from Paris.'

'Oh, I bet Bob enjoyed that. Always a lady's man our Bob. What's she like?'

'Tall, with a stick-like figure, a face so narrow one eye would have been enough, too much hair, too much make-up and too little flesh. And she wore floozie shoes.' Sharonne drained her glass.

'What are floozie shoes?'

'Don't you know anything?' Sharonne replied, and flounced off to bed.

She ignored him when he came into their bedroom. She tossed and turned all night long, sleeping in short spells and then waking with thoughts of Françoise foremost in her mind. She didn't know why she was so angry, why she had hated this woman on sight, why she'd felt so threatened. Then, she admitted the reason to herself. She was jealous. She didn't want to share Christian with anyone.

TWENTY-ONE

It was Friday. Trish didn't know how she had got through the past week. She managed to avoid Rory's nightly phone call by making sure she had something planned that meant she had to leave the house before seven – not a difficult thing to do with teenagers, who always needed ferrying to and fetching from somewhere or another.

The kids were well settled into their school routines after half-term and were preoccupied with their PlayStations. Normally banned on school nights, Trish didn't care – she didn't care about anything really, except deciding how she should handle the dilemma in which she now found herself.

She'd had a call from Conor to know if she'd like him to talk to Rory.

'Not yet, please, Conor. Don't say a word to him or anyone. I'm still not sure if I'll let him know that I know. I feel that if he thinks no one has an inkling, that it will be easier to put it behind us. If we want to.'

Liam called too, leaving a message, 'I'm here if you want an ear or just someone to shout at. Please call me if you feel like it – anytime,' or something like that, she recalled, unsure of the exact wording, because, although she knew in her heart she wasn't imagining things or blowing them out of all proportion, hearing his message just reiterated her deepest fears.

She had a plan. Rory would be home tonight. She went grocery shopping, buying all their favourite foods. She set the table in the dining room, something they usually only did on high days and when they entertained on a formal level, since they had the conservatory and sunroom enlarged. When the kids came in from school, they all asked what the occasion was, but she answered with enigmatic mutterings.

Rory arrived home from the airport, dropping his bag and briefcase in the hall. He was met with a deluge of pleas from Louise, glossy brochure in hand, looking for €750 to go on ski camp during the Christmas holidays.

'Whoa, I'm just in the door. Don't you women know anything? Rule number one in taming the male, and getting what you want, is that you never tell him anything until after he has been fed, never mind asking for money. Besides, €750 is outrageous.'

He breezed into the kitchen and kissed Trish on the back of her neck as she stood at the cooker. 'Speaking of feeding, that smells delicious and I'm starving. I've only had a bowl of soup at lunch, the flight was delayed because some old dear fainted in the departure lounge and they had to get the paramedics to certify she was OK before allowing her board. I fell asleep on the plane and missed their gourmet offerings, even the disgusting coffee.'

'Well, this'll be ready in a few minutes,' she said, as normally as possible.

He's guilty as hell, thought Trish, barely able to control her anger. He's rabbiting on about nothing. Too tired from bonking his mistress and keeping up a banter because if he stops, he might let his guard down. He reeks of that new aftershave too.

'I'm ready for the feast. Where are the others?'

'Doing their homework,' replied Louise, determined not to lose his attention. 'I've done mine. Look, Dad, we'll be staying in these wooden ski huts. They're right on the side of the mountain just minutes away from the ski lift.'

'Sounds cool.'

'The lifts don't stop – you just jump on and they keep moving.'

'It's very, very expensive.'

'It could be my Christmas and birthday presents together, Dad. And the lessons are included in the price, and the hire of ski boots, skis and passes. Those add-ons can be really dear when you have to pay extra for them.'

'Add-ons no less. My daughter is growing up. Let me see that brochure,' he said, directing all his attention to the glossy pages.

Trish's sixth sense was alert to every nuance, her antennae responding. She sent them all into the dining room and started to serve up. She studied her husband as he sat at the end of the table, with Louise on one side, still trying to wheedle a commitment from him. Barry was on the other side, in his now-normal catatonic state. In between shovelling the food into his mouth, he muttered how Louise was 'Daddy's girl' and how she could get anything she wanted from him. She was the favourite anyway.

'Mind your manners, Barry, and don't talk with food in your mouth,' said Rory.

'Who invented manners anyway?' asked Louise. 'They're silly old-fashioned rules designed to keep the classes in their places.'

'They are not silly,' said Rory.

'I think they are. Who dictated whether you should put milk in your tea first or not? Before they had cutlery they used their fingers.'

'You can do that in McDonald's,' said Barry.

'You might be interested to know that it was only the hoi polloi who put milk in first and the upper classes looked down on this practice,' said Toni.

'Who cares?' said Barry. 'You midget know-it-all. Anyway, what about my motorbike?' he turned to his father. Barry wanted a motorbike, well a scooter really, for his sixteenth birthday. According to him everyone had one!

'Don't speak to your sister like that,' said Trish.

'She's just trying to impress and change the subject. I had the floor. I was talking about my scooter,' he said, looking from Rory to Trish at the other end of the table.

'But will I get it? No! Why? Because I have over-protective parents who don't want me to enjoy my life. Why? Because they don't want me to have a life. Why? Because they have none of their own!'

'That's what you think. Some day you'll know better,' said Trish.

Toni then piped up, 'If Louise gets her ski trip and Barry gets a scooter ...'

'He won't,' said Rory.

'Well, if he gets something half decent, what will I get in compensation?'

'Compensation for what?'

'For not having had as many birthdays as the others?'

'Nice try, chicken,' Rory laughed. 'Your turn will come too.'

'Yeah! Nice try, chicken,' echoed Barry.

Trish sat observing her family, capturing the image, although it was no longer a happy family snapshot in her eyes. It was smudged and sullied. It would never be the same. They might sit around the table, but the man at the other end was no longer the man she trusted implicitly, loved more than anyone, even her children, her abiding passion for nearly twenty years. Now he was a lying stranger, a cheat, a guilty man with secrets, traits he has always abhorred in others.

'Perhaps you'd like to tell us about your week,' she said to him, trying to keep her voice from trembling and holding her shaking hands out of sight on her lap.

'Busy. Busy as usual,' he said, avoiding looking at her. 'It's been rather hectic. How's Maeve been doing?'

'She's as puzzled as I am.'

'Puzzled? Over what?'

'Over your carry-on.'

The three children were suddenly interested in their parents' conversation.

'What are you talking about?' asked Rory, shifting in his chair.

'I'm talking about your carry on with Anna Maria and your tryst in the Radisson Hotel last Saturday and Sunday.'

She hadn't known for sure if he'd seen Anna Maria on the Saturday too but decided to throw it in anyway.

'I don't know what you're on about,' he said, sitting up straighter in his chair.

'I suppose you know nothing about the text messages she sent you.' She looked him directly in the eye. 'I took your phone to the party by mistake, Luver.' She stopped. She watched him blanche and, before he could compose himself, she said, 'And I got those billets-doux she intended for you.'

'What's a billet-doux?' piped up Toni.

'Not now,' said Trish to her youngest and, looking back at Rory, she continued in a slow, steady voice, even though her heart was pounding.

'You remember I left early – well I answered her texts and went to the hotel on Saturday. I saw you together. I wiped the messages off and left the phone back after the party. I knew you'd find it there. You can be so smart sometimes and so stupid at others. You thought you'd got away with it, didn't you?'

He said nothing.

'Mum, Dad—' started Louise, but Trish stopped her.

'There'll be plenty of time to talk to me tomorrow. I'm not so sure it will be the same with your father.' She stood up, watched in bewilderment by the four of them, and said, 'I'm going out now, and while I'm gone, Rory, I'd like you to explain to our children the nature of your relationship with this woman – here and in Brussels – and tell them perhaps how it will affect this family's future.'

The children stared at her in astonishment. Addressing them she said, 'Don't worry, I'll be back later. I promise.' She wanted to yell – you can trust me and not that lying bastard, but she held back.

She walked out into the hall, picked up her handbag and jacket, and went out into the night.

Trish's whole body was shaking as she put the key in the ignition. She turned the heater on full. By the time she reached her destination, she was still shivering. She'd told Maeve earlier in the day about her plan and she and Conor were expecting her. Although Maeve had serious reservations about involving the children at this stage, there didn't seem to be any way to stop them from finding out for much longer. Trish and she had spent endless hours talking during the week. Maeve listened as the realisation of what was happening to her friend's marriage sank in. She went over the sequence of events again and again and she had to stop herself from issuing platitudes. There were no words to comfort Trish or make things any better. Nothing would make any difference, but that did not stop her from wishing that Trish wouldn't turn up on their doorstep – that she and Rory would have managed to talk things out, maybe even sort them out or come to some sort of compromise. But here she was.

Conor opened the door, having heard the car on the gravel outside, and gave her a huge hug. He ushered her into the lounge where Maeve was waiting. He poured them both a drink and sat on the other side of her on their big, squashy sofa.

'How did it go? Did he admit anything?' asked Maeve.

'No. I didn't wait to hear his excuses. I left him to explain to the kids. I was afraid if I started I'd kill him – in front of them all. I don't know what to do,' she said, bursting into tears. 'There's no blueprint for this sort of thing, is there?' she asked.

They let her cry, partly because they felt she needed the release, partly because they were at a loss for what to say. They were hurting too. Rory had let them all down.

'Did you tell Liz?'

'No, I didn't. Can you believe I feel so ashamed and embarrassed that I can't even tell my own sister?'

'There's nothing for you to be ashamed of,' said Conor.

Maeve announced, 'I'm going to make a large pot of tea.'

Trish actually managed a smile. She felt safe here. 'She always does that – make large pots of tea – anytime we have anything serious to discuss. And it does help sometimes, but I think it will take more than that this time.'

When the tea was poured Trish started to talk again. She didn't seem to be able to stop. In what seemed hours later, she was aware that Maeve was wilting. Conor seemed to notice at the same time and said, 'Maeve, you look done in. Take your tablets and off you go to bed. I'll look after Trish. In fact I'm going to drive her home in a little while.'

'No you're not,' said Trish. 'I'm quite capable of doing that, I've only had one drink.'

'I know that – and he is bringing you home. You're too upset to drive,' insisted Maeve. 'I'll come around and get you in the morning and you can take your car back then. You know you can sleep over if you want,' she suggested.

'No. I promised the kids I'd be back and I don't want them waking up in the morning to find I'm not there. I should imagine they've enough to deal with without thinking I've done a runner.' She hugged Maeve before she went upstairs.

'I'm sorry to dump all this on you. You've enough on your plate, both of you. I've been very selfish.'

'Oh, yeah, like you planned this to happen … Just remember the phone's beside the bed if you need to talk when you get home.'

'Thanks. For everything. I don't know how I would have got through the past week without you.'

'And I wouldn't have got through the past few months without you both – so we're quits. Night darling.' She blew Conor a kiss.

Conor said, 'Trish, sit down for a few more minutes. I want to tell you something.'

'About Rory?'

'No, about me actually,' he said, sitting down beside her on the sofa. 'I know. No, I'll rephrase that. I don't know, I can only imagine how you must be feeling.'

'You can't. Believe me. You can't. How should I feel? Should I be the forgiving little wife? Go home and say it's all right, pet, you had a little moment of lust and men must get satisfaction when they need it? Come on, Conor, give me a break.'

'I didn't say that. Rory's been my buddy for years and I've never known him do anything like this in all that time. Perhaps it was nothing more than a moment's weakness.'

'Don't try to make excuses for him. He's as guilty as they come.'

'That's as may be and I'm not trying to make excuses.'

'Look, it's even worse that it's that Finnish slapper. She knew he was married. She can't pretend she didn't know about his wife and kids. She's even met me. Could she not get a man of her own without hitting on someone else's? Remember the week in Spain? I thought it was Liam she had her eye on. What an idiot – I must have been blind.'

'I don't think anything happened in Spain.'

'That makes no difference. It's too late. He's destroyed our love, that bond we had. I'd never trust him again. Ever. Right now, I hate him with a violent hate I never knew I was capable of.'

'Trish, listen to me for a second, please. I can understand that, but I want to tell you something that might make *you* understand – a little. I'm not sure if Maeve ever told you, but I was unfaithful to her, once, a long time ago.'

'Christ. I don't believe it. You too. What is it about you men that you can't be faithful – any of you? You're all the same.' Jumping up, she shouted, 'Anything in a skirt and you're off. I trusted Rory. I trusted you, for God's sake, Conor.'

He said quietly, 'I'm not proud of what I did. I was drunk, but I can't blame that. That was my excuse and my defence. I love Maeve, always have. There has never been anyone else for me. I almost lost her when I slept with that woman.'

'Did you not think of that before? Did it not enter your head as you unzipped and undressed, that it might be wrong or that you might damage your marriage? Did you think of Maeve at all? Did you think she wouldn't mind? Even afterwards?'

'No, it didn't and no, I didn't. I often think about it since and try to analyse why I did it.'

'Surely it was a bit late for that then. Why *did* you, as a matter of interest?'

'Please sit down, Trish. This isn't easy for me. I don't know why I did it – curiosity, lust, availability, opportunity, maybe a bit of all those things. I met her at a conference. I can't even remember her name, except her surname began with an L, because they had seated us alphabetically. I can't even remember what she looked like. It meant nothing to me.'

'Maybe it did to her. Did you ever think that?'

'No. I'm ashamed to admit I never did.'

'How did Maeve find out?'

'I told her. The guilt was eating me up and I needed to confess and I think that may have been the wrong thing to do. She was devastated. It almost finished us. However, she agreed to give me another chance. I know I didn't deserve it.'

'No. You didn't. I won't take Rory back because I know this is not a one-night stand. It's a full-blown affair. He's had to plan around this – plan his deception. He's been in Brussels for a whole week. You know him, he never stays away more than a few nights.'

'I know that only too well. Look, it took some hard work before things were right between me and Maeve again, and a lot of time. What I'm trying to say is perhaps in time you two can do the same.'

'Never!' she said emphatically. 'Never! You know what really hurts? We used to say the most awful thing you can do to another human being is to destroy their trust in you. When trust is gone, there is nothing left. And, do you know what's even worse about it all? He lied to me. He's been lying for weeks now, maybe even since Spain. He goes mad if the kids tell lies.'

'Give him a chance to explain.'

'Did he ask you to say that?'

'No. We haven't discussed it. I promise you.'

'You know Conor, he has tainted everything we ever had. It all feels defiled and dirty. I can't look back on the good times, because it hurts too much. I can't face the future because I'm terrified of the consequences, of being on my own with the kids. And the now is unbearable, because *she's* there. Oh my God, how she is there! What's it going to do to the kids? I want to kill her for being so available – for not having the guts to say, "Go home to your wife and family." What sort of kick do women like that get out of destroying other people's lives and homes?'

He remained mute, nodding in agreement with her arguments.

'Was it worth it, Conor? Can you answer me that? Is a furtive fuck really worth so much to a man? If you put that and your marriage on a weighing scales which would you choose?'

He didn't know what to say to her.

Eventually, she went home, declining his offer to drive her. She was furious with him too. Did he think because he confessed that it changed anything, made it alright? She was so confused. She was sure Rory was waiting up for her as the lights were on all over the house, even though it was past one o'clock. He always turned them off when he left a room. But there was no one about. There was no sound, so she crept upstairs, first opening Barry's room to check on him. She stepped over his discarded clothes to pull his duvet up on his shoulder. He was curled up in a ball snoring loudly, her uncommunicative teenager safe in sleep.

Toni was stretched out on her back with a discarded book by her side, her arms behind her head breathing so quietly Trish could hardly hear her. She turned her bedside lamp off before she left the room. Next door, her older sister Louise was lying rigid in her bed and as Trish went to close the door she heard her call.

'Mum. Mum is that you?'

'Yes darling.'

'I thought you'd gone away.'

Trish rushed over to comfort her daughter.

'Lou, I'm not going anywhere. I promise you that. You're stuck with me.'

Louise cried, 'Mum what's wrong? Why doesn't Daddy love you any more?'

'I don't know,' she said, sitting down on the edge of the bed, tears running down her face. She rocked her older daughter like she had done when she was small and was frightened in the dark or had a bad dream. Now she was rocking her to dispel her own horrific thoughts and to take whatever comfort she could from her child. Fourteen was too young to have to deal with all this, she thought, as she wished someone could hold her in their arms and make things better. But with a frightening calm she also knew in the dark of the night that she had absolutely no control at all over what was happening to them.

'Hush, hush, we'll talk about this tomorrow', she said with a composure she did not feel. Stroking Louise's hair she asked, 'Have you a hockey match in the morning? I've forgotten.'

Trish felt her daughter relax as she answered, 'Just a practice at eleven.'

'Well, I'll collect you and we'll talk after that.'

The dirty sneak. How could he do this to us all? Telling the kids he doesn't love me anymore. Did that excuse him cheating on his kids and was that how he was going to excuse himself? She really wanted to hurt him, to let him see how it felt to be betrayed. Instead she said, 'Daddy and I have to sort some things out between us.'

'Will we have to move? When Jacqui's parents split they had to move and she and her sisters had to change school and everything. I don't want to have to do that.'

'Like I said, there are lots of things to be discussed yet. You try to sleep. Look, move over and I'll lie down beside you till you drop off.'

'I can't Mum. I'm afraid.'

So am I, thought Trish. So am I.

TWENTY-TWO

Trish got Barry up for rugby and the girls for hockey. She cooked a fry and tried to keep a bit of normality in their Saturday morning routine. Rory stayed out of sight. He had slept in one of the guest rooms, but it had made no difference to Trish, who ended up staying all night beside her daughter. She slept in snatches between bouts of palpable anger, drawing meagre comfort from Louise's closeness.

Barry came over to her at the sink and gave her an unexpected hug. 'Mum, we're going to stick together in this. Dad's a prick.'

'He's still your father and deserves respect.'

'Hah. That's rich. He's always going on about having to earn that, and I don't really think he has, do you?'

She was torn. She so badly wanted to share her thoughts with her children, but felt it was the wrong thing to do. 'He and I have to talk and try to iron things out. We'll do that later. This is between him and me.'

'No it's not. It's about us too. Don't we have any say?' asked Louise.

'I don't want you to separate,' said Toni, 'and I don't want to move.'

'We're moving?' asked Barry.

'No, we're not,' Trish said, suddenly realising that perhaps they would have to. My God, what had he told the children and where was this going to end? 'Come on you lot. Get your kit, or you'll all be late.'

When she came back Rory was sitting at the kitchen table. He had tidied away after the breakfast and had a pot of coffee on the table in front of him. The dishwasher purred and whooshed in the background.

'Trish, this isn't easy …' he started.

'You're absolutely right there.'

'I never meant it to happen.'

'Oh yeah, like you said to that woman, "No! I'm married. I have a wife and children and I am their world, so leave us alone. Get a man of your own." Is that how it happened?'

'I don't know how it did.'

'Don't give me that nonsense. You're not one of the kids trying to worm your way out of the homework you didn't do. You know how it happened. You had to arrange meetings and trips. How did she happen to have your mobile number? Come to call you 'lover'? To be in the Radisson in Dublin waiting for you? Don't give me that … that bullshit.'

'I wanted …'

'So what are you going to do about it? Right now you offend me so much I can't stand the idea of you being near any of us, or even using a bathroom in this house, after where you've been, but we have three kids together, a matter you seem to have chosen to forget, so we have to do the right thing for them.'

'I would never do anything to hurt them or you.'

'You sanctimonious prick. Don't you realise you already have?'

'I love the kids. I love you too Trish, you know that.'

'No! I don't. I did know that, but I don't any more.'

'This doesn't change my feelings for you.'

'Well it bloody well changes mine for you!'

'Look Trish—'

'What are you suggesting? That we should all live as one happy family? Perhaps you could ask her to stay. Wife sharing, is that it? Only Rory, you do realise that you must treat us all equally, the other wife would have to have a Jeep and a detached house and all her children would have to go to private schools. You wouldn't be able to discriminate. I can't see those expenses appealing to you!'

'This is nonsense.'

'No it's not! What are your plans? Because, mate, if you think you are staying here and continuing your liaison with that woman, then you are mistaken. We have to think of the children. This is not just about the two of us. If you can promise that you'll have no further contact with her – and that means getting someone else in the office to look after Brussels too – then maybe we can go to counselling and try to make it work again. We all have too much to lose. If—'

'Trish, I can't and won't promise you that.'

'Then you can pack your bags and go.'

'For Christ's sake woman, you can't do that. What about the kids?'

'What about them? Shouldn't you have thought about little things like that first?'

'That's not the way things work.'

'Oh, there are rules are there? Well, no one gave me the manual. Am I supposed to say come back to my bed – lover? All is forgiven? Well, I can't. I'm not that big. I don't know if I can ever forgive you, but I am prepared to try to make things work for the kids' sake but only if that woman has no contact with you or you with her ever again.'

'Trish, I told you, I can't do that.'

'Then get to hell out of here, now! I'm going to collect the kids and I'd like your stuff out of my bedroom when I get back – all of it.'

'Trish, you're being unreasonable …'

'Me, unreasonable? Do you honestly believe that? Do you? Just go to hell and never, ever, come back.' She shouted as she made for the front door.

TWENTY-THREE

Trish was always delighted to see Liam, who popped in at odd times to check on how she was doing. Today, he whisked a big bunch of lilies out from behind his back. 'What on earth are these for?' she asked. She didn't even buy flowers for the house any more.

'Just for being you. The sun is shining and I thought you could do with some cheering up.'

She hugged him there on the doorstep, taking care not to crush the flowers or let their vivid pollen get on their clothes.

'People are going to start talking if you take to kissing men on your doorstep,' he said. 'Will you be able to cope with the gossip and the ruined reputation?'

She laughed, a rare enough occurrence these days. 'Yeah, they'll be calling Joe Duffy and it'll be in all the tabloids, asking how the poor woman whose husband ran off on her managed to snare Dublin's most eligible and, dare I say it, elusive bachelor?'

'And what would you tell them?'

'Forget about the facelifts, healthy eating regimes and dressing sexily. Simply cry every time he calls, look puffy-eyed and emaciated, be depressed and despondent and dump all your problems, and your kids' problems, on him. It works every time!'

'Well I'm glad I picked the right day to bring the flowers,' he said, following her into the kitchen.

'What a waste you are. Why haven't you been snapped up by now anyway, Liam Coffey?' she said as she filled the percolator.

'I've been waiting for the right one to come along.'

'And have you had any success?'

'I might, yes, I think I might just have.'

'Oh, Liam, that's great news. It's not Agneta is it?

'No. It's someone you have never met.'

'Would I approve?'

'Now, of that I'm not too sure.'

'Why? Is she married – with a load of kids?'

'No, neither, but I'm not prepared to talk about it just yet. The last time you all knew every scintilla of detail about my relationship with Helen. This time until it's official, this is my secret so you'll just have to wait. Trust me, Trish, you'll be one of the first to know if it goes anywhere. I promise.'

Liam had called that day because he had seen Barry in town and he'd looked as though he was wandering aimlessly and it struck him that he should be in school. Now he was there, he didn't want to broach the subject directly with Trish – she's enough to deal with, he thought – so he just asked casually how the kids were doing.

'You don't really want to know. Barry's been mitching occasionally, but I think we have that sorted now. He has also stopped going to rugby on Saturday mornings. Says he feels the odd one out with no Dad to support him. He's exaggerating of course, but I can identify with him. I feel all wrong anywhere with couples. I feel as though I have a big sign over my head saying "deserted" or "alone" – and it feels all wrong being alone.'

'And the other two?'

'Always fighting over clothes. Louise won't talk to Rory. She was even prepared to let her school trip go because she wouldn't ask him for money again and you know the way he held the purse strings.'

'I'll pay for her – she can't not go – she'll feel even more left out. She is my godchild after all.'

'Liam you will not. It's all been organised. I do have my running away money – although I don't think that's what it'll be used for now. It's all organised and she's madly excited. Toni, of course, is madly jealous.'

'Have you heard from Rory?'

'Oh yes. He rings the kids all the time, and they don't know what to say to him. It's unreal. I just stand there with the phone in my hand, thinking am I supposed to ask how he is? All I really want is for him to die squirming and with no morphine to alleviate whatever horror has befallen him. He's brought out a side in me that I never knew existed and I'm in danger of becoming a twisted man-hating bitch.'

'No you're not. You're still in shock, Trish. We all are.'

She told Liam about a time recently when Barry had bunked off school and she had had a call from his form master. When Rory had phoned and she had told him about it, he absolutely dismissed the seriousness of it, in case any of the blame could be apportioned to him, no doubt. 'That's normal. All boys bunk off school at some time,' he'd said. 'Put him on to me.'

She'd passed the phone to Barry, then heard him shout, 'Don't give me any of that crap.'

She'd had to restrain herself from telling him not to use language like that.

'If you cared a damn you'd be here to make sure I went to school, wouldn't you?' Barry had said before slapping the handset down on the counter and Toni, the youngest, had picked it up. Trish told Liam how she had listened to her daughter's half of the conversation.

'She told him that things are bad here. That Mum's crying all the time and Louise won't come out of her room …'

There'd been a pause. Trish had almost choked when she'd

heard what Toni said next. 'The girls in my class say you ran off with a whore. Did you, Dad? … I do know what it means. I looked that up in the dictionary. I thought it was spelt h-o-a-r but that's a frost. I didn't know it had a w. Did you know that, Dad?'

There'd been an even longer pause.

'Well, it also said bint and tart … Well, I'm just telling you what everyone in school is saying … Of course I'll behave for Mum. She's here for us.'

At the end of the phone call, Toni had shouted, 'Don't tell me you love me. You used to say that to us and to Mum. And you didn't mean it. Anyway I have to go – *X Factor* is on … Yeah, yeah, whatever. See you in McDonald's with the other weekend dads.'

Trish told Liam she had to hold back when she heard these exchanges.

'One part of me is proud that they are standing up to what Rory did, but I'm afraid of what all the bitterness will do to them.'

'They have to get it out and it's better that they do it on him rather than you. Remember they are teenagers, so those mood swings are normal at that age, I seem to remember, absentee parent or not.'

'Fine, I suppose you're right. I have lots of anger I'd love to get out too, but what's the point? It would be lost on him. I'm history as far as he's concerned and it looks as though the kids will have to learn to live with part-time affection when it suits him. It's very unfair.'

'Wasn't it John Lennon who said something about life being what happens between the plans you make?' he asked.

'I'm not sure but it sounds pretty apt to me.'

'Have you been to a solicitor yet?'

'No, I've held off partly because I haven't a clue who to go to and, really, because I honestly can't believe this has happened. I was convinced Rory would wake up some morning and realise he's made a dreadful mistake, that he couldn't live without me and the kids, and that he'd come running back to us. I have had to accept that you can't make someone love you. That they can fall out of love as easily as into it. I thought what we had was special. Isn't that sad and delusional?'

'No. Would you take him back?'

'Liam, I still love the bastard. I don't know if I could ever forgive him or indeed trust him again, but I'd take him back for the kids' sake and try and work things out. They are totally lost without him. Why? Do you think he might change his mind?' she asked, clinging to any morsel of hope and praying he might be offering some.

But Liam soon quashed that. 'I don't, but then I never thought he'd go either, so I'm a poor judge. You have to go and talk to someone, suss out where you stand legally in all of this. Look, Jim McConville is a good friend of mine. He specialises in family law. Can I give him a call for you?'

'His name is always in the papers. I don't think I could afford anyone like him. He charges the earth.'

'Don't worry about things like that. I'll—'

'I won't take charity.'

'Who said anything about charity? Look on it as a thank you for all those meals you've cooked me over the years. It'll also be an insurance that you'll continue to feed me occasionally for the rest of your life,' he smiled. 'Besides, old Jim owes me quite a few favours.'

'You're just saying that.'

'I'm not, you know. I'll ring him in the morning and set something up for you. In the meantime, try not to worry about the kids. They'll come through OK. They're hurting right now and, tough as it may be, they'll take it out on you because they know you're not going anywhere. If it's any consolation to you, all my friends with teenagers are going through hell with one or more of them. It seems to be a rite of passage and it takes a little time for things to level out, but they will. Really.'

'I hope you're right. It's just that I feel so helpless. I'm too caught up with what has happened here, and with Maeve, to be any use to them.'

'That's nonsense. Tell them their Uncle Liam is here if it all gets too much for them, or if they want to sound off at anyone other than you.'

'I'll do that and thanks again for just being here.' She felt safe in his bear hug, 'Oh, and for the lovely flowers.'

'My pleasure. I'll call you tomorrow after I've spoken to Jim.'

TWENTY-FOUR

Trish was tidying Toni's room a few weeks later. From a shelf, she picked up the old jack-in-the-box that the children had all loved when they were small. Just like me, she thought. I've spent the last month nodding and jumping to the rhythms of the children and going into hiding. And they're probably the only things that have kept me sane.

If they needed buoying up, she buoyed; if they needed a cuddle, she cuddled; if they needed to shout, it was usually at her and she let them. Once they had retreated into their boxes, she closed the lid on hers and withdrew into the dark space that enveloped her, a space that started in an indefinable gap in her innermost self – until she could almost pinpoint the spot in her very soul. She felt she had been robbed of any hope; the void filling up with fears she had never known existed. Terrors of not being able to cope alone, of trying to steer her children on an unbiased path. How could she possibly be capable of guiding them without bitterness and malice? How could she do this when her whole world was consumed with revulsion, despair and the need for revenge?

Rory had simply vanished from their orbit with his impromptu move to Brussels. Yet he was still everywhere in their home. He was in the paintings they'd bought together, in the apple trees he'd planted in the garden, in his favourite mug, his car magazines, the photographs that were dotted around the house, in his gym equipment in the spare room and in the unspoken feelings and sense of abandonment they all felt. His accelerated move left Trish wondering now that he was free and available would Anna Marie still want him, or did she only go after married men.

She didn't want to hear the platitudes from well-meaning friends, who only said them because they didn't know what else to say. She rationalised that they couldn't just greet her and say, 'Sorry your husband has run off on you.' So, instead, they all muttered variations of the time-will-heal-all adage. Time was the only thing she seemed to have plenty of, and every minute dragged like an hour, every hour like a morning or afternoon and the nights, darker than ever, just never seemed to end.

That was her worst time. She'd pull her duvet around her seeking comfort in its softness, but it failed to warm her. She couldn't wait to get her children out to school so that she could cry out loud, releasing some of the pain that engulfed her. She couldn't wait for them to return to put some normality and noise back into the emptiness in her life. She'd stopped listening to the radio: every song was about love, requited and unrequited – of lovers' hopes and dreams. Was it all a myth this loving someone for ever? Did it really exist? Or had she, sensible and practical Trish, bought into a fictitious idyll that all teenage girls believe? No! She refused to believe this. She knew she'd known the real thing but now, just like the spring on the old jack-in-the-box, it was broken. It had snapped and she knew there was no way to put the life back into it.

Rory's affair had firmly destroyed their marriage. She might have been able to cope with a one-night stand as Maeve and Conor seemed to have done, but a relationship was infinitely worse. It was a deliberate decision, one, whether he'd realised it or not the first time he'd been unfaithful, that he'd decided to forge ahead with. He had put normality in jeopardy. He had gambled and won. His family had turned out to be the losers. Trish hoped fervently that he would live to regret it and come crawling back, begging forgiveness.

Yet, she still loved him so much that she wanted their lives to work out. But, she wondered, would it ever be possible to trust him again? To let him make love to her without the thoughts of him in bed with someone else? She also wondered how her kind husband could be happy, knowing the hurt he was inflicting. Never mind her, didn't he look into his children's eyes and see his betrayal there too?

Was one person's happiness worth sacrificing everything for?

She didn't think so.

***

Conor sat at his desk thinking. He stared at the monitor, read and reread the figures on the file in front of him, without absorbing a single line. The screensaver popped up after several minutes, showing a photo of Maeve and him on the front terrace in Mijas – taken just this summer – before they knew.

He felt his body tense in panic. He was in uncharted territory. He was used to having control over his life, while not necessarily needing to control it. He'd had a charmed life. He'd spent summer holidays trekking in South America, Morocco and island hopping in Greece, herding sheep, washing dishes and doing bar work when his funds had run out. The only real crises that he'd ever had to deal with were the deaths of his parents and, of course, his and Maeve's inability to have a child. While disappointed each time they had failed, he'd never had that bond that Maeve had developed almost the instant she knew she was pregnant, and so his sorrow when they miscarried was more for Maeve and what she was going through than for himself. They had just about given up on ever carrying a baby to full term, when she had discovered she was pregnant, naturally and miraculously. But that was not to be; the complicated, ectopic pregnancy rubber stamped any chance of ever conceiving again.

'Have you considered adoption at all?' their consultant had asked.

'We've talked about it a lot,' Maeve had replied. 'But I have a real fear that after losing our own babies I might have difficulty accepting someone else's so I, we, keep putting it off.' She'd looked at Conor, who'd nodded in agreement.

'Then you're right not to rush into it,' the consultant had said. 'You've had a lot of problems, so take time out and forget about it for a while.'

Now the problems they were facing were infinitely worse than infertility. Yes, Conor had to admit his life had been pretty damned good up till that summer.

He stared at his screensaver. They had had fantastic times in Spain. They loved it there, so did their friends and it had become a cherished place for them, all together and separately. Maeve thoroughly enjoyed having guests, revelling in the trips to buy fresh food from the local market. She brushed up on her au pair Spanish and was now able to banter back, colloquialisms and all, with the stallholders as she bargained for fresher fish or less ripe tomatoes from their colourful displays.

Conor knew he was navigating in uncertain waters, where the final port of call, whenever it came, would not be one of refuge and comfort, but loneliness and trepidation. It was at this point that his mind always shut down. Just like his computer screen, as though programmed on autosave, not allowing access beyond a certain point. He couldn't allow himself to think of what the doctor had said would happen, perhaps hoping that if he didn't, he could will his wife to a full recovery.

'She's having the best treatment,' Stan assured him time and time again. Working at the clinic means she's among friends and colleagues. These medical people are up to speed with the latest trials and drug treatments – and we all have her personal interests at heart. And, Conor reasoned, weren't scientists and pharmaceutical companies always coming up with new solutions and cures? Advances were being made all the time. He had to keep hoping.

He couldn't give up. He clicked on the mouse, bringing the screen back to life again, and tried to concentrate. He had a meeting at noon and had to read several transcripts thoroughly by then.

***

Maeve and Trish held each other up. Maeve had now become a prop for Trish. Her love for her friend allowed her to step out of her own private fears when they were together, which was a lot. She never made judgemental remarks about Rory and Trish respected that. She let her rant and rave when she needed to and they often cried together. They talked about how Maeve had coped when she learned about Conor's one night stand and how hard it was for her to forgive him. Trish felt she'd never get to that stage with Rory. They laughed too.

Maeve was the only person Trish laughed with that winter.

TWENTY-FIVE

Bloody Frenchmen – they think they are great, Sharonne thought. Christian had been in Dublin several times since the meeting when he had turned up with the knitting-needle-like PA and introduced her as his Françoise. Since then, he had flirted outrageously with Sharonne on the phone, that French accent activating the tiny hairs on the back of her neck, making them quiver to some unknown melody every time he lingered over her name. Each time, too, he promised her a gorgeous dinner when next he came over – 'Just the two of us – somewhere special.'

He was coming in on Tuesday. She had booked Chapter One, her favourite haunt in the city, and she had spent a small fortune on a new linen suit in black with a red trim. She hadn't even looked at the price tag hanging from the sleeve. When she found some red strappy shoes, which were an exact match, she just knew she had to have them. The shoes reminded her of Minnie Mouse in their on-trend round-toed perfection. She then found a black clutch bag with a large red dot as its clasp.

'I just had to have them,' she told Sadie when she arrived back in the office with all her bags.

'I just wish I was your size – then you could pass them on when you tire of them,' she laughed.

Work was going well, even if it was very demanding, and

Sharonne knew Christian would be pleased with the progress. The FitzGerald-Reglob enquiry was on target and although they had enough to sink the dishonest owners and directors, they knew there was more to come. Sharonne and her team had managed to keep everything away from the press. She loved working on this account. It was much more challenging than some of her other ones. She had hated Morrera Ceramica, with its persistent pushy sales manager who used to ring her every Monday to ask, 'Well, did we get any publicity last week? Why can't you get us into the daily papers, the Irish Times property pages? What about The White Book? I want you to get me into that.'

She used to want to tell him, 'Because you've been in all of them, several times, and you never advertise with anyone, you mean sod. You've used up your goodwill quota. You just want free publicity everywhere, but it doesn't work like that.' The cheapskate had given her a bottle of some obscure budget-bin Spanish cava and a set of ceramic coasters with their brand logo on them for Christmas last year and she hadn't forgiven him yet.

No, the FitzGerald-Reglob account was a challenge, and no one rose to a challenge quite like Sharonne. That Tuesday she'd rushed home from the office, popping into Hervé on the way to have her hair washed and dried. Once home, she'd sat down with the twins and Sabine, the au pair, while they had their meal and heard about their day.

'Are you going out again tonight, Mummy?' came the plaintive question as she left the table to go upstairs.

'Afraid so, my angels, but it's work. Daddy will be home before I leave though.' And he was. He came upstairs as she was getting out of the shower.

'A business do?' he enquired.

'Yes, but over an early dinner for a change, so it won't be too much of a trial,' she replied. 'How was your day?'

'The usual. I'll probably have to go off to Cyprus next week for a few days. Why don't you think about taking a bit of time off and we'll do a long weekend – just the two of us?'

'I can't. I'm in the thick of the takeover, or should I say the takeover and cover-up. Maybe some other time, as soon as this business is finished.'

He didn't seem too disappointed, she noticed.

'Nice suit.' He had spotted the purchases spread out on the bed. 'I'm going back down to the girls. Have a good night,' he said, pecking her on the cheek.

There was a time she would not have got away from him, standing there wrapped only in a bathrobe, and she was glad he hadn't seen her frivolous purchase of the scanty undies she had picked up in the Westbury Mall on her way back to the car that day. They were lying on the bed under the suit.

She said goodnight to the twins and gave Derek a peck goodbye on the cheek. The taxi called promptly and she clip-clopped out in her new shoes, knowing she was getting the once-over from the driver, but pretending otherwise. Black was good on her and she felt vampish in the red shoes. She studied her nails as the car snaked its way to the hotel to collect Christian. His flight had come in at five. He was waiting on the steps and then it happened again, the little hairs doing Riverdance on her neck. He slid into the seat beside her.

'You do look quite delicious,' he said kissing her, not on both cheeks, as was his wont, but directly on her lips. She felt herself flush.

'Cherie, we are going to have a lovely night, just the two of us.'

'Evening, Christian,' she corrected him. 'We're going to have a nice evening.'

'We'll see,' he said, taking her hand.

She withdrew it. She'd show him she was no pushover. Derek was driving her mad, going on and on about Rory and work. They hardly made love any more because they were always so tired. She felt he didn't value her either, didn't even notice her. Who would blame her if she wanted a bit of excitement?

She walked sideways down the steps in her skinny heels, which accentuated the length of her legs. Christian followed, looking at her wiggle and smiling the smile of a man who knows that every head is turning to see who the lucky guy is with such a gorgeous creature. She was welcomed as an old friend by Martin at Chapter One and they settled down in the lounge for a pre-dinner drink.

'We'll have Kir Royale,' ordered Christian. As they waited, they studied the blue and white glass wall panel.

'If you can name all those twelve Irish writers there's a bottle of champagne on the house,' said the maître d'. 'I have to warn you, though, not many people have actually managed to do it to date.'

'Hah, I see you are bringing the Writer's Museum into the restaurant?' Christian remarked. Sharonne was impressed. How the hell did he know so much and always seem to be so damned sophisticated?'

'No,' said Martin, 'but many of our guests will have been up there before coming in, or across the road at the Gate, so it seemed a good idea to have a literary connection, hence the window and our name too, of course, Chapter One.'

Christian was easily able to identify Yeats, Joyce, Beckett and Synge. They argued over Synge. Was it Gogarty?

'I don't know. I haven't seen many pictures of Gogarty. In fact, I haven't a clue what he looked like,' said Sharonne, 'but he has to be there, doesn't he?

'I don't think I know any of his work, but perhaps your latest Nobel literature winner, Seamus Heaney, is here too, non? Or has the window been here longer?'

'I think so,' said Sharonne, not sure. They identified nine of the panels before being ushered to their table. Christian guided her, putting his hand on her back, letting it slide down a fraction too low for propriety.

I'm playing with fire here, she thought, and now I'm thinking in clichés. This man has really gone to my head, but, hell, it feels good to flirt and he is very easy on the eye too.

How had things gone so seriously wrong between her and Derek? Solid, dependable Derek. And since when? He'd been very off everything since Rory had left. That affair had changed all their worlds and she wasn't about to do anything as stupid, no matter how enticing it was. Perhaps she should go away with him to Cyprus for a few days to get their lives back on track. They'd had good times together, very good, and he was a caring and considerate man. The sex had been great too, until lately. Well, really until she had made that stupid show of herself in front of everyone. She still remembered the way he had looked at her that night – with disgust at how she had treated his friends. She also remembered the feeling of rejection when he had slept in the spare room for a few nights. She felt he would have stayed there if it hadn't been for what their daughters would think.

'You are far away, cherie?' Christian muttered as they studied the menus. He flattered her openly, made her feel special and desirable. The gingery scent of his Roger & Gallet aftershave excited her. He ordered a Sauterne to accompany the foie gras.

'That is a gastronomique marriage that is made in heaven!' he said. When they began to eat she had to agree. They then had succulent lamb with a wine she didn't recognise. When Christian ordered a second bottle she protested, 'No, Christian, I have had enough. I have to work tomorrow.'

'So do I, cherie, but tomorrow is a long way away,' he whispered. 'If you prefer we could go back to my hotel and have a drink there.'

Voicing what was in her head she said, 'I bet that's not the first time you've used that line.' He laughed out loud but didn't answer. Later in the taxi to his hotel he said, 'Seriously, Sharonne, I don't like to mix business with pleasure, but I do have some papers for you to study before the meeting on Thursday. Come up with me and collect them?'

She looked at her watch. It was ten thirty. She was going home to Derek – she had some talking to do. She'd make sure to take time off and have that long weekend with him, make a fresh start and do a bit of work on her marriage.

'No, thank you – I'll wait here.'

She saw a flicker of annoyance cross his face, but he quickly recovered his composure, obviously not used to anyone turning him down, she thought. He took the steps two at a time, ignoring the liveried doorman as he went by. She opened her bag to check her phone. There was one voicemail from Derek.

'Hope you're having a good evening. The girls are asleep and I'm off to a poker session with the lads at Conor's. Don't wait up for me. It'll be a late one.' Sharonne felt let down. Derek didn't often do the lads' night thing and he was entitled to some time off too and Conor needed his friends now. But she had agonised about her decision to try and fix things up between them and had come to some conclusions. Now she felt as though she had been stood up and this sense of being let down made her make a snap decision. Fumbling in her bag, she pulled out a twenty-euro note and handed it to the taxi driver. She eased herself out of the car and made her way up the steps of Christian's hotel, smiling at the doorman as he held the door open for her.

TWENTY-SIX

As promised, Liam talked to his solicitor friend Jim McConville, who agreed to see Trish. He had phoned her and she liked the sound of his voice. They had had what he called 'a preliminary chat' and he reassured her he would take care of everything – if she wanted him to. She phoned Liam to thank him and he offered to go along with her but, much as she said and thought about Rory since his hasty exodus from their lives and his home in Ireland, she didn't want to say any of those things in front of anyone else, least of all one of his mates. She made a few notes before she left the house: joint bank account details, name of their mortgage provider, joint insurance policies and the like. In her conversation with Jim on the phone he told her, 'Don't agonise over these things too much at this stage, they can all be supplied later.'

She parked on Merrion Square, the parking meter gobbling up a handful of one-euro coins, and then she made her way up the stone steps to the Georgian door. A gleaming brass plaque caught the sun and she was quite close before she could read McConville Solicitors at Law in black lettering. The receptionist seated her in the plush waiting room.

'Mr McConville's two-thirty appointment is just leaving so he'll be with you in a few minutes,' he said as he went back behind his enormous desk. There was another man sitting there answering a high-tech switchboard. How times have changed since I was at work, she thought. Obviously they feel a male voice has a greater degree of gravitas and projects their firm in a more serious light than a frivolous woman's would. She was feeling anxious and was glad when Jim McConville presented himself moments later.

'Hello, Trish. Sorry to have kept you waiting. I'm Jim. Will you come this way?'

He led her up the stairs to a half landing and up again to the front of the house. She could have sworn the stairs were not level and thought not only is my life out of balance, but now my world is tilting. As though he had read her mind, Jim McConville explained, 'The stairs are uneven. These old houses are beginning to show their age. They were built without foundations, you know, so they are sagging a little bit here and there.'

'I thought it was just me – that I was losing the plot altogether,' she laughed nervously.

He paused, pointing to the elegant architraved doorframe, indicating how it leaned perceptively to the right too.

'There's one house over there on the corner and you can actually see the sag on the stairs where it turns. It's much grander than this. Quite unnerving really as it's cantilevered. Any time I'm in there, I have visions of it disintegrating some time and the occupants being stranded on the top floors.'

'That's fascinating,' she said.

'You know they weren't as magnificent as we imagine – these Georgian rows. The Wide Streets Commission of the time had to threaten the residents of this square and others with hefty fines if they didn't sweep up outside their houses three times every day, because there were no fine pavements there, just muddy paths, and people's clothes got destroyed, especially the ladies' long skirts.'

'I never knew that. I always thought I'd love to have lived then, although I'd probably have been a parlour maid.'

'And I a stable boy, for sure.' He indicated to a room at the front of the building.

'That ceiling is magnificent.'

'Yes. Yes, it's one of the better ones on the street, done by some Swiss brothers who probably didn't make a fortune at the time, but who should have. Anyway, Trish, we're here to talk about you. Sit down please and I'll ring for coffee, or tea, which would you prefer?'

He led her to two leather armchairs beside the fireplace, all antique furniture, she noticed, enormous pieces which would not fit anywhere into modern houses.

'I did meet your er, husband, em, in some golf match or other, but that was some time ago. Tell me how I can help.'

'I don't know if I can afford your services and I don't want to waste your time. But Liam …'

'That's not the issue at the moment. We have to protect you and your children and their interests. What ages are they?' He started to make notes. They chatted on for a while and then he said, 'Good, good. We need to write to your husband and his solicitor, advising him you will be seeking a judicial separation, if that is your wish. According to Irish law that means you will have to wait until you have been living apart for a year before that can be made legal. Meantime, we will be looking for maintenance and security for you and your family.'

'I never thought our marriage would come to this – discussing maintenance and separation,' she said, getting visibly distressed.

'No one ever does, and it's often the sudden break-ups that cause the most heartache. Those of bad marriages are often a release to both partners and, indeed, to the children too. The end of a marriage is a bit like bereavement with the loss of dreams and expectations. In my experience, cases such as yours, where there's another person involved and someone is having to deal with rejection, can sometimes be the hardest to come to terms with.'

He paused as she nodded, not trusting herself to speak. She foraged in her bag for a tissue and blew her nose. He asked, 'Has Rory been contributing to the household expenses since he left?'

'Well yes, he has. Well, in a manner of speaking. He sent me cheques for the school fees, and most of the other bills are on direct debit and it seems they're being paid since he left. I've been paying for other things myself.'

'Good. Well we'll have to formalise these arrangements.'

'To be honest, we haven't actually sat down to discuss it – or anything else for that matter. It's very degrading to have to ask for money for housekeeping and petrol when you haven't ever had to do it before. I feel it brings the marriage to an even lower low and I don't want him to think I am ripping him off.'

'He won't, but you have to be realistic. What would you do if he stopped those payments? Could you manage?'

'No. Absolutely not. I'd probably have to go back to work, but I don't know what I'd do. It's been so long. I think I'll get something part-time. I can't let three teenagers come in to an empty house, or "free gaff" as they call it, every day. Who knows what they'd get up to or who they'd bring in.'

'No. No. Of course not. But he has responsibilities, whether he chooses to admit them or not at this point. You have to think of day-to-day expenses and then factor in the unexpected. What about doctors' bills, bus fares, school books, trips, holidays, pocket money, your car insurance and tax, the central heating oil. What happens when the washing machine packs in? You must be realistic. Running a house and having teenagers is like having siphons on your bank account. Money doesn't last very long.'

'You sound as if you are speaking from experience.'

'No. No. I have no children. I never married, but I see it all the time with my clients. They forget that their children's needs change as they mature and that things will need to be maintained and replaced. It's a very long route ahead and one

to which you do not need to add financial worries as well.'
Almost as an after-thought he added, 'You will have to agree
on access rights and visiting times too.'

'Oh I wouldn't object to that – for their sakes. I'm not going
to restrict access or let the kids be collected on street corners
when he comes to take them out. I want that part to be as
civilised as possible. But I don't want *her* in their lives either.
She paused for a minute. 'What about the house? Will we have
to move?'

'That's in joint names and one would hope he will not wish
to sell it. He has a responsibility to provide a home for you all,
but that does not mean the existing family dwelling. Your
husband is a comparatively wealthy man so I can't see him
making you leave, but there are no guarantees.'

He continued in this vein, opening her eyes to aspects of a
marriage, or rather a marital break-up, that had never entered
her head before.

'Have you thought about counselling or mediation? I have to
advise you about them. They do work for some people, but if
Rory is adamant that he doesn't want to come home, there may
not be much point in going down that road.'

Jim suggested that Trish should withdraw a certain sum from
their joint account and put it in a new account in her name – as
a kind of insurance policy that she could draw on if things got
messy.

'You don't have to touch it and it can always be re-lodged to
his account if everything else is agreed on amicably.'

She seemed doubtful.

'Trust me. It's for the best. I've seen things go horribly
wrong in these situations so it's better to be protected. You are
not just dealing with the man you thought you knew, but with
his mistress too. That often colours their perspectives and
indeed their actions.'

'Will we have to go to court?'

'Hopefully we can agree on these things without having to do that. If it comes to a divorce, and that would be four years away, you may have to. Unfortunately, I always feel, the Irish people voted for a 'no fault' divorce in the last referendum. Effectively that meant that no matter who is at fault, the division of the estates is equal. In my mind, there is no justice in that – especially in clear-cut cases of adultery, as this seems to be.

'That seems unfair.'

'It is.'

'I didn't vote. I felt I had no right to make that choice for others. Besides, I never thought I'd be in this situation. Maybe I should have. Makes you think that pre-nuptial agreements may be the way to go, although we had nothing to agree on when we married. We weren't exactly Tom Cruise and Katie Holmes.' She smiled, remembering the old sofa they inherited and lived with until they could afford to buy a brand new one. It had then been passed on to some other newly-wed friends in the same situation.

'I think there is a place for pre-nuptial agreements and they will come in too, especially now that family splits are more and more common, and often not just once in a lifetime either.'

'So what do I do next?'

'Go home and do your sums. I'll give you a fact sheet with some guidelines and that'll give you some idea of what it costs to sustain your lifestyle.'

'I don't seem to have one of those at the moment.'

'I know,' he said kindly,' but you will have again, I guarantee you that. The months after a break-up can be very bleak, but it will get better. Meantime we have to get your affairs in order. I find peace of mind on these matters always helps.'

'I hope you are right.'

'Trust me, I am, Trish. You'll see.'

TWENTY-SEVEN

Maeve was in her element as Christmas approached and delighted in all the preparations, even this year's scaled down ones. She shopped when she felt strong enough and put all her efforts into wrapping.

'This year I'm doing brown paper with red and green tartan bows as my theme,' she told Trish. 'I found some lovely little felt poinsettias and I'm using them too.'

'You'll show us all up,' Trish said, as she saw the ever-growing pile of presents under the tree in Maeve's hallway.

Conor had decorated it, or at least put the lights and the highest decorations in place. He wasn't looking forward to Christmas at all knowing that Maeve's cancer could return. He hated what had happened to Maeve and how she shied away from him when he made any advance to her. He told Derek, 'I still don't know how to handle this. Maeve says she feels unattractive and no amount of reassurance seems to make any difference.'

'You can understand that,' replied Derek, always philosophical.

To Conor, she was still his beautiful and desirable Maeve. In his book, she had survived and that was all that mattered – and he was optimistic about her future too.

'I know I shouldn't be so pessimistic. She's doing OK. Her

energy levels are way below par and but they are getting better. She seems to hit a low a few days after the treatment, and then she perks up again. They told her this would start to improve once she finished this course. Then they'd have to wait a few months for it to work its way out of her system before they carried out more scans.'

'That's hard on both of you.'

Conor agreed. He found the waiting was the worst part.

***

'Let's head off to Mijas. A bit of warm weather might perk you up,' Conor suggested to Maeve while they were having their breakfast the next day. 'Sharonne and Derek are off on holidays to celebrate her fortieth.'

'Love, don't take this the wrong way. I'd love to go away, but I'd rather be here for this Christmas, as usual.'

'What about going to a hotel instead?' Conor asked.

'No, I just want things to be as they always are. Besides, I feel we should be around for Trish and her kids too. She's dreading it. I'd love to ask them here for dinner …'

'No! That's not even up for discussion. I won't let you take that on. It would be madness.'

Both lost in their thoughts, they sat drinking tea and looking out at the garden, which had an icing of frost on the lawn, broken only by paw prints where some adventurous cat, or maybe even an urban fox, had intruded during the night.

'Doesn't it look beautiful out there this morning?'

Conor didn't answer immediately and when he did break the silence it was to tell Maeve, 'I had a phone call from Rory yesterday.'

'You never said anything last night.'

'No. I've been mulling it over in my mind. He kind of asked if he could stay here at Christmas, as he wants to be near the kids.'

'Well, he has some nerve. I hope you told him to take a hike.'

'I didn't. I thought we might be away and he could have come here if the house was empty. He's in a real mess. He was – is – one of my closest friends and now when he needs a hand, I feel I'm not there for him.'

'He should have thought of that before he went. He's putting you in an impossible position and he's lucky to have any friends left.'

'I think he's hoping Trish will let him join them for Christmas dinner.'

'Then he must be mad. Why should she? Where is his fancy bit – off rolling around the snow in Finland?'

'Maeve, you're beginning to sound like Sharonne!' he laughed. 'But, seriously, do you not think the kids would want to see him?'

'I'm quite sure they would, but what about Trish? Do you think he wants to get back with her? Has the novelty of having a mistress begun to pall or does he not like having to spend money on her?'

'I didn't go there.'

'Well I would. I don't know how I'd react seeing him again, knowing what he's put her through. It'll be very hard to be civil to him. I'll feel I'm betraying Trish by being nice to him.'

' … nice to him? Don't think I don't have reservations too, not least because I don't know if it's fair putting you through this. We're going to have to confront this situation at some stage anyway and perhaps it's better sooner than later. Maybe we can help smooth things out.'

'I'm not sure we would be – smoothing things. And how will the kids feel? Is it not another betrayal for them too, that the people they trust are now siding with him?'

' … siding with him. It's not a case of taking sides, Maeve.'

'Well, they'll probably not see it like that. I know I wouldn't. He's putting us in a spot here.'

'He is that. Look, I have reservations too. It's a tricky position for everyone. You know how I feel about what he did.'

'I know that. Should I sound Trish out to see how she'd react before we tell him he's welcome, although I don't think that word quite fits?'

'That would be great.'

'I feel like a collaborator – and – if he comes here – he'd better be prepared for a piece of my mind, because he'll get it – with bells on – and they won't be nice jingle ones either. I won't be able to hold back.'

***

Trish was making some Christmas puddings when Maeve arrived for coffee.

'That smell brings me right back to childhood. It's great. Can I make a wish?' she asked, grabbing the wooden spoon. 'We always did that when we were kids.'

'So did we,' said Trish, 'but I haven't bothered this year. There are so many things I want that I can't have and I know it will take more than a few wishes to put them right.'

Maeve closed her eyes and stirred the heavy spicy mixture three times, before opening them again.

'What did you wish for?'

'You're not supposed to tell, but seeing as you asked, I wished that you won't pour the whole thing over me when I tell you what I'm about to.'

Trish wiped her hands on her apron and looked at her friend. 'You've not had more bad news.'

'No. Nothing as sinister as that. Things are going well on that front for a change. There's a "chemo holiday" in sight and I can't say I'll miss the ordeal. But I'm not sure how you'll take this – Rory rang Conor yesterday and asked if he could stay with us at Christmas – so that he could be near the kids.' She watched Trish's shocked reaction.

'And what did Conor say?' Maeve could sense her hostility.

'He didn't commit us to anything. I feel so annoyed that I don't want anything to do with him, yet I can understand. I don't want him staying after what he has put you through, but he is Conor's best friend and Conor feels he should be there for him. What do you think?'

'Isn't that just typical? What did I ever see in that selfish prick? He rides roughshod over his family and now he feels he can pull the friendship card when it suits him. Where's yer wan gone? Has she thrown him out? Was he too mean for her?'

'I don't know. I asked Conor if she was going off to Finland to roll in the snow and he told me I sounded like Sharonne.' They both laughed, before Trish got serious again.

'He loves plum pudding – perhaps we should put some arsenic in it and send some over to her with our good wishes!'

'Good idea.'

'Do you think he's coming back because he's heard from my solicitor and has realised how much it will cost him to separate?'

Mentally Maeve thought that was a very likely possibility. She let Trish fume, agreeing with everything she said, but she also knew she'd most likely agree with Conor and let Rory stay with them.

Why, she wondered, did friendship have to be such a balancing act?

***

Rory was feeling terrible. He had had a difficult conversation with Conor and knew it had not gone down well when he asked if he could stay with him and Maeve over Christmas. Conor had not given him a straight answer, making some excuse or other about checking to see if Maeve would be up to it and then came straight out and told him he'd have to talk it over with her before he'd give him an answer. That left him in limbo.

He didn't want to go to a hotel. It would cost a fortune at Christmas time and he'd feel like a fish out of water. Maybe he'd get a B&B in Killiney or Glenageary, not too far from the kids. Besides, he wanted to talk to Conor about the letter he had had from his solicitor – enclosing the one that Jim McConville had sent him but he thought it wiser not to mention that just yet. He was reeling at the speed at which Trish had acted.

Barely a few months on and she had gone to the most expensive legal eagle in the land. That would cost him dearly, he thought, and as he was clearly the guilty party he would, in all probability, be hit with her legal fees on top of his own. He had no intention of selling the family home. If he did he'd end up paying huge stamp duty on another one and, anyway, it would be too disruptive to the kids, he admitted to himself guiltily.

He took the envelope out of his pocket and read the contents again. It had been delivered to his office in Brussels. He wouldn't mention it to Anna Maria yet. He'd wait until after Christmas to deal with that.

TWENTY-EIGHT

Sharonne was sending out her corporate gifts, cases of vintage wine to the more important clients and bottles of Moët & Chandon in their own stylish chiller cases to those of lesser value in her pecking order. On a whim, she added Trish to her list and hand-wrote the card. 'This is for a frivolous moment when you feel there is something, no matter how small, to celebrate. Enjoy! Sharonne.' She placed the card beside the brown and cream container and left it on the side table in her office along with others that two of her staff were wrapping and addressing.

After the courier company had collected the last of the gifts, she received one herself. An enormous arrangement of flowers with pink ginger, white lilies, red berries and some exotic double-leafed eucalyptus and greenery that had leaves that looked as though they had been pleated. She could hardly see her PA behind them as she brought them through to her.

'Somebody thinks a lot of you, and it's not even your birthday until next week,' Sadie said as she placed them carefully on the floor. 'They are magnificent. I can't see any card though,' she added. 'Would you like me to ring the florist to see if it fell off in transit?'

'No. Thank you. I know who they are from.'

Her heart raced and she couldn't stop a grin from spreading

across her face. She'd known who the sender was when she saw the ginger flowers. That night in Christian's suite at the Merrion, she had inhaled his aftershave as he hugged her. It was Gingembre – which he told her was pronounced something like 'jan-jambre'.

'Have you ever seen the flowers?' he had asked as he released her.

'I don't think so.'

He had taken her by the hand to the showy arrangement on the side table in his suite and shown her the spiky, waxy, pink ginger plumes that she could not recall ever having seen before. They only had a hint of an aroma, but that did have a distinct resemblance to the scent of his all-too-close face.

'Close your eyes and remember this fragrance. The smell is so potent. It brings you back to those intimate moments and to secrets which no one but those involved know about, n'est-ce pas?' And then he'd kissed her, slowly and gently, before leading her to the bedroom.

Now the floral arrangement had awakened all those thoughts, the memories of his hands moving on her body, of her wanting him so badly and of the guilt afterwards, a guilt made even worse by knowing she wanted to do it again and again.

That guilt saw her spending even more than ever on presents for her precious twins and on Derek. Bob had warned her that Christian gathered trophies wherever he went, and she was not stupid enough to think this would be different than his other conquests, but there was nothing to stop her wishing it would be.

Was there?

TWENTY-NINE

Rory was flying in on the twenty-third and Trish was on tenterhooks. She was just getting to grips with being alone, always tetchy, but trying to hide her anger from the children while getting through the days. She normally enjoyed the run-up to Christmas, but this year every day was an endurance test. It was hard to pretend to be jovial. She had forced herself to put up the decorations, send cards and make the place look festive. But her heart hadn't been in it. She had been surprised to receive the unexpected gift from Sharonne and she realised when she took it from the courier and read the card that she'd actually smiled, something she didn't do too often these days. She didn't really do frivolous moments that often any more either. She rang her and thanked her and was surprised at how kind and concerned Sharonne was.

On the twenty-fourth, Trish braced herself. She hadn't seen Rory for over seven weeks. She knew he would have received Jim McConville's letter but neither of them had mentioned it during their difficult phone conversations. He was coming to take the kids out to go shopping. Probably to try to buy them off, she thought maliciously. It was the season of goodwill and she had to give in – but she was not prepared to make it easy for him. Every time she thought of him in bed with Anna Maria, she felt her blood pressure rise. Now she even felt hypocritical at the thought of trying to be pleasant to him in what she now thought of as *her* home.

Determined to keep busy, she had all the usual last-minute things to do. She'd decided she'd wrap the presents when she had the house to herself. She had everything else in and had avoided the shops almost totally this year.

The wall-to-wall carols made her even sadder. Johnny Matthis's 'When a Child is Born' really got to her. It had always been her favourite. Now she couldn't listen to any of the Christmas songs at all, especially Chris Rea's 'Driving Home for Christmas'. A few days earlier, it had come on when she was in the supermarket, she'd panicked and had just abandoned her stacked trolley in a checkout queue and run for the seclusion of her car to escape the world of festivity and happiness all around her. She'd persuaded the girls to go with her the following night to stock up – the idea of midnight shopping appealed to them – and much to their surprise, Barry said he'd go along too. She had gone to town a few times with Maeve and they had shopped for the girls together. That was easy – they had practically written out their wish lists. Liam had come to the rescue when it came to buying the latest games technology for Barry. He'd also insisted on paying for his godchild's skiing trip too.

For her the word 'home' had taken on a new meaning – instead of being a safe haven, it had become somewhere to hide, metaphorically, not somewhere cosy and comforting.

Santa Claus was never meant to be a woman, she thought, remembering previous Christmases when they'd always gone to Grafton Street as a family and had had lunch together.

She wondered would she ever be happy again. The doorbell went and Toni was first down the stairs to answer it.

'Dad, Dad, Happy Christmas.' She threw her arms around him. The other two followed, Louise holding back a little while Barry barely accepted a manly pat on the back – after he'd rejected the usual bear hug. Trish came out of the kitchen.

'Hello there,' he said, looking distinctly uncomfortable, 'Happy Christmas.'

Is he for real? Happy Christmas? Happy Christmas! Happy bloody Christmas!

'Whatever,' she muttered.

'The tree looks nice,' he said. 'Were all the lights working OK?'

'I checked them first,' said Barry, implying he was now in charge of those things. Trish almost felt sorry for Rory. She offered him tea.

'I never drink tea,' he replied. 'Have you forgotten that already? Must be some other man in your life,' he said.

'Fat chance,' muttered Barry. 'I'll have some tea before we go, thanks Mum.'

'If you'd got out of bed for breakfast you wouldn't be holding us all up now,' said Toni to Barry.

Trish could see from the expression on their faces that the children were not exactly easy in their father's company. It was going to be a hard day for all of them.

'How are Liz, and Brian and all the kids?' he asked.

'They're all fine,' she replied, not wishing to let him in to any part of her life again. Her sister promised her she'd be ready with the carving knife if he showed up at her door.

Louise asked, 'Dad, do you remember last year we saw Joe Duffy in Grafton Street?'

'Of course I remember.'

'Dad, do you remember what you gave me for Christmas last year?' she asked.

'What's with the twenty questions? I haven't been gone that long you know.'

'Long enough,' said Barry.

Rory decided to ignore this remark and tried for a bit of levity. 'Right then, troops. Have we all been saving our yo-yos to spend? Where are we off to? Grafton Street? Dundrum? Where would you like to go?'

'We'll be going into town with Mum when the sales start,' said Toni, 'and Auntie Maeve.'

'That'll be nice for you,' he said, as he ushered them out, pausing briefly. 'You wouldn't like to come along too, would you?' he asked Trish, as an afterthought.

'I don't think that would be a good idea,' she said. 'Spend the time with the kids. See you later.' She had to force a smile as she said, 'Now don't go spending all your pocket money on presents for me. I don't need anything' – that money can buy, she thought. Then she noticed the car he had hired, a Nissan Micra! Cheapskate! He'd had his own BMW shipped to Belgium. I hope he's not going to be mean with the kids too. She caught Barry by the arm as he passed and whispered, 'Make an effort, love. I know it's hard for you.'

'Like it's easy for you,' he muttered, and slunk out to the car. As she waved them off she saw her son ignore the open front door and squeeze in the back beside his sisters. She went back inside and sat down with a cup of coffee, her mind a mix of emotions. Who was this stranger that she had thought she knew inside out? He had taken on a one-dimensional quality. She couldn't read him any more. Maybe she never could, she began thinking, her thoughts interrupted by the doorbell. One of them must have forgotten something. But there stood Liam, Conor and Maeve.

'Come on, girl, get you glad rags on – we're going out to lunch,' said Liam.

'I can't! I still have shopping to do.'

'Who hasn't?' said Maeve.

'I promised Liz I'd bake the ham for tomorrow.'

'You can do that tonight or even in the morning!'

Outvoted, Trish agreed reluctantly to go along.

'We're meeting Stan in Café en Seine for a drink first,' said Conor.

'That's nice. I haven't seen him in ages.'

'He's trying to persuade Maeve to go back to work in January.'

'Just part-time – well job-sharing really – and I think I will. I miss them all in there and I'm feeling ready to face the world again.'

Derek and Sharonne had gone away skiing with their daughters and no one mentioned Rory as they made their way into the foray that is Christmas Eve in Dublin. Grafton Street hummed with carollers, some wearing Santa hats and flashing reindeer antlers. Collection boxes were shaken for the Simon Community, the St Vincent de Paul Society, the Children's Hospital and numerous other good causes. People jostled by each other, clutching their last-minute purchases and parcels. Overhead garlands of silvery lights glistened, adding to the wonderful atmosphere and, for a while, Trish forgot that this was no ordinary Christmas. Someone had put a holly wreath on the statue of Phil Lynott and as they walked by the flower sellers on the corner of Harry Street, Liam scooped up four bunches of vibrant gerberas and presented them to Trish and Maeve.

'To two of my favourite ladies.'

'Did you hear that? We're only two in a crowd? I'm not sure we should accept these. What do you think, Trish?'

'Well I'm taking mine! They'll be the only ones I'll get this year! Thanks, Liam,' she gave him a big hug.

'Where is your mystery love today?' she whispered to him.

'Family commitments,' he replied, but Conor had heard.

'You're keeping this one a great secret,' he said.

'Yep. I am!' he laughed and said no more.

They cut through South Anne Street and went to rendezvous with Stan, dashing as ever, even with his flashing Rudolf tie. 'I have socks to match,' he laughed, pulling up his trouser leg to show them. He called for a round of drinks and had even managed to get a table too.

'So what are you doing for Christmas?' Trish asked Stan, as they had all divested themselves of their coats and squashed on the little stools.

'Same old, same old. Going back to my mum to be fed and to listen to her tell everyone how we don't celebrate Christmas but Hanukkah! Then she'll proceed to put on a traditional meal that will be the talk of the bridge club for months.'

'Isn't that typical of mothers,' laughed Liam.

'You know, she was quite happy to let me live my own life when I was married to Breda, who couldn't boil water, but since that broke up she feels it's her duty to mother me again. It's not too bad, so long as she's not matchmaking. Her ideas and mine for an ideal mate don't exactly tally. She's determined that I won't make the same mistake again. Mind you she's right there!'

'There's a pair of you in it – you and Liam,' Trish laughed. 'I hear Maeve's going back to work in the New Year. That's great news.'

'Yeah, she's doing well. By the way, I wanted to talk to you about that. Would you be interested in sharing the job with her? Conor doesn't want her doing full-time just yet and I'm inclined to agree with him. The temp we kept on will only be working for another month or two. Maeve could train you in and you could work out your hours between you?'

'I don't know if I'd be able for it. I'm really rusty. I haven't used computers in any serious way at all.'

'There's nothing to it, and you wouldn't have to write up reports or anything like that. My secretary does those. You'd be more front of house, so to speak, looking after the diary, making appointments for follow up consultations, that kind of thing.'

'It sounds just what I need. A new interest.'

'I think so too.'

'What does Maeve think? She won't feel I'm pushing her out will she?'

'Will she what – it was her suggestion!'

'Well, thank you, sir, that's the best Christmas present I could have got,' she said and she gave him a peck on the cheek. Conor caught Trish's eye and winked at her.

They didn't leave town until the crowds had started to thin. On a whim, Trish asked them all back in for mulled wine and mince pies when they dropped her off. They needed no persuading. She was just adding the spice to the wine when the hall door opened and in came the kids with their purchases, followed by Rory. There were greetings all around. He looked pale and ill at ease, and so did Barry. *Oh God, I hope he didn't upset them even more,* she thought.

Stan hadn't seen him since he'd left. 'How's life?' he asked, sticking to a safe topic. 'Getting in any golf over there?'

'Yes, eh, not bad at all. There are a few good courses to choose from, not as challenging as we have here though. I think the best one I've played is in the Brabant Wallon Valley, near Waterloo.'

'Abba sang that, didn't they?' said Toni.

'Know-all,' interjected Barry.

'Do you two never stop?' chimed in Louise. 'Why don't you grow up?'

'Screenagers!' laughed Liam.

'Screenagers? I never heard that before,' said Stan.

'Yep,' said Liam. 'They're the next generation – the ones who spend their time looking at screens – computers, DVDs, Xboxes and iPods.'

'Can I do anything?' Rory asked, not knowing where to put himself. 'Looks like you're having a bit of a party.'

'No, we're just having a drink and everything's under control,' Trish said. Barry asked if he could try some mulled wine.

'No, you're underage,' said Rory.

'Dad – that's if you still want to be called that – don't think you can come swanning back in here and order us around. You forfeited that right when you walked out.'

There was an awkwardness in the kitchen and Liam said, 'Come on, Barry, the season of goodwill and all that – besides mulled wine is for sissies. Save your—'

'Oh, leave me alone,' Barry said, slamming the door before pounding up the stairs. The bubble had burst. The tensions they had all been ignoring exploded. Toni started to cry. Maeve put her arms around her.

'I had hoped Mum and Dad would get back together over Christmas. I don't want loads of presents. That's all I want.'

'Me too,' said Louise, not trusting herself to say any more. Trish felt her eyes fill up. She wouldn't let him see her like this. She turned back to the worktop and sliced some lemons. Maeve just wanted to get away to diffuse the situation, but she couldn't catch Conor's eye. Rory was suddenly the focus of everyone in the kitchen.

'Perhaps I should go.'

Perhaps you should, thought Trish, but with a huge effort she heard herself say, 'There's no need for that. Let's all be civilised and have a drink. After all, it *is* Christmas and the mince pies will be ready in a few minutes. Lou, the napkins are over there.'

Rory went to lift the tray, but she said, 'I'll do that. This is my home, and don't think you can walk back in and play host, because you can't, mate!' She'd have to make more of an effort for the kids' sake, she thought. Stan gave her arm an understanding squeeze as he passed and she said to him, 'If Rory sits in his usual chair I'll pour the mulled wine over him.'

'And I'll help,' said Stan.

He didn't.

They all left in his hire car, teasing Conor about what being seen in the back of a Micra would do to his image if they were spotted by the paparazzi.

'They'll definitely think you are in cahoots with the underworld, going about incognito!'

'I'll pick my jalopy up in the morning,' said Conor.

It had been arranged that they would all go to Conor and Maeve's house the next day. Trish thought it was too much for Maeve, but Conor had whispered that she really wanted to have a normal Christmas – especially after the past few months, so she agreed to go even though her heart wasn't in it. The kids ought to see their dad. Who knew where he'd be next year? They were then going to Liz and Brian's for Christmas dinner and as Liz only lived a five-minute walk away, they didn't have to bother about designated drivers. At least the kids would have some fun with their cousins too.

'See you all tomorrow.'

'Keep the chin up,' said Liam. 'It'll all be over in a few days.'

'I wish it was that simple,' she said.

THIRTY

They had all survived Christmas in their own way. New Year had come and gone with drinks at Conor and Maeve's. After lots of champagne, they'd drunk with optimism to the year ahead, all of them wanting to put the last one behind and willing everything good for the months ahead. Conor, as always, had made sure everyone's glass was topped up and Liam had had the witty quip, to lighten things if they seemed to be in danger of becoming morose.

Sharonne had even behaved herself – she'd never liked New Year's Eve. She and Derek had been away for Christmas with her mother, skiing in Austria where she had celebrated her birthday.

'It's not my favourite time,' she'd said. 'I always find it reflective and sad and, you know, I usually decline invitations to go anywhere to ring in the new one. I often prefer to go to bed before midnight and wake up when celebrations are well and truly over and the New Year's already arrived.'

'Then let's make this one extra special,' Conor had said, trying to shake off an unvoiced fear of what could be ahead.

Trish had got through the holiday season, with everyone making a fuss over the kids and trying to make it good for her. Friends had rallied around and she got more invites than ever. How was it she had never noticed how cosy she had been in coupledom? Now she felt so out of her depth, even among her own friends. She felt they pitied her and she didn't want pity.

***

Rory had gone back to Brussels after five days in Ireland. Nothing had been the same. His being around had put a dampener on Christmas for everyone. His kids were strangers to him and they didn't seem to like him very much any more. He'd felt like a stranger too. Trish was distant and he could see the hurt in her once-sparkling eyes. The only times they seemed to sparkle now was when they were brimming with unshed tears. Gone too was the easy closeness and camaraderie that he had enjoyed with his friends.

Had he made a terrible mistake? If Trish hadn't found out the way she did perhaps things would have been different. Lots of men had mistresses. He could have kept this affair a private matter and if the novelty had worn off, then he would still have had his marriage to go back to. What disgruntled him most of all was that deep down he knew Anna Maria had told Agneta they were seeing each other – knowing that it would get back to Dublin and that, once it did, the proverbial would hit the fan. On one level he knew he had been forced into a decision, on another his male pride would not allow him acknowledge that even to himself. Not yet anyway.

But when he was in bed with Anna Maria these niggly thoughts evaporated completely as he gave himself up to the passion of the moment. Then it all seemed worthwhile. And so right. She was beautiful, desirable and very, very sexy. She was also very demanding. When she was in a relationship nothing else mattered except enjoying herself and going out on the town. She was a woman who was used to getting her own way in everything, it seemed.

He'd continued the habit of phoning the kids a few evenings a week and that often coincided with their mealtimes.

'Do you have to do that just when we are going to eat?' Anna Maria asked.

'Yes I do,' he said, 'it's very important,' staying on longer, trying to engage his family in conversation. He'd given up everything for her so he wasn't going to let her dictate when and for how long he could talk to his children.

Living in the apartment was taking some getting used to and it was all proving to be a bit of a strain. There was no space. There was nothing of Rory's about the place apart from his clothes and his laptop. It was very much a single gal pad, with her make-up potions and lotions filling the bathroom cabinets and her shoes and handbags the closets. It felt more like a hotel than a home.

He missed having the garden to look out at, with footballs and bald patches and vestiges of teenagers strewn about and he found it hard to be comfortable, especially at weekends. He also missed golf in his own club. Paying green fees and being an outsider in the various clubs around Brussels had added to his sense of aloneness. Perhaps he should ask someone to propose him for membership to help him integrate. Funny, he had never minded being away, but he knew deep down that he would never consider this place his home, no matter how long he stayed. Anna Maria and Agneta still went back to Finland every other weekend – to her other life, and it was quite clear that she was not prepared to share that with him yet.

'I must have my own space. This apartment is very small for two people living here all the time,' she had said pointedly, on more than one occasion. Was she trying to tell him something? Was she hinting they should find somewhere bigger? If she was, he decided, he was going to ignore those hints.

'I need to get out into the country and to see my mother too. Besides, you can go home to your family when I am away,' she'd suggested.

He could, but he also knew he couldn't depend on a bed in Conor and Maeve's every time he went back to Dublin. When he'd gone back the last time, he'd stayed in one of the airport hotels. The room there had the same impersonal feeling he got in their apartment in Brussels. Just remembering that made him realise how lonely he was, desperately lonely in fact, for the first time in his life.

Conor, Liam and Derek had all told him the sex-itement would wear off. It hadn't – yet – but he was beginning to question if it was worth the sacrifices. He was also very unhappy at how quickly Trish had gone to a solicitor, and to Jim McConville too. Knowing that he'd have to pay that robber's costs hurt him. He knew he already paid all the bills, but somehow when they were itemised they seemed to amount to so much more. On top of all that he had the commute to and from Dublin – although he could write some of that off against company expenses – but now he had the added car hire and hotel expenses on top of everything else when he visited.

Perhaps he could look at investing in an apartment in Dublin, but with property still going off the scale he was reluctant to even think about that yet. He'd need one large enough for the kids to come and stay, so it would have to have a minimum of three bedrooms and even that would mean the girls would have to share. Trish had made it perfectly clear that she would not allow them stay with Anna Maria, even if they wanted to, which they didn't at the moment anyway, so he would have to put them up in a hotel too and stay there with them himself when they came to Brussels, as he had promised, at Easter. He'd have to try and mend some bridges then and give them a special weekend. He felt he had lost all connection with Barry, and it wasn't a lot better with the girls either, if he was really truthful.

Anna Maria hadn't been at all happy that morning when he told her he didn't want to introduce her to the children just yet. She'd given him the silent treatment ever since and had gone to bed early with a face pack and eye mask, which spelled a very definite Keep Off message. Rory took out his laptop.

There was nothing on the television, apart from the endless repetition of the coverage of yet another atrocity in Afghanistan or Iraq, where suicide bombers had killed indiscriminately again. Both CNN and BBC World News irritated him. They seemed to deal only in fragmented sound bites. In his present mood, he even missed programmes like *Prime Time*. He sat on the leather sofa looking at the shots of his family that Toni had taken on her new digital camera over Christmas. Eventually, he fell asleep there.

***

By the end of January, life had settled down a bit. Maeve had started back working with Stan in the clinic. Delighted to be among her friends there again, she had had a constant stream of visitors all morning. She had to wait five more weeks for her next scan and she did so with trepidation. It was a weird feeling to think that something could be invading your body and you hadn't a clue it was happening. It was even worse wondering if these rogue cells were active again. She had always thought rogue was a rather benign word – a loveable rogue, a charming rogue, a feckless rogue but there was nothing loveable or charming about rogue cells. She put these thoughts aside for more constructive ones. She was feeling much stronger, very positive and certainly much more energetic than she had been coming up to Christmas. She was also looking forward to Trish coming in to work with her.

Trish just wanted things to be normal again. Whatever normal was. In the supermarket she had met a so-called friend at a neighbouring checkout, who, at the top of her voice, had enquired, 'Is he supporting you?' She had felt herself redden, something she hadn't experienced since she was a teenager. What gave people the right to feel they could pry like that? Trish thought later. She thought a lot of things these days, but most of all she realised how important real friendship was. When Sharonne had phoned one day, Trish was being particularly introspective. She'd waited for Sharonne's own brand of insensitivity to follow, along with her theories and suggestions as to what had gone wrong in Trish's life. She had been really surprised by how genuine she had been. And by the apology.

'Trish, we've all been friends for a long time and I know I am often arch bitch when I don't get my way. Rory going has shaken us all and I can't begin to imagine how awful it must be for you having to deal with that and with the kids' emotions too. If you ever want to go out for a few drinks, or come over for a chat, I'll be here. I do mean that.'

Trish had been so overcome she'd just burst out crying. Within an hour, Sharonne had been on her doorstep, with a hamper of make-up from one of the clients she represented.

'I didn't mean to upset you,' she'd said.

'It doesn't take much to do that these days, Sharonne. It wasn't you. It's just that everyone is being so kind and I can't cope with that. I seem to be able to hold on when the kids are around and once they are out of the way I fall to pieces.'

They'd talked for most of the morning.

***

When Trish presented herself at Stan's consulting rooms to learn the ropes, she was as nervous as she had been in any first-day situation, even though she knew Maeve and Stan really well. She had even got to know him better since Maeve had got sick as he often popped in to visit her on his way home when she was there too.

'No need to be apprehensive, Trish,' he said as he welcomed her. 'Siobhan here does all the medical reports, usually from my dictation. No one, least of all me, can read my own handwriting.'

'And his dictation is just as bad,' said Siobhan, turning around from her keyboard. 'He doesn't know a sentence from a paragraph.'

'Well, that's a relief. I'd never be able to spell all those medical terms,' said Trish. 'I'd end up sending guys off for mastectomies and women for vasectomies.' They all laughed.

'Well, we do get some guys in here for mastectomies,' said Siobhan.

'No!' said Trish incredulously.

'Oh yes,' said Stan, 'more often that you ever hear about.'

'Well, what about vasectomies?'

'Now they are still a male exclusive – but we do have some female sterilisations, not routinely but where there are other problems. See how much you've learned already and you're only through the door. You'll be a natural,' said Stan as he went in to his room to await his first patient.

Trish worked three mornings that week, with Maeve in the role of tutor. She learned who to ring to arrange scans and chemotherapy as well as for referrals when patients needed to be sent to another hospital for follow-up treatment. She was astonished at how many patients they got each day from GPs and at just how many people needed to be checked. As the weeks went by, she was also pleasantly surprised at how many of Stan's patients got good news and walked out of his consulting rooms with a reprieve and a new lease of life.

'I love being back in the real world,' she told her sister. 'It's a real escape.'

An escape from her beautiful home, albeit filled with the trappings of three teenagers and which was no longer a refuge for her. She hated it with a passion. It was an unhappy place filled with too many memories. Once she walked through the door sadness enveloped her like a big heavy overcoat. That day, she picked the post up from the carpet noticing there was still nothing from Jim McConville's office or from Rory's solicitor. She wasn't sure who would respond or when she would hear anything, but she felt sure Rory had had time to reflect by now and she wanted to know what was happening.

She felt she was suspended in some sort of time bubble where the future didn't exist and the present was all that mattered. Yet even in this protected zone, she knew in her innermost being that she would have to make changes and accept things that she wasn't yet ready to tackle. She decided to give Jim a ring. She made a cup of tea and then took out the phone directory. He was free to take her call.

'Jim, I am so sorry to bother you.'

'You're not bothering me, Trish, I assure you. How can I help?'

'Have you heard anything from Rory? Anything at all?'

'No, nothing. I ran into his solicitor on Monday in the courts and he says he has been pushing him to reply. I know it leaves you in an untenable situation, waiting and wondering, but I'd advise you to hold on for another few weeks and then we'll send a reminder letter. At least he's not making irrational and hasty decisions.'

'Do you think he may want to sell the house?'

'I have no idea at this stage but, as I said, he's not acting in haste.'

'He already has.'

'Is he still paying the bills and giving you enough to live on?'

'Yes, he hasn't changed any of that to my knowledge.'

'Good. Good. Well we must be thankful for that anyway, Trish. You know the wheels of the law grind very slowly and in my experience that is not always a bad thing, unless there are more children in the interim.'

That hit Trish like a rocket. It hadn't even entered her head that he might start a family with Anna Maria. 'You don't … Do you … Is he?'

'No, no. But we can't rule out that possibility and very often women who get involved with married men become pregnant as a way of keeping them. Sad but true in my experience, especially as it often has the opposite effect.'

She replaced the receiver and wondered for the umpteenth time if he had any regrets at all. Whatever about falling in love with someone, she couldn't grasp how he could just turn his back on his children. Now she had the added fear that he might start another family. She didn't know how the kids would react to that – or indeed how she would either. That, she felt, would be the ultimate betrayal for them all.

THIRTY-ONE

Sharonne and Derek were muddling along in much the same
way as many married couples do. They were cordial and
friendly with each other, in the way that good friends or
siblings were, but not as lovers or a wife and husband should
be. Their relationship had definitely improved but they both
knew it was not back to where it used to be by any means.
They had just eaten dinner. The twins had finished their
homework and they were doing what many families do to
avoid issues – watching television – before going to bed. The
phone rang and there was the usual squabble between the girls
to get to it first.

'It's for you, Mum.'

Sharonne hated to get calls at night. This was her downtime
and, to her, the phone was a work tool.

'Yes?' she said. 'Oh Bob. Hello … No, it's all right. I
understand … Yes, the time difference always gets me too. I
forget they are working now.'

There was a pause before she asked, 'When are you talking
about? Next Wednesday? Just a sec and I'll run it by Derek. It
shouldn't be a problem, but I want to make sure.'

Putting her hand over the mouthpiece she said, 'Derek, Bob
needs me to go to New York for a few days. You are around
next weekend, aren't you?'

'Yes. No problem, I'll be here,' he said, looking at his daughters. The girls were animated with delight.

'Mum can go shopping for us!' said Sandy.

'No, she can't!' Sharonne said putting the phone down. 'She'll be working!'

'When Rosie's mum went over to the States before Christmas she was working and she bought her Abercrombie & Fitch jeans and sweatshirts. Rosie looked them up online and gave her mum a printout of the ones she wanted,' said Megan.

'That was enterprising of her,' said Derek.

'That's what Siobhan and Ciara did too,' she added.

'I don't want anything with big writing on it. I don't want to be an advertising board,' said Sandy.

'Spoiled brats! We were lucky to get a T-shirt,' laughed Sharonne, 'and not from the States either.'

'How long will you be away for, Shar?' Derek asked.

'I think only until Monday night, but Bob will let me know tomorrow. He's sorting the details out. We're nearly at the end of this business and I assume they want me to test the mood and prepare some press releases for them over there. It's vital that we are ready to make announcements on both sides of the Atlantic simultaneously, but I need to meet with their legal people over there so we get the spin just right, and in American as well as English!'

'It's been a lot of work. I bet you won't be sorry when it's wrapped up.'

'No, I won't,' lied Sharonne, sitting back down on the far end of the squashy sofa, willing Christian to be needed in New York too. That way, at least, they would be able to spend some time together.

***

Conor was working late. He'd had a day of meetings and was just getting his papers together when his private line started bleeping. He looked at the number. If it was Maeve, he'd answer – if it was anyone else, then Conor had definitely left the building. It wasn't Maeve. It was Rory. He hesitated for a moment before picking the phone up and saying, 'Hi, there. How's it going?'

'Not so bad. Just wondering how Maeve is doing?'

'She's well, really well. They are all delighted with the way she has responded to the treatments and she's kept her good humour throughout. How are you getting on?'

Conor sensed there was more to this call than an enquiry about Maeve's health.

'Oh, you know, it's quite strange being away from everyone. I've just been on to the kids and they're coming over for a visit next week and quite honestly I'm terrified. Suddenly, I can't talk to them anymore. They treat me as a pariah.'

'I suppose it will take a while for things to settle down for all of you.' He paused before asking, 'Don't you have any regrets at all, Rory?'

'Of course I do. Lots of them. But I made my decisions.'

'You know it's not a crime to admit you made a mistake. We all do, maybe not as publicly as you did, but you can always come back.'

'I haven't made a mistake. Why? Has Trish said she would have me?' he asked.

'No, and that's not what I meant. I meant you could always come back to Dublin, let someone else run the Brussels office. You'd be among friends and close to the kids. They'd appreciate that, you knowing their friends and what's going on in their lives day to day. You must miss them like mad.'

'I don't know. It's not that simple. I do know what's going on in their lives by the way, I'm just not flavour of the month.' There was an edginess creeping into his voice.

'Try sounding them out when they're over. Have you given them a chance to tell you what they want from you?' There was an awkward silence before he filled it by saying, 'No matter what, it'll do them good to have some time with you. How do they feel about meeting Anna Maria?'

'They won't be doing that, not yet. I gave Trish my word, so we're all staying in a hotel in town. Anyway she'll be in Helsinki.'

'Do they want to meet her?' asked Conor, knowing he was pushing him.

'I don't know. I haven't asked. She's not too happy at not getting the chance to, but I had to agree with Trish's demands – that's the condition she's allowing them to come over at all.'

'I suppose she has a point.'

'Do you really think so?'

'I definitely do. If it doesn't work out, it would mean that they had got to know and maybe even become attached to someone else who may disappear from their lives.'

'She not going to disappear, as you put it,' he said defensively. 'And ... I haven't disappeared either.'

'I didn't mean it like that,' said Conor,

'I know what you meant,' he said, 'Look, I have to go now. Say hi to Maeve for me.' And he hung up.

Conor wondered – what was *that* all about?

THIRTY-TWO

'I'm so glad the flight's at a civilised time,' said Sharonne as she shared an early breakfast with Derek, Sabine, and the girls. 'I hate those early transatlantic ones with the scramble at the Aer Lingus check-ins.'

'I know, it's such a pain,' agreed Derek. 'That drive to the airport takes forever, in spite of that extra lane on the M50.'

'Mum, you do have our lists, don't you?'

Sabine laughed, 'Your mother is going to work, not to shop.'

'But New York is full of shops and you can't come back with nothing. What would our friends say?'

'If you're lucky, I'll bring you back some candy!'

'You can't,' said Megan.

'I can!' said Sharonne.

'Mum, you so-ooo totally can't,' said Sandy. 'Besides, I put the list in your laptop case so you'll know where to find it.'

'Come on or we'll all be late,' said Derek. 'Have a good trip and I'll see you Tuesday.' He kissed her cheek and gathered up his things. He'd drop the girls off at school on his way to work. Sharonne saw her taxi arrive.

She hadn't heard from Christian since Bob had asked her to fly to the States. She looked at her watch. If he was going to be in New York, he would probably be on a plane by now. It was already nine o'clock in France. She was excited and had packed carefully, just in case. There was no reason why he should not be there, she reasoned. After all, he was the one who handled European affairs and if they were to get their facts aligned in preparation for the revelations, then they would have to liaise.

***

As she filled in her visa waiver and customs declaration forms she bumped into an acquaintance who worked at another public relations company. They joined the endless queue to get by the US officials. Clearing immigration in Dublin meant she would be able to go straight through at the other end.

'I think we've seen the halcyon days of travel,' she said. 'Do you remember when you dressed up to fly, especially in first class?'

'I do indeed. And no one was ever upgraded wearing denim or runners – before they became trainers. Now they're the height of designer chic.'

'We didn't have to go through this rigmarole either. It was all very civilised then in the good old days.' They laughed.

'I'm off to visit my sister in upstate New York, but she's coming to town for a few days first. Are you going on business or pleasure?' the other woman asked.

'Oh, just for a bit of shopping,' said Sharonne, determined not to let anything out, 'and the kids have even printed out their lists for me.'

'So have mine. What are they like at all? Are we raising little monsters?'

They eventually got through the formalities of fingerprinting and having their photos taken before they were cleared. Sharonne was relieved to see that they wouldn't be seated together on the Continental Airlines flight. She was directed into business class, and there was even a vacant seat beside her. She had thought she would do a bit of work but when seated, a glass of champagne and orange in her hand, she realised she felt tired and gave it a miss. Once airborne she plugged in her headphones and tuned in to the classical music channel and started to think of Christian. But she was quickly asleep.

***

The driver was standing waiting with her name printed on a card when she emerged in Newark. She had managed to avoid her friend in the melee of baggage reclaim. It was a damp lunchtime in New York as the traffic wove its way through the streets. Sharonne was always surprised at how hick and dowdy the approach was – clumps of little huckster shops and old wooden houses, an enormous cemetery and lots of fast food outlets, acres of billboards and webs of overhead wires. Then, as always, the skyline of Manhattan emerged ahead and she admired its jagged-tooth appearance and looked forward to the glamorous sophistication of downtown. She loved this city and it was a while since she had been there. Lost in her reverie she was outside Fitzpatrick's Hotel on Lexington before she realised it.

'Welcome back, Mrs Lenihan,' said the receptionist. 'Your colleagues are in the dining room waiting for you. Would you like to go up to your suite to freshen up first?'

'That's a good idea,' she said. 'Please tell them I've arrived.'

The lift doors opened immediately. She knew exactly where her suite was as this hotel was always her home from home in the city. Popping her laptop case and handbag on the sofa she went through to the bedroom. She unzipped her case, hung her garment bags in the walk-in closet, applied some deodorant, put on a fresh top, ran her fingers through her hair and refreshed her lipstick. Picking up her room key card, she headed for the lift again. She could feel the adrenalin pumping through her, her heart rate making its presence felt in the silence. She was sure she was about to see Christian again. They had only talked, albeit very seductively, numerous times since the night they had got together. She felt a surge of guilt whenever she thought about it, yet the heady excitement she now felt in anticipation of a repeat performance swept all such annoying thoughts from her mind. What was it theatrical folk always say – what happens on tour stays on tour? No one need ever know.

Entering the dining room, she glanced around, missing the table where the three men were waiting for her, until they stood up buttoning jackets as though choreographed. They welcomed her to the city. Ed and Marty from the New York office and Jonathan Whyte from the London one.

Where was Christian? There was no sign of him and she noticed the table was set for four and felt really let down. Perhaps he'd been delayed.

'Sorry, I didn't hear what you said,' she uttered as Marty held her chair out for her. 'They've changed this place since I was last here.'

'Yes, they have,' Marty said. 'Now let's get down to work.'

'Yes, let's,' she muttered, remembering such directness was the way they did business in this town. No pussyfooting about the weather and traffic as was mandatory preamble in Dublin. They praised her for the successful smoke screen she had conjured up to keep the shareholders unaware of what actually had happened prior to the original FitzGerald-Reglob merger.

'Just to clarify things,' said Ed, 'I'll recap and if you have any questions, Jonathan, feel free to interrupt. So far our investigations have uncovered accounts in Jersey, the Cayman Islands, some investment in the developments of the Dubai Towers as well is in a block, possibly two, in the Sport City developments in Dubai. There are also considerable cross-border investments in Belfast and Derry, made in anticipation, no doubt, of the inevitable rising prices as devolution became effective and trends in property prices there followed those in the UK and the Republic.'

'But how did no one twig what they were up to?' asked Jonathan?'

'Cleverly, when Reglob and FitzGerald amalgamated some years ago, they took advantage of the business culture in Ireland. I'm not sure how much FitzGerald knew of what was going on then. Reglob is a formidable character and he apparently made it quite clear that he would deal with some of his clients exclusively. That all seemed perfectly logical and, once it was accepted in the company, no one thought anything more about it. That was just the way things were done there.'

'They know all the tricks of company laws and avoidance,' said Sharonne.

'He covered himself well. He subdivided the business so there were several operations doing different things. It was the small hedge fund management one that he put Jim Murray in charge of that set the alarm bells ringing. Murray kept trying to ferret out information but Reglob always said, "They're my clients, old friends, you needn't concern yourself about them." An overheard conversation at the golf club led Murray to become suspicious. A few guys in the locker room were discussing the stock market wobble of a few months earlier and one, an actuary, said, "I had my funds with FitzGerald-Reglob and I lost nearly everything." Another one said he did too.

'Jim Murray knew for certain that neither of their companies was registered with the fund management company he was heading. Nor had he ever come across their names in other documentation. When he left the clubhouse, he drove to his office and started to check the records. Not a mention of either one of them. He concluded that perhaps they were just bragging to their friends, to make it look as though they were higher rollers than they were, but he was bothered by the conversation just the same.

Ed continued, 'It burrowed into Murray's mind and he decided to ask Reglob about it on the following Monday. Reglob said they were still listed with them since before the merger and that he looked after them personally as they were friends who had had some outstanding tax issues and asset liabilities which he was trying to sort out, without these becoming general issue in the office. Murray accepted this but he had a hunch that something was not quite right. And he kept searching away when everyone had gone home in the evenings. He was to discover that those two accounts and numerous other companies were registered to a small fund management company in Luxemburg.

'How did they get away with it for so long?' asked Marty.

Sharonne replied, 'You have to remember that in the nineties corporate governance was not such a big issue in Ireland. We had just come though a terrible decade with excruciating interest rates, huge emigration and then the country was suddenly awash with cash. The Celtic Tiger was roaring across the land and the onus on tax compliance was not regulated like it is today. There were many companies then that were not compliant and the subsequent tax amnesties allowed many of them avoid penalty and prosecution altogether.'

Ed nodded in agreement, 'It was at that point that Murray started to record things when he realised that the accounts technicians had been told by Reglob himself that nobody was to have access to certain accounts without his written permission. It transpired that FitzGerald was the only other one with their banking information.'

Sharonne interrupted, 'The directors of the subsidiaries were such in name only and paid well enough to prevent them making waves. Murray talked to a friend of his in the Garda Bureau of Fraud Investigations – that's the Irish police – and he told him there was no point in letting any of this out until he had an unbroken chain of evidence. Once, and only if, he could get that could they move. Hence the need for such secrecy over the past months.'

'Did no one else suspect anything?'

'No. Apparently not. Both Reglob and FitzGerald are very persuasive and personable guys. They never let anything slip. FitzGerald has been very clever with the way he has divided the portfolio as well – mostly in property and practically all in tax-free zones.'

The discussion continued through the morning. It transpired that FitzGerald had also taken a director's loan against client monies and that offence alone was enough to have him jailed. Murray went to the financial regulator and after several weeks discovered there were numerous other clients whose accounts did not reconcile with the disclosed figures.

'To think they almost got away with it,' said Jonathan.

'And the sweetest part is that the pair of them still think they have,' said Sharonne.

'You'll have to make sure they're both in Ireland when this goes public, otherwise they'll just do a runner to somewhere that has no extradition agreement with the EU and where, no doubt, they have funds secreted for just such a contingency,' Jonathan replied.

'That shouldn't be difficult,' said Sharonne. 'Let Reglob think he's up for some business award and he'll be there, chest puffed out and surrounded by his acolytes. His ego wouldn't be able to resist.'

They all laughed as they visualised the scene of Pieter Reglob and his associates arriving ready to collect an award, only to be handed a bench warrant for embezzlement and fraud instead.

Marty shuffled some papers, took a drink of water and said, 'We're ready to roll with that now so we need you all, in New York, Dublin and London, to be up to speed and to issue a joint statement when the arrests are made, or at least when the news of pending charges break in the next few weeks. And that's really why you're all here. We'll treat this as a dummy press conference so that we have all the right answers to the awkward questions those bastards in the media will bombard us with once the story breaks. There's a hell of a lot of money at stake and some of these investors are seriously high players. They're not going to like the fact that they will be seen as incompetent by their clients, so they will be looking for a scapegoat to blame, any scapegoat.'

'That's true,' said Jonathan. 'But it'll be a pleasure to nail fraudsters like them.'

'It certainly will,' Ed agreed.

'Well, Sharonne, we have you to thank in no small measure for not letting anything out. Some of those decoys you dished out to the media were mightily impressive. And you should take a bow – the CIA could do with your skills,' said Marty.

'It has been quite a challenge and I have to admit I am really looking forward to the reaction when we do the reveal, as you would call it. By the way, shouldn't someone from the European office be here?'

'Oh they should be by now,' he replied, looking at his watch. 'We'll all meet at 8.30 tomorrow in the boardroom at the office for the run-through. Meantime if you come up with any angles you think we may not have covered make a note of them.'

With important documents saved, a gathering of papers, and a scramble for laptop cases, they went their separate ways. Sharonne stopped at the reception desk to enquire if there were any messages. 'No Ma'am, nothing for you.'

Dejected, she made her way to the lifts. Typical of the Americans, she thought. If they had come to Dublin we'd have made sure they had company on their first night in town. They never even thought to ask where I would be eating. Then she rationalised she had already lost six hours, so an early night would be no bad thing. She decided to order room service and go over her paperwork in bed. While eating, she watched some noisy game show with lots of shouting and even more ad breaks than at home. She hated American television. She pressed the remote control and the flat screen darkened.

She had some tidying to do to ensure the months of work drew to a satisfactory conclusion for her clients. Their company was heavily involved with the prestigious annual Irish Business and Corporation Awards. She would invite both partners of FitzGerald-Reglob along, with a nod and a wink that they may just be among the main recipients, and they'd be sure to turn up. However, she knew she needed to come up with a contingency plan just in case they decided to flit off to Barbados or somewhere for a few rounds of golf in the sun.

She would have to make time to buy the girls' presents and something for Derek too. She really had been a bitch to him, and the fact that she could pinpoint the night when things had really started to go wrong didn't make her feel any better about it. She knew she should have handled that differently. She had let herself down badly and behaved like a spoiled child – she had acted in a way that she would not have tolerated from Megan or Sandy or indeed in any of her staff. She also knew she had always been jealous of Maeve. Now she admired her courage and optimism and she wouldn't trade places with her for anything.

THIRTY-THREE

Maeve was still wrapped in her favourite fluffy dressing gown. She was being lazy this morning and had stayed in bed to finish the book she was reading. Her hair re-growth was just beginning to appear, itchily admittedly, and she enjoyed the freedom of not having her wig on for a while. She came down and made some toast and a pot of tea and sat at the counter, savouring her surroundings.

Conor had had a very early start. He'd told her they were about to embark on interrogating a senior politician and the media were baying for more revelations. This one was a slippery character, whom everyone knew had been behind many shady dealings, bribes in brown envelopes and illogical rezonings of land, netting enormous sums of money for various cartels and the like.

It was one of those mornings when everything seemed clear and bright. Maeve could see things with a Technicolor feel to them. On the windowsill, the crimson cyclamen held their heads up defiantly from the little galvanised containers she had bought in Bercy in Paris. They were joined together with a wooden handle and she had had to stuff her underwear into them to make them fit in her suitcase and stop them getting bent on the way home. The blue and white milk carton on the countertop seemed to be more vivid than ever and the red writing on the yellow wrapper on the sliced bread was almost violent in its contrast. Outside, one part of the sky was a postcard blue with a dense menacing grey creeping over from the sea. The blue reminded her of Spanish days.

She walked into the conservatory, her favourite room. What was it they said about conservatories in the interiors magazines in the waiting rooms at the clinic – 'the latest must-have is a room to bring the outside in'. Well, she thought, it certainly does that. Outside the daffodils stood out in their intensity against the dark wood chipped beds and, although she had always liked the paper whites and paler varieties best, she had to admit that sprinkling the more vibrant narcissi between them had been an inspired decision. The clematis that had been pruned almost to extinction for winter were bravely pushing themselves up to reach the lower supports on the walls. Another few weeks or so and I'll be able to stake those up, she thought. From the tubs on the steps of the conservatory, the tiny faces of the purple and yellow winter pansies nodded and seemed to wink at her as the icy winds sporadically gusted savagely. Suddenly a few snowflakes started to fall. Beautiful large white fluffy flakes. They stopped after a few minutes.

She decided to spend the morning planting some sweet pea seeds. She got the potting compost and the little individual pots she had bought the week previously. She remembered her father steeping the seeds first and checked the instructions. These ones didn't require such treatment. The packet said: 'Unwins Old Fashioned Mixed – Lathyrus odoratus "grandiflora mix", so popular in Victorian times. Their delicious scent will transport you to a more romantic world.' She knew it would. Her father's always had, and sweet peas had been her mother's all-time favourite.

She moistened the compost and filled all the individual pots as directed; then she took five of the round black seeds and placed them, evenly spaced, in each container. Topping them up with a further light covering of more soil she carried them back into the conservatory. When she had finished, the leaden cloud had almost totally obliterated the blue sky and the snow was falling again, heavily this time, cloaking her garden unevenly as though with a loosely woven fabric. She opened the door and walked outside into that special silence that only accompanies falling snow. She stretched her arms out and looked up towards the swirling spots, feeling them fall on her head, her nose and cheeks, only to melt seconds later. Just like bubbles. She closed her eyes as the flakes landed on them. It's good to be alive, she thought, and whirled around and around like a child. The sound of the doorbell brought her back to earth. She didn't know how long she had been there but the tallest blades of grass were completely covered and she realised she was shivering. She ran back inside to open the door.

It was Trish. 'Oh I hope I didn't get you out of bed. I should have rung first,' she said, taking in the dressing gown.

'No, I was in the garden.'

'You were what? Are you mad? You'll get pneumonia.'

'Don't be a fusspot. I was just savouring the feeling of being a child again. Besides, I may never get another chance to see the snow.'

'Now I really am worried about you. You never talk like that. What brought this on? You haven't found anything else have you?'

'No. I promise. Just a feeling I got when it started to snow. You know, despite all the places I've been in my life, I never went skiing and I began to think that maybe it's too late to do it now.'

'There you go again, being all morbid on me. I'll tell you what we'll do: we'll go skiing next winter – to some super luxurious resort with great après-ski and gorgeous instructors – well they're for me really – you can have the après-ski. Now that I'm earning, I'll save every cent for that. What do you think?'

'That's definitely one of your better ideas.'

'Now get upstairs and have a hot shower, I'll put the kettle on.'

'Two good ideas in one day. Work must be good for you.'

'Cheeky bitch!' Trish swiped a tea towel at her, as she began clearing the compost off the worktop.

THIRTY-FOUR

Sharonne had picked at her meal, stepped out of her business suit and the frilly flesh-coloured underwear she had put on in anticipation of a rendezvous with Christian. The room was overheated and she turned the temperature down before climbing into the oversized bed. She spread her paperwork around her and perched the laptop on her knees. It wasn't long before her eyes started closing as she tried to concentrate. Her phone rang on the locker. She realised immediately that it was late at night at home and a panic rose inside her. Could something be wrong?

'Cherie, did I wake you?' came the seductive tones through the receiver.

'No no, just drowsy,' she said, now totally awake. She sat up straight in bed and several sheets of paper floated to the floor; she managed to grab her laptop before it followed them.

'I am so sorry. Go back to sleep and I'll call you tomorrow.'

'No really, I'm wide awake now. Where are you? Are you in New York?'

'Just downstairs, actually. Can I come up?'

She jumped out of bed and said, 'Yes, but give me ten minutes.'

'OK cherie, à bientôt.'

She hung up, gathered all the papers in a bundle and shoved

them into her briefcase. She'd sort them in the morning. The phone rang again. Damn, who is that? she thought, and thought about ignoring it.

She didn't. It was Christian. 'Room number, cherie? You wouldn't want me going to the wrong one, would you?' he asked. She laughed and gave it to him then ran into the shower, tucking her hair up into the polythene shower cap.

In seconds, she was out from under the powerful jets and drying herself off. She took her flimsy underwear, black with blush-coloured lace this time, from the drawer and put it on. She pulled her brush through her hair, added a spray of perfume, a touch of tinted moisturiser, lip-gloss and she was ready. She liberated a slinky robe from its hanger, straightened the duvet and kicked her high heels to touch under the bed. She heard his knock as she dimmed the lights. She opened the door. She could hardly see him behind the enormous bunch of flowers he was holding up.

'Room service, madam,' he said, as he lowered them and leaned forward to kiss her, moaning softly as he did so. She didn't hear the lift door open just around the corner. The passengers it disgorged walked towards the room next door to Sharonne's.

'Come in, come in,' she said, tugging at Christian's arm but not before she caught a glimpse of Cathy Walshe, the woman she had met at the airport. 'Shit, bugger and damn – of all the places in all the world, why did she have to come along just then,' she raged, as she closed the door behind Christian. The other woman with her must be her sister. She explained to Christian who they were. Guilt and shame at being caught and fear of being found out by anyone else sent panic through her. Had she seen her? Or Christian and his flowers?

'The bloody Irish are like homing pigeons – they all come here as though it was the only hotel in Manhattan,' she said illogically, offering Christian a seat. She put the flowers on the coffee table.

'That's a bottle of red from the hotel owner. He always does that when I stay. I usually never got around to opening it and usually give it to the person who services the room.'

Christian picked it up and read the label. 'This looks good but I'll only open it if you'll join me.' She nodded. Deftly he uncorked the bottle and poured, sniffing the contents before he came towards her and handed her one of the glasses. He kissed her again. A slow, tantalising kiss. She waited for the tingle, the tingle she felt whenever she remembered the last time and when she envisaged this moment. But there was none.

She sat down on the sofa. She was really shaken by what had just happened. Suppose this got out in Dublin. What if Derek found out? How would she explain kissing a man laden with flowers, when she was in a sexy robe, and then bringing him into her hotel room? It even sounded seedy and cheap, and she was neither. The mood had changed completely. She just wanted Christian to go. She had too much to lose.

Ever the practised lover, he read the situation and decided to bide his time. He put his jacket on a chair, turned his phone to silent and sat down beside her on the sofa, not too close but not too far away either. He put his arm along the back and crossed his knees in her direction.

Sharonne was very aware of his presence and she began to talk of safe subjects. 'Thank you for the flowers – they're lovely. When did you get in?'

'This afternoon. I couldn't make the meeting as Françoise and I had to tie up a few things in Paris before we left.'

'Françoise is with you?'

'Of course. I can't live without my right-hand woman.'

'Where are you staying?'

'I had hoped it might be here,' he said, moving slightly towards her, stroking her neck with feathery strokes. Nothing happened.

She didn't know what to say. He continued, 'We're in the

Marriott Marquis in Times Square. Not my favourite place but alors, it was all very last minute.'

The 'we' again rattled her.

'Today's meeting was very successful, I think. Marty, you know Marty, he was very—'

'Let's not waste time talking about business, cherie.' He moved closer still and she could feel the heat of his body next to hers. Her heart was pounding.

'You'll be very happy with the results.'

'Stop talking work – this is *our* time.'

He raised his hand, sliding it under her wrap, and began to fondle her breast. She recoiled, flustered and stood up.

'I can take a hint. You have a headache, is that what you say in Ireland when you want to put your man off?' he asked, and she sensed annoyance in his voice.

'Christian you are not "my man" and I have been up since six this morning and it's now half eleven at night at home – add six hours to that for the time difference and it means I have missed a night's sleep already,' she said.

'You haven't. Your watch has,' he rationalised.

'Explain that to the others when I fall asleep at the breakfast meeting tomorrow.'

He downed the rest of his wine in one long swallow and said, 'Then I'll be off.' He stood, picked up his mobile, and checked the screen, muttering something about a missed call. He tapped a number and kept looking at Sharonne. It was answered immediately,

'Françoise, cherie, sorry I couldn't take your call. I was otherwise engaged … Non, nothing important, nothing important at all,' he said, holding Sharonne's gaze. 'Oui, oui, I'm on my way now … Be ready for me. À bientôt…'

'You bastard. Get out!' she said evenly to him. 'And before you go, you might like to remember that just because you're French that doesn't automatically make you a good lover. You were pathetic that night in Dublin and that's why I have, as you say "a 'eadache". I didn't want you to be an embarrassment to yourself – again.'

He blanched, took his jacket, picked the bouquet up from the table and said, 'I don't suppose you'll be needing these …'

The frame shook as he slammed the door behind him. Sharonne sat back down again and stayed on the sofa for a long time, wrapping her robe more tightly around her. She was shocked at his reaction, his insensitivity as to how she might be feeling at being caught out and at his dismissal of her. What a fool she had been. She was mad with herself for having allowed this situation to happen in the first place. How had she been so easily flattered? If Derek found out, her life and that of the girls would be ruined. She eventually went to bed but didn't close her eyes all night.

THIRTY-FIVE

Liam phoned Trish to see how things were going. 'Any news from the solicitor or the great adulterer?' he asked.

'No, nothing at all, but I got tired waiting and phoned Jim McConville the other day. He seems to think that no news is good news as it may mean Rory is really thinking things through and not making hasty decisions to sell the house. I feel like he hasn't really grasped the fact that Rory rushed into this relationship like a tornado and rationale doesn't seem to be part of his psyche any more.'

'Well, for what it's worth, I'm sure Jim knows what he's talking about. He has a lot of experience with marital breakdown and although he doesn't come across like a fierce terrier, believe me, he is.'

'Anyway, thank you for asking. Lou is still talking about her ski trip and her benevolent godfather.'

'I hope you told her that it's her sixteenth, eighteenth, twenty-first and wedding presents all rolled into one!'

'I did!' she laughed. 'And thanks for taking Barry to the car show too. He loved it. Anyway, how are you and what are you up to?'

'Not a lot. Loads of travelling. I seem to be living out of my suitcase these days. I'm trying to block off a few weeks for myself in May.'

'And the love life?'

'I wondered when you'd ask about that.'

'Well …'

'Like I told you, you'll be the first to know – that's a promise. It's early days yet and I'm still not sure how I feel.'

'OK, I won't ask again.'

'Promise?' he laughed. 'Give the kids my best and let me know if there are any developments.'

'I will. They're off to Rory for the weekend and I know they are dreading it. Mixed feelings all around.'

'Ah so you'll have a free gaff – can we have a party?' he joked.

'You know, that's not a bad idea. I haven't done any entertaining since he went. Maybe if I did, I'd start to feel a bit more normal again. Are you around – and your friend?'

'Me, yes; my friend, no – but if you're cooking you won't keep me away.'

'Right. Saturday 7.30 it is.'

'Why don't you just do drinks?'

'Because I have this awful feeling that I will hate the emptiness in the house and it'll give me something to do. It's very short notice though.'

'No it's not. Sounds like you've got a plan. I know Derek is on his own – Sharonne's away on business. You could ask Stan – he'll go anywhere for a good meal.'

'Was that supposed to be a compliment?'

'That kinda came out the wrong way. I'll come around early and give you a hand.'

'No way – I'm one of those Gordon Ramsay types who will take my bad temper out on my assistants, so you're better off staying out of my kitchen.'

'OK, I can take a hint.'

'See you about half seven Saturday then – and thanks for being there for us, as always.'

THIRTY-SIX

Sharonne forced herself out of bed. She had a real headache, a pounding-over-the-eyes-hurts-to-even-blink kind of one. She still had to sort out the papers she had put away so hastily the night before. It was only 6.45, but she knew she needed to look her best and appear on top of things this morning. She wasn't going to let that French prick think he had upset her.

Although she usually skipped breakfast, she rang down and ordered some juice, tea and toast to her room. She took care with her make-up and clothes, and tonged her hair to give more movement to her bob. Glancing in a full-length mirror on the way down in the lift she thought – you certainly look a hell of a lot better than you feel.

She was early, but that was part of her game plan – to get there first and be in control. She took the documents out, positioned the laptop in front of her and was quite settled when Christian and Françoise arrived, followed seconds later by Marty, Ed and Bob. She smiled at them all as they exchanged morning greetings. Christian asked how she was feeling. 'Not too jet lagged I hope?'

'No, not at all,' she lied. 'I had a wonderful sleep last night.'

The other parties arrived and they got down to business seriously, playing out every possible scenario that could ensue when they went public with their findings. Fortunately for Sharonne, she became so immersed in the matters in hand that she forgot about Christian. When they broke at twelve, Marty suggested they all lunch together.

'Sorry, but could I be excused? I have to do some shopping for my girls or I needn't go home. I haven't been to New York for a while and as all their friends have been with their mothers I'm already in their bad books.'

'I know the feeling,' said Marty. 'I get the same instructions when I go to Europe. I don't know who is worse – my wife, my kids or my sisters.' They all laughed. 'Off you go and we'll see you tomorrow morning.'

'Enjoy your lunch,' she said to everyone. She took a cab back to the hotel, deposited her things and walked the two blocks to Bloomingdales. She took the nearest escalator and found herself facing a department filled with Easter bunnies, chickens and decorated eggs. The colourful displays drew her in and, on impulse, she bought a whole lot of the decorations. She knew the girls would love them and she could just visualise them hanging on some twigs on the console table in the hall at home. Delighted with her purchases, she wandered through the swanky store – posh and sophisticated on one hand, while still managing to be hick and out-dated on the other. She smiled at the price tags on some of the handbags, resisting all temptation to add to her ever-growing collection. She'd have to do some pruning when she got home but these days she never seemed to have time to get around to sorting out her wardrobe.

When it came to shoes she was not as disciplined. It was her ever-rising number of these that had made her convert one of the bedrooms into a dressing room. She knew she would have to visit the designer shoe department. Immediately one pair caught her eye – black with cheeky striped bows, peep-toes and very tall heels in the latest spindle shape. The inside of the heels was lined with the same stripe as the bow detail. She took them up to try on when she spotted Cathy Walshe and her sister at the other side of the department, laughing together. They had lots of shopping bags between them. They must have started early, she thought. This was the perfect opportunity to put things straight about last night. She made a beeline across the floor to them.

'Sharonne, doing some damage to the credit card?' Cathy said when she saw her.

'Possibly. Isn't it all very tempting? We just can't buy shoes like this in Dublin.'

Introductions were made and Sharonne said, 'I do hope my visitor didn't disturb you leaving last night. I'm afraid he got carried away. We had worked on a deal some time ago and when he heard I was in town, he decided to surprise me with flowers. I think he may have visited one cocktail bar too many on his way, and I had to threaten to have him removed from my room. He was so offended he took his flowers off with him when he left and he nearly took the door off the hinges.'

'I don't believe it!' Cathy said.

'Well you can. He's French you know – fragile egos.'

'Did he really take the flowers back with him?' asked the sister.

'Word of honour! But that was after he'd phoned his PA to see if she was available.' They all laughed and, relieved, Sharonne felt a weight had been lifted.

'You ladies look as though you have been busy,' she said, eyeing their booty. 'Do you fancy stopping for a little lunch or have you eaten already?'

'No, we were just about to find somewhere.'

'There's a great little deli around the corner that I've been to before. They make an amazing array of sandwiches there.'

'That's a great idea. Lead the way,' said Cathy.

They headed for the busy elevators, merging with the lunchtime shoppers, and were just leaving when a suited man put his hand on Sharonne's arm.

'Will you accompany me, ma'am?'

'Who are you?' she asked, looking at this clean-cut individual.

'Store security.'

'But what do you want with me?'

'If madam will accompany me I will tell you,' he said, looking at the others. 'I think you had best come along too.'

He indicated to the elevators and the three women walked in ahead of him. Sharonne looked at the other two in puzzlement and then saw she was still carrying the $725 shoes she had picked up to try on.

'Oh my God,' she said. 'I never put the shoes back when I met you two.'

'No, ma'am, you didn't,' said the store detective evenly, muttering under his breath, 'funny that happens quite a lot.' It was only when he turned around in the lift that she noticed the discreet earpiece.

They all looked at her. She could see disbelief in their eyes. They had to know she was innocent. They had no plans to meet. This was a terrible mistake. For one second, she expected to see a camera and one of those cheesy television presenters pop out from the opening lift doors shouting, 'You've been pow-azzed' or zapped or whatever word they used now for being set-up, but she knew that wasn't going to happen. They were escorted along a corridor and through a maze of offices where they got funny looks from staff working behind the windows en route.

'Look, I can explain,' Sharonne began.

'Not to me,' the suit drawled. His nametag said Chuck Decker Junior. She'd never forget that. 'You'll have plenty of time to do that later, lady, but not to me.'

She looked at Cathy, who seemed to be very embarrassed by the whole situation. Could she really think I was trying to steal the shoes – that I was using them as a decoy? Sharonne was lost for words. She knew only too well why she had forgotten to put them back, or even try them on. Her worries about making sure that Cathy didn't carry any tales back home had blocked everything else from her mind. But how could she convey this without letting everyone know what she had almost been up to with Christian? They were shown into a room with numerous chairs, a large table, several screens, a phone and precious little else.

Chuck Decker Junior spoke into his mouthpiece. 'I have the suspects from the shoe department in the interrogation room now.'

'Look, there has been an awful mistake. These women have nothing to do with this … I just met them by accident. I wasn't …'

'Save it, lady. Like I said, I don't need to know the details. I just know what I saw.'

That was what worried Sharonne. She ran this nightmare scenario back in her head as they waited for whoever was on the other end of the little radio to turn up. This trip was turning into a disaster.

'Look, you are mistaken,' said Sharonne.

'Like I said, lady, save it.'

Neither Cathy nor her sister said anything. Sharonne waited, more panicked than she had ever been. Who do you call in a strange city? Would she be arrested? Could she explain that she was upset? A woman carrying a bag full of Easter bunnies, decorated eggs and other seasonal trinkets? She looked down at her hands and they were shaking.

The doors opened eventually and a sombrely dressed woman came into the room, followed by a burly guy with an egg yolk yellow tie, who wouldn't look out of place as a bouncer in Leeson Street. Chuck Decker Junior gave his side of the story.

'I saw the suspect,' pointing at Sharonne, 'pick the shoes up, admire their fine craftsmanship, seeming to consider what they would go with and decide to try them on.' He was enjoying this. You'd think he was on *Judge Judy* instead of at a backroom questioning. 'But she didn't do that. Instead she made a dash across the department to two women who seemed to be waiting for her to join them and together they went to the escalators.'

'That's not true,' said Cathy.

'He put his hand up to silence her and continued, 'I followed them down and stopped them leaving the store. The suspect was still carrying the shoes and had made no attempt to open her pocketbook for money or to go near a cash desk to pay for them. Neither had her accomplices.'

Cathy tried, 'We're not accomplices …'

The shoes sat on the table between them, and although Sharonne was well used to reading people, she knew they were the ones being assessed here. Three shoppers from out of town, well dressed, with money in their pockets, buy a few things then steal a few others, then move on to the next store.

'Where are you staying in New York?' asked the uniformed man.

'In Fitzpatrick's – just up the street,' they all replied.

'Convenient. Room numbers?' he replied.

They gave them.

'When did you arrive in New York – you came together I presume?'

'No. Well, Cathy and I did – I mean we were on the same plane, but not together.'

'I'm from Upstate New York, West Seneca,' said her sister.

'You didn't come to New York together, but you just happen to get two rooms beside each other in a city with 72,000 bed spaces?'

Sharonne felt she was drowning – everything she said seemed to damn her even more.

'I think you may need to find an attorney,' the woman said.

She'd asked them to call Marty or Ed – they would know how to sort this out.

'Now let me get this straight,' said the security man again.

'You flew in yesterday with this lady, but you didn't sit together on the plane; you just happen to be staying in the same hotel next to each other, but you say you're not together.'

'We're not,' interrupted Cathy.

'I've not finished yet, lady,' he continued, turning his bug-eyed gaze back to Sharonne. 'You pick up a pair of shoes, very expensive shoes and these women, your accomplices …'

'We're not …'

'Your accomplices just happen to be waiting for you at the other side of the department. You all go downstairs and try to leave the store, together, without paying for the item' – sweeping his hand in the direction of the offending spoils – 'or were you going to come back in and pay for them later?'

'I never even tried them on,' Sharonne said, hoping to make sense of this ridiculous situation. And at the same time wondering how she could ever even have liked them.

'I noticed that,' agreed the man who had followed them. Before she could answer, he had turned to Cathy and her sister. 'May I see all of your purchases and receipts. One at a time, please.'

Cathy tried to explain what had happened but Sharonne knew she was having doubts herself – wondering if Sharonne could really be a shoplifter fortuitously involving them in her sordid game. She had told her she was going to New York to shop, now she knew Sharonne was here to work and had lied about that to her. Yet Cathy knew she was not lying about the guy with flowers and that she had heard the door slamming a little while later as he left her suite. Oh good God, perhaps she thinks he is in on this shoplifting racket too?

Cathy turned out her purchases on the table; they matched her Visa receipts and satisfied the inquisitors. Her sister did the same. Their garments amounted to hundreds of dollars. Then Sharonne displayed her goods and the forty-five dollar receipt that she has shoved in the bag with them.

'Your pocketbook too,' he ordered.

What a stupid name for a handbag, she thought, as she unzipped the fastening and pushed it across the table for closer scrutiny. The guy with the yellow tie pushed it back and said, 'Ma'am, if you wouldn't mind …'

'Of course,' she said, sounding much more confident than she felt. The first thing that came out were the A4 sheets of paper her children had given her – with colour printouts and style numbers – their shopping lists for Abercrombie & Fitch.

'What are these?' asked the woman, who had not said much until then.

'I have twin girls with very different tastes and they gave me their shopping list before I left.'

'Convenient,' was her enigmatic reply. Sharonne was now convinced that they thought she was stealing to order.

'Will you please let these people go? They have nothing whatsoever to do with this predicament.'

'We can't do that just yet,' explained the woman quietly. That was even more unnerving. New Yorkers were seldom quiet.

She ordered coffee for them while they waited for Marty or Ed to arrive. Sharonne was so shocked she could think of nothing to say. She had done nothing wrong. She had been so het up about her stupidity that the relief of seeing Cathy across the department presented the opportunity of staving off any gossip back home. She had just acted on impulse, the fact that she had just picked up the shoes had been forgotten completely. She knew she would have noticed she was still carrying them when she sat down in the restaurant and she would have gone back to pay for them.

It seemed like hours before the door opened to admit her colleagues. To compound the chain of events, Christian was with them. Sharonne felt the blood draining from her face and thought she was about to faint. He smiled at her and she wanted to scream at him, This is all your bloody fault.

Everyone seemed to be talking at once in the crowded office. They handed their business cards to the woman, who scrutinised them, while Sharonne sat there, watching as though this was happening to someone else. She was numb. She had said her piece and it hadn't made any difference. Now they were arguing and suddenly it was only Christian's voice she heard.

'I am the European lawyer for the company Sharonne is working with. She is a woman of impeccable integrity. I know because I have been at the wrong end of her high standards. She isn't capable of stealing. I can verify what these ladies say about Sharonne being upset. I know she had an unpleasant experience last evening.' Ed and Marty were watching him closely, not sure what was coming next. 'These ladies saw me trying to impress Sharonne at her hotel. I didn't succeed,' he said, looking at her. 'I didn't succeed at all.'

'You know them too?' asked Chuck Decker Junior, looking at the sisters.

'No, I have not had the pleasure. I never saw them before last night and I only got a fleeting glimpse of them then.'

His story matched what both Cathy and Sharonne had told them earlier.

'Will you just excuse us for one moment?' The people from Bloomingdales stood up and left the room. As they did, Christian asked if he too could have a word with them in private. They agreed and he followed them outside. About ten minutes later, they all returned.

'You are all free to leave now,' the yellow tie said. 'We must apologise for the inconvenience we have caused you, but we acted on what evidence we had and I am sure you will understand our position. We have our jobs to do too. Theft is a real problem for us. We get all sorts of operators and shoplifting rings who work in groups and gangs – the more successful they are the more plausible their stories tend to be.'

Christian had told the Bloomingdales head of security that Sharonne was working on a very sensitive project for them and was stressed out about work. He had managed to use his persuasive powers on them.

Sharonne turned to apologise to Cathy and her sister for ruining their day. There was awkwardness between them all, but Marty stepped in to try and smooth things out.

'Ladies, you've had a dreadful experience, all three of you, and I insist you all join us for dinner tonight. We can't have you leaving our town with a bad taste in your mouth, can we? By then, you'll be able to laugh at this misunderstanding and you'll dine out on it for years to come.'

They knew he was right, but it took a little more cajoling before they agreed. They had missed lunch and now needed some down time to recover from this ordeal. As they left Bloomingdales, Sharonne found Christian at her elbow.

'Sharonne, I must apologise for last night. My conduct was unforgivable.'

She said nothing, still feeling as though she had just stepped off a rollercoaster.

'Would you rather I did not come to the dinner tonight?'

'No, Christian, it doesn't matter. I am so relieved to be out of that situation. Besides, I feel so guilty about the others.'

'Don't. It was a genuine faux pas. You are innocent.'

'I know, but the frightening part was trying to convince them of that. They just didn't seem to believe a word I said.'

'Did you want to buy the shoes?' he asked with a grin. 'I could go back and get them for you.'

'Don't ever mention them again,' she said, a smile breaking on her face. 'I'm going barefoot after this. I'll probably have flashbacks every time I walk into a shoe shop for the rest of my life.'

'So will I,' said Cathy.

'That's better. See she's laughing at it already!' said Ed.

Arranging to meet up again for cocktails at six-thirty in Fitzer's Bar, the women walked the few blocks back to their hotel reliving the nightmare.

When Sharonne got back to her room, she rang Derek and

broke down as she told him what had happened. He was sympathetic and she mentioned the flower episode, omitting the real reason for Christian's visit. When they had talked it over and over again, they began to laugh at the absurdity of it all and at the idea that the girls' printouts had been mistaken for a steal-to-order list.

'I can't wait to tell them that in the morning,' Derek said.

'Don't you dare. Some things are best left unsaid.'

***

After they had finished talking, Derek sat and thought. It had been a long time since Sharonne had shown her vulnerable side to him. She always seemed to be on the defensive these days – a mode he too had adopted to deal with her, but it hurt that their easy camaraderie had got lost somewhere along the way. He then went up to his study and sat in front of the computer. Logging on, he punched in a few combinations on the keypad, found seat availability and booked three tickets. They were in business class – the only ones he could get for a flight to New York the following morning. He went back downstairs into the kitchen where the au pair was making a cup of coffee. And he asked her to pack a few things for the girls.

'I know it's very late, but they won't need much – just big suitcases, Sabine, and a change of clothes will do. I imagine there will be a bit of shopping involved when we get there.'

'I'm sure there will,' she laughed, 'lots.'

'And if you have any special requests …' he began, stroking his beard, but Sabine said, 'I've already sent those with Sharonne.'

'Good, good, then I'd better throw a few things in my own case too.'

He couldn't wait to see the girls' faces the following morning when they found out where they were going. He would have to wake them up at some impossibly early hour. He typed a few emails and instructions to his PA to explain his unexpected absence and went to bed. He usually kept Fridays as meeting-free days to catch up on his paperwork.

***

Sharonne was first to arrive at the swish New York office the following morning. She was in a completely different frame of mind than the one she had been in the previous day. Her colleagues had insisted on taking her with Cathy and her sister to enjoy the New York cocktail tradition. Then after a round of Manhattans in Fitzer's, to a delicious meal in midtown west at the Venetian restaurant Remi, where they made light of the misadventure in Bloomingdales. Christian reined back on his charmer role and there was no sign of his assistant either. Sharonne was surprised at how easily she relaxed. Now that they were at the final stages of making sure that this fraud would not go undetected, she needed to be able to focus on the business in hand.

Sharonne had done her homework and put her plans to the table. She looked around to see how they were being received and there were nods of approval from all of the partners.

'I'll stress that secrecy is of the utmost, and that is why we'll be meeting in my offices rather than at theirs,' she said.

'I think that's a great idea,' said Ed.

'Good,' she said. 'I'll confirm the date and time with you early next week and it's up to you to do the rest.'

'You're a genius,' said Marty.

That out of the way, they immediately went into rehearsal mode, going through the documents Sharonne had drawn up again to make sure they had covered every angle. 'I'd appreciate if you legal eagles would go through these with a fine comb, mindful of the clauses which may differ from one jurisdiction to another. I don't need to tell you that they have been worded very carefully so as not to prejudice the further legal proceedings that are bound to follow once these crooks are apprehended.'

She passed photocopied documents around. There was always a hack out there somewhere who would pose an awkward question so vigilance at this stage was paramount to the success of this exposé. The morning sped by and they had wound everything up satisfactorily by noon.

'I won't ask you to join us for lunch today, as I know you still have your shopping to do,' said Marty with a smile.

'Don't remind me,' said Sharonne.

They all shook hands formally and Christian's parting words to her were, 'I'll see you in Dublin.'

'That you will,' she answered, including them all in her smile.

When shaking her hand and holding it slightly longer than was necessary he whispered, 'You owe me one, cherie.'

That's what you think, you smarmy bastard, she thought, still smiling. What did I ever see in him? She hailed a cab, deciding to get out of her business suit into something more casual before she hit the shops. She remembered the first time she had called a cab like a proper New Yorker. It was during college holidays and she and dozens of others from her year had got their holiday visas and were going to work in bars and restaurants for the summer. She had felt like a film star standing on the kerbside, hailing down one of these iconic symbols of the US. She smiled at the memories of that summer – when she really grew up and became independent. It was there that she'd discovered designer chic and what money could buy. Everyone in this city seemed to walk with intent, giving the impression that they had to be somewhere important at a fixed time. There was no ambling done here.

Back in her suite, the ring of the doorbell startled her. In puzzlement, she wondered if it was Christian. He wouldn't have had the gall to follow her, would he? You're being stupid, she thought, it was probably room service with more towels or toiletries. Stony faced, she opened the door just in case … but it was her daughters who rushed into the room, followed by a grinning Derek. 'Surprise, Mum, surprise,' the twins shouted.

'What are you all doing here?' she asked, looking at her husband, and in panic thought about what she would have done if Christian had been there.

All talking together, she heard Derek say, 'We've come to take you out shopping, as you seemed to have had problems doing it on your own.' He gave her a wink.

'You didn't tell them, did you?' she asked at the first opportunity, horrified that Megan and Sandy would go home and tell all their friends.

'Of course not,' he answered. 'Relax. We just felt they would be better able to find what they want if they were here to help. We know how busy you've been and besides, it's time these young madams saw the Big Apple for themselves.'

'Well, your timing is perfect. I have finished what I needed to do. Where are your bags – have the girls got a room?'

'It's all taken care of. There are some late checkouts still to happen and they are getting one of those, but you better make room in your wardrobe because I'm moving in here.'

'Mum, we want to go to the Top of the Rock,' said Sandy. 'They have this space at the top that gives you a colour when you walk in and everywhere you go it follows you.'

'I bet I'll be green. That's my favourite,' said Megan.

'Yellow's mine, but that's not how it works.'

'Well how does it?' Derek asked Megan, giving Sharonne a what-on-earth-are-they-taking-about look.

'Motion-detection technology tracks your movements and the colour you are designated changes with you when you move. It's cool. The floor, ceiling and the walls light up and your colour follows you around.'

'Where did you hear about that?' asked Sharonne, always amazed when her kids knew things she didn't.

'I read about it on the web; besides, everyone goes there when they come over,' said Sandy.

'Well then, we've got to too,' said Sharonne. 'The Rockefeller Center it is.'

'Isn't that where those old black-and-white photos were taken of the guys having their sandwiches out on a beam fifty or so storeys up?'

'Dad, that was seventy storeys up.'

'Even worse,' said Derek. 'And to think they built that with no safety harnesses, hard hats or tomes of health and safety regulations to protect them, either. I wish I could get away with working to those standards on our sites. It would cut costs considerably!'

'Are you hungry?' Sharonne asked her daughters, changing the subject.

'No, Mum. We were in business class and we had a huge meal on the way. We watched two films too.'

'Business class, no less. I'll have to go travelling with your daddy more often,' she said, looking over their heads to Derek.

He winked back at her.

THIRTY-SEVEN

The timesheet was posted on the notice board for the Captain's Prize in July. It had gone up that morning and already several places were filled. It was only May but members liked to book the places before they went on holidays.

'Will we give it a go?' said Conor. 'We can't let Derek have it all his way; he may have a title to defend, but let's not make it easy for him. Who'll we get to play instead of Rory?'

'I know a bloke who's only been a member here since January,' said Liam. 'Had dinner with him the other night. He was a member in Druid's Glen before, but it was just too far out with the traffic for him to get full use of the time he has. Will I ask him?'

'Yeah sure, why not?'

'He plays off nine. His name is Kevin Breen.'

They pulled their caddy cars alongside to the first tee. Liam did the honours, swinging a drive that soared beautifully, mirroring the gentle curve of the fairway, plugging a respectable distance from the green for his second shot. This was a deceptive par four.

'Wow-ee – you're on form.'

Conor lined up his shot, took a practice swing, moved closer to the target and hooked to the left into the long grass three-quarters way down. An expletive followed. His next shot wasn't much better.

Liam's second took him just short of a clump of trees but in perfect position to avoid the bunkers on his third.

'I've had a bit of practice – in Cyprus – over the past few weeks.' He laughed as he saw Conor's expression. 'That new course is shaping up beautifully. Takes thousands of tonnes of water to keep the greens green and some of the hoteliers and locals are complaining, especially with water rationing in high season.'

They continued chatting as they walked between shots. 'What's the standard going to be like?'

'Quite spectacular, although the new course will put the original one back in the time of niblicks!'

'When's it opening?'

'It'll probably be a year to eighteen months. They're building a whole complex of luxury villas at the same time, but they do archaeological surveys on every scrap of the terrain there before a sod can be turned.'

'So unlike us. We wait until work is in progress before we countenance even the thought of such things. Then we have to go billions over budget to give wide berth to a historic monument or burial ground.'

'And you know we never seem to learn,' said Liam.

Conor went to locate his ball in the rough and hit it closer to the green.

As their paths converged again Liam asked, 'Do you ever wonder where it all went wrong, and why?'

'All the time.'

'This time last year we were all one big happy group – well, apart from Sharonne and her tantrums, but, generally, I think she enjoys life – she just won't admit it to Derek.'

'She's a power freak. There isn't a glass ceiling tough enough to stop her breaking through it and it won't matter who she flattens or flatters to get there. But, if I remember rightly, you were still mooning around after Helen this time last year …'

'Let's not go there. That, at least, was fixable. But, hell, what went wrong with Trish and Rory – or should I say with Rory?'

'Male menopause, lust, insanity – the dirty dog. I don't know. I spoke to him recently. It's like talking to an automaton. He'd called to ask about Maeve and then he casually enquired if I'd seen Trish and how she was coping, but he didn't want to know, really. Just switched off when I suggested he should ask her. I also told him he should consider coming back to Dublin again – to be near his kids – and he virtually hung up on me.'

'It's as if someone wiped his master disc and replaced some vital information and components. He's not the same guy any more.'

'That's a good way of putting it. He's over there now in his glossy new world, where the sex is unfettered. He has no responsibilities, only satisfying Anna Maria. He keeps saying how happy he is. Why the hell wouldn't he be? Wouldn't any of us, given half the chance? But for Christ's sake, doesn't he remember that's how he felt about Trish – for years – and that happy is not a place she – or the kids – are in right now?'

'Did you know Barry has been bunking off school? I saw him in town one day and confronted him about it afterwards and do you know what he said to me? He said, "Anyone can be a father, but it takes a man to be a dad." I was floored. I didn't know how to answer the poor kid.'

'Yeah, it's really awkward. I want to kill Rory on their behalf. I don't know how Trish is holding up, I really don't.'

'It's sinking in that he's not coming back. I think when the legalities are settled, it may be a bit easier for her. But, hell, what do I know? I've never been married or had kids.'

Liam took another straight drive down the fairway. 'She's lucky to have Maeve,' he said, putting the driver back in his golf bag.

'They are very good for each other. Women have this knack of being able to talk straight and of getting right to the problem. We mere males on the other hand run as far and as fast as we can. They seem to be able to share more easily than we can. I envy them that. I'm sure Trish knows how Maeve is feeling better than I do.'

'That's probably only because she's protecting you, doesn't want you to worry. She is doing OK, isn't she?'

'Yeah, she's great. Her last results were very positive but she has another check-up in about six weeks and I know they're happy with her, but I can't help being anxious about it.'

By the time they reached the seventh hole Liam was leading.

'Damn and blast, I can't seem to get one shot right this morning,' Conor muttered after hitting a fresh air. 'It's ages since I did that!' A little further down he said, 'I was thinking of sending Trish and Maeve off on a little break together. I can't get away just at the moment with this bloody tribunal at such a critical stage. What do you think?'

'I think that's a great idea. It would do them both good to have some girly time together. They love the villa.'

Liam holed his putt, level par; Conor went three over.

'Actually I thought about sending them to Scotland. Maeve's never been there and it's one of those places she's always wanted to visit. I read about a cruise on a small ship, a floating country house sort of thing, and I've emailed for the brochure. It only has something like fifty guests and almost as many staff. I think the pampering would be a tonic for both of them. I don't think she'd be into one of the huge liners with thousands of passengers.'

'Sounds idyllic. I could do with a piece of that myself. I seem to spend my life going through security checks at airports these days.'

Conor's next shot went to the far side of the green, rolled merrily along and off the edge into another bunker. It took him two more shots to get out.

'You know what they call that?' asked Liam, who was streaking ahead.

'Pathetic!' he laughed.

'Well that too! It's an Adolf – two shots in a bunker – and you'll have to do better than that, lad, if we're going to show Derek how it's done.'

'I'll practise, I promise,' Conor, said gesturing a salute.

'And this year, for everyone's sake, warn Maeve to check what Sharonne will be wearing on the night!

'You can bet on that, too, sir!' he laughed.

THIRTY-EIGHT

It was only mid-afternoon when Conor arrived home from work. Maeve was in the garden deadheading and weeding. The sweet peas she has planted had taken well and she was encouraging their tentacles to curl around the metal wigwams at the corners of the patio. Everything that was in flower was in blue, white and purple. She straightened up to admire the overall effect. She had always done all the work in the garden herself, but since she had become ill, Conor, for whom grass cutting was the height of his green-fingered skills, had got someone to come in once a week to do the heavy work. She was suddenly aware of being watched and when she turned around she saw her husband framed by the French doors.

'What are you doing home so early?' she asked. 'Is everything OK?'

'Yep. The sittings finished earlier than expected, so I decided to head home – no point in getting stuck in traffic going back into the office for a few hours and out again.'

'How long have you been there?' she asked. 'I never heard the car.'

'Just a few minutes.' He kissed her and handed over the roses he'd been holding behind his back.

'Coals to Newcastle and all that,' he laughed, 'but I know how you hate cutting the ones in the garden.'

'I always feel I'm murdering them. I nurse them and feed them and it just seems too cruel to behead them as soon as they open up.'

He'd heard her theory before and had to agree she had a point. They only flowered for such a short season. Everything else was fair game, but the roses were off limits. She smelled the bouquet.

'Mmm – they have a lovely fragrance. Thank you. What's the occasion?'

'Oh just a surprise. There's a note in there for you. If you'd been out I was just going to leave them on the table for you to find.'

She poked her fingers down between the tissue and the cellophane and found a small pink envelope. Handing the flowers back to Conor, she tore it open. 'Much as I love you I'm sending you away for a week. Pack your bags, you're off next Monday.'

'Where? Where am I going and why aren't you coming too?'

'Now don't get too excited – you won't need factor thirty or a new bikini – just your walking shoes and lots of midge repellent. You're going to Scotland – cruising!'

'Oh, Conor. That's terrific I've always wanted to go there, but a cruise? And why can't you come? It won't be any fun on my own.'

'You won't be on your own – Trish is going too. It's all arranged.'

'What about work?'

'That's all covered. Stan says it will do you good to get away.'

'You're amazing.'

'I know,' he said, 'and modest too.'

'Trish never said a word.'

'She was working undercover,' he grinned. 'By the way, you can put the kettle on because she's on her way over now with the brochures. When I saw your car in the drive, I called her.'

Trish arrived, as if waiting off-stage for her cue. As they drank tea on the patio, they discussed what they would pack, and what sort of people would be on the cruise with them. Would sneakers be out of place? Should they bring proper walking boots and wet gear?

'You'll have to posh up for the captain's dinner too,' said Conor.

'I'm glad my hair is long enough again not to have to wear the wig. Being blonde was a novelty, but I have to say I'm pleased to be back to my own colour again.'

'You remind me of Audrey Hepburn with that short hair. It really suits you,' Conor agreed.

'Anything would be an improvement on being bald. You've no idea the sense of freedom there is in not having to wear that thing. It was OK in the winter but as the weather got warmer, it really irked me.'

'I can't even begin to imagine,' said Trish. 'Now I have to go and collect the girls – they were playing tennis at Liz's, and as she'll be minding them when we're away, I don't want them outstaying their welcome before I leave.'

'Liz loves having them,' said Maeve. 'Besides, with her brood another two for dinner would hardly be noticed.'

'I know that, and she has two French exchange students at the moment, boys as well. I think that may explain this sudden passionate interest in the game and why mine raised no objections at all when I told them I'd be missing for a week! And Barry's delighted to be going to David's.'

'That probably has something to do with it all right,' said Conor. 'I used to love when my aunt took French students – and always girls – they always seemed to be much more exotic then the girls who lived in our cul de sac.'

***

Six days later, Trish and Maeve joined their vessel in the seaside town of Oban. They were shown to their stateroom by a steward who talked them through some housekeeping details. As he turned to leave, Trish said, 'Did you give us a key?'

'No. You'll notice there are no locks on the doors. It's perfectly in order for you to leave your tiaras on the bedside tables as you would at home!' he said with a glint in his eye. 'Of course, there is a safe too and, if you ladies would like, afternoon tea is now being served in the lounge.'

When he was gone Trish, spotting the gold-foiled neck of a champagne bottle protruding from an ice-filled bucket, said, 'Look at that. Conor did pull out all the stops.' Some chocolate-covered strawberries sat on a dainty plate with tiny linen napkins folded beside it.

Trish then jumped on one of the squashy beds, laughing. 'Is this luxury or what?'

'What are you like at all?' laughed Maeve. 'You've been spending too much time with your teenagers.'

'Tell me about it. I feel liberated and I'm really going to enjoy it.'

'So am I.'

Passing the wood-panelled library on the way to the lounge, Trish whispered, 'I feel I'm in an Agatha Christie mystery.'

'Let's go and check out our travelling companions. We'll see if there are any potential murderers and we can decide who should be watched.'

***

Time slipped by and the captain did as he promised – he changed the scenery daily – all they had to do was relax, go for long walks ashore, enjoy their porridge and morning coffee, both served with a 'wee dram of whisky to keep the cold out'.

They visited a different island every day and the transfers to them were done by tenders when the waters were too shallow for the *Hebridean Princess* to dock in the little harbours. By the end of the week, they were best friends with the two men who manned these operations. They had bought bottles of twelve-year-old malt whisky at a distillery for both Stan and Conor, and Trish had got a beautiful mohair wrap for her sister for minding the kids. Conversations had roamed from spirits to the afterlife, quizzes to grouse shooting, old movies to history.

A bearded bird watcher, who never seemed to be separated from his binoculars, even at mealtimes, pursued Trish actively. 'He must be at least ninety,' she said to Maeve. 'How can he keep up?'

On one of the really sunny days she announced, 'I have a plan. Today I'm going to leave last and he'll think I've gone on ahead.' She managed to lose him by lagging behind, talking to a photographer whose photos of penguins in the South Pole and of polar bears in Alaska had appeared in *National Geographic* and other authoritative publications. Trish and the photographer stopped in silence as she lined up a shot of an otter that seemed to be playing with them. Just as the camera was ready the otter ducked away, jooking around some rushes before coming back to tease again. Trish inhaled deeply, breathing in the fresh air and admiring the tranquillity of unspoiled nature as the photographer set up yet another angle. Eventually satisfied with her shots, the photographer folded the tripod and they headed off to join the others.

They came upon a little church where some stray daffodils were still blooming in the graveyard. Pushing the door open they found the others standing in a knot around a tiny wooden organ. Behind it sat the wonderfully eccentric opera singer from middle Europe, who had kitted himself out in plus fours and thickly knitted socks for this holiday.

'Oh you missed it Trish,' Maeve exclaimed as they rejoined the group. 'Pavel just played the most beautiful piece of music. It was so moving.'

Maeve blossomed as they walked around the breathtaking countryside. 'Oh, Trish,' she said, inhaling the fresh, clean air and admiring the tranquillity of the lake they had just come across. 'It makes me realise how lucky I am to be here.'

'Only for Conor …'

'No, that's not what I meant. I mean I am so lucky to be alive and well and here to enjoy all this.'

'I know,' Trish said, giving her a squeeze. On the way back Maeve was quiet and Trish left her to her thoughts.

***

Later, as they sat sipping gin and tonics on deck, they decided on the victims in their ongoing murder mystery plans.

'I definitely think those two sisters have to be bumped off,' said Trish.

'I like them.'

'So do I, but the way they 'oooh' and 'aaah' at everything is beginning to grate.'

'I think I'd murder Janet,' said Maeve.

Janet was on her eleventh cruise. Uniform spotting, it seemed, was her main pastime. She always insisted on a place at the captain's table before she booked. She never went ashore on the side trips, preferring to stay behind in the hope of snatching some time with an officer, any officer, when there was less competition around. She shot them threatening looks when they were joined by an officer at dinner and he regaled them with tales of other cruise lines where he had worked.

Maeve nudged Trish, who could already feel Janet's stare on her neck.

'Has she tried pursuing you too? Or does she just go for captains?' whispered Trish to the officer.

He laughed. 'Oh no – any stripes will do. They're like magnets, the more you have the more magnetic you are! She's the only woman I have ever lied to about my personal life. I told her I had seven children and was really devoted to my wife, whom I fell in love with at sixteen. Even that didn't scare her off.'

'You should have told her you were gay instead.'

'Oh, that wouldn't have worked – women like her have very finely tuned gay-dar – they can spot a fake from miles away.'

Later, some others joined them in the lounge for an after-dinner drink and, little by little, everyone retired.

'I can't believe we're going to bed so early,' said Trish, looking at her watch. It's only half ten!'

'It's the fresh air,' their officer friend told them. 'Walking and being busy doing nothing can tire you out. Tomorrow will be a later one. We have our formal night and I have the honour of performing the ritual of addressing the haggis for you. That's always fun.'

The next day, having spent the afternoon on the beautiful island of Crinan, they returned to the ship, not on one of the hardy tenders, but on the speedboat, which usually sat on an upper deck beside the wheelhouse. They bounced across the loch at what seemed to be frightening speed and arrived, exhilarated, hair wet and tangled and with their faces glowing.

'It's glam night tonight, Trish, and it's going to take some work to make us presentable after that jaunt.'

'It's going to be tough going back to the kids after all this. Isn't that an awful thing to say? I love them to bits, but it's great being away from them.'

'No, it sounds perfectly natural to me, especially as you have them all the time now. You needed a break and I'm so glad you could come. I wouldn't have missed this for anything.'

'Neither would I.'

***

Their finery was laid out on their beds – Maeve was in the shower, Trish was drying her hair – she didn't hear Maeve come out but saw her in the mirror. She looked pale and distracted. Turning the switch off, she asked, 'Are you all right?'

'I feel a bit funny, light headed. I must have jumped up too quickly.'

'Put your head down. I'll get some water.'

After a few minutes, she seemed to be a little better.

'It must have been the speed boat or something,' she said.

Trish sensed there was something more; Maeve seemed agitated. She sat on the bed beside her, putting her arm around her shoulder.

'There's something else you're not telling me, Maeve,' she said softly.

Her friend looked at her through brimming eyes. One tear escaped and ran down her face. She wiped it with the heel of her hand and nodded. 'I've just found another lump. I wasn't even looking. It's under my other arm.' The tears ran freely now. And the friends hugged each other.

When she had quietened down, Maeve begged Trish not to say anything to anyone, especially not to Conor.

'I was dreading this happening at some stage and I need time to let it settle before I can talk about it. Let's get through the next weekend, the golf club do and I'll see Mary on Monday, I promise. But I don't want to talk about it again until then. I mean that!' she insisted as Trish was about to protest. 'Not one word.'

Although she didn't think Maeve was right, Trish felt she had no choice but to agree. 'OK,' she muttered, 'it's your body.'

They went to dinner and Maeve gave a star performance. Anyone looking on would have thought she hadn't a care in the world. She even ate the haggis with gusto and had a go at some of the Celtic sayings of Rabbie Burns. Later that night, she actually slept.

THIRTY-NINE

It was a couple of weeks before the dinner for the Captain's Prize at the golf club and Liam and Kevin Breen were having a drink in a wine bar in town when Kevin asked him if he intended to take anyone to the dinner for the Captain's Prize in the golf club.

'I haven't really thought about it. Have you someone in mind? For you, I mean?'

'I have, but the problem is her sister has just arrived from the States and I'm in a bit of a bind because I had asked her before her sister decided to visit. They're identical twins actually, originally from Sneem, but now living in LA.'

'Tell me more,' said Liam, thinking that with Maeve and Trish drooling for any hint of who he was seeing, twins would confuse them even further. 'Why not invite the two of them?'

'These are not your average girls, I have to warn you,' said Kevin. 'A bit Hollywood and OTT.'

'They sound perfect. I can't wait to see the reaction they'll cause,' he laughed.

***

As anticipated, when Liam announced that he and Kevin were bringing two sisters along to the captain's evening, there was great speculation among the women. Were they going to meet Liam's new lover at last? Trish, who had promised not to mention the subject again, restrained herself several times from asking questions. She had also been resolute about staying away from the golf club because of all the memories. However, she had been the subject of an intense campaign, led by Conor, backed up by Maeve and, surprisingly, Sharonne, to come along.

'We're all mates and Derek and I want you there with us,' Sharonne had said when she'd phoned a few weeks earlier. Even Stan was in on the campaign. Although he belonged to a different club, he played regularly at theirs as a visitor, so he knew the group and had been asked along. He jokingly threatened to stop Trish's pay cheque if she were 'unco-operative'.

'I can't sit at a table full of couples and look like a sad old bachelor on his own, now can I?' he'd said. 'You've got to come along as my decoy to keep all those predatory golf widows at bay.' After much cajoling, Trish capitulated.

Trish hadn't found it that difficult to make her entrance. Flanked by Conor and Maeve, they steered her to the veranda, where Stan greeted her warmly. Liam and Kevin were already there, sipping champagne with two women who looked like clones of each other. They were very tall, with lots of jewellery and dresses that lifted and clung in all the right places. Just then, Sharonne and Derek arrived, laughing together. New York had put their relationship back on track and Sharonne seemed much happier of late.

'Allow me to introduce you to Kimmy and Jayden and, for those of you who haven't met him before, Kevin,' said Liam. He ran through the names. 'There's a prize if you can remember all the names,' he laughed.

'Charmed to meet y'all,' the sisters said in unison.

'Isn't this quaint?' Jayden remarked, as a match concluded on eighteenth green below them.

'Don't they have golf carts here?' asked Kimmy, as the players retrieved their clubs.

'Yes, but most of us still use caddy cars. It's not exactly a mountainous course,' said Kevin.

Stan joined Derek and Conor on the way to the bar, 'Not Liam's usual sort, eh?'

'Nope,' Conor agreed. 'Could be an interesting evening all the same.'

After the speeches and presentations, they sat down for the meal. There were no major prizes for them this year, only a trophy for the longest drive and that went to Liam.

The twins were identical in every way apart from their manicures. Kimmy didn't drink and had her unnaturally long nails painted in royal blue to match her dress, while Jayden's were square at the tips, decorated in scarlet with a tiny white flower on each. Their hair had a rigid varnished look and had wispy bits arranged around their temples and ears. Both hovered on skinny heels and were a good few inches taller than the Irish women – and some of the men too.

'Do you play golf?' Trish asked.

'Yes, we're in the country club at La Jolla, with our parents, but we both prefer tennis actually.'

'What brought you over here?'

'We were born in Kerry, but our Mom's from Texas. We moved to the States when we were five,' said Kimmy, 'and I'm back and forward all the time. Jayden just came along this time for the ride.'

Kevin interrupted, 'Kimmy's a life coach and she is doing some training with some companies in Ireland. That's how we met.'

'And Kevin introduced me to her and then along came Jayden,' Liam said, putting his arm around Jayden's shoulder, a gesture missed by none of them. 'So we're spoiled for choice.' They made their way to the table.

'It must be fun being twins,' said Trish.

'It has its moments,' said Jayden.

'Are you telepathic – do you know when the other one is in trouble or has a pain?' asked Maeve.

'Sometimes we do,' said Kimmy.

'And before you ask,' interrupted Jayden, 'yes, we have swapped boyfriends and gone on each others date's …'

'I wasn't going to – I was about to ask what does life coaching involve?' Sharonne asked Jayden.

'Oh, don't ask me. Kimmy's the intelligent one. She's always ranting on about the sea and life cycles, balance and movement. I've no idea what she's on about most of the time.'

'What do you do?'

'I have a cosmetic therapy, dental and beauty studio. It's called Perfection,' she said, extending her fingers unselfconsciously, admiring their tips. 'I just took on two more cosmetic dentists before I came over.'

'In a beauty parlour?' asked Trish.

'Oh, lord, yes. Teeth are the new eyebrows.'

'Pardon?' asked Sharonne.

'Teeth – they're the new eyebrows,' Jayden drawled. 'Everyone is having those tattooed on now, and in the same way as eyebrows frame the eyes, the mouth frames the teeth so they have to look good. I mean, you wouldn't frame a picture of rotting bananas would you?'

'I suppose not,' said Sharonne, unimpressed by this skewed reasoning. She looked at Derek, who had a don't-you-dare-bring-me-into-this-conversation look on his face.

Sharonne turned her focus to Kimmy. 'How would you go about life coaching me?' she asked.

'Well, I'd get you to write your own obituary. That's where I'd begin.'

'My obituary?'

'Most people see how little they have achieved when they write their obituaries, and they get a shock, which makes them want to improve. It's a good starting point for me to decipher where your inadequacies and failures are. That way we both get to work on your goals together and on the things you never achieved. It can change the whole way you think about yourself and how others will judge you.'

'Is that not all a bit extreme?' asked Derek, thinking failure was one word he'd never associate with Sharonne.

'No, I don't think so. Often all people need is a good dose of reality, but we don't tell them that. We do a lot of dance, too, using the Butoh techniques.'

'Botox?' asked Conor.

'No Butoh – it's a Japanese system that was devised after the war so that people could forget the horrors they had witnessed.'

'So they dance their way to a new life?'

'Well, there's more to it than that, but, in some ways, yes.'

'Speaking for myself, I think it's much easier to change someone's nose or chin or boobs than their personality,' said Jayden.

'I don't try to change their personality,' snapped Kimmy. 'I just give them options and it's up to them to accept or reject them.'

'See what I mean – she's the intelligent one. I find the results are much more instantaneous with a surgeon's knife or implants.'

'Would you actually have surgical work done for beauty purposes?' asked Kevin.

The two sisters exploded. 'Would we?'

Kimmy said, 'We've both had Brazilian butt lifts and boob jobs.'

Trish looked over at Maeve. This was not where the conversation should be going. She tried to steer it on a tangent but Jayden was having none of it.

'I definitely chose the wrong discipline,' Stan whispered to Trish as he poured some wine. She just rolled her eyes heavenwards.

'We had our boobs done at the same time so we could empathise with each other on our bruises and pain …'

Maeve sensed the discomfort around the table and said, 'I'm thinking of having implants myself.'

Trish smiled at her. Good on you girl, she thought.

'Go for it, there's nothing like a pert pair to make you feel rejuvenated,' said Kimmy.

'Jayden is an interesting name,' Liam cut in.

'Our Mom made it up.'

Sharonne's face had a well-why-isn't-that-a-surprise look about it.

'She's Jayne and Dad's Dennis, so it's short for the two.'

There was a pause in the conversation.

'May I ask,' said Stan, 'what in God's name is a Brazilian butt lift?'

'They take fat from your flanks and stomach and insert it in your butt cheeks to give them a perkier appearance.'

'They didn't show us that in the College of Surgeons, but it sounds a lot easier than what I do. I'm definitely in the wrong job.'

'No, you're not, you save lives,' said Sharonne.

Trish was sitting on his other side and she asked, 'Does no one grow old any more in LA?'

'Absolutely not,' said Jayden. 'Old is so out of fashion at the moment.'

Liam cut in, 'I'm glad I'm a mere male – where my car says more about me than my figure.'

'Oh, you get used to it,' Jayden went on. 'The bruising looks worse than it is and you forget the pain when you see the results, especially with boobs. We only had those done in January, but they're really natural. Feel,' she ordered Derek, pushing her chest towards him.

'I don't think …'

'Go on. Could you tell? Could you … honestly?'

Sharonne grinned across the table at him as Jayden moved even closer.

***

The following day, Liam phoned Trish, Sharonne and Maeve and invited them to his apartment for drinks at five.

'The guys will have finished their game and will come straight here.'

He lived in a sprawling penthouse which showed Dublin at its best – from the early-morning sunlight and the twilight creeping over the Dublin hills, to the reflections on the glass towers across the River Liffey and the twinkling lights at night to the constant movement of the water below. He was comfortable here, high above the world, and when he was out of the country, he looked forward to such leisurely Sundays, poring over the newspapers out on the roof garden.

The taxi picked Sharonne up first and then went on to Trish's where Maeve was already ensconced, carrying out a post-mortem on the proceedings the night before. 'You were great,' Sharonne said to Trish. 'I know it can't have been easy for you going there on your own.'

'It wasn't, but Stan was so solicitous – he never left my side for a minute. He's so considerate. I can see why he's so popular as a doctor.'

'He's kinda easy on the eye too, isn't he?' Sharonne said mischievously.

'Now stop that. I'm off men for ever. I'd never trust anyone again the way I trusted Rory.'

'Tell me that in five years' time when you've met someone new, have a second family – your own and probably a step child or two – maybe even another one together …'

'A yours, mine and ours scenario,' teased Maeve.

'God forgive you for even wishing that on me. You know you two should be writing novels!' said Trish.

In the taxi Trish mused, 'Do you think the twins will be there?'

'I hope not,' said Maeve. 'I couldn't take any more of the Botox and new eyebrows malarkey, never mind dancing away my war wounds, or surgical wounds in their case.' They all laughed.

'Could you imagine going to either of them if your self-esteem was low?' asked Sharonne. 'You'd end up on Prozac sandwiches for life.'

'Do you think Liam is really smitten?' said Maeve. 'And if so, have either of you figured out with which one? I just couldn't pick up on the messages.'

'I think I know,' said Trish.

'Please tell me it's not Jayden,' said Sharonne. 'I'd rather have to do my obituary than listen to more LA-lifestyle drivel.'

'No, I don't think it's either of them' said Trish.

'What do you know?' asked Sharonne.

'I'm saying nothing!' she answered.

'She knows something!' said Maeve as they arrived at the entrance. They paid their fare and Sharonne keyed in the code. The gates opened slowly and the pair pushed Trish for more information but she refused to be drawn.

'Just wait and see. I know Liam, and he's up to something. I can sense it.'

Liam buzzed them in and was waiting for them by the lift, an iced jug of margarita in his hand.

'I always feel I'm in a movie when I come in here,' said Trish, waving her arms about the classically decorated hallway. 'Sophistication in pale vanilla with black, grey and yellow accents. I expect to find a string quartet in the corner behind the double doors, or see some famous pianist sitting behind the grand piano playing mood music.'

Liam grinned, 'Sorry to disappoint, but if you're very good, I might play something later on. Meanwhile you'll have to make do with background Leonard Cohen.' Glasses filled, they made straight for the roof garden where Kevin, Stan, Derek and Conor were gathered admiring the views, while some noisy seagulls bickered overhead.

'Ladies, I owe you an apology,' said Liam. 'I'm sorry about last night and all that talk about breasts and implants. Maeve, I know that must have been difficult for you, but our guests obviously didn't know about your surgery and we just didn't seem to be able to move away from the topic.'

'I know you can do just about everything, Liam, but even you can't control conversations,' said Sharonne. 'This is the real world. I put my foot in it all the time. Anyway, I'm more interested to know about you and – the ladies! Is it serious, with one of them I mean? And if so, with which one?'

'With neither, you'll be pleased to hear, but I do have something to tell you all.'

'I knew it,' said Trish. 'I should have taken bets from you two in the taxi.'

'Kevin and I decided to bring Kimmy and Jayden along as a lark and we regretted it as soon as we were all together. However, I did want to get you all together to tell you something. I have' – he paused for effect – 'met someone' – another pause – 'with whom I want to spend the rest of my life. And it's time for the formal introductions.' They all looked at each other, waiting for someone to appear from inside.

'I'd like you to meet my partner, Kevin.'

'I knew it,' Trish jumped up. 'I knew it!' she said, hugging Liam and then Kevin. Sharonne and Maeve exchanged glances with their spouses. How had they not seen that one coming? Of course Liam was every woman's idea of the perfect gay man: eloquent, funny, debonair, witty, carefully elegant about his dress and always caring. It was so obvious, but they knew him so well they had missed it.

Everyone talked at once, but Kevin shushed them, saying, 'I too must apologise for last night. It was my idea to bring the twins along, as a sort of disguise. They were so awful I felt that I wouldn't be such a let down after them,' he laughed.

'Well, Kevin, you were right there,' said Derek.

'We want to know everything, don't we girls?' said Maeve. 'Where and when did you meet? How long has this been going on?

'You know by taking on Liam you are taking us all on too?

We're part of his baggage and we won't be going away!' said Trish.

'I've noticed that,' Kevin laughed. 'But from what I've seen so far, that doesn't seem to be such a weighty lot to carry. Besides, you haven't yet met my eclectic bunch of friends and family! They come with a health warning.'

FORTY

The letterbox made a loud bang as Trish downed the last of her coffee and went into the hall to collect the letters. The long legal envelope was an immediate giveaway. She brought it back to the table, licked the marmalade off her knife and used it as a letter opener to get at the contents. It was from Jim McConville and had a document attached with the terms of the settlement Rory was proposing. Her hands shook and her heart raced as she scanned it.

… the family home to remain in her name. School and college fees and expenses to be paid until their children's chosen courses or further education would be completed. School trips and an annual holiday would be paid for. Health insurance for them all to be covered. The 4x4 was to be hers until she decided to dispose of or replace it and it was her responsibility to maintain it. She would receive a monthly payment by direct debit into her account. She was to relinquish any prior claims to monies, insurance policies and investments.

… If she remained single and non-cohabiting.

'If she remained single' – she felt her blood pressure rising – 'or non-cohabiting'. It was all right for him but not for her!

… the mortgage would be cleared on agreement of these terms but his name would stay on the deeds of the family home. If, however, she co-habited or remarried, the house would be put in trust for the children and when the youngest reached twenty-five, it would be sold and the proceeds divided between the children and their father.

She sat amid the remnants of the breakfast and rationalised – it could have been worse. She wanted nothing from him for herself, just wanted him gone out of her life, with all the hurt, betrayal and pain, but she knew this was unreasonable. Rory was and would always be the father of her children. Jim suggested in his letter that she should contact him so that they could discuss the contents. She looked at her watch. She'd call Jim later. She picked up the phone and rang Maeve to wish her luck. She was meeting her oncologist at eleven.

Maeve had earlier insisted that she really wanted to go to the specialist on her own this time because she had questions to ask and she wanted time to digest the answers, whatever they might be.

'Conor knows,' Maeve told Trish, when she answered her call. 'I didn't mention it, but he walked in on me in the bathroom last night. I was examining myself for the hundredth time to see if that bloody lump had magically disappeared.'

'How did he react?'

'He was mad for a bit, but eventually said he understood where I was coming from, but he's insisted on coming with me.'

'I'm glad.'

'So am I – now. He's not due in to the tribunal until two today, but he's gone into the office early to arrange a few things and he's meeting me here. Look, I'll call in on my way home. I promise.'

'Don't you dare forget. I have things to tell you too, but they can wait.'

'What things?

'Nothing that can't wait. I'll be thinking of you. Good luck.'

FORTY-ONE

Breakfast time at the Lenihans was as hectic as always. Derek was dropping the twins to school before heading to a planning meeting in the Docklands and Sharonne was preoccupied with all the things that might go wrong at this critical – and, hopefully, final – stage of the whole FitzGerald-Reglob fraud. As she listened to Christopher McKevitt read the business news on the radio, she knew he'd have some story for the following morning, and it would be more than just reporting on who had won the overall Irish Business and Corporation Awards.

She was confident that they were all well prepared for the climax of the project. She had a hair appointment en route to the office where Sadie had all of the paperwork ready for her. She gathered her things and headed out for her day.

Bob was there before her, along with Christian, Marty and Jonathan, who had just flown in. They were already seated at their table, keeping their distance so as not to be seen together, just yet. The Dublin solicitors were waiting in the wings too. The Irish Business and Corporation Awards ceremony was due to start in the State Apartments at Dublin Castle at 11.45 am.

Everything was going according to plan. When Pieter Reglob and Pat FitzGerald climbed the elegant marble staircase together, they were escorted, not to their table as expected, but to a side room on the pretext of a briefing on the running order of the proceedings. They gushed compliments and platitudes to Sharonne for a few minutes about her appearance, the choice of venue, and the way she handled such events. Several members of the Garda Bureau of Fraud Investigation (GBFI), who had been waiting in another room, came in and identified themselves.

Warnings were read aloud on their rights and the pair were arrested on the grounds of 'suspicion of fraud and embezzlement, tax evasion, insider trading and undeclared off-shore interests'. One of the detectives was despatched to find someone from their firm of solicitors, who were represented among the guests sitting under Valdre's ceiling paintings. Many in the gathering were hiding their own secrets, negotiating tax avoidances and omissions with great skill. The irony of the depiction above them of Ireland with her harp, Justice and Liberty sitting in attendance, was probably lost on them all.

The guest speakers were ushered into their places, heralding the commencement of the awards ceremony. As soon as everyone was settled, the two offenders, the members of the GBFI and some very uneasy-looking solicitors were escorted discreetly off the premises by a back entrance.

Nods and knowing looks were all the signs that passed from table to table as Sharonne's team exhaled in triumph. She had delivered the sheaf of press statements to the media room en route to the hall, and was assured that once the award winners had been named, these were ready to go to all the radio and television stations as well as the newspapers. She slid into her place as the first course was being served.

The awards ceremony honoured a list of familiar and respected business people from around the country, as well as a few new entrepreneurs. The guest speaker was a well-known personality from *The Business* programme and his witty delivery went down really well. The food was good, the wine flowed, congratulations buzzed through the air with much backslapping and hand-shaking. With all the formalities out of the way, the guests trooped out of the banqueting hall. Sharonne, Marty and the rest of their team joined them. Reporters and photographers immediately swamped them. The others deferred to her, and Sharonne replied with her prepared statement.

'The information we are happy to impart is contained in the press release we issued earlier. It is now up to the legal system to do its part. We would like to extend our sympathies to those who have lost their investments and stock portfolios and who have been affected. However, we are not at liberty to make any further revelations at this stage, in case we prejudice the course of justice. Thank you.'

A few of the pushier members of the media shouted more questions, but she stemmed their efforts with her hand. 'That's all I'm at liberty to say. Thank you.' She turned and retreated down a corridor. She felt great.

The day continued in the same vein, with a deluge of phone calls, texts and emails. The stock markets blinked, many companies' shares fell radically. Several banks and investment brokers issued statements of their own and some small investors panicked. Amid the mayhem, she got a text message from Derek.

'Well done, Shar. Really proud of you. Celebrate later. D XX.' It was the only personal message she replied to all day.

They headed back to her offices. It was too risky to be heard discussing details in a busy foyer. Now that the scandal was out in the open, there would be spies everywhere. Christian was shadowed by Françoise, whose presence didn't bother Sharonne at all any more.

'Well, we did it,' said Marty. 'Got those seedy embezzlers behind bars where they belong. Well done everyone. When all the facts become public, no one connected to those deals will ever hold their heads up again. All their nouveaux riches friends in the yacht clubs and golf courses will never mention their names either. I just feel sorry for the smaller investors.'

'So do I,' agreed Bob. 'Many of the larger ones knew right well what was going on and they were quite happy to enjoy the benefits; they don't need our pity. They are probably cross-invested with funds that will more than cover their losses. For some it'll be a blessing, as they will be able to write it off against the tax bills they never intended paying anyway.'

'All this will probably result in a few more reforms in the banking and financial world, and that will be no harm. They're long overdue.'

'Let's drink to that.'

Sharonne buzzed Sadie, who came into the boardroom with glistening cut glass flutes and Cristal champagne. Sharonne glanced at this quizzically. She knew she hadn't ordered Cristal. Christian caught her eye and bowed slightly, 'This is on me.'

She returned his smile, glad they had got over the awkwardness. A while later, she saw him slip an envelope to each of the two lawyers they had worked with, and for one awful moment she wondered what the hell that was all about. Surely things were not about to go wrong. Not now. Not when fourteen months of work had just been concluded successfully.

'No bribing the counsel,' she joked, moving towards them to investigate, before the young men had a chance to open the envelopes.

'You still don't trust me, I see,' he said. 'I'm not bribing anyone, merely passing on a fee. I promised these legal eagles that if they managed to unearth all the facts we needed, they'd be off to the Grand Prix in Brazil, and I'm just keeping my word. Without those vital documents they revealed we would not have been able to nail down this case.'

They were speechless. So was she.

Bob interrupted, 'Let's go and celebrate properly. I've booked two tables at the Shelbourne.'

'This is very nice of you,' Sharonne said to Bob, as she walked into the hotel.

Christian flanked her other side and said, smiling down on her, 'I am very nice, too!'

She moved ahead of them as they joined the smart and the desperately seeking set, as Derek often called them, that made up the glitterati who frequented this venue. There was always a good sprinkling of over-tinted, over-tanned and over-collagened women of a certain age, who read everyone from head to toe and back up again as they arrived, before passing comment. Sharonne sensed someone staring over at them, but she refused to turn her head. Christian was still hovering just a little too close to her elbow, so close that the heady smell of his aftershave – the same gingery scent which had made her skin tingle before – now repulsed her. She turned to move away and caught the stare of the people-watcher she had sensed. It was Breda, Stan's ex. Sharonne wondered how long it would be before she made a move – seven men and only three women and the certainty of an introduction to them all. Before she had even finished formulating this thought, Breda was making a beeline over to say hello, with no interest whatsoever in engaging Sharonne in conversation. She totally ignored Sadie and Françoise too. Sharonne did the formalities as Breda moved in on Christian.

'I believe Frenchmen make great lovers. Is it true?' she said.

'Perhaps we can find that out later, cherie,' he purred back at her.

Sharonne excused herself and went to the ladies' room. He had said in New York that she owed him one, maybe she'd just paid him back and with interest too. Perhaps Christian de Villepin had just met his match.

FORTY-TWO

Conor had walked in on Maeve in the bathroom the previous night, and found her examining herself in the mirror.

'You're not seriously contemplating a reconstruction yet, are you?' he had asked.

'No, of course not, but I have a check-up tomorrow.'

'… a check-up. Tomorrow? How could I have forgotten that?' he said, annoyed with himself. He knew his work schedule was at overload levels, but, Christ, this was way more important than any planning tribunal.

'Because you didn't know – because … because I didn't tell you. I didn't tell you because it's not a check-up,' she argued unconvincingly, with the logic she had used on herself as her reason for not telling him. 'It's a consultation.'

'I thought we agreed we were in this together,' he said, and she could tell he was annoyed with her.

They had talked late into the night. Now here he was with a great sense of foreboding, parking in the grounds of the clinic. Maeve was chatting to Mary's secretary when he got out of the lift and it wouldn't to be too long before his – their – worst fears were realised. There was a definite lump, and possibly the beginnings of another one beside it and this was not a good sign. The chemo and radiotherapy had not halted the spread of these offending cells and Mary booked Maeve in immediately for further tests and treatment.

Conor was amazed at how calmly Maeve took all this, as though she wasn't shocked by it. Slowly, he began to realise that she'd known what it was before the results were delivered – feminine intuition perhaps – or simply being in tune with her body. Further surgery might still be an option, but for now it was back to the waiting game. He wanted to ask questions, but felt he couldn't. Perhaps his wife didn't feel the tightening of fear that had gripped him, but he couldn't project that on her, not now. He could always phone the doctor later or talk to Stan about it.

'Normally we wait for six months to do these tests as the chemo keeps working for that length of time, but I think we have to be realistic,' Mary explained. 'We'll do an MRI and that will tell us much more.'

Conor hardly heard anything else. He tuned back in again as she concluded, 'We are definitely dealing with new activity here.'

FORTY-THREE

It was just over fifteen months since she had been first diagnosed and Maeve had had good times in between. Her hair had grown back, thick and curlier than before. She told everyone she was doing fine – even hinting the last series of chemo had zapped the illness altogether. In tackling it though, it also seemed to have zapped her energy. Mary got up from behind her desk to greet them. After they had exchanged pleasantries, she told them she had Maeve's scan and blood test results. She held them purposefully and Conor, alert to every nuance, noticed a slight tremble in her hand. Maeve hadn't missed it either.

Without allowing the doctor to speak first, she said, 'Mary, I know the cancer's back. I want to know what the prognosis is. How much time can I expect, and how much of that time will I be reasonably well?' She reached over and held Conor's hand. 'It will be easier for me to cope if I know what's ahead.'

'It's never possible to give definite answers, Maeve. You know that. You're obviously very much in tune with how your body is working. Yes, the cancer is back and it has spread, is spreading.'

She tapped her keyboard and turned the monitor around to face them. She zoomed in on certain areas and explained what she was looking for and what they had found.

'It's gone into the bone here,' she indicated, 'and I'm afraid there are other secondaries here and here, and that's not good. We can, of course, give you more treatment, followed by some radiotherapy, which will stop it spreading as rapidly. But that's all it will do,' she said, taking total control of the situation. 'I would be lying to you if I promised any more than that.'

'Conor, I don't think I'll go down that road again. I'll let nature take its course as it seem determined to win this battle.'

'You … we … can't just give up like that,' he said.

'Please, Conor …'

'We can, of course, control the pain and discomfort and I will respect your decision whatever you decide. Why don't you two take some time to talk about this? You don't have to make any decisions right here.'

'I don't know how I feel about this, Maeve. Shouldn't we at least give the treatments another go? Mary, are there any other avenues open to us? If we went to the States or Europe?'

'I honestly don't think so, Conor. Cancer is very well handled in Ireland, despite the bad press our hospitals get. But being quite frank with you both, Maeve, you have had the most aggressive treatments we could give you. Having more will definitely take its toll on the quality of life you can expect and will have very little benefits in arresting the cancer.'

'Conor, I don't need any more time to consider, I have my mind made up. I just need to live what's left to the full. Can you give me any indication of how long I have, Mary? Are we talking about eighteen months, a year, six months? Please, be honest with me.'

Conor felt sick. He knew now with conviction that he was going to lose Maeve, but he had never let himself think about when, dismissing such thoughts every time they crossed his mind.

'Less, I'm afraid, if we can't halt the progress. Conservatively, I would say around six to nine months, but there are many factors, not least your will power. People sometimes go into remission for no apparent reason too and you can't rule that out.'

Conor was speechless. He wanted to roar, to rail against their calm acceptance that Maeve's death was inevitable – something to be discussed like the closing date of some house sale. But he couldn't trust himself to talk. It was as if the awful truth was filtering through to him properly, for the first time. They left the consulting rooms and, while waiting in silence for the lift to arrive, Maeve suggested they go up to Stan for a few minutes.

'Maybe you could persuade him to take us to lunch?'

He didn't answer, but she pressed the fourth-floor button anyway.

FORTY-FOUR

Trish had been to see her solicitor to talk over Rory's proposals. It was coming up to a year since she has discovered his affair with Anna Maria. It was a date she would never forget. The shops were already decked out with Halloween masks and the traditional reds and greens of Christmas were beginning to creep in to the shopping centres. Would she ever enjoy these things again? The very word 'traditional' brought a surge of pain. They – she and Rory – had made their own traditions with the kids. They had always gone together to the bonfire in the local park and watched the fireworks on Halloween. She loved fireworks. Of course she could still go, but knew she wouldn't as she'd just feel lost and alone among all the couples they met and chatted to over the years and she couldn't, wouldn't, expect the kids to mind her.

It still amazed her how being part of a couple had metamorphosed her into something that meant she could no longer function as a single person, and she wondered if these feelings would ever go away. Would she ever regain her whole self and be able to attend parent–teacher meetings and other school events without feeling so ill at ease and so different that she could hardly think or talk coherently? Would the broken bits of her re-fuse and mend in time? If Rory had been a real bastard perhaps the transition would have been easier. But he must have been a bastard, mustn't he, she rationalised, to walk out on his kids like that? At this point, she consciously pushed away such thoughts as they only led to a dead end. She had lost her husband and soulmate: now she was going to lose her best friend.

She and Jim McConville had worked their way, item by item, through the proposals put by Rory's solicitor. He advised on certain points, put her mind to rest at some and abjectly refuted others. She took most of his advice and argued fiercely about the co-habiting clause, feeling it was unfair as Rory was already co-habiting. What right had he to sentence her to a life on her own?

'None, absolutely none. It works both ways,' Jim explained, 'and it really has nothing to do with you having a life of your own. It's the children who must be protected – it's their home that's at stake. It's yours too, but it has to be safeguarded for them first and foremost. It also means that he cannot decide to sell it from under them whether you both, or either of you, remarry or co-habit,' he argued logically. 'He's not saying you can't co-habit – he's saying you can't in that family home.'

They batted back and forth.

'I know it may not seem fair, but for someone with such a reputation for being, shall we say, cautious with his money, these proposals are quite generous,' he pointed out.

After some more deliberation, they finally worked their way through the document that would to go back to Rory's solicitor.

'Well now, what do you think of Liam's news?' he asked.

'I'm delighted. Kevin seems to be a really nice guy and they are good together. I've been meaning to have a dinner to celebrate some night. Will you come along?'

'Try and stop me,' he laughed. 'I've heard about your cooking. Meantime, don't worry about this business. Rory, despite everything, seems to be acting with good heart, and believe you me, whether it's from guilt, remorse or goodwill, that doesn't happen in many separation cases, so let's strike while he's still in that frame of mind.'

FORTY-FIVE

The weeks trundled on and Conor found it very hard to concentrate on work. He was devastated and wondered how he'd go on when the inevitable happened. Increasingly he handed over more of the workload to his partners and took to bringing files home so that he could spend more time with Maeve. She had finally given up working in the clinic altogether, and, despite her best efforts to keep smiling, was not always in good form. She got a bad flu; her resistance had been lowered by the earlier treatments and from the ongoing battle her body was waging against the cancer. The coughing was an effort and after two weeks with no improvement and a lot of discomfort, Mary decided she should be admitted to hospital and put on an intravenous antibiotic.

Trish spent a lot of time with her and although Maeve didn't seem to be winning this bout, she tried to keep her upbeat, visiting every day, massaging her feet and arms to try to ease the pain when it got bad.

One day when Sharonne visited, Maeve asked her to tell Derek to pop by, on his own. 'It's not that I have designs on him or anything like that, and while Conor is still around I'll stay on the monogamous road for a while longer – although maybe a little fling before it's too late might be an idea. What do you think?' she asked. 'I'd hate to die wondering!'

'That's what we used to say about the nuns at school,' said Sharonne. 'We used to think they knew nothing about sex and were all virgins. Now I often wonder if any of them actually were and did any of them really die wondering.'

'Probably not!'

A nurse came in to check on the drip and write a remark on Maeve's chart. 'What beautiful flowers, can I put them in water for you?'

They thanked her and Maeve said, 'Sharonne, I have to tell you something. Derek and I never had anything serious going on.'

'That doesn't matter now, Maeve.'

'It does, because I have to confess I used to like seeing you being so jealous. That was horrible of me. Derek never loved me and I never loved him in that way. We had great fun together for a few months, but that was all and it was all a long time ago. I value and have always valued his friendship, but only that, so you never had any need to worry. Besides, you know, he loves you very much, never stops talking about you and the twins.'

'I do know that,' said Sharonne, taking Maeve's hand. 'And I was the horrible one, especially to you, and you never deserved it.'

The nurse came back in with the flowers, beautifully arranged.

'Maeve, you look tired. Why don't you try to have some sleep?' she suggested, and Sharonne took the hint. They hugged warmly.

Sharonne called Derek from the hospital car park. She didn't like to dwell on what was ahead either. It reminded her of losing her father and she couldn't bear to think what she would do if it was happening to her or Derek. What would happen to the girls? She was also full of admiration for Maeve's coping skills and her unfailing good humour and sense of fairness.

'Oh, Derek, I don't think she'll be with us for too much

longer,' Sharonne told her husband. 'No, I don't know if anything is going to happen immediately. She's gone awfully scrawny though and has asked if you could go and see her – on your own!'

'Oh,' he laughed. 'A private audience. Interesting. I'll drop in on the way home from work.'

***

Maeve held Derek's hand, wanting to tell him something before Conor came in on the way from the office.

'He has to move on when I'm no longer here.'

'Maeve, don't talk like—'

'Let me speak, Derek. Let's be honest with each other. We've always been able to be that. You know and I know that I'll be gone soon – where to I'm not too sure about, but I won't be around here and that's a certainty.'

'But no one knows … '

'No, hush, Derek, I have to say this. I know and I have accepted it, but Conor hasn't. At least I don't think he has. Perhaps he's trying to pretend for my sake. Make him sell the villa in Mijas.'

'You know he won't want to do that. He loves that place.'

'Spain's where we've always been happiest and I know he'll hang on to that. That's why I wouldn't go over this autumn, I only want him to remember me strong and well when he thinks of it. It will take some persuasion to make him leave it, but I know him and he'll not move on as long as it's there. Besides, we've hardly used it this year and it's full of memories. You'll have to use all your influence to convince him that in selling it, he's not jettisoning our memories.'

'He won't want to sell it.'

'I know, and you'll have to talk him round. Going somewhere new on holiday doesn't obliterate the places you've been before, does it? Promise me, Derek, that you'll do your best.'

'I don't know if I can promise you that.'

'I'll not pretend it will be easy, but he has to have a life after me. Any time I bring the subject up, he talks about something else. I don't want him to waste his time moping around on his own and I need to know that he'll have what we had again.'

'I'm sure the thought never crossed his mind. Conor has never looked at another woman since he met you, Maeve. You know that.'

'That's not important,' she said. Conor had never told anyone but his wife and Trish about his one infidelity. 'I need to know that he'll meet someone else and have new places and new memories to cherish. He's a young man. His life won't be over and he could still have the children he always wanted. Promise me you'll tell him that, as soon as you think he's ready to hear it. But make him wait six months,' she added, attempting to lighten things up. 'I hate men who parade their new wives with indecent haste!' She smiled at him and squeezed his hand.

Derek felt tears behind his eyes and knew he couldn't look away to avoid Maeve's intent gaze. All he could do was reach out and wrap his arms around her and rock her gently. He was shocked at how thin she had become, afraid his hug would crush her.

'I'm going to miss you,' he said, 'an awful lot.'

'And I you.'

He released her softly back onto the pillows. She closed her eyes for a few minutes, hoping to dispel her own tears.

'We've been so lucky, you know? And if Conor and I had another ten or twenty years, we may have ended up hating each other. Who knows? I may have gone off with George Clooney. He may have eloped with J.Lo or Beyoncé. This way I get to exit first and that's hard, but we've had a great life together.'

***

Maeve got home again, but not for long and, a few weeks later, she was back in hospital. Trish witnessed Maeve struggling, and on her good days they laughed and joked as though there was no tomorrow. On her bad ones they just sat together, with no need for words. These women made an occasion of everything that needed to be celebrated. Even the staff commented on it. On Maeve's last birthday, her thirty-ninth, a week before what was to be her last Christmas, Trish brought in a fistful of helium-filled balloons and tied them to the bedpost. They had popped open a bottle of Prosecco that Conor had left in earlier. Trish had brought a second one. 'Let's celebrate – just in case I'm not here to ring out the old,' Maeve had insisted.

'Don't even joke about it,' Conor said, unable to cope when she spoke like that.

All the nurses came by. Mary, her oncologist, who had been tipped off by the ward sister, had left some of her patients waiting in her private rooms to add her best wishes and join in a toast. When they had all left, Trish sat up on the bed beside Maeve, sharing her pillows. With red Christmas hats on, they wrote a letter to Santa, asking for outlandish presents for everyone.

Maeve asked for a Mercedes for Conor – a sporty one in dark green with cream leather upholstery and a soft cream top. For Liam it had to be a Lamborghini – red – it was time he changed from his Ferrari. For Trish, they asked that the drop-dead-gorgeous waiter in their local Italian would come and read the phone book to her every night. He couldn't speak English and she had often said that would be the next best thing. She was a sucker for all things Italian and was always threatening to learn the language! For Rory, despite his absence, they asked for a lock and key for his trouser pockets, so that none of his loose change would fall out, or indeed his notes either, as he rolled with Anna Maria in the snow. They asked that she would get fat, grow a beard and get spots. For herself, Maeve asked to get through Christmas and, if possible, the New Year too.

'I hate people who die at Christmas, because they ruin that time for anyone who cares for them,' she said. 'If I go before, please put me in storage and have the funeral in February – that's a dreary month anyway.'

'Shut up and stop talking like that or I'll ask Sharonne to arrange your funeral for you! One with a Barbie pink theme.' They fell back on the flattened pillows laughing, the effects of the fizz beginning to work.

'Now I'd hate to miss that, and if you dare, I'll come back and haunt you,' threatened Maeve.

'She's really changed for the better, hasn't she? What will we ask Santa to bring her.' They thought for a second and simultaneously said, 'A designer handbag.' They laughed again and Trish, putting her finger up to her lips, said, 'Shusshhh, we're behaving like bold kids. They'll throw us both out and I'll be barred for bringing in alcohol.'

Maeve used one of the blank envelopes from her cards for their letter and addressed it to 'Father Christmas, North Pole, The Arctic Circle, The Earth, The World, The Universe, Outer Space, The Cosmos', as she had done as a child. She sealed it just as the chaplain popped his head around the door.

'Anything I can do?' he enquired.

'Yes please,' said Maeve who had rejected any such offers previously. 'Can you post this for me please? It doesn't need a stamp.'

Glancing at the address, he just smiled and said, 'No, I don't suppose it does. Have you written one to God too?'

'There's not much point if he doesn't know what my wishes are by now. Besides, he's the one carrying the map,' she answered. 'I'm just following along behind.'

***

It may be true that time heals, thought Trish, but no one actually told you how long it takes. The kids had settled down somewhat and in many ways she felt they were more resilient than she was. But would what they had been through screw up their chances of having sustainable relationships later in life? Barry was working in school and attending regularly, thanks in no small way to Liam's encouragement. His mocks were looming early in February. Louise had made it onto the school's hockey team and her life seemed to be a round of matches and practices. Toni seemed to have dozens of friends and Trish often used to wonder if she was surrounding herself with them to stop herself from feeling lonely. Trish knew her days with Maeve were numbered and her sister had offered to do the Christmas dinner so that she could spend this precious time with her friend.

Sharonne, Derek and the girls decided to go to the Caribbean for the holidays to spend some quality time together. Since she had had such success with the very public FitzGerald-Reglob debacle, her company was inundated with work and she had had to take on a new partner. That was when she decided to take more down time and spend more of it with her family. Liam and Kevin were now living together and the whole holiday period had a surreal feel to it. Everyone seemed to be preoccupied – waiting and wondering and dreading.

***

Maeve did see the old year out and the new one in. Conor didn't go back to work after the Christmas break. He used to watch her as she slept, something she seemed to be doing more and more. He knew she was heavily drugged to keep the pain managed, but there were many lucid moments. While she slipped into her own little world, he found himself holding silent conversations with her as her chest rose and fell with an even, slow rhythm. 'Will your heart just stop?' he wondered. 'What happens at the end?' 'Will you know?' Occasionally she'd take a long slow inhalation followed by an awful silence and he'd think she'd finished breathing altogether, causing his own heart to race, only for her to start again in a regular steady pattern, allowing his own panic to subside for another while.

She wanted to die at home and Mary agreed that with hospice nursing that could be arranged. Maeve was losing body weight and mass before their eyes, and she'd developed quite a tummy. It was the palliative care nurse who alerted Conor to the fact that her kidneys were coming under serious stress and that her time was shortening. It was on Saturday night that he phoned their closest family and friends. They were all gathered in her bedroom when she opened her eyes, which were now far too big for her thin face, and she smiled. 'Thanks, guys, for being around me.' And they all talked at once, breaking the hush that had fallen on the room before that.

She never said anything else. She simply stopped being there with them at that second.

Conor stood up, kissed her forehead and said, 'Goodbye, darling. Sleep peacefully.' Then he left the room.

Trish, who felt she had no heart left to break, was inconsolable. 'We never got to go skiing together,' she muttered as she stroked her friend's forehead and wondered where that ridiculous thought had come from.

FORTY-SIX

The days went by in a blur and a muddle of arrangements, which somehow came together in time. Funeral notices, readings, flowers, making sure no one was forgotten. Rory arrived from Belgium without Anna Maria, everyone was relieved to see. He stayed with Conor, their rift unmentioned, just two long-term friends who needed each other. Trish got through the days, looking out for her children who had loved Maeve as much as their real aunts. She could sense their disbelief and bewilderment as their world was rocked again. Flanked by her daughters in the church, her son looking manly and dependable in a seldom-worn overcoat, blazer and chinos, Trish sensed rather than saw her ex-husband slide into the end of the pew.

That evening, when they had returned home after another exhausting day, her phone rang. It was Rory. 'Can I come around? I need to talk to you.'

'No. Not tonight. I am wiped out emotionally. I don't want to discuss settlements and things like that right now. I just want to go to bed. '

'I understand,' he said and arranged to call the next morning.

Trish felt like an alien in her own world. Something was missing and would never be the same again. She wanted to ring Maeve and tell her all about the funeral – her own funeral – the meaningful readings, the hauntingly beautiful music, the things people said, the memories that had been dredged to the surface for so many of those who knew her. And she knew she couldn't. She would never be able to tell Maeve any of those things. This emptiness was totally different to when Rory had packed and left. He was still alive and although she'd wanted to kill him, he was still around. Maeve was gone.

***

'How dare you. How bloody dare you even suggest such a thing?' Trish said evenly, although her heart was racing. 'You lowlife, coming back here thinking you can get around everyone, worming your way back in with your friends who are all distressed and vulnerable. Can't you see they are just being nice to you because of me and our kids? They don't like you anymore – they don't like what you did to us or to them. Just because we've managed to be civil to each other and, believe you me, it's not that easy, that doesn't mean that there is anything left between us.'

'Can we not try again?' he urged.

'Try what? Try allowing you move back in and pretend you never left us? You abandoned your kids. Can you get your head around that? When they wake up every morning, you're gone. You're not exactly down the road so that they can pop in and talk to you about their life. You chose to move to another country, for God's sake. Could you not even have stayed where you could be close to them?'

'I don't think—'

'No – you don't think. That's your trouble. Did you ever think of the long-term effects of anything you do?'

His phone rang. He looked at the screen, turned it off and put it back in his pocket.

'Does she know you're here? Does she know you're asking me to take you back?'

'She has a name.'

'Oh, I know that.'

'Being back has made me think about things. I know I made a mistake. I treated you badly, you and the kids too. I can't explain it, but I think I'd like to try and work things out.'

'Well, you'll have to do that with the kids, but count me out of this scene. I cashed in everything when I married you and I did it willingly. I gave up my career to be a stay-at-home wife and mother.'

'You wanted to do that.'

'Yes, I did, and you wanted me to do that too. I would not swap one minute of that time, but what I *would* change would be the fact that I totally surrendered myself to you. You were my life, my first priority, and I thought I was yours.'

'You were, Trish. You know you were.'

'I know I was until you decided it was over. You were tired. You wanted a new toy so you threw away the old ones. Not just me, Rory. You traded Barry, Louise and Toni for that woman too. You ruined four people's trust, love and loyalty and that can never be restored.'

'Can we not try to rekindle what we had?'

'You're not listening. How can you sit there and ask me that? You destroyed my faith in everyone. I'll never trust anyone again because I was so sure about you. What we had was supposed to be for ever. If you were not happy why didn't you say so?'

'I wasn't unhappy.'

'When was it no longer enough?'

'I don't know. I never thought about it.'

'No. You never thought about anything only making money and trying to keep up with Conor and Derek. There's Barry ashamed to go anywhere where there are fathers. He doesn't even go around to David's any more. He's dropped out of rugby and games at school.'

'He's a teenager. They're all moody.'

'Yes, he's a teenager, who shouldn't have to cope with his father running after a blonde from Finland. The biggest crisis in his life just now should be teenage acne, or whether some girl will go out with him if he had the courage to ask her. Not being ashamed of his father.'

'I'll talk to him.'

'You can talk all you like. Nothing, and I mean nothing, will ever make up to them for what you did. Your daughters will probably never trust a man in their lives either. They adored you, Rory, now they don't know how to act around you. Have you any idea what it's like trying to tell them you still care and that they are still important to you when you just fly in, spend a day or two and leave them again to go back to someone other than them? How do I answer them when they say, "He must love her more or he wouldn't have left us?"'

'That's not true. It's not like that.'

'Can you answer me this then, what *is* it like? Because I've tried. I've tried not to be bitter and not let them see my feelings, but they have their own. They have their own sense of betrayal and abandonment. They feel cheated and they are hurting too. And that breaks my heart.'

'Don't you think I don't know that, Trish? But it's not too late.'

'It is for me.'

'Are you seeing anyone?'

'Have you heard nothing that I've said? I don't think I'll ever go out with anyone again. I'll never get close enough to give anyone the chance of a repeat performance of what you did to me, to us.'

'You don't know that.'

'Oh yes, believe you me, I do. I so do. I've erected a barbed-wire fence around me and inside that, there's an electric one. No one will ever get inside them.'

'I was hoping we could sort things out. I'm lonely over there.'

'I've been lonely since I read those wonderful text messages from your lover. Now I'd appreciate if you'd finalise the legalities so that I can get on with my life.'

'The reason I've been dragging my heels is because I didn't want to rush in to anything in case I was coming back.'

'You bastard! How can you sit there and tell me we're just part of your great life plan, option B if things didn't go according to Rory's divine plan A; pawns to be moved around a board at your bidding. Well, I want things sorted so that I can move on. Talk to the kids and see how they feel about their home. I don't want your money, but I do want them to feel some sense of security.'

'I'll talk to the solicitor before I go back to Brussels,' he said in a deflated voice. 'I don't want the house. I'll sign that over and I will support you all.'

'Why does that not give me a warm glow – make me feel confident? That could be more lies.'

'I never lied to you.'

'No? Just think what you are saying. You lied when you went on those so-called business trips. You lied when you said you were playing golf that morning when you went to the Radisson. You lied to your friends too. Are you really so deluded that you honestly can sit there and believe you never lied to any of us? Rory, get real. You've probably lied to Anna Maria about why you're still in Dublin. I'll only believe everything you say when I see a court seal on it.'

'Let's do this civilly. Why hand out a fortune to the solicitors? They'll take a whopping percentage.'

She was exhausted. It was back to money again. Everything in his life came back to that base line. 'Just go, Rory. Just go,' she said, getting up from the table.

As he was leaving he said, 'I am really sorry about Maeve. You'll miss her.'

'I know. I will.'

She leaned against he door after he drove off and cried for herself, for Maeve, for her children and for everything that was gone for ever.

FORTY-SEVEN

Eighteen Months Later

A white cat with patches of ginger was poised for attack, eyeing two birds as they skirted the palm trees. The cat blinked, changed its mind, stretched and lay back down in the parched grass.

From a hundred metres or so off the beach, the squeals of excitement carried as a group of youngsters whizzed by, towed at speed on a banana boat. Every so often one fell off – followed almost immediately by the whole lot. The speeding leader boat slowed to a halt while the pantomime of trying to mount the banana again began, amid more shrieks of laughter and much splashing and grabbing. Further out, the intermittent whone-whone-whone of jet skis could be heard as they made contact with the water. The sound reminded Conor of the dentist.

Conor was in Cyprus – staying at a hotel that reflected the up-market side of the island in one of the five-star resorts that dotted the eight-mile-long stretch that is Limassol. Derek had come out with him. They had meals served by a Hercules, cooked by a Socrates and met a wine merchant called Herodotus; his son was Calistus. The solicitor they dealt with that morning had a wonderfully unpronounceable name, which was shortened to Harris.

Derek had just bought a new villa on the golf-course complex that Liam had been involved in developing. It would be ready for use in a few weeks. They had completed their business, signed the contracts and, with those out of the way, Conor felt a great sense of fulfilment. Liam was on his way back to Dublin for a meeting but Derek and he were staying on for a few more days before returning home. The tribunal was over, at long last. Conor had made an obscene amount of money out of it. All sorts of dirty dealings had been unearthed, yet it had no power to prosecute anyone involved. He had been glad of all its prevarications, because they had kept him from falling apart after Maeve had died. He had worked every hour God sent and was finally able to go home in the evenings and sit down to watch the telly. He hated their house now and would have put it on the market, except he felt it would be disloyal to her memory if he did.

Derek was going to have a thalassotherapy treatment – in the line of research, he'd claimed. 'I feel I deserve this, after traipsing around that site all morning with you,' Derek had said. 'And as I spend so much time drawing up the plans and costings for such developments, I think it's now time to see if they really do live up to the glossy brochures.'

'Enjoy, Derek. I'm just going to take time out and sit in the sun doing absolutely nothing.'

'Seriously though, I know you've done the right thing buying here. It really is a wonderful spot and the views are spectacular. Aphrodite is supposed to have risen from the waves right there. I wonder did they add anything on to the asking price for that legend?'

'Ever the romantic soul,' he laughed. 'I hope Sharonne appreciates you.'

'What do you think?'

He had encouraged Conor to go for the villa in Cyprus, for all sorts of reasons.

'From a purely personal point of view, I feel I do deserve

this,' said Conor. 'It's been a rough few years, even though I was afraid to admit that to myself at the time.

'Just as well you don't suffer from triskaidekaphobia,' said Derek.

'What the hell is that?

'A fear of the number thirteen. Today's the thirteenth.'

'You and your big words. That sort of thing doesn't bother me. I'm not the superstitious kind. Anyway, don't people say 'lucky thirteen'?

'Lucky for some …'

This was Conor's third visit to the complex, but he had been sold on the idea the first time he'd seen it. Still incomplete, the course was due to open in one month's time. Set spectacularly on either side of a deep gorge, the seventh hole sat right in the middle on a tiny plateau with ravines surrounding it. On one side the golf cart pathway ribboned precipitously down the steep side of the hill to the uncharacteristically green fairway and hole.

Harris had said, 'This par four is what we call the crown jewel of the course.'

It was as spectacular as it was difficult, and it was where prospective investors and buyers were first taken for the sales pitch. No one could fail to be impressed.

'Dane Merrel will make his name as a course designer with this playground. It'll certainly pander to those in pursuit of the hardest hit, the lowest handicap and the biggest boast in the clubhouse afterwards. Even I can see that and I don't play golf!'

'You'd never guess with that spiel,' Conor had laughed, as he and Harris had agreed that this fledgling course builder seemed to have got it in one.

Conor sat up on the lounger and watched a tanned Adonis do intricate moves on water skis as he rode the waves in the wake of a powerful motorboat. The birdsong was crisp and different;

the cat had long since given up the inclination to hunt and was slumbering supinely.

I need to cool off, he thought, and looked towards the pool and back to the sea. He was equidistant from both. The pool won. This hotel had a dozen of them in all, albeit many in the spa facilities. He did a couple of lengths. He waved to some kids who were looking up from the window below the bottom of the pool. Then he headed towards the row of bar stools in the water and ordered a beer. He watched his feet making shadows on the blue tiles beneath. When he got back to his lounger, the cat has made itself comfortable on his towel. Shooed away, it took up its position alongside his flip-flops and went back to sleep.

Conor stretched out again and began a virtual tour in his mind of his new property. The show villas were decked out in the best of everything and he had decided to use their interior designer to do up his one. They had left nothing out – the stylist had even stocked the freezer with mock cartons of ice cream. There was a hammock in the garden. He didn't like hammocks: he had fallen out of one while showing off in Derek's house years ago. That in itself was not remarkable enough to remember all these years later. However, it was the fact that it had been in that same garden and on the same midsummer's night that Rory had introduced him to Maeve that had made it unforgettable.

He felt sad when he thought of Rory. He'd had it all – the perfect house, family, wife, body and personality. Then he lost the plot and walked out on everything. When he'd upped and left, he'd burned all his bridges. On one of the occasions that he had come back to Dublin, he had even played a round in their golf club. That had been a bad call. Meeting him had embarrassed everybody. His discomfort had shown and there were plenty of awkward pauses and self-conscious banalities. Frankly, they were all relieved when he had flown back to Brussels.

Conor didn't know whether he would have Rory out to stay at the new place. They sometimes kept in touch, but not so much since Maeve's funeral. Although affable, Rory took everything he got and more besides. Despite having plenty of money, he never spent any unless he had to. He had improved a bit though, because when Rory had set up his fledgling practice, Barbara, a friend of Maeve's, had worked there and had regaled them with tales of 'skinny' toilet paper and of how he'd always turn off the water heater before he'd leave for the day. They'd always been able to tell when he wasn't coming back – by checking the switch.

Despite everything that had happened between the friends, Rory probably wouldn't wait to be asked, he'd invite himself to the villa. That was for sure.

Derek had been Conor's staunchest friend through Maeve's illness, through the ups and downs of radiation and chemo, the false hopes, the total despair, the desolation. He was the one who had finally persuaded Conor to think about selling the villa. Liam had joined in counselling him to make a fresh start.

'Maeve'd want you to move on,' they'd urged, and after much arm-twisting, Conor had agreed. Today he'd made everything legal and last month had tied up the sale of the Spanish property – but not without mixed feelings. He rationalised, 'Mijas was good to me. It netted me four times what I paid for it, so this was a no brainer really. I'll still have plenty of change in my back pocket.'

'Wise man,' said Derek.

'I'd never have borrowed to fund this. It would be madness with all the uncertainty around.' Derek had agreed.

'This is an investment in my future. I wouldn't mind retiring here someday,' Conor said.

'You could do a lot worse.'

The sun cast lengthening shadows as it lowered to meet the water off Limassol. Umbrella- and fruit-adorned cocktails were appearing on tables around the pool. The couple next to Conor whispered and laughed intimately and he looked up instinctively. The laugh was like Maeve's. He felt so alone, surrounded by people – lost – a singleton in coupledom.

He'd managed a whole day until now, five-forty on September thirteenth, not to think of Maeve – even once. No! That was a lie! He had thought of her, but had managed to divert his thoughts, actively channelling them to the figures and the legal clauses, the green fees and to his new best friend, the ginger and white cat. Now the way the young, bronzed girl twisted her hair, expanded the elastic and tucked in the stray strands brought him back with a physical pain. Maeve had done exactly the same thing.

It was easy for others to say 'get a new interest, make new friends' and to offer the kind of advice that his friends had showered on him when the cancer had finally taken Maeve. It was not so easy to do though.

Besides, Conor didn't want to forget. He didn't want to move on either. He was scared he would forget – forget her dark eyes and the long, dark lashes, her boyish figure and sallow skin. He was afraid he'd forget the golden beaches they had shared, their favourite spot in Mauritius at the St Géran, where they planted flags in the coral sand when they wanted a drink and the waiters appeared from nowhere to take the orders for their pina coladas. These had arrived with the pineapple pieces cut in the shape of parrots and the waiter had taken a photo of them sipping and laughing head-to-head. He had that snap in his wallet still – their fifteenth anniversary and their last trip before her illness.

Focus, focus, focus, he said to himself, standing up and walking towards the sea. Maeve had tried to make him promise he'd get on with his life. He knew she'd have loved the new villa with its high-tech kitchen and tall windows, the bougainvillea, the beds of roses and the aqua-tiled pool. He waded into the tepid, almost waveless water till he found his depth. I can see her there on the patio. If she were still alive, I'd know she'd have fallen for the outdoor Jacuzzi too.

I have to move on and think about something – anything– else, he willed his mind as he lengthened his stroke. Derek should be out from the spa soon and we'll head off for some more of Socrates' specialities and wit. Remember the floor plan of the villa. How many jets had that Jacuzzi? What will the neighbours be like? Where will they be from? Will the course be up to scratch for the opening in four weeks' time? What is that yellow flower that is blooming everywhere?

He didn't hear the speedboat, hadn't noticed passing the warning red marker buoys. In fact, he hardly felt the impact at all. Suddenly all thoughts of Maeve were gone.

The white cat with the ginger patches opened her eyes, looked out to sea, blinked twice, and jumped onto Conor's lounger.

***

Derek presented himself at the reception desk in the Wellness Centre in their hotel, which had just won another world leader award. His company acted for a rival international hotel chain, which was now diversifying its attractions and adding luxurious spas as part of the conference and leisure packages at their five-star-plus resorts. He wondered when someone would call a halt to these decadently luxurious add-ons, which every hotel seemed to see as essentials nowadays. Back home even the smallest ones were constantly advertising their spa packages and weekend breaks. A recession was beginning to bite and if it came as predicted it would be a much bigger crash than anyone expected. Spas would be the last thing on many people's agenda then, but he was interested to see what the opposition was doing. Besides, he and Conor had been given complimentary use of all the amenities here for the duration of their stay, thanks to Harris, who, it seemed, knew everyone in Cyprus.

He was impressed as he looked around, wearing a monogrammed wrap. Modern-day monks and nuns all dressed in similar robes, but instead of pursuing self-deprivation and sacrifice, these modern orders were worshipping at the altars of the gods of pampering.

'That's a very futuristic workstation.' he said to the perfectly coiffed and flawless assistant as she checked his name in the appointment book. She smiled back. Her name badge said 'Colette, South Africa'.

'Isn't it special? There is nowhere else like it in Cyprus. It is a lovely place to work. If you take a seat over there, your therapist will be with you in a moment.'

The wall behind her looked more like the bridge on a luxury liner, with brass-framed cases protecting brass-finished wheels and gauges, all controls and monitors for the various pools. He went over to the window and took in the vista below. The lawns were dotted with blue-and-white-striped sun umbrellas and loungers. The hotel-issue towels were striped to match. There was lush foliage everywhere. Beyond, the beach was in full use and the sea shimmered in the Mediterranean sun. He could see there was a lot of activity going on at the complex's marina too.

A therapist arrived to escort him to the first of the thalassotherapy pools.

'Have you had this sort of treatment before?' she asked Derek.

'Just once, but I've been on the other side a lot. I work in the development business and spend a good deal of time on new properties and although I do get to see lots of spas, they're usually still pretty raw when I am on site.'

'Then let me show you the facilities we have.'

After a walk through manicured gardens, past statues and beneath arches and pillars, they ended up back at the first pool.

'This is filled with natural minerals and nutrients – all derived from seaweed,' the therapist explained, handing him a little inflatable neck ring. 'It's very nice; you just lie back and enjoy the feeling. I'll come for you in about ten minutes and we'll move you on to the next one. Each pool has different properties and temperatures and as you work your way around them, you'll find jets of water to tone the various parts of your body.'

Taking off his robe, he hesitated as he walked down the steps. The lukewarm water seemed to have an oily, murky skin.

'It's just the additives. They are all natural, and they are very good for you,' she added, as though willing him to feel the benefits. She sashayed off.

'It pongs too,' Derek commented to himself.

Disembodied heads floated around him, jutting up with closed eyes on their little cushions. Whatever these nutrients are they certainly add buoyancy to the water, he thought, as he adjusted his pillow. He felt himself float into the shade and looked up through the spaces in the psychedelically vibrant bougainvillea to the bright-blue sky above.

This is the life. I should have insisted that Conor come with me – this is just the sort of relaxation he needs. He knew that this morning had taken its toll on his friend: moving on was never easy, but he was equally sure that buying that villa would be the start of a new life for him.

Although none of them dared bring up the subject, his friends felt it would only be a matter of time until he met someone else. Already in the golf club in Dublin, the ladies were circling at social events, although none had yet issued invitations to him. They had all known and liked Maeve enormously.

Derek couldn't wait for his wife's reaction when she came to check the place out. Sharonne had an opinion on everything and it was usually at variance with the general consensus. They'd have to get Trish out too. They hadn't spent a holiday together since Maeve had died.

As Derek sank down into the second pool he thought, 'Well, Maeve, girl, if you are out there in the great blue yonder, I've managed to persuade your very stubborn husband to move on – somewhat. It took a year before he would even talk about it.

He's sold Mijas and has just bought a new villa out here in Cyprus, which you would love. Sharonne will never come home once she sees it and I'm tempted to take early retirement and move over here altogether.'

His thoughts were interrupted by a group of noisy women who joined him in the pool. Moving from one underwater spout to the next, they yelled to each other, 'You must try this, it's great for your back' or 'Stretch out your legs and feel the pressure on the bottom of your feet.' They included him in the banter and proceeded to tell him they were Dutch, and their employer was paying for all their treatments and for their two-week holiday, prescribed by the company doctor as an insurance against stress in the workplace.

'I think I need to get a project in Holland!' he told them. They laughed and said he'd be most welcome. He'd need to be fluent in three other languages though, apart from English. That brought him back to reality. His prowess in linguistics was limited.

The peace broken, he decided to abort the thalassotherapy rituals and head back to the beach to find Conor. Skipping the indoor steam and relaxation rooms with their background music of gently dropping water and vague ethereal sounds, he stood on the steps outside enjoying a different view of the resort than the one he had earlier. There seemed to be some commotion just off the beach. Two speedboats joined a few others out at sea. Along the shore's edge people gathered, talking in small groups. In the distance, he could hear sirens. He took the stairs two at a time.

Logic told him it had nothing to do with them. Conor was a strong swimmer, always on the water polo teams in college. Yet some premonition hit him like a fist to the solar plexus. Some primeval inner sense told him that the commotion concerned Conor, somehow.

He broke into a run.

FORTY-EIGHT

Trish was just walking out to her car to go to her Italian-language class when the phone rang. She paused for a second, trying to decide whether to pick up or let the answering machine take the call for her. If it was Liz she could expect a twenty-minute invective on her children's fortunes and lack of. Not that her teacher would have minded, but she was due to pick up one of the others en route and she hated to be late for that. She really enjoyed these classes and she was going to join an Italian wine appreciation one in the autumn too.

Let the machine take it, she decided, and then thought it might be her friend to say she'd been delayed.

'Trish, it's me,' said Derek, and some instinct made her shiver.

'I'm afraid I have some bad news.'

'What's happened? Are you OK?'

'Yes, I'm fine. It's Conor – there's been an accident.'

'What happened? Aren't you in Cyprus?'

'Yes. I really don't know what happened. He was swimming in the sea and was hit by a jet ski or a motorboat, I'm not sure which. He's in a bad way.'

'Oh, no. My God, no. How bad is bad?'

'I'm at the hospital now and he's in surgery, but they have warned me he may not make it. He was taken by helicopter from the hotel about two hours ago and the police brought me by car.'

'Oh Derek. Can I do anything?'

'There's nothing to do at the moment, until I know more. Sharonne's trying to get on to Dee and tell her to clear my diary for the rest of the week. There's no way I'll be back, whatever happens.'

'Derek, be positive. I was just going out, but I'll stay at home to be near the phone. Should I come out there?'

'I don't know what to say. I've been trying to get in touch with Liam. He flew back there this morning. Could you tell him?'

'Of course. Call me or get Sharonne to as soon as you have any news.'

'Of course I will. Straight away,' he said.

'You take care.' She hung up, thinking why the hell does life have to be so shitty? It seemed to wait until things just started to go well, and then wham!

***

Derek paced the corridor of the hospital, not understanding any of the snatches of conservation going on around him. White-clad figures came and went, businesslike, about their errands while visitors in summer clothes passed by on their way to the wards. A large clock over the door marked the seemingly slow-motion passage of time. When he glanced at the hands, they had barely moved at all since his previous look.

Why did this have to happen now? he thought. Conor was just getting his life back on track and the purchase of the villa was a huge step for him, and now this. The swing doors on the right opened together and two doctors came through, striding with intent towards him.

'You came in with Mr Conor D'Alton, didn't you? Is he a relative?' the swarthiest of the two asked in a heavily accented voice, with American undertones. He tugged at the tabs on the back of his blue surgical headgear, which for some ridiculous reason reminded Derek of the blue and white fabric of the washing-up cloths Sharonne used.

'Yes, I did. Conor and I are like brothers, but we're just friends. How is he?'

'I'm afraid the news is not so good. He is by no means out of danger and it is only fair to say that he is alive, but only just. I am Spiro Theopolus. I'm a neuro specialist. Dr Dimetri Stephanides here is a general surgeon,' he said, introducing him to the second, taller doctor. Derek noticed his headdress had sprigs of flowers printed on it.

'He and his team have done all they can to correct the physical damage for the moment – the broken bones and lacerations. But we are more concerned with the damage to his spine and his head. We do not know the extent of brain injury from the bleeding caused by the impact and it is impossible yet to say if he will have paralysis from his spinal injuries. We must now play the waiting game, no?'

Derek found himself lost for words.

'When … How long will it be before we know if …' he hesitated, afraid to voice his greatest fears, 'before we know if … he'll pull through?'

'I am sorry. I cannot answer that. We don't know. Every hour he survives is crucial, but it may be days before he comes out of the coma, if, in fact, he does.' He led Derek gently towards the reception desk. 'We will need to get some more particulars of Mr D'Alton, his nearest relatives and some contact numbers. Can you supply us with those, please? Does he have any family or friends in Cyprus?'

'No, just business contacts, but I'll get in touch with those tomorrow. Can I see him?'

'He's still in recovery in the operating area, so I'm afraid not yet, but we'll be moving him to the intensive care unit in a while and you may go in for a minute then. May I say, I am sorry your friend should have such a terrible accident when visiting our island.'

Derek mumbled something, which he hoped was coherent, and the surgeons retreated to their world behind the swing doors, leaving him lost, bewildered and very much alone.

***

Liam answered his phone after only a few rings.

'Well, Trish, this is a pleasant surprise. What's the occasion? Are you ringing to invite us around for one of your delicious feasts?'

'Afraid not this time.'

Trish broke the news.

'I just can't believe it. Do you think we should go out there?' he asked her. 'Or can we do anything this end?'

'I'm waiting to hear back from Derek or Sharonne. He said he'd call and let me know if there's any change. I'm almost afraid to say it, but it's not looking good at all. I was going to wait until the morning and see if I could get a flight. I don't want to hold up the telephone line now in case he's trying to ring again.'

'OK. I'll get back to you later. Will you be able to get away?'

'Conor has always been there for me and I'm going to be there for him. Anyway the kids are all away, as luck would have it. The girls are in the Gaeltacht and Barry is still in the States! I wish he was here because he's a computer wiz and he could magic up flights from the internet in a flash.'

'Don't bother about doing that. I'll sort them out at this end and come with you. Should I book one for Sharonne too? No, she's probably already on to it herself. I'll call Aldora and ask her to go to the hospital, she'll be able to help with translations and such if needed.'

'That's a great idea.'

'Whatever happens, I'm sure Derek will be glad of some company if he's keeping vigil there. I'll see if I can get some seats, something direct from Dublin if possible. I'll get back to you. I'll use the mobile number to keep the landline free. If Derek rings ask him for the name or the phone number of the hospital and his hotel, will you?'

Derek phoned Trish again at eleven. 'There's no change,' he said in a flat, tired voice. 'They've moved him into intensive care and he seems to be wired up to loads of machines and drips. He's still in a coma, but they tell me that's a good thing. They keep saying it's much too early to know if he'll survive.'

'Did they let you in to him?'

'No – just let me look in from outside. There was no room for anyone else, as they seem to have a huge team looking after him. Liam's friend Aldora came in. She's just left.'

'Why don't you go back to the hotel and try to get some sleep?' she said. 'You've had a hell of a shock too. I'm coming out tomorrow – how I'm not yet sure – but I'll let you have all the details later. Liam is arranging things and he's coming too. Whether we manage to get the same flight or not I don't know, as it's the height of the season.'

'It will be great to have you here. Sharonne can't get away for a few days as the au pair is on holiday and her mother is in Spain. She's going to try to send the girls out to her there tomorrow. They were due to go over next week anyway.'

He gave her the relevant phone numbers and she had no sooner replaced the receiver than Liam called to say he had secured seats on an early-morning flight, via Amsterdam. 'I'm sorry about that, but it's the quickest way for us to get there.'

Trish didn't mind where they hubbed, so long as they could get there in the shortest time possible. She went upstairs and threw some clothes in a bag, trying to remember where she had left her passport.

***

The ICU nurses had three-hour shifts, observed Derek, and he presumed that was to ensure their alertness at all times. They recorded every peak and fluctuation on the charts and passed every variation in the readings to their successors. Dr Stephanides, whose day should have ended before this last emergency had been helicoptered in, stayed on stand-by all night, occasionally taking advantage of the narrow bed in the cubicle off the ER department to snatch some sleep.

Conor had an unhealthy pallor, despite his recently acquired tan. His breathing was laboured, at odds with the eerie stillness of his body and the hush with which the professionals did their jobs. Derek eventually went back to his hotel in the early hours and ordered room service – but he was asleep before it was delivered. The persistent knocking on his door woke him eventually and he opened it, took the tray and placed it on the bedside table. He lay down on the bed again and was asleep in seconds, the food untouched.

There was still no change when Liam and Trish boarded the plane at Dublin the following day. The flight took them to Amsterdam and with a short delay they were airborne again, flying above Vienna, Budapest and Rhodes, before turning over the sea to make their approach to Arnica, a long, slow descent which gave a very real impression that they were going to land in the water. The sea seemed to disappear only seconds before the wheels made contact with dry land. Derek was there to welcome them.

'I didn't think you'd be at the airport,' she said, as she hugged him tightly.

'I'm so glad to see you both,' he said, hugging Liam too. 'There didn't seem to be much point sitting in the hospital. At least coming out here I feel I'm doing something. There's no change. I booked you into the same hotel I'm in. We pass it on the way so you can both drop your stuff off there, unless you'd prefer to go straight there.'

They decided to do that and were shocked when they saw the state Conor was in.

'I didn't realise he had so much wrong with him,' Liam said, when he came out of the technology-heavy environment.

'Well, from what I can gather, he has a hairline fracture in his skull, a fractured shoulder and broken arm, a punctured lung and lots of soft tissue injury,' said Derek.

'If he makes it he'll have a long road to recovery ahead of him,' said Trish, her voice breaking. The others agreed.

'But, you know, the biggest fear is that because of the impact his neck took, he may have some paralysis and they won't know that until he wakes up – if he does.'

They kept a vigil from the anteroom, stepping outside into the heat every so often for a change of scenery. They were there when he woke. The nurse on duty had noticed his fingers twitching and a movement in his arm. She waited a few minutes, mindful that it may just be an involuntary muscle spasm but, no, there it was again, more purposeful this time. She called his name and his eyes moved beneath the shut lids. She beckoned to his friends to come in.

'He may be a little confused,' she said reassuringly, in perfect English, 'but don't worry about that. That can be normal after a head injury and also after some concussions.'

'Conor? It's Trish. Liam and Derek are here with me.'

Without opening his eyes, he moved his head towards her.

'Maeve's gone. Isn't she?' he said.

'Yes, she is,' she said. 'You've had an accident, but you're going to be all right.'

His eyes opened wide and he asked, 'Where am I?' What happened? Did Maeve …?

'You're in hospital, in Cyprus. Don't try to talk. There'll be plenty of time for that later. Just rest now.'

Trish looked at Derek and Liam and saw they were almost afraid to speak for fear of breaking down. She stepped aside and let Liam talk to him.

'You're in good hands, dude, in intensive care and we are

only allowed stay a few minutes, but we'll be outside. We're not going anywhere.'

'But Maeve, she's really gone, isn't she?' he insisted.

'Yes, Conor – she's really gone.'

The nurse picked up a chart and indicated that their time was up. Trish kissed his forehead, the other two gave his good hand a squeeze and his eyes followed them as they left. Minutes later, the doctors arrived and after a lengthy consultation came out to talk to them.

'It's all very positive. He's regained consciousness quicker than he might have and that's always a good sign.'

'What about his back?' asked Derek

'It's really too early to say. He does have some good movement in his left arm and in his legs. That's very positive too. The next few days will give us a better indication as to the extent of his injuries and if indeed he will regain the use of his right arm. That's where most of the damage seems to be.'

Seeing how distressed Trish was, he added, 'Just be positive for him. Bruising can often account for temporary paralysis. His will to live and to recover will do more than we can. If he sees despair around him, he'll begin to feel it too, and that's not good. May I suggest you go for a walk, go to the beach, have something to eat and come back later? Rest is very important for the patient and you will also have had some time to let this shock wear off.'

Reluctantly they took this advice and went back to the hotel. None of them had eaten all day. They sat by one of the pools and ordered food that they had no appetite for and went over and over again what could have happened.

'Thank goodness they all speak such good English. Could you imagine trying to get information if this had happened in some remote place?' said Derek.

Liam next took them all by surprise, 'It couldn't have been a suicide attempt, could it?'

Astonished, Derek said, 'Absolutely not. He was full of the new villa and planning when to have you all over. He was in great form when I left him and we were planning to go to dinner in a great little place that we dined in last night.'

'He hasn't recovered from losing Maeve,' Liam said.

'If he was going to do something like that, surely he'd have done it after she died,' Trish said, thinking, he couldn't – wouldn't. Would he? No way. He had held *her* together when her life had fallen apart, in a completely different way than Liam had, with his good humour and art of distraction. Conor was the sensible one, looking at the practicalities for her kids and making sure they were considered in anything that mattered. He had become somewhat of a surrogate father to them, even taking Barry to the driving range to hit buckets of balls when he felt he was missing Rory. No. Conor would never do anything like that.

They sat, immersed in their own thoughts, each feeling that no matter what happened, Conor had passed some kind of watershed – that he had finally accepted that his wife was not coming back – and that his accident had been just that, an accident.

Over the next few days Harris and Aldora, with their network of contacts and friends, rallied around and seemed to be there in the background, anticipating their needs. Aldora had met them all in Dublin at Liam's birthday and remembered Maeve fondly. She proved to be the link they all relied on for the assurance that everything possible was being done for Conor. Progress in the beginning was very slow but gradually they began to see some daily improvement in Conor.

Once Sharonne had arranged flights for Megan and Sandy to go to Spain, she flew out to join Derek. She and Derek came in to visit Conor a week later and found Aldora sitting by his bedside animatedly discussing the furnishings for the villa with him. Derek had been afraid to broach the topic in case his accident had coloured the whole idea of his ever coming back to Cyprus, if indeed he'd be able to at all. But Aldora had turned out to be a real stalwart for him. Here she was, talking about the reality of when he got out of hospital, her infectious chatter putting some semblance of normality on the unreal situation.

'If I were you I'd go with the designer who did the show villa and just tell him to do exactly the same for your one. You liked it, didn't you?'

'Yes. It was impressive,' Conor agreed. 'And, would I be right in suspecting that there's more to your relationship with this designer than a purely professional one?'

'Now that's for me to know!' she laughed. 'I'll talk to him for you and get the interiors sorted out while you're in here.'

'I don't know how to thank you, Aldora, You've been amazing.'

'Then don't,' she said. 'It's my pleasure. Now I'll leave you with Derek and Sharonne.'

***

Once he began to recover, Conor's progress was steady and it was soon apparent that he had suffered no lasting nerve injury. His temporary confusion disappeared altogether and his short-term memory came back, although he still had difficulty remembering the accident that had put him in hospital. The shoulder was a different matter. His doctors told him that without complications the shoulder blade should recover in about six to eight weeks, however the socket injury would take longer and it was therefore imperative that he rested this to avoid long-term consequences or complications.

'No golf, no driving, in fact as much inactivity as possible – that's the prescription,' Dimetri Stephanides said.

'Now, I could live with that,' said Trish.

Conor's reflexes reacted the way they should to hammer

tappings, to pinching and to tickling stimuli. He was moved into a private room and was given gentle physiotherapy. The doctors started talking about releasing him, not to fly back to Ireland but to a few weeks' recuperation in the sunshine first. When Harris heard this, he set some wheels in motion and arrived in one afternoon with Derek and Aldora. Trish was already there. He handed over some papers and said, 'Your villa is ready for you whenever you want to move in, but I have to tell you something. It's not the one you purchased so I'll need you to sign more papers, when you're up to it. We've switched your one for the show villa – the one you wanted to buy originally.'

'But—'

'Everything is arranged,' said Aldora. 'All we have to do is remove the fake ice-cream cartons from the freezer, stock it up with real food and you can go to your new home.'

Before he could react, Trish added, 'Harris is letting me have one of the ones that's ready to be rented and the girls are coming out next week to be with me, so we can all keep an eye on you until you are ready to go home.'

It had taken a bit of persuasion to get Harris to hand over that villa. Although it was open to offers, he really wanted to hold on to it for himself. He was being pestered by an international banker to let him have it, but so far he had not given in to the temptation of accepting an over-the-asking-price figure.

Harris told Liam, 'He's a very wealthy Frenchman who seemed to be very taken with Aldora. I'm not sure if all his haggling is a way of spending more time with her or of acquiring the property. I do hope he doesn't sweep her away from me.'

'It he does, you could probably have another sideline to your many businesses – matchmaking!' laughed Liam.

FORTY-NINE

Conor couldn't believe Harris' generosity and was still amazed at the turn of events that saw him get the villa that overlooked the seventh hole on the tiny plateau with the ravines surrounding it. He would be quite happy to recuperate there. Liam and Derek went back to Dublin and flew out the odd weekend with Sharonne and Kevin, to check up on progress. Rory was in constant touch by phone, but sensing his presence would not add anything to Conor's well being, he declined to visit. Stan arrived and stayed in the villa with Conor for a week, wining and dining them all. Sharonne and the twins spent seven days on the island before the term began and, in some ways, it was just like old times – with al fresco meals and barbecues that reminded them all of Mijas, but without Maeve and Rory. Louise and Toni arrived at the same time, delighted with this unexpected holiday, and with an extra week off school.

Trish felt happy again because she had a cause. She hired a car and became quite proficient at driving on the right-hand side of the road, once she had mastered the roundabouts. As Conor regained his strength and the pain in his shoulder subsided somewhat, they all went exploring the Greek part of the island, up to the cobbled streets of the medieval villages that were dotted about in the Troodos Mountains. In one of these, they visited a Greek Orthodox church with numerous gilded icons and were shocked when they were told that women with their periods were not allowed close to these shrines, and had to stay in the general part of the church.

'So much for women's lib,' said Trish to her daughters when they left.

'What's that?' asked Toni. 'What's women's lib?'

'It was an aspirational dream of the sixties and seventies – of women having equality and choices, of being able to burn their bras and stay at work after they had married, if they wanted to. It was not supposed to allow everyone in the village know when and if you had your period or to make you feel unclean because you did!'

Toni and Louise laughed at their mother's explanation.

'Why would you want to burn your bra anyway?' Toni asked Trish.

They liked seeing her becoming again the mum they remembered – the laughing, joking mum of pre-Anna Maria days. Trish enjoyed shopping in the colourful local markets, experimenting with all sorts of strange vegetables. Aldora and Harris sometimes joined them too, both getting involved in giving them a cookery lesson on how to make the perfect moussaka, which they all devoured with gusto.

'You must use potato,' said Aldora.

'No, the secret is no potato!' argued Harris.

'It's not real moussaka without it!' she insisted.

'Yes it is!' he retorted, having to have the last word.

They discovered little taverns and restaurants and dipped their bread into bowls of cracked green olives with coriander seeds. They tried watermelon with halloumi cheese and Trish grew to love the sweet Commandaria wine. They feasted on mezedes and walked about the town squares in Larnaca, Vasilikos, Episkopi and Paphos. They even visited the breeding grounds of the endangered green turtle.

It was a surreal time, though. No one had planned that summer – it seems it had made its own plans for them all. They spent hours by the pool, Conor becoming an expert at one-armed swimming. Aldora cooked for the girls one evening so that he could take Trish to the restaurant where he and Derek had had meals served by a Hercules, cooked by a Socrates and where the wine waiter was called Herodotus.

By the time he was well enough to travel home, Conor felt more contented than he had for a long time. Still quite dependent, he knew he'd need help when he returned to his own surroundings, which he did with a file full of correspondence for his doctor and letters of referral to orthopaedic specialists for follow-up care. His shoulder was still strapped up and consequently his movement still quite limited.

On the plane home, Trish sat with her girls, Conor was farther up and had two seats so that his shoulder wouldn't get knocked about.

'Mum, can Conor come and stay with us for a while?' asked Louise.

'I don't think that would be a good idea,' she said.

'Why not?' said Toni. 'I think it would be cool.'

'It would not,' Trish said, scrambling around to find a plausible answer for her daughters. 'I think Conor needs to get back into a routine. We can visit as often as you like and we'll keep an eye on him.'

'But that would be much easier to do if he's living with us. He can't drive yet and we can help do things for him.'

Outnumbered, she knew it made sense, but she couldn't tell the girls that she was beginning to have feelings for Conor, feelings that were wrong. He was her best friend's husband. Whatever he needed, she knew she had to put some distance between them. She had got used to having him in her life, filling a void, including him in her every thought. Now she needed to break away from that. Realistically, they couldn't abandon him to an empty house with a twice-weekly housekeeper to help him recuperate, could they? Louise kept on until Trish surrendered and Toni made her way up the plane to where he was sitting and issued the invite to Conor. He accepted without any hesitation.

Once home, Trish immersed herself in getting the girls' uniforms and filling book lists for their late return to school. Barry got his Leaving Certificate results and, to even his own surprise, he had got enough points to do engineering in UCD. He stayed in the States until just three days before registration, came home and presented Trish with a wad of dollars.

Trish hardly recognised her son. He seemed to have stretched even more and had filled out. He was tanned and confident. 'I can't take that,' she argued.

'You must. It's a thank you for keeping us all together – and it's for you, Mum. Not to be spent on anyone or anything else.'

He seemed genuinely delighted to see Conor.

'You gave us all a right fright, dude,' he said as he greeted him.

'Not half as great as the one I gave myself,' Conor laughed back.

FIFTY

The December morning was late dawning, but it was bright and crisp and there was a dusting of frost on the lawns. Conor had moved back home five weeks before and was still following a rigorous physiotherapy programme to get him fit again. It was Maeve's birthday today. She would have been forty. He remembered so many things as he looked out on their garden and sipped his coffee in the empty house. He sighed and wondered how they would have celebrated her big four zero. She had been much too young to die. He missed her every day, despite the fact that his life had somehow taken on a steady pattern and he had managed to fill some of the voids. His buddies had rallied around, making sure he had no time to mope. Trish still phoned to check on him, but there was a distance between them now that was awkward, and it unnerved him very much. They had always been great friends. Now he couldn't describe their relationship. It had tilted and was decidedly off balance and he was afraid to take steps to put it right in case he changed it even more radically.

One evening, while he was still at her house, they were sitting at the table after dinner, laughing at something he had said, an unfinished bottle of wine between them. They hadn't heard Barry come in. He stood in the doorway and said nothing for a few seconds, then muttered 'cosy' and left the room, grinning. That was the moment that things altered between them. They looked at each other, both realising that there was no going back to when Conor was her best friend's husband and she was an abandoned wife. The ground had shifted beneath them so imperceptibly that they hadn't really noticed, although all the signs were there in front of them. That tiny utterance 'cosy' was the deciding factor in the timing of Conor's move back home – to the space he and Maeve had shared.

He needed to be where he could still feel her all around, in her conservatory, their bedroom, amid the décor she had chosen so carefully for their home, and in the photographs on the tables. He needed to embrace these things, so that he wouldn't forget anything of their togetherness and intimacy.

Trish had protested half-heartedly that it was still too soon to be living on his own. 'We all love having you here with us,' she'd said, deliberately stressing the 'we'.

'And I love being here, but it's time I went, time we all got back to normal.'

'You're right,' she agreed. 'It is.' She knew that he did not belong to her. It was time for her to let go.

Now that he was back in his familiar surroundings, he had many unresolved issues. He missed Maeve and all the things they had had and done together – but, disturbingly, he also missed Trish, more and more. He felt disloyal. He had never had any intention of replacing Maeve. He no longer knew where he was going in life and found the confusion very hard to deal with. He also felt guilty, well perhaps guilty was too strong a word, but he felt ill at ease when he found his mind wandering more and more in Trish's direction with each passing day.

***

Trish pottered around her kitchen, tidying up after the breakfast whirlwind. She could never understand how the quickest meal to be eaten left the most mess. She had no work today and she wanted to visit Maeve's grave. She felt out of sorts, uneasy and upset, and had done for some weeks past. She still grieved for her friend and still frequently thought of things she wanted to tell her. She went into the garden and picked some lingering Michaelmas daisies from the flowerbeds. They were nothing as showy as her friend's had been, but many of the plants had come originally from cuttings and seeds Maeve had potted up, so they meant a lot to her. She had bought large, white pom-pom chrysanthemums the day before and now arranged the purple flowers with these and some ivy. She found a straw ribbon in a kitchen drawer, one she had saved from another bouquet. She tied the stems together and she set off for the cemetery.

The sun cast long, wintry shadows on the paths and headstones and, in the distance, she could hear the gardeners cutting away at some shrubbery along the far side. She stood before her friend's resting place, reading the inscription, as she tried to conjure up Maeve's vivacious smile, wondering if she knew what had happened since she'd left them all behind.

Her stream of consciousness meandered through thoughts that she had been storing up to tell her friend. 'You'd be very proud of me. I started learning Italian too. Do you know that Conor had an accident and almost died and we all wondered if he had tried to kill himself just to be with you again? Of course, we know he didn't, but he still misses you terribly. He sold Mijas, just like you wanted him to, and has a new place in Cyprus, which you would love.'

She placed the flowers reverently, straightening the floppy heads of the chrysanthemums and fixing the bow. 'I miss you so much. He came to stay with us too. For a while. To recuperate. Did you know that?'

She traced her finger across the gold lettering that spelled her friend's name, and the dates of her birth and her death.

Her silent tears began to fall on the shiny black marble as she realised the only person she could have discussed her real feelings for Conor with was Maeve. She spent several more minutes remembering the good times they had shared.

'That's when I began to realise … Oh Maeve, I promise … I never, ever saw this coming … I never meant this to happen … really I didn't.'

Eventually she dried her eyes and stood up to walk away. It was only then that she spotted Conor standing close by. She hadn't heard him arrive above the noise of the gardeners working on the shrubbery.

'You know something, Trish. I really think she did,' he said, as he stretched his arms out for her. She walked towards him, smiling.